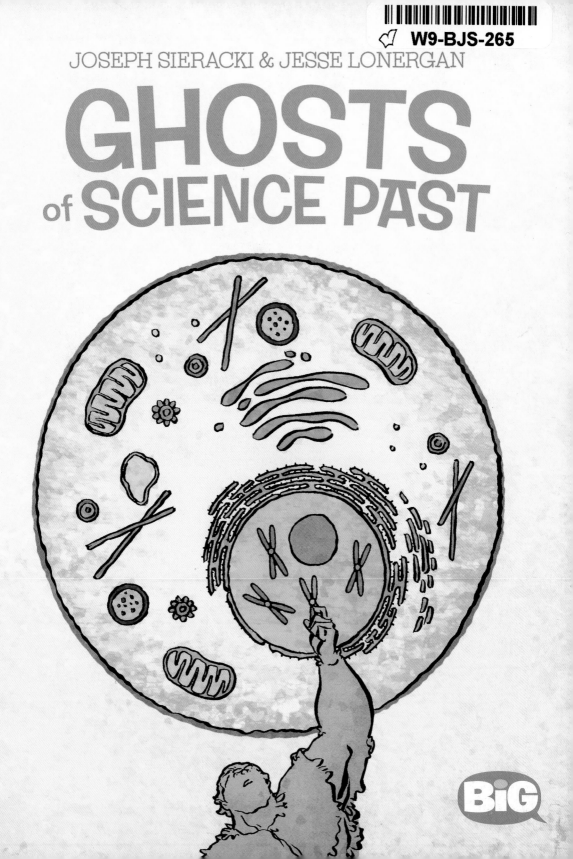

JOSEPH SIERACKI & JESSE LONERGAN

GHOSTS
of SCIENCE PAST

BiG

STORY
JOSEPH SIERACKI

ART
JESSE LONERGAN

COLORS
JESSE LONERGAN

LETTERS
DAVE LANPHEAR

EDITORS
ROB LEVIN & JAKE THOMAS

DESIGNER
SANDY TANAKA

SENIOR ART DIRECTOR
JERRY FRISSEN

PUBLISHER
MARK WAID

SPECIAL THANKS
JASMINE WALLS

Rights and Licensing - licensing@humanoids.com   Press and Social Media - pr@humanoids.com

GHOSTS OF SCIENCE PAST. First Printing. This book is a publication of Humanoids, Inc. 8033 Sunset Blvd. #628, Los Angeles, CA 90046. Copyright Humanoids, Inc., Los Angeles (USA). All rights reserved. Humanoids® and the Humanoids logo are registered trademarks of Humanoids, Inc. in the U.S. and other countries.

Library of Congress Control Number: 2021951701

BiG is an imprint of Humanoids, Inc.

Stave One: Darwin's Ghost

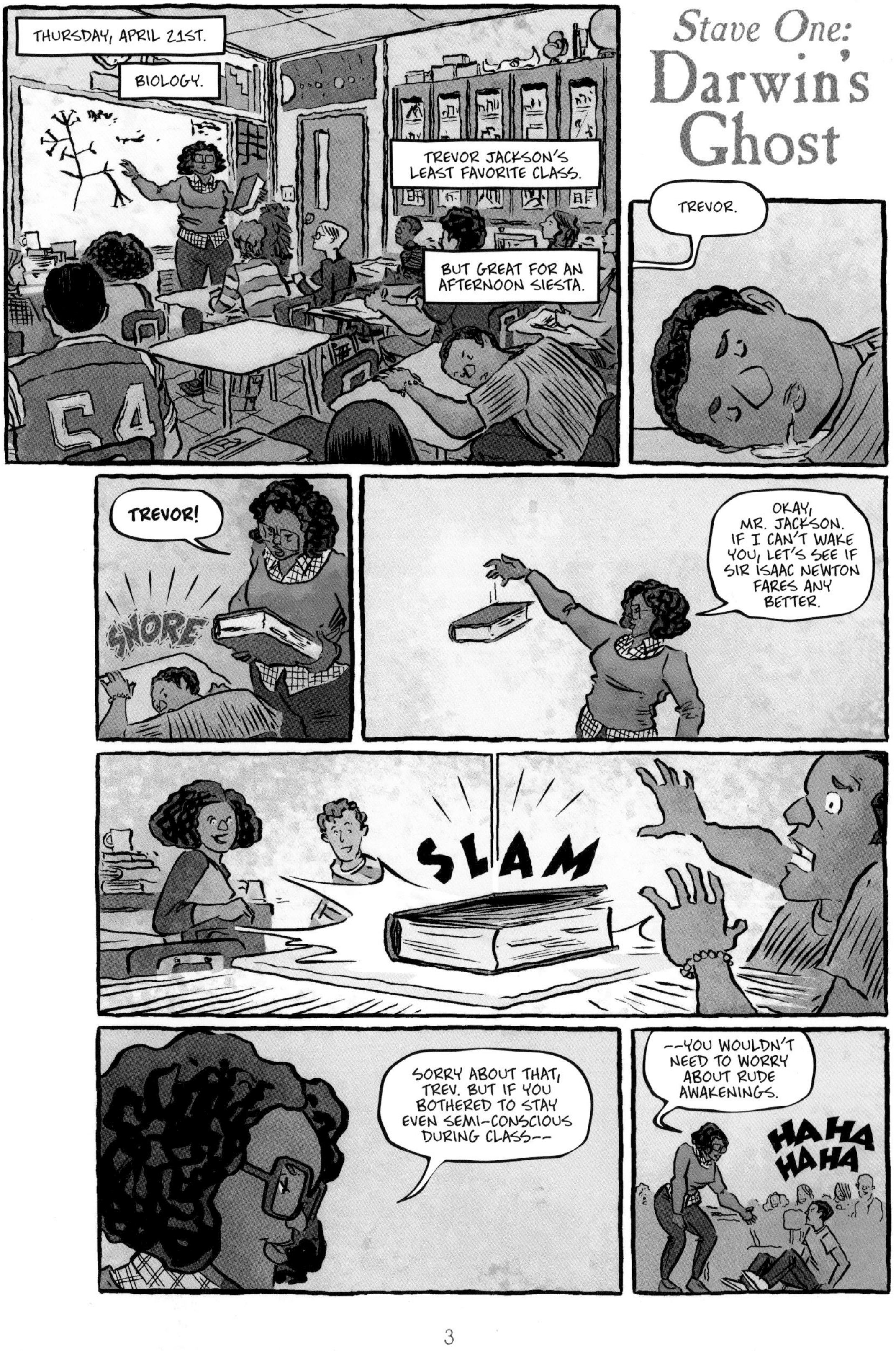

THURSDAY, APRIL 21ST.
BIOLOGY.
TREVOR JACKSON'S LEAST FAVORITE CLASS.
BUT GREAT FOR AN AFTERNOON SIESTA.
54
TREVOR.
TREVOR!
SNORE
OKAY, MR. JACKSON. IF I CAN'T WAKE YOU, LET'S SEE IF SIR ISAAC NEWTON FARES ANY BETTER.
SLAM
SORRY ABOUT THAT, TREV. BUT IF YOU BOTHERED TO STAY EVEN SEMI-CONSCIOUS DURING CLASS--
--YOU WOULDN'T NEED TO WORRY ABOUT RUDE AWAKENINGS.
HAHA HAHA

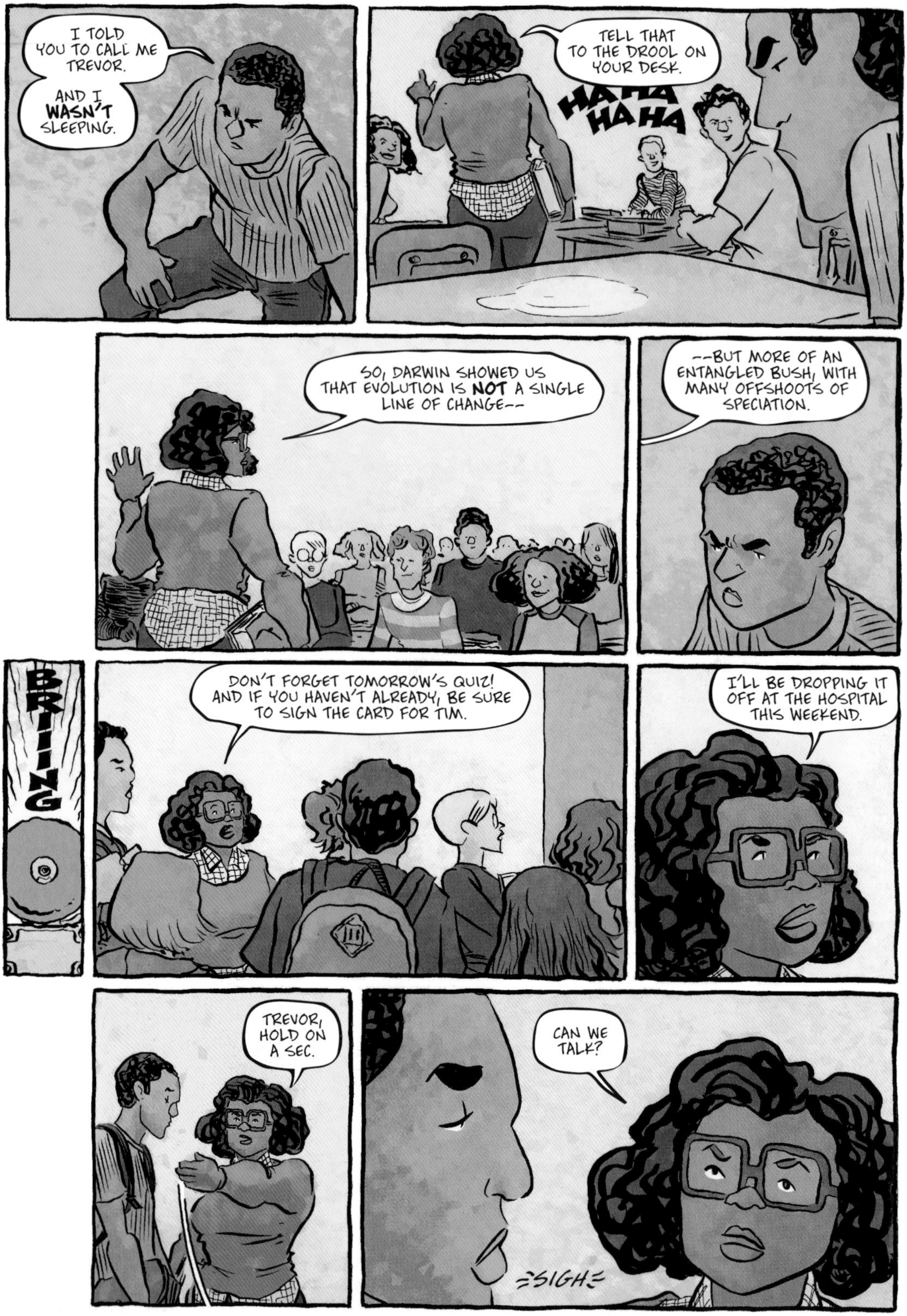
I TOLD YOU TO CALL ME TREVOR.
AND I **WASN'T** SLEEPING.
TELL THAT TO THE DROOL ON YOUR DESK.
HAHA HAHA
SO, DARWIN SHOWED US THAT EVOLUTION IS **NOT** A SINGLE LINE OF CHANGE--
--BUT MORE OF AN ENTANGLED BUSH, WITH MANY OFFSHOOTS OF SPECIATION.
BRIIING
DON'T FORGET TOMORROW'S QUIZ! AND IF YOU HAVEN'T ALREADY, BE SURE TO SIGN THE CARD FOR TIM.
I'LL BE DROPPING IT OFF AT THE HOSPITAL THIS WEEKEND.
TREVOR, HOLD ON A SEC.
CAN WE TALK?
SIGH

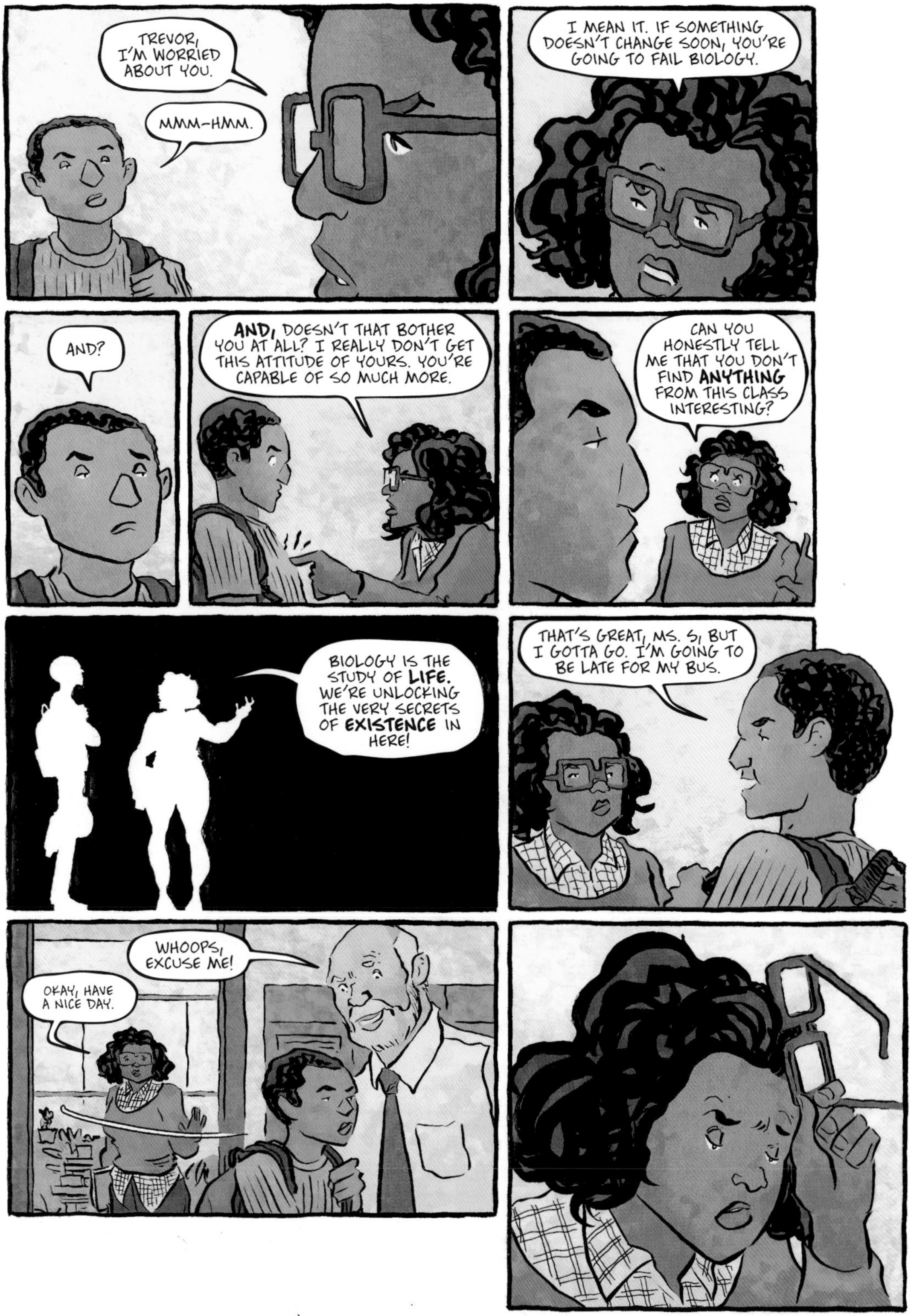
TREVOR, I'M WORRIED ABOUT YOU.
MMM-HMM.
I MEAN IT. IF SOMETHING DOESN'T CHANGE SOON, YOU'RE GOING TO FAIL BIOLOGY.
AND?
AND, DOESN'T THAT BOTHER YOU AT ALL? I REALLY DON'T GET THIS ATTITUDE OF YOURS. YOU'RE CAPABLE OF SO MUCH MORE.
CAN YOU HONESTLY TELL ME THAT YOU DON'T FIND **ANYTHING** FROM THIS CLASS INTERESTING?
BIOLOGY IS THE STUDY OF **LIFE.** WE'RE UNLOCKING THE VERY SECRETS OF **EXISTENCE** IN HERE!
THAT'S GREAT, MS. S, BUT I GOTTA GO. I'M GOING TO BE LATE FOR MY BUS.
WHOOPS, EXCUSE ME!
OKAY, HAVE A NICE DAY.

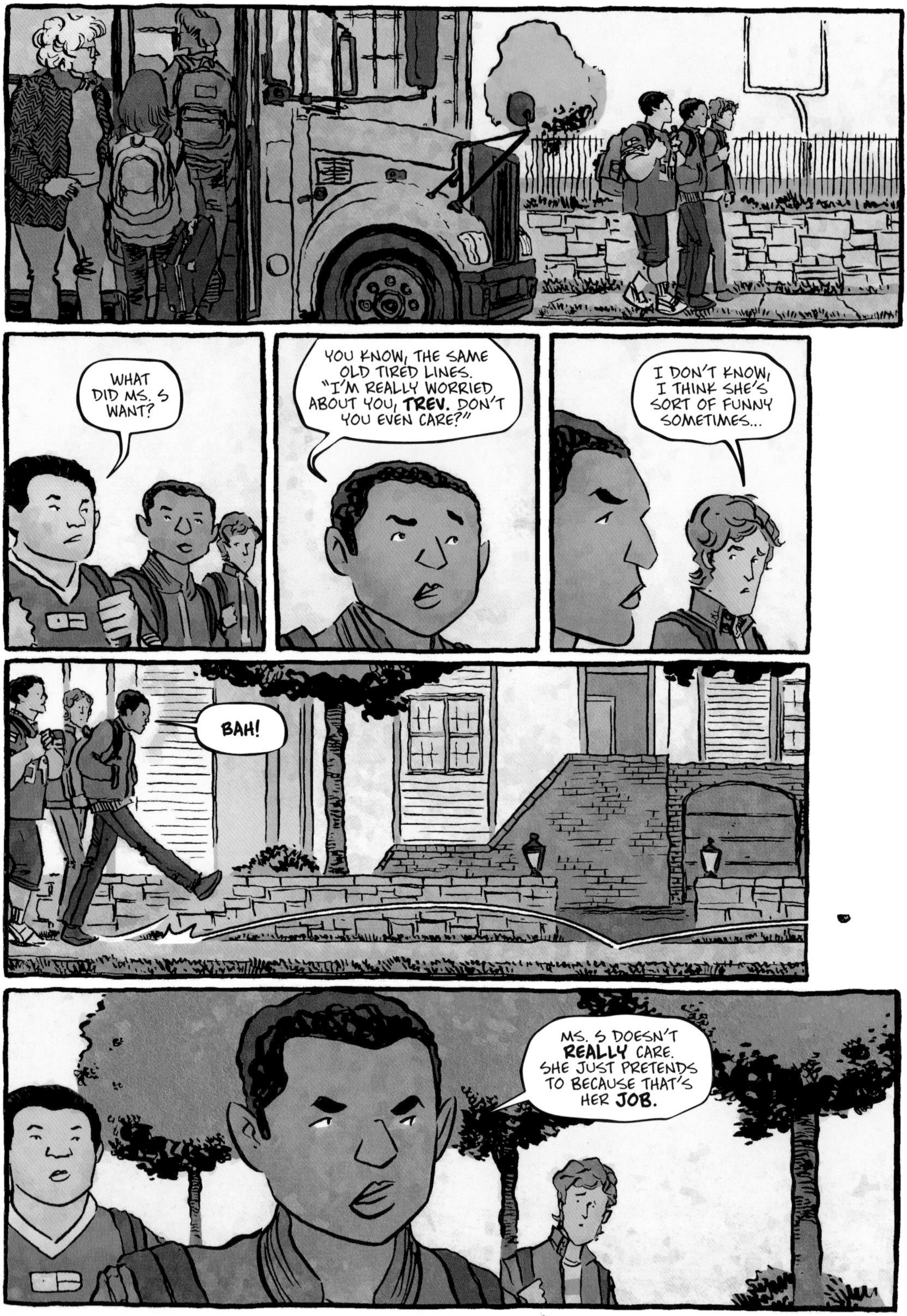
WHAT DID MS. S WANT?
YOU KNOW, THE SAME OLD TIRED LINES. "I'M REALLY WORRIED ABOUT YOU, **TREV.** DON'T YOU EVEN CARE?"
I DON'T KNOW, I THINK SHE'S SORT OF FUNNY SOMETIMES...
BAH!
MS. S DOESN'T **REALLY** CARE. SHE JUST PRETENDS TO BECAUSE THAT'S HER **JOB.**

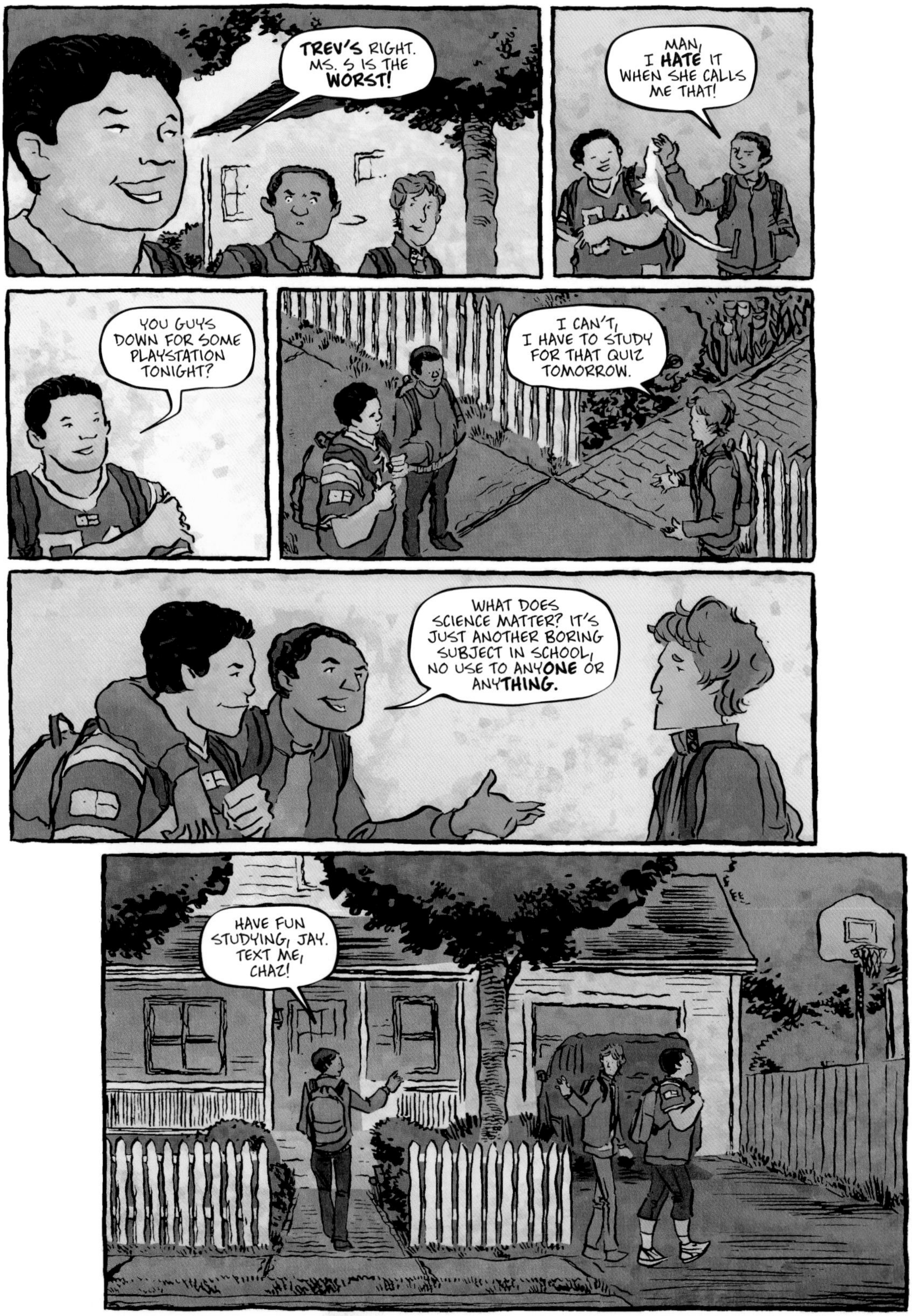
TREV'S RIGHT. MS. S IS THE WORST!
MAN, I HATE IT WHEN SHE CALLS ME THAT!
YOU GUYS DOWN FOR SOME PLAYSTATION TONIGHT?
I CAN'T, I HAVE TO STUDY FOR THAT QUIZ TOMORROW.
WHAT DOES SCIENCE MATTER? IT'S JUST ANOTHER BORING SUBJECT IN SCHOOL, NO USE TO ANYONE OR ANYTHING.
HAVE FUN STUDYING, JAY. TEXT ME, CHAZ!

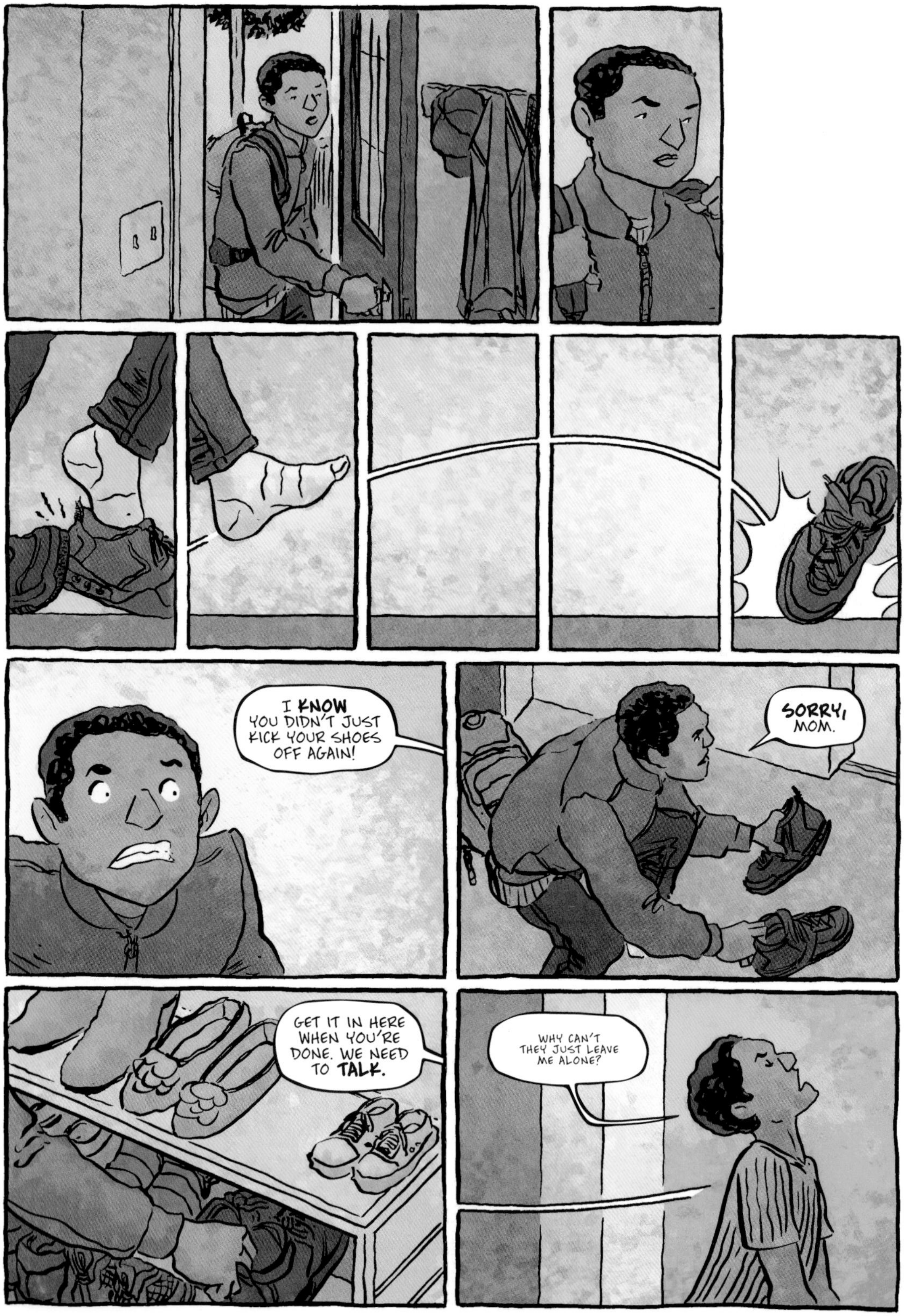
I KNOW YOU DIDN'T JUST KICK YOUR SHOES OFF AGAIN!
SORRY, MOM.
GET IT IN HERE WHEN YOU'RE DONE. WE NEED TO TALK.
WHY CAN'T THEY JUST LEAVE ME ALONE?

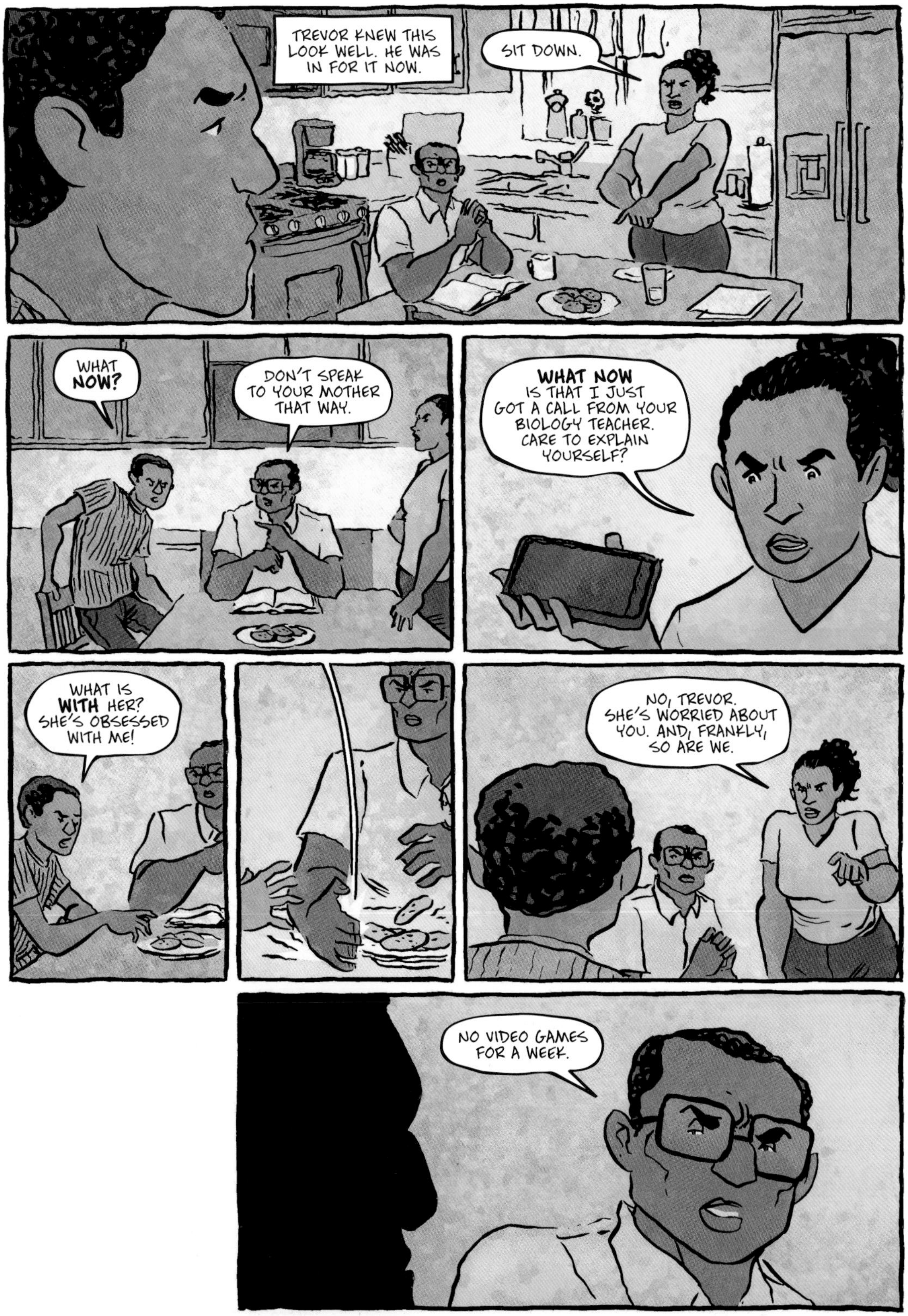
TREVOR KNEW THIS LOOK WELL. HE WAS IN FOR IT NOW.
SIT DOWN.
WHAT NOW?
DON'T SPEAK TO YOUR MOTHER THAT WAY.
WHAT NOW IS THAT I JUST GOT A CALL FROM YOUR BIOLOGY TEACHER. CARE TO EXPLAIN YOURSELF?
WHAT IS WITH HER? SHE'S OBSESSED WITH ME!
NO, TREVOR. SHE'S WORRIED ABOUT YOU. AND, FRANKLY, SO ARE WE.
NO VIDEO GAMES FOR A WEEK.

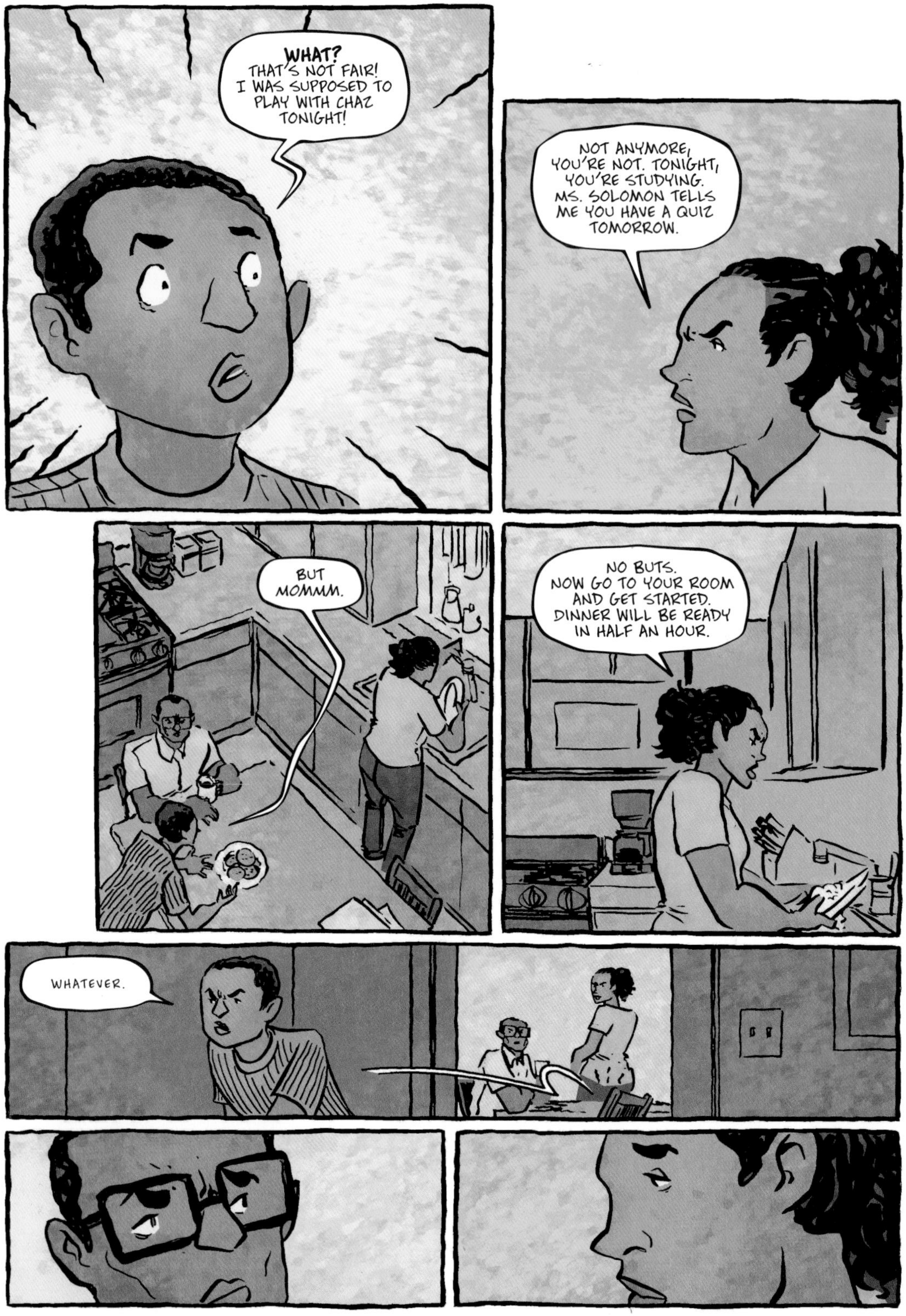
WHAT? THAT'S NOT FAIR! I WAS SUPPOSED TO PLAY WITH CHAZ TONIGHT!
NOT ANYMORE, YOU'RE NOT. TONIGHT, YOU'RE STUDYING. MS. SOLOMON TELLS ME YOU HAVE A QUIZ TOMORROW.
BUT MOMMM.
NO BUTS. NOW GO TO YOUR ROOM AND GET STARTED. DINNER WILL BE READY IN HALF AN HOUR.
WHATEVER.

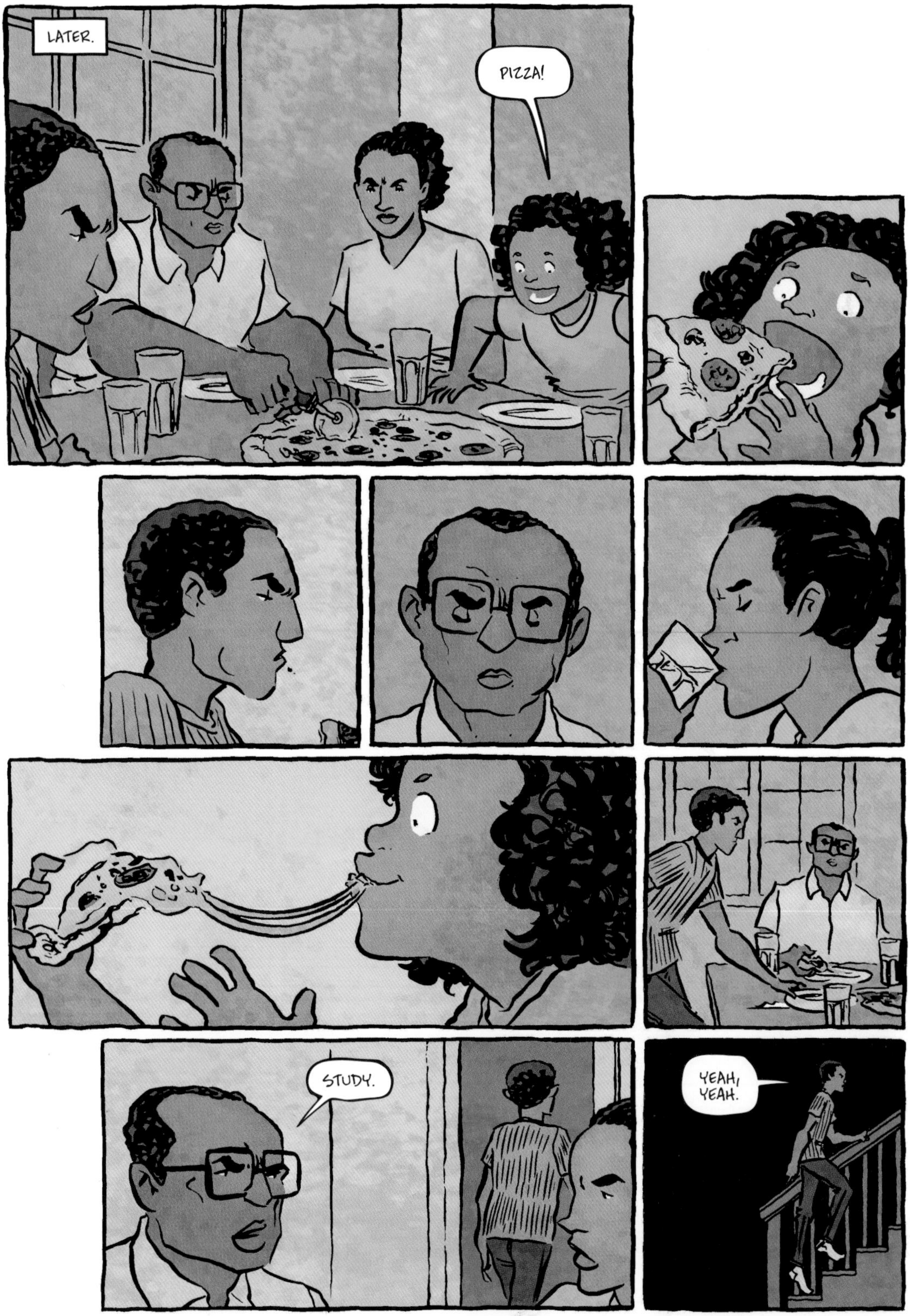
LATER.
PIZZA!
STUDY.
YEAH, YEAH.

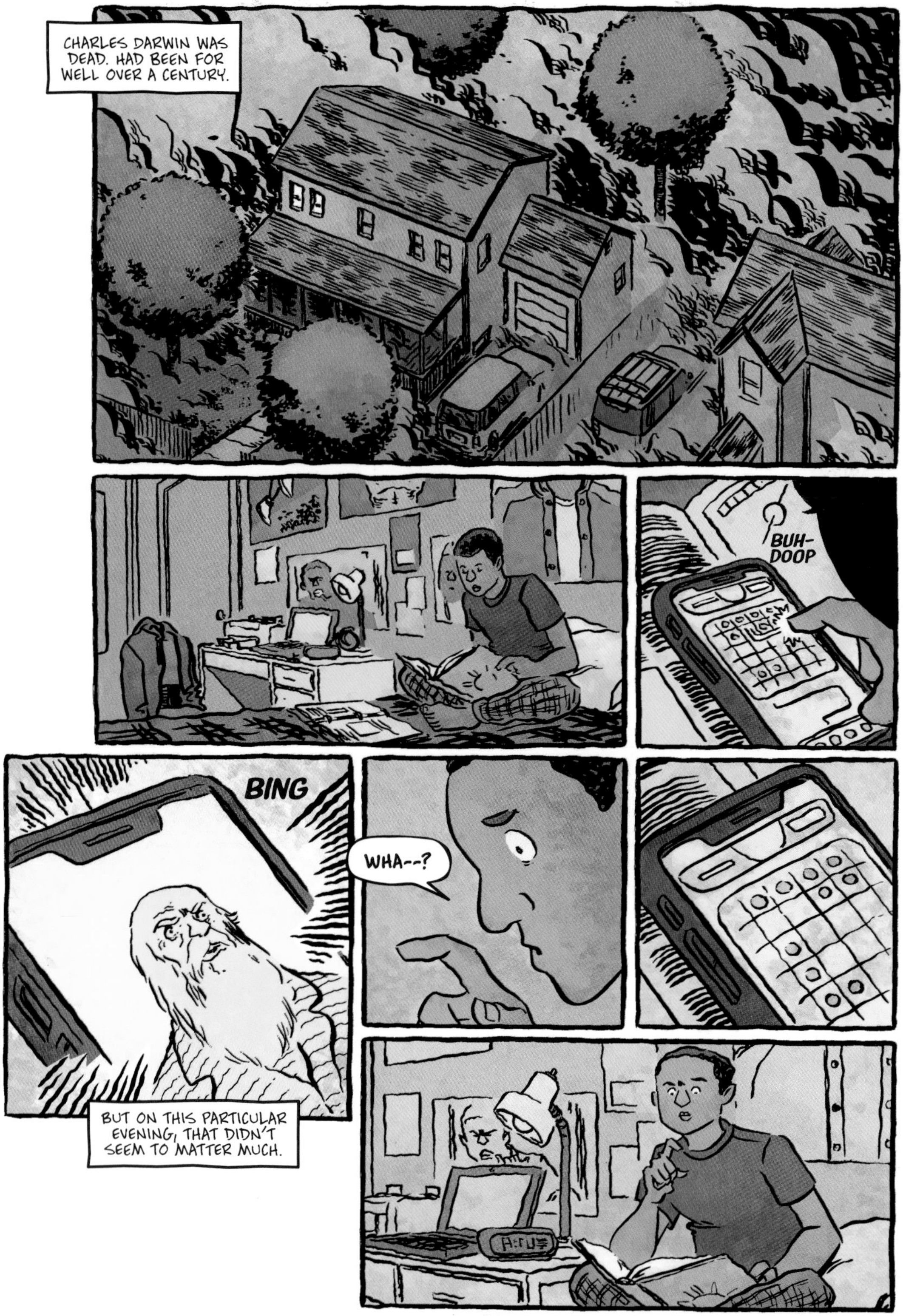
CHARLES DARWIN WAS DEAD. HAD BEEN FOR WELL OVER A CENTURY.
BUH-DOOP
BING
WHA--?
BUT ON THIS PARTICULAR EVENING, THAT DIDN'T SEEM TO MATTER MUCH.

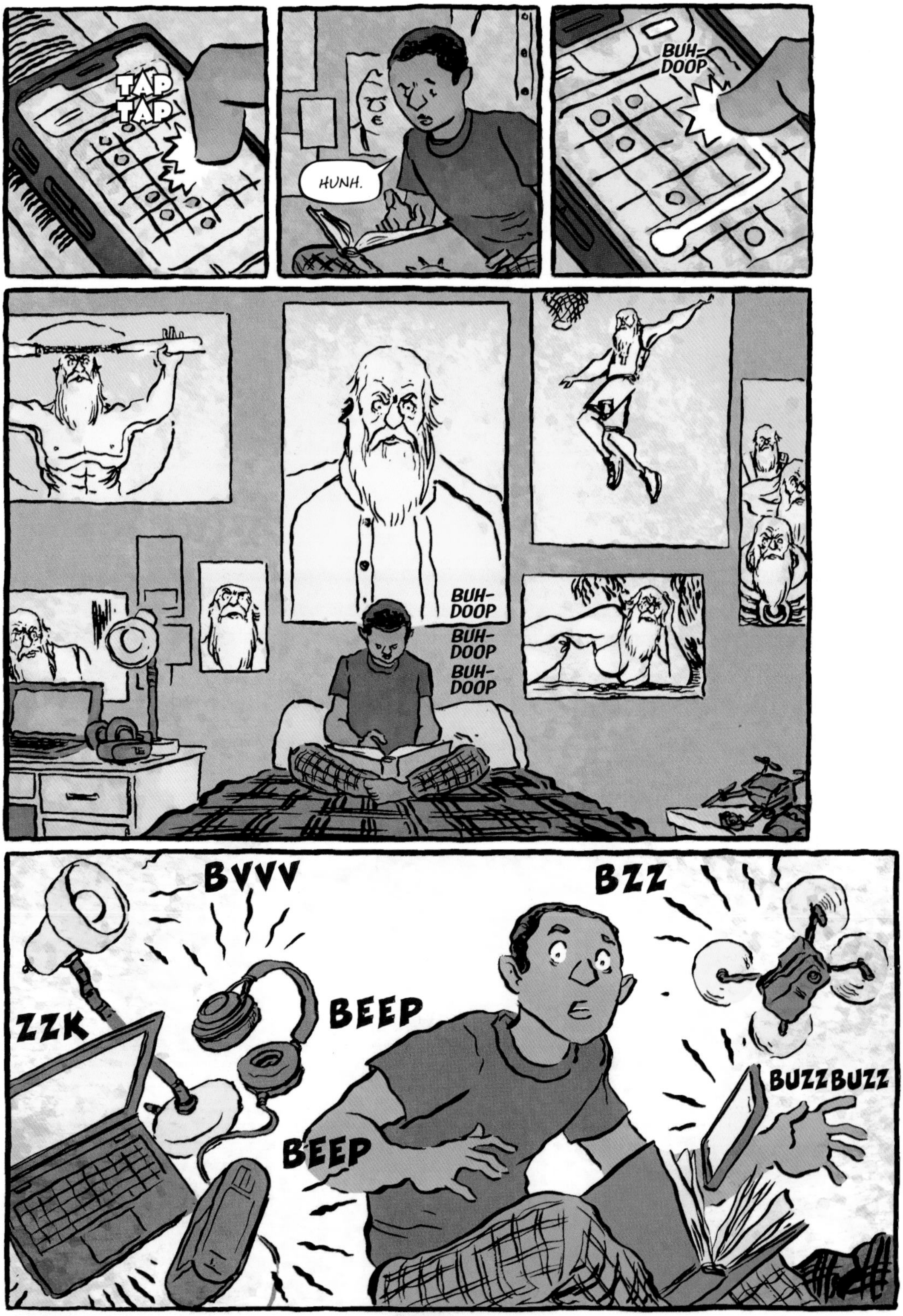
TAP TAP
HUNH.
BUH-DOOP
BUH-DOOP
BUH-DOOP
BUH-DOOP
BVVV
BZZ
ZZK
BEEP
BEEP
BUZZBUZZ

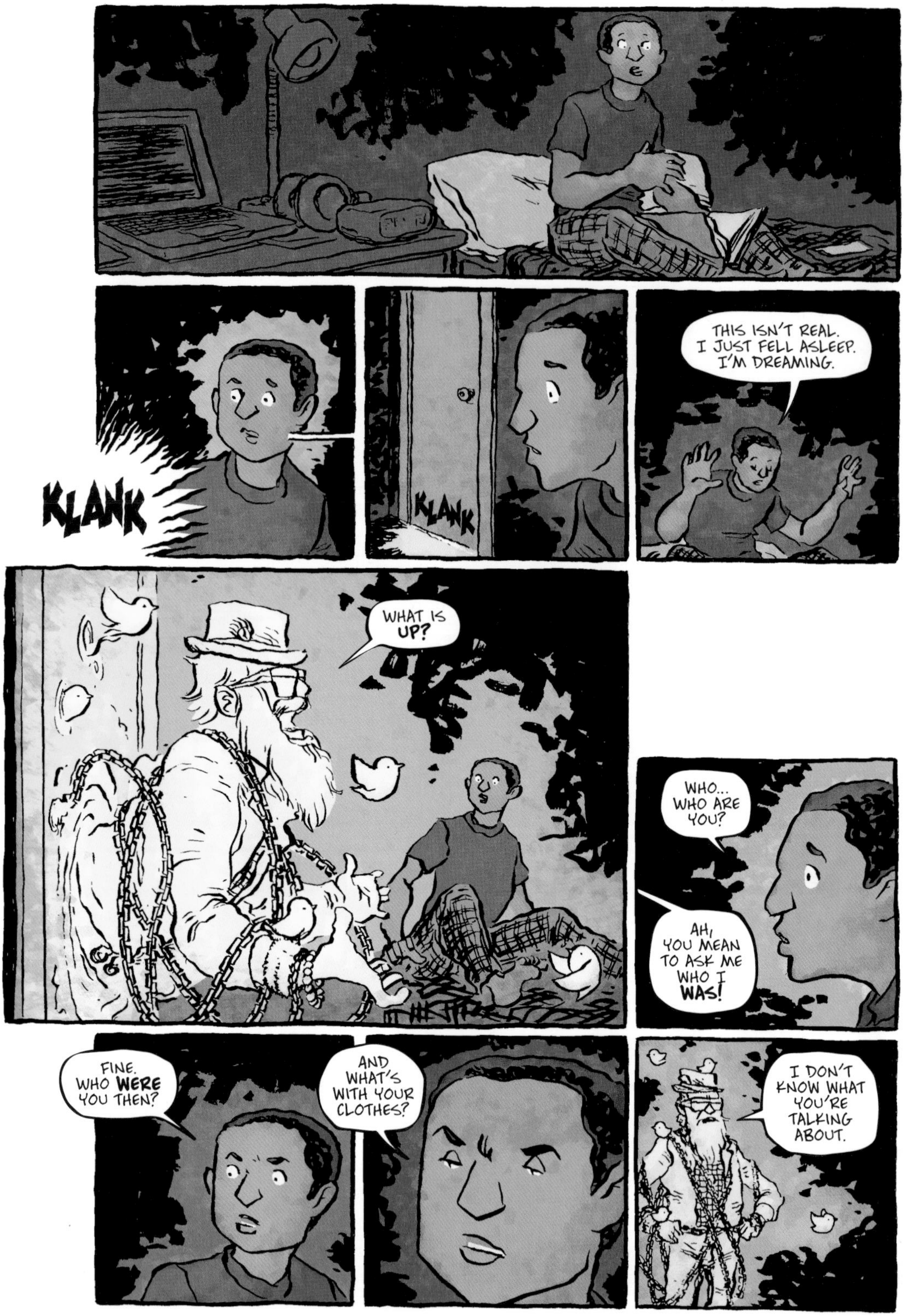
KLANK
KLANK
THIS ISN'T REAL. I JUST FELL ASLEEP. I'M DREAMING.
WHAT IS UP?
WHO... WHO ARE YOU?
AH, YOU MEAN TO ASK ME WHO I WAS!
FINE. WHO WERE YOU THEN?
AND WHAT'S WITH YOUR CLOTHES?
I DON'T KNOW WHAT YOU'RE TALKING ABOUT.

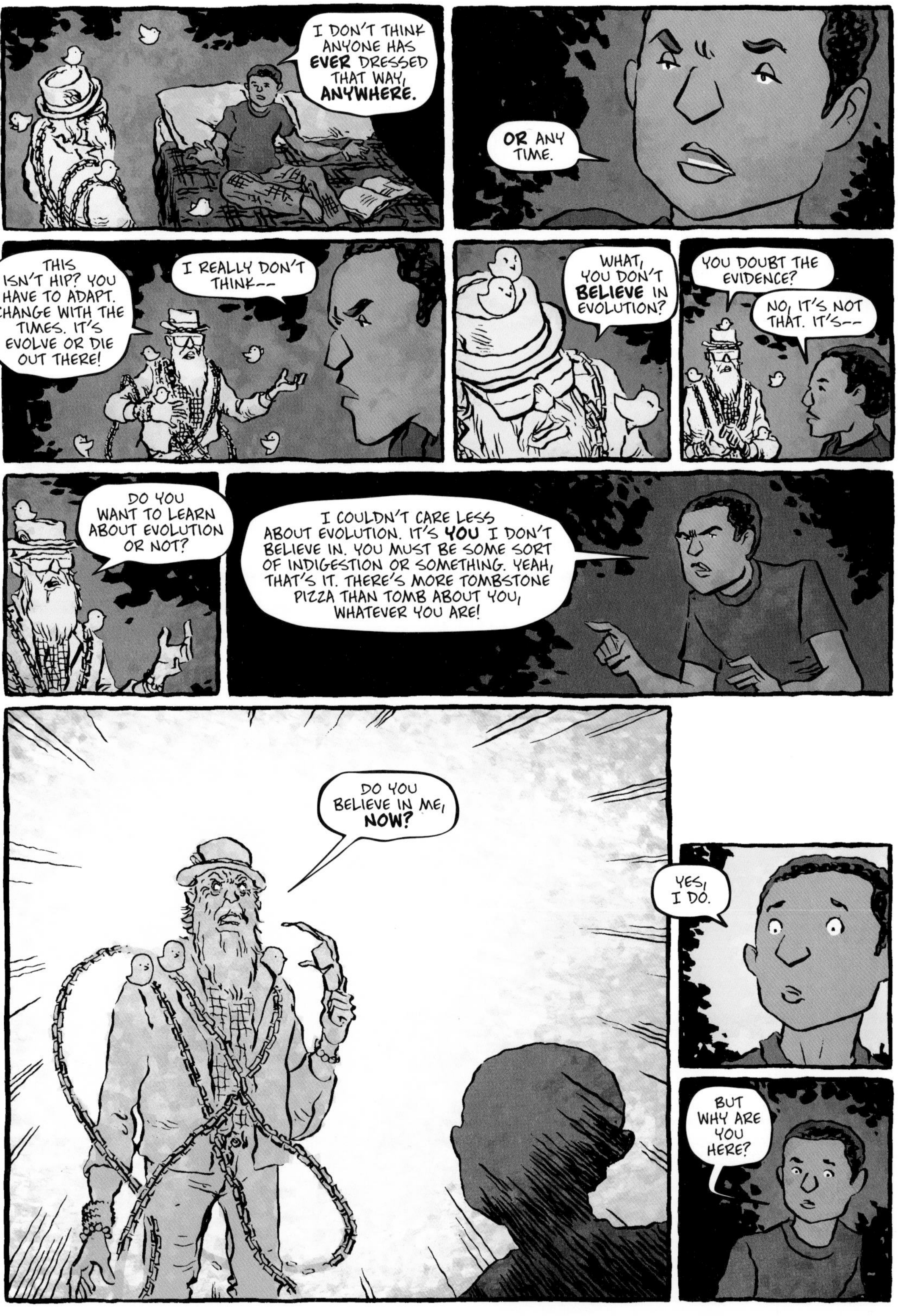
I DON'T THINK ANYONE HAS **EVER** DRESSED THAT WAY, **ANYWHERE.**
OR ANY TIME.
THIS ISN'T HIP? YOU HAVE TO ADAPT. CHANGE WITH THE TIMES. IT'S EVOLVE OR DIE OUT THERE!
I REALLY DON'T THINK--
WHAT, YOU DON'T **BELIEVE** IN EVOLUTION?
YOU DOUBT THE EVIDENCE?
NO, IT'S NOT THAT. IT'S--
DO YOU WANT TO LEARN ABOUT EVOLUTION OR NOT?
I COULDN'T CARE LESS ABOUT EVOLUTION. IT'S **YOU** I DON'T BELIEVE IN. YOU MUST BE SOME SORT OF INDIGESTION OR SOMETHING. YEAH, THAT'S IT. THERE'S MORE TOMBSTONE PIZZA THAN TOMB ABOUT YOU, WHATEVER YOU ARE!
DO YOU BELIEVE IN ME, **NOW?**
YES, I DO.
BUT WHY ARE YOU HERE?

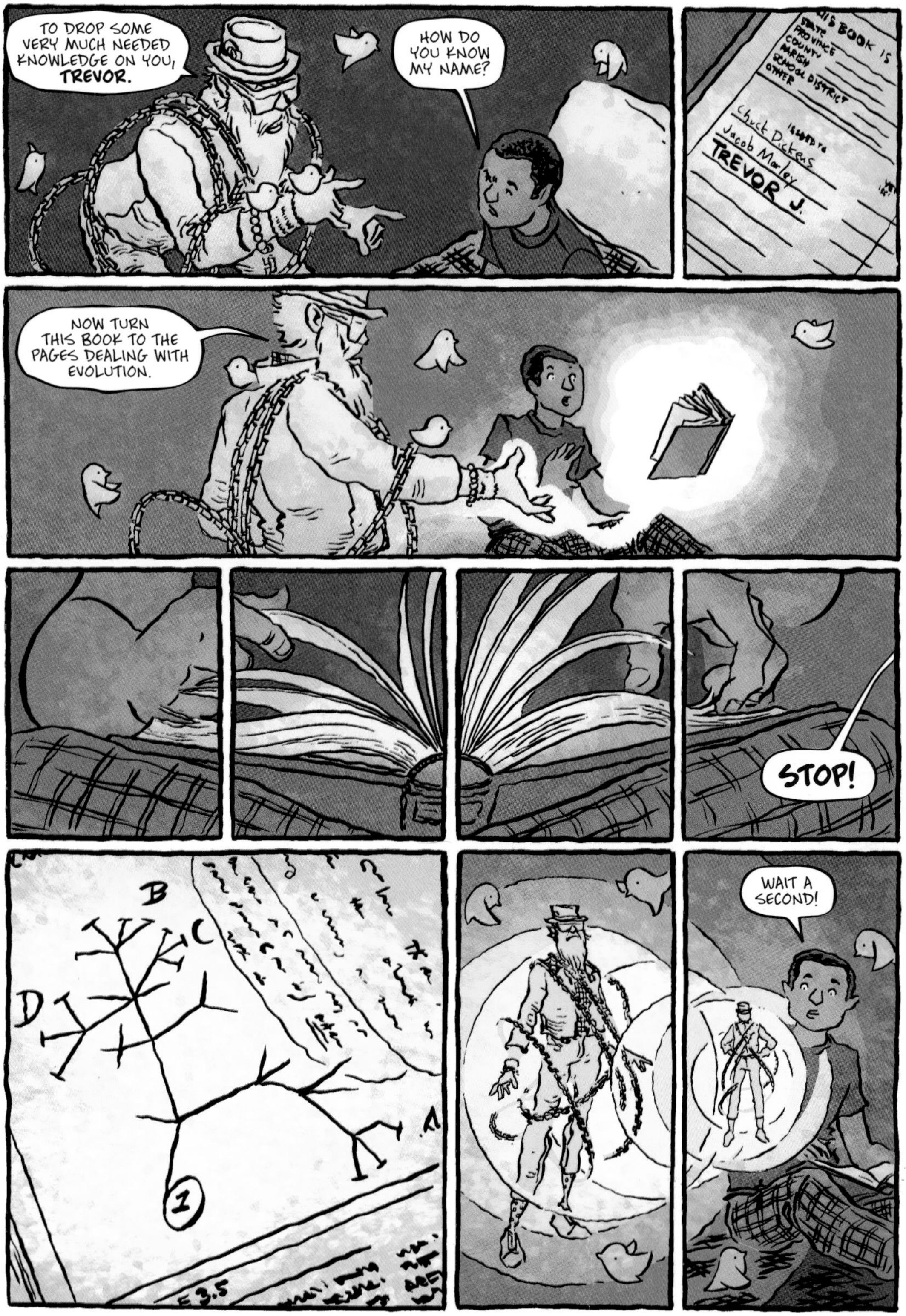
TO DROP SOME VERY MUCH NEEDED KNOWLEDGE ON YOU, **TREVOR.**
HOW DO YOU KNOW MY NAME?
BOOK IS
STATE
PROVINCE
COUNTY
PARISH
SCHOOL DISTRICT
OTHER
ISSUED TO
Chuck Dickens
Jacob Marley
TREVOR J.
NOW TURN THIS BOOK TO THE PAGES DEALING WITH EVOLUTION.
STOP!
B
C
D
A
1
WAIT A SECOND!

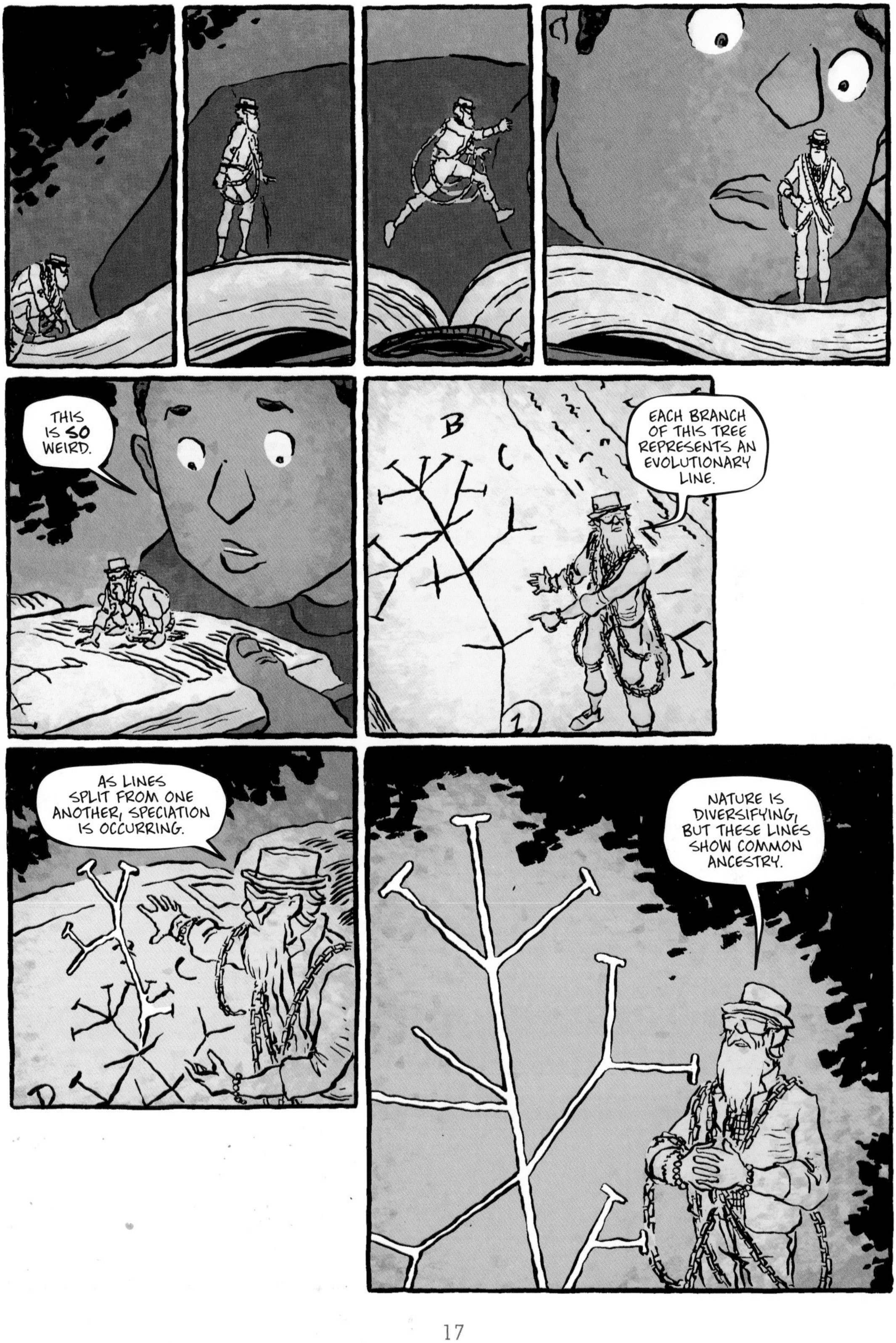
THIS IS SO WEIRD.
EACH BRANCH OF THIS TREE REPRESENTS AN EVOLUTIONARY LINE.
AS LINES SPLIT FROM ONE ANOTHER, SPECIATION IS OCCURRING.
NATURE IS DIVERSIFYING, BUT THESE LINES SHOW COMMON ANCESTRY.

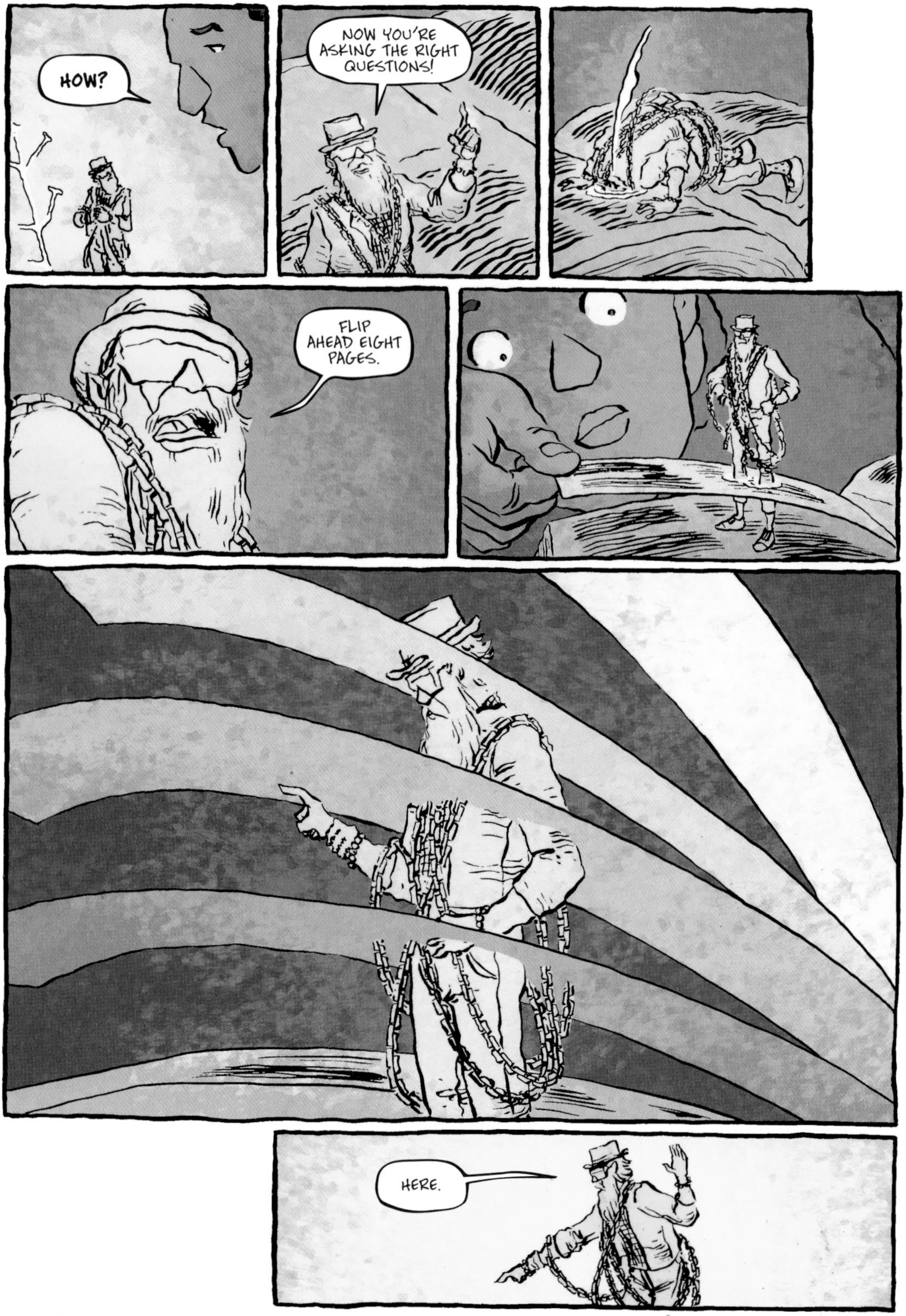
HOW?
NOW YOU'RE ASKING THE RIGHT QUESTIONS!
FLIP AHEAD EIGHT PAGES.
HERE.

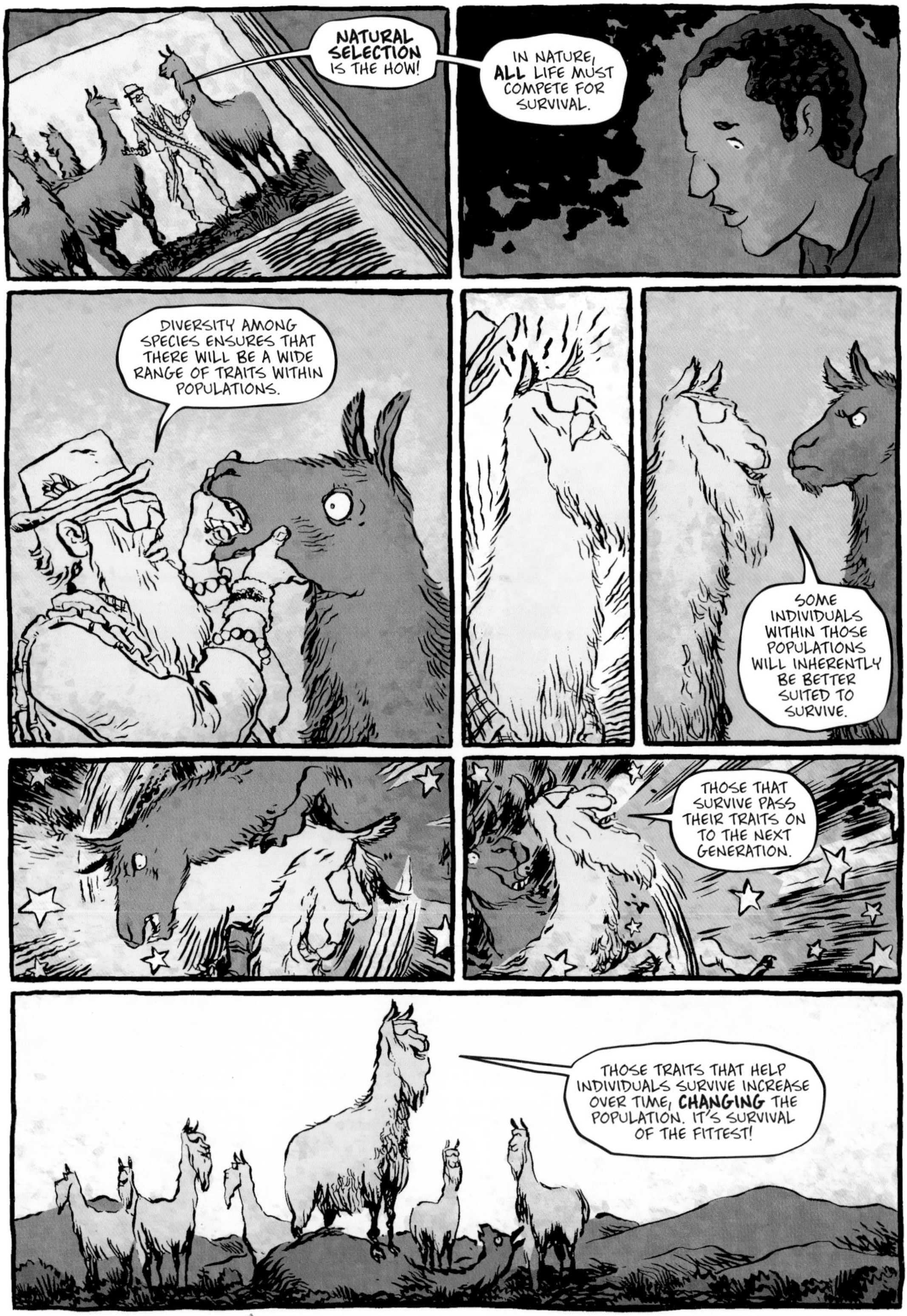
NATURAL SELECTION IS THE HOW!
IN NATURE, ALL LIFE MUST COMPETE FOR SURVIVAL.
DIVERSITY AMONG SPECIES ENSURES THAT THERE WILL BE A WIDE RANGE OF TRAITS WITHIN POPULATIONS.
SOME INDIVIDUALS WITHIN THOSE POPULATIONS WILL INHERENTLY BE BETTER SUITED TO SURVIVE.
THOSE THAT SURVIVE PASS THEIR TRAITS ON TO THE NEXT GENERATION.
THOSE TRAITS THAT HELP INDIVIDUALS SURVIVE INCREASE OVER TIME, CHANGING THE POPULATION. IT'S SURVIVAL OF THE FITTEST!

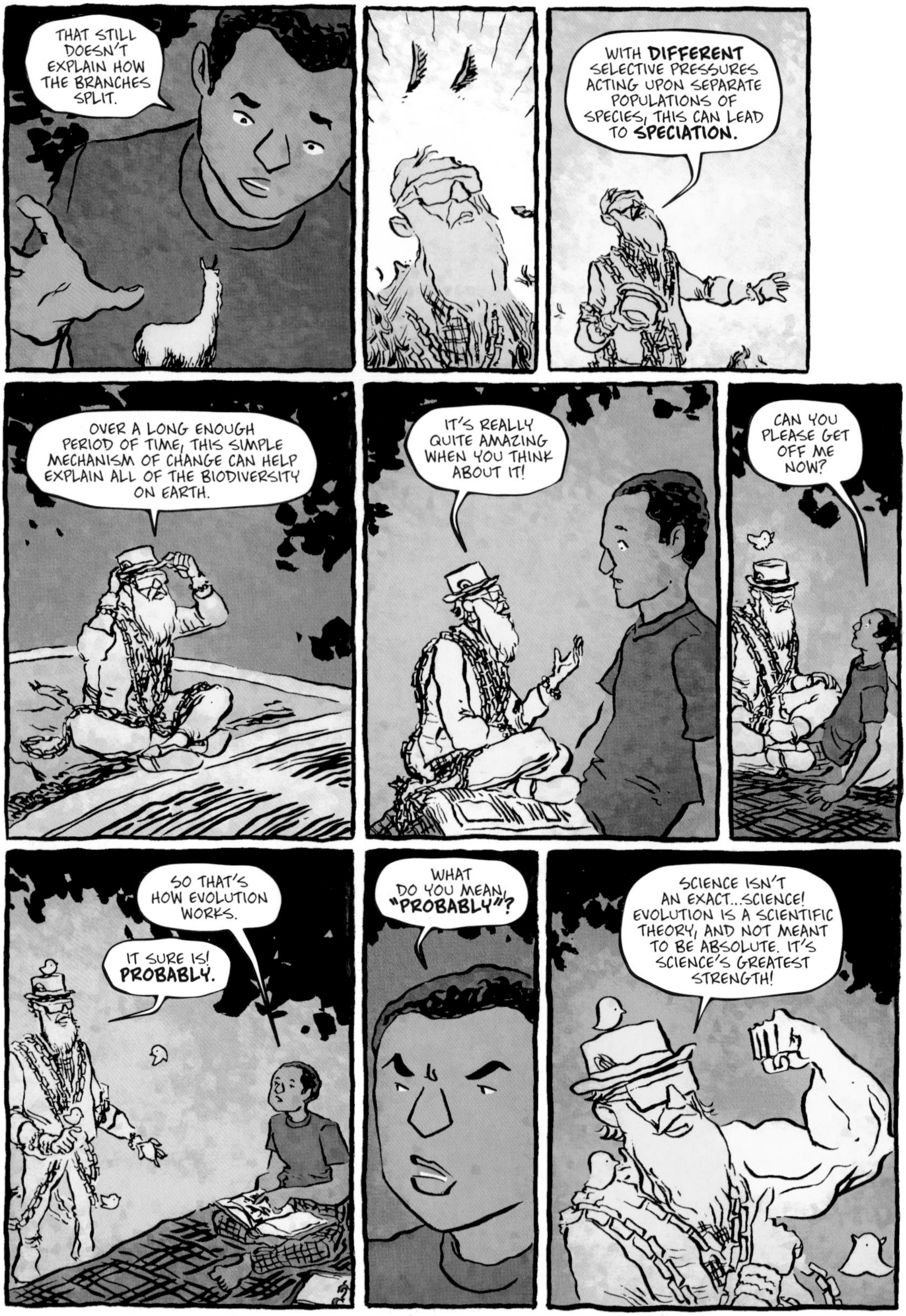
THAT STILL DOESN'T EXPLAIN HOW THE BRANCHES SPLIT.
WITH **DIFFERENT** SELECTIVE PRESSURES ACTING UPON SEPARATE POPULATIONS OF SPECIES, THIS CAN LEAD TO **SPECIATION.**
OVER A LONG ENOUGH PERIOD OF TIME, THIS SIMPLE MECHANISM OF CHANGE CAN HELP EXPLAIN ALL OF THE BIODIVERSITY ON EARTH.
IT'S REALLY QUITE AMAZING WHEN YOU THINK ABOUT IT!
CAN YOU PLEASE GET OFF ME NOW?
SO THAT'S HOW EVOLUTION WORKS.
IT SURE IS! **PROBABLY.**
WHAT DO YOU MEAN, **"PROBABLY"**?
SCIENCE ISN'T AN EXACT...SCIENCE! EVOLUTION IS A SCIENTIFIC THEORY, AND NOT MEANT TO BE ABSOLUTE. IT'S SCIENCE'S GREATEST STRENGTH!

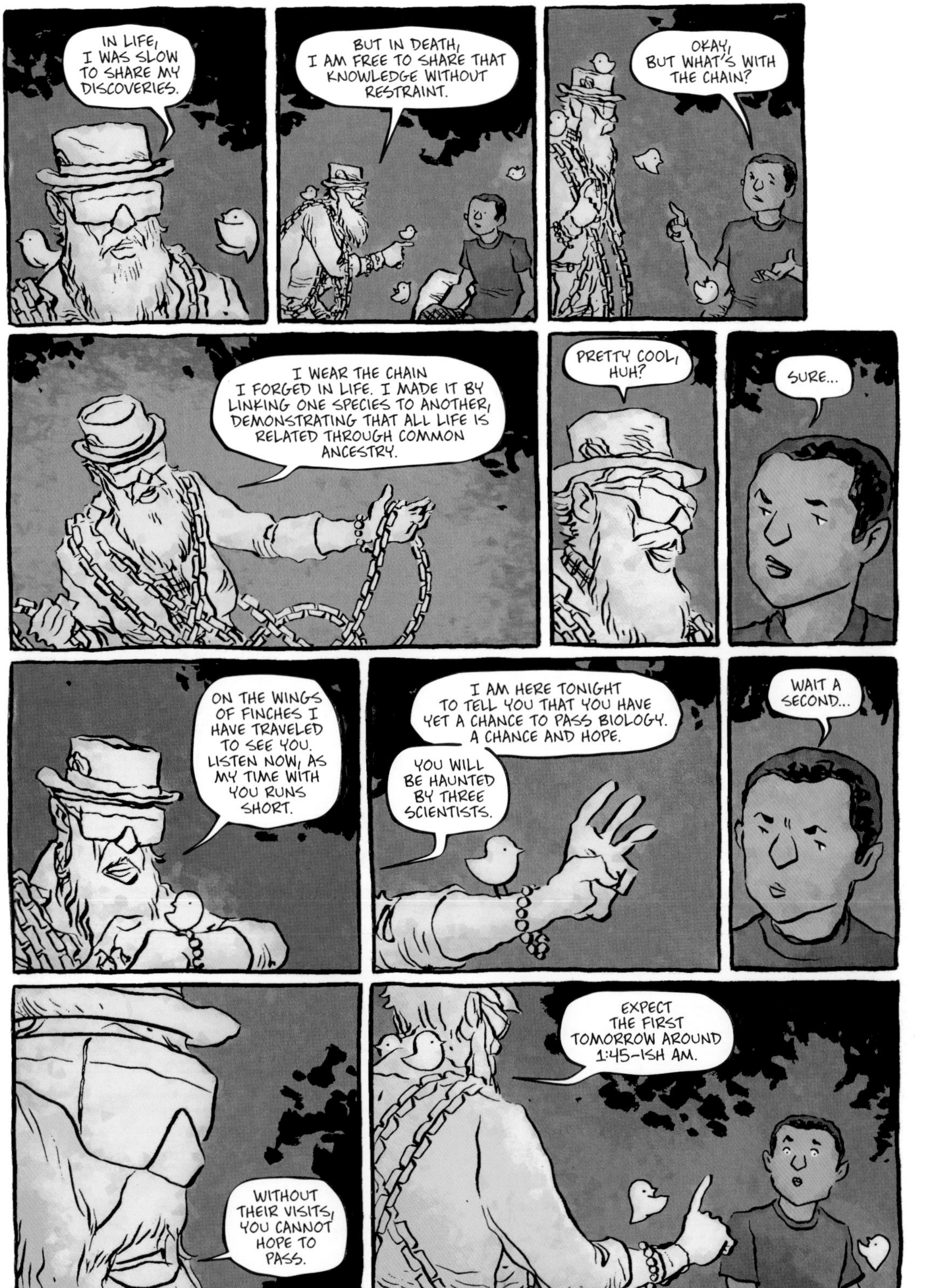
IN LIFE, I WAS SLOW TO SHARE MY DISCOVERIES.
BUT IN DEATH, I AM FREE TO SHARE THAT KNOWLEDGE WITHOUT RESTRAINT.
OKAY, BUT WHAT'S WITH THE CHAIN?
I WEAR THE CHAIN I FORGED IN LIFE. I MADE IT BY LINKING ONE SPECIES TO ANOTHER, DEMONSTRATING THAT ALL LIFE IS RELATED THROUGH COMMON ANCESTRY.
PRETTY COOL, HUH?
SURE...
ON THE WINGS OF FINCHES I HAVE TRAVELED TO SEE YOU. LISTEN NOW, AS MY TIME WITH YOU RUNS SHORT.
I AM HERE TONIGHT TO TELL YOU THAT YOU HAVE YET A CHANCE TO PASS BIOLOGY. A CHANCE AND HOPE.
YOU WILL BE HAUNTED BY THREE SCIENTISTS.
WAIT A SECOND...
WITHOUT THEIR VISITS, YOU CANNOT HOPE TO PASS.
EXPECT THE FIRST TOMORROW AROUND 1:45-ISH AM.

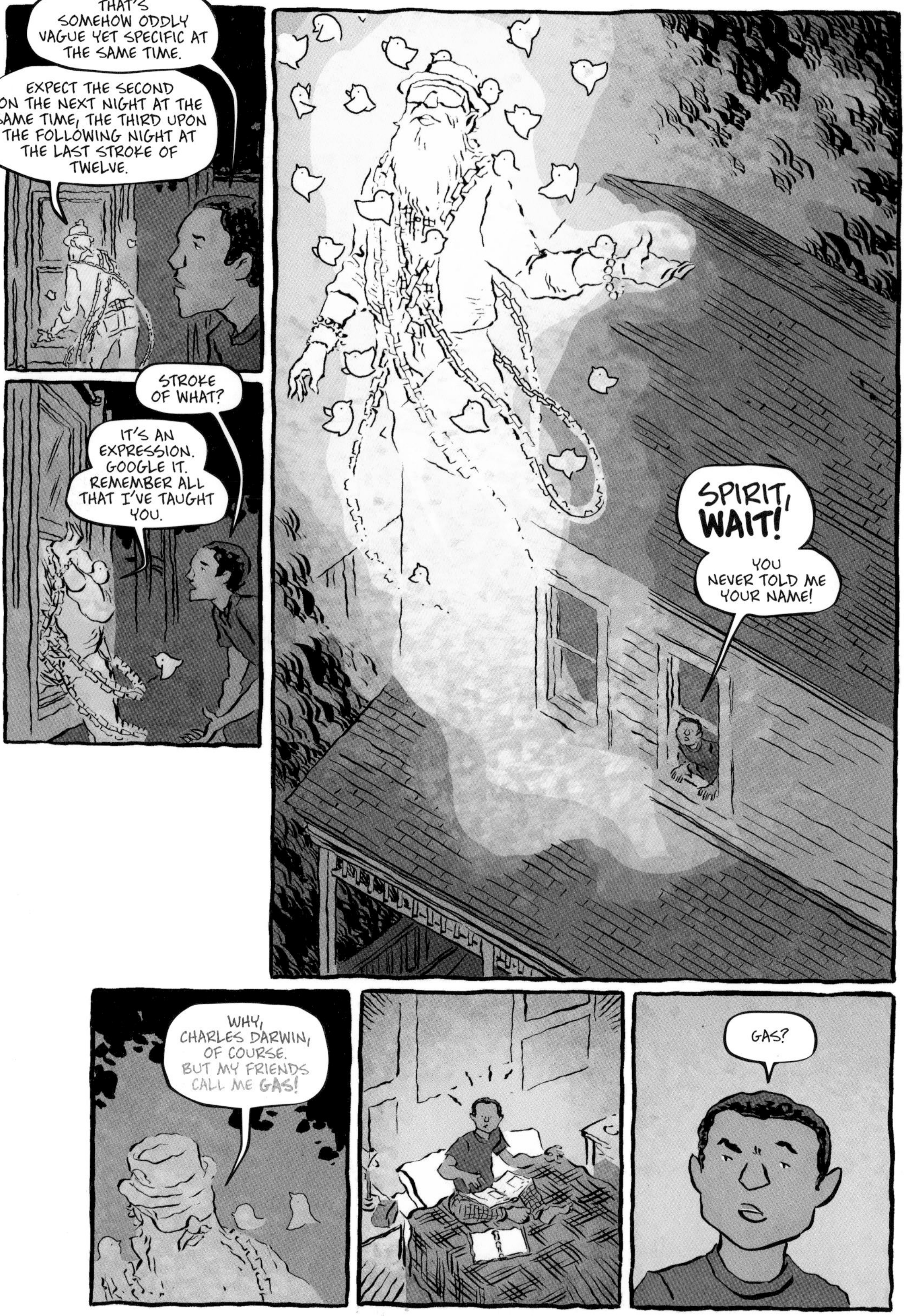

THAT'S SOMEHOW ODDLY VAGUE YET SPECIFIC AT THE SAME TIME.
EXPECT THE SECOND ON THE NEXT NIGHT AT THE SAME TIME, THE THIRD UPON THE FOLLOWING NIGHT AT THE LAST STROKE OF TWELVE.
STROKE OF WHAT?
IT'S AN EXPRESSION. GOOGLE IT. REMEMBER ALL THAT I'VE TAUGHT YOU.
SPIRIT, WAIT!
YOU NEVER TOLD ME YOUR NAME!
WHY, CHARLES DARWIN, OF COURSE. BUT MY FRIENDS CALL ME GAS!
GAS?

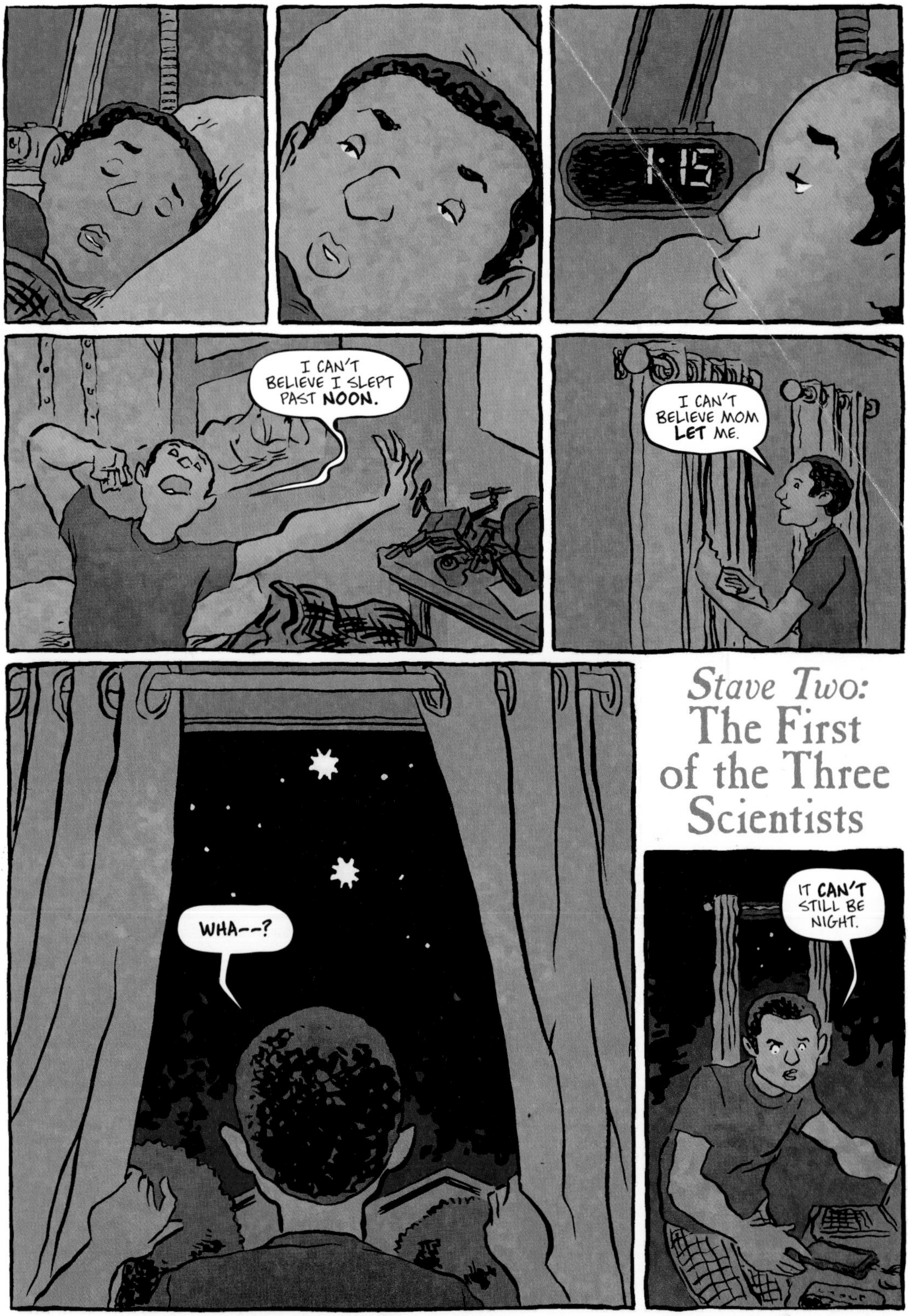
1:15
I CAN'T BELIEVE I SLEPT PAST NOON.
I CAN'T BELIEVE MOM LET ME.
WHA--?
Stave Two: The First of the Three Scientists
IT CAN'T STILL BE NIGHT.

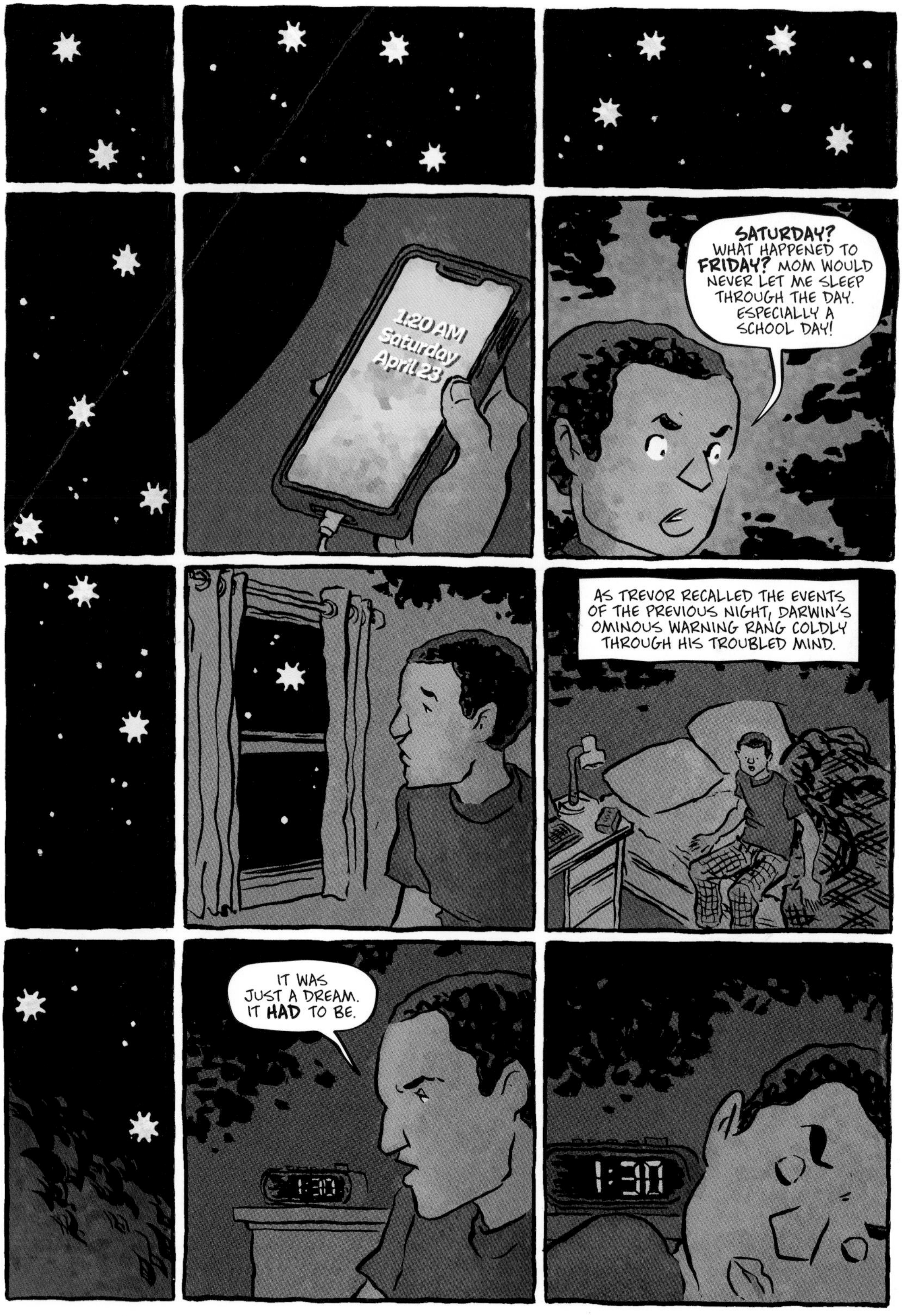
1:20 AM
Saturday
April 23
SATURDAY? WHAT HAPPENED TO FRIDAY? MOM WOULD NEVER LET ME SLEEP THROUGH THE DAY. ESPECIALLY A SCHOOL DAY!
AS TREVOR RECALLED THE EVENTS OF THE PREVIOUS NIGHT, DARWIN'S OMINOUS WARNING RANG COLDLY THROUGH HIS TROUBLED MIND.
IT WAS JUST A DREAM. IT HAD TO BE.
1:30

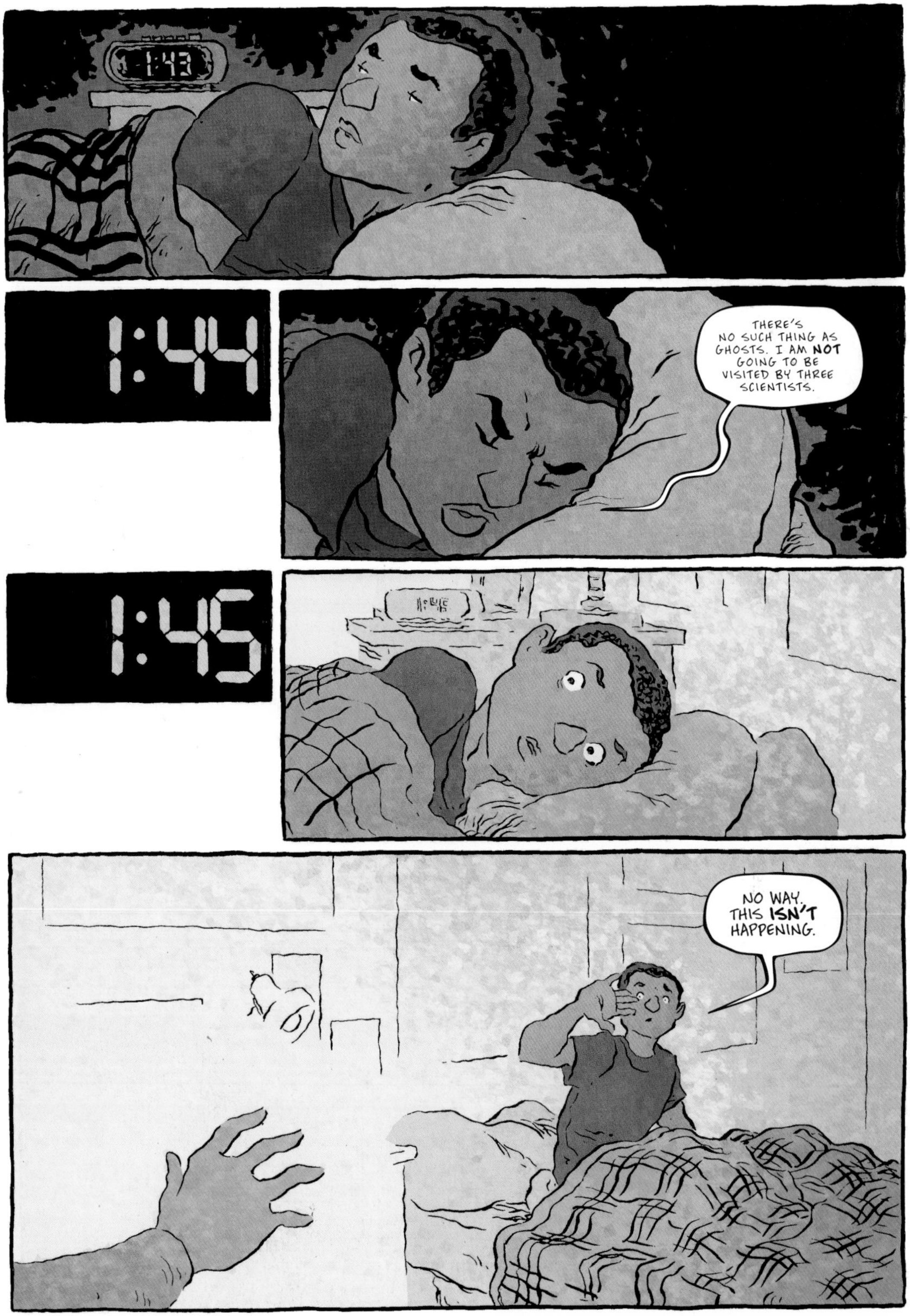
1:43
1:44
THERE'S NO SUCH THING AS GHOSTS. I AM **NOT** GOING TO BE VISITED BY THREE SCIENTISTS.
1:45
NO WAY. THIS **ISN'T** HAPPENING.

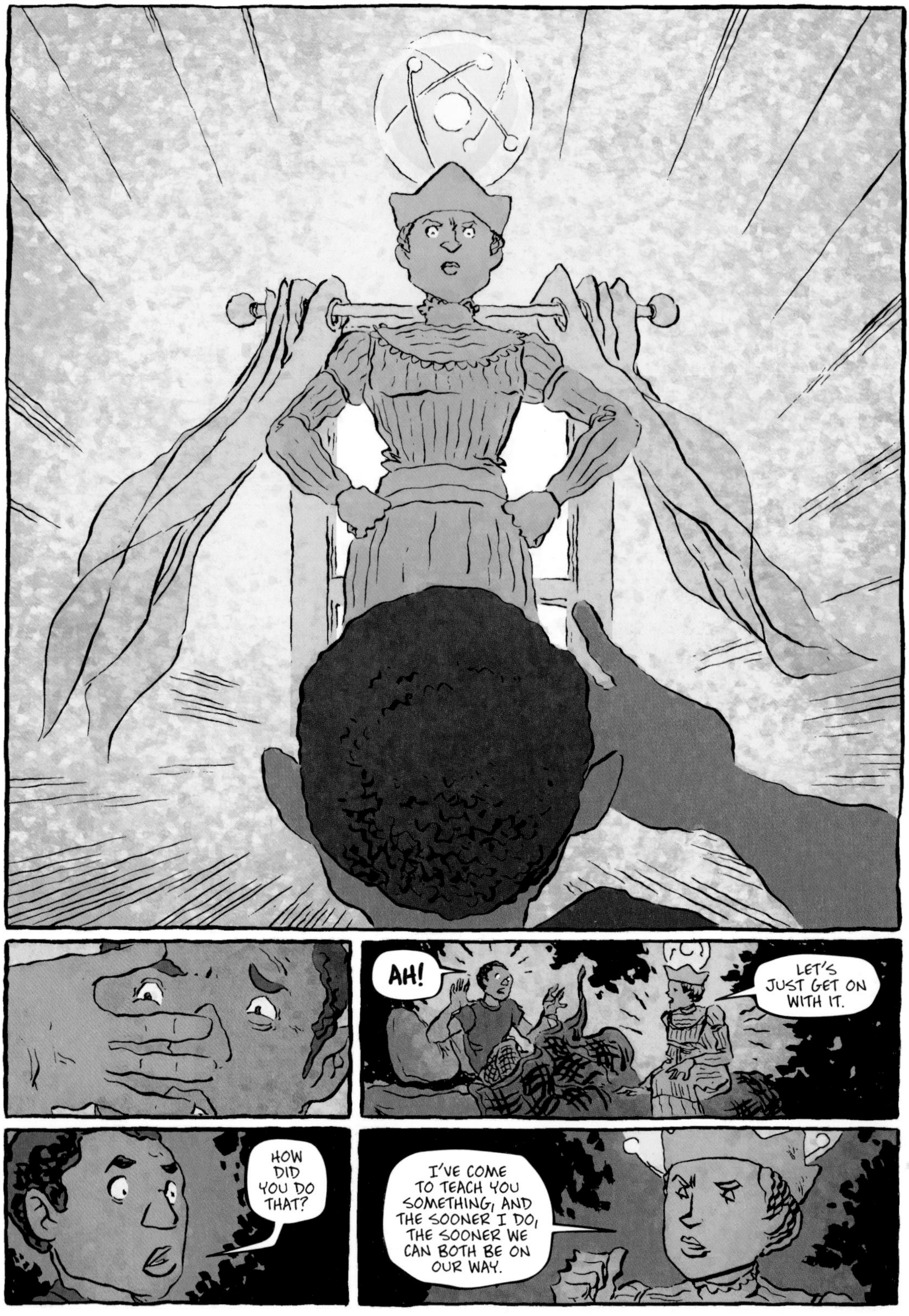
AH!
LET'S JUST GET ON WITH IT.
HOW DID YOU DO THAT?
I'VE COME TO TEACH YOU SOMETHING, AND THE SOONER I DO, THE SOONER WE CAN BOTH BE ON OUR WAY.

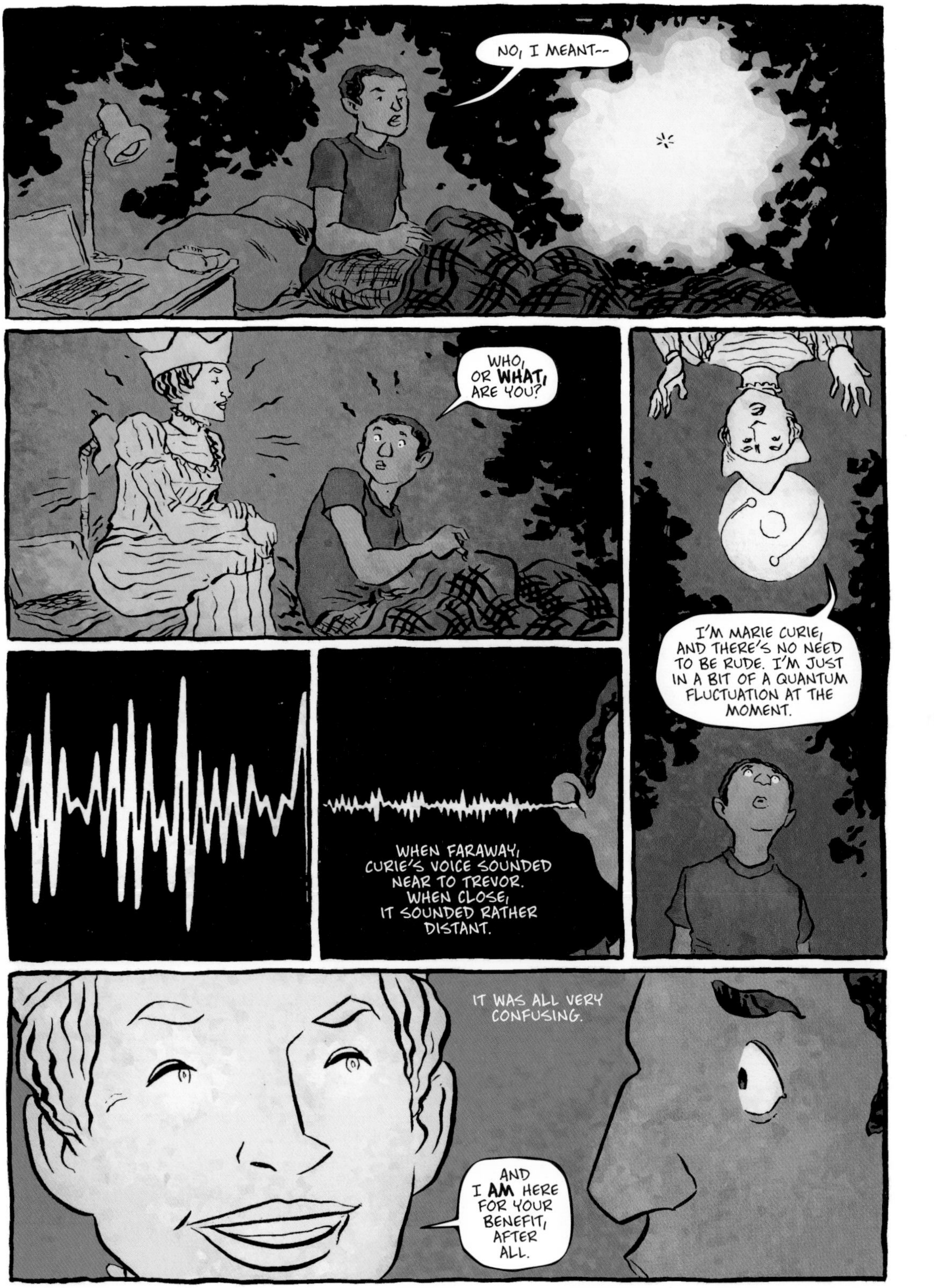
NO, I MEANT--
WHO, OR **WHAT**, ARE YOU?
I'M MARIE CURIE, AND THERE'S NO NEED TO BE RUDE. I'M JUST IN A BIT OF A QUANTUM FLUCTUATION AT THE MOMENT.
WHEN FARAWAY, CURIE'S VOICE SOUNDED NEAR TO TREVOR. WHEN CLOSE, IT SOUNDED RATHER DISTANT.
IT WAS ALL VERY CONFUSING.
AND I **AM** HERE FOR YOUR BENEFIT, AFTER ALL.

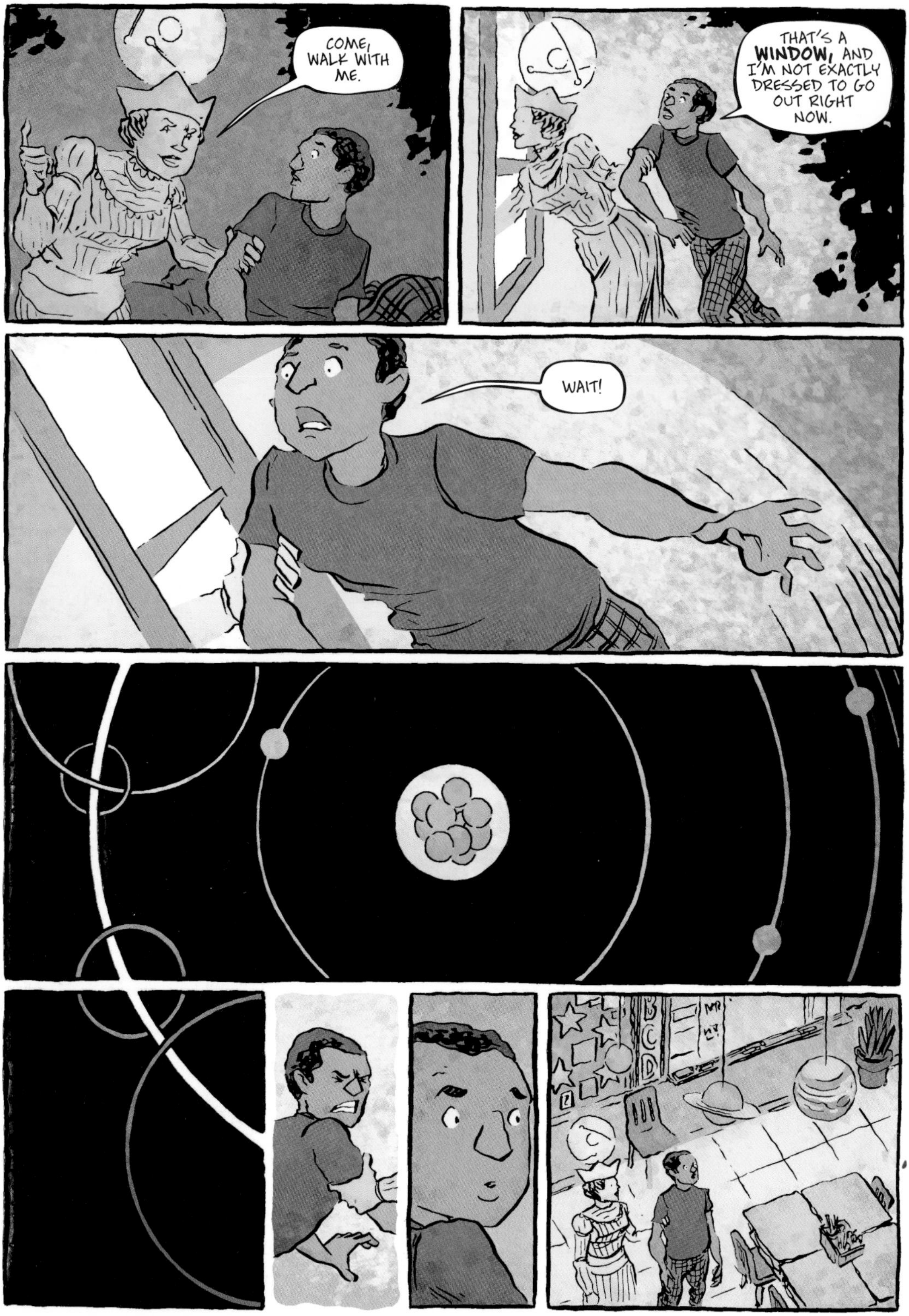
COME, WALK WITH ME.
THAT'S A WINDOW, AND I'M NOT EXACTLY DRESSED TO GO OUT RIGHT NOW.
WAIT!

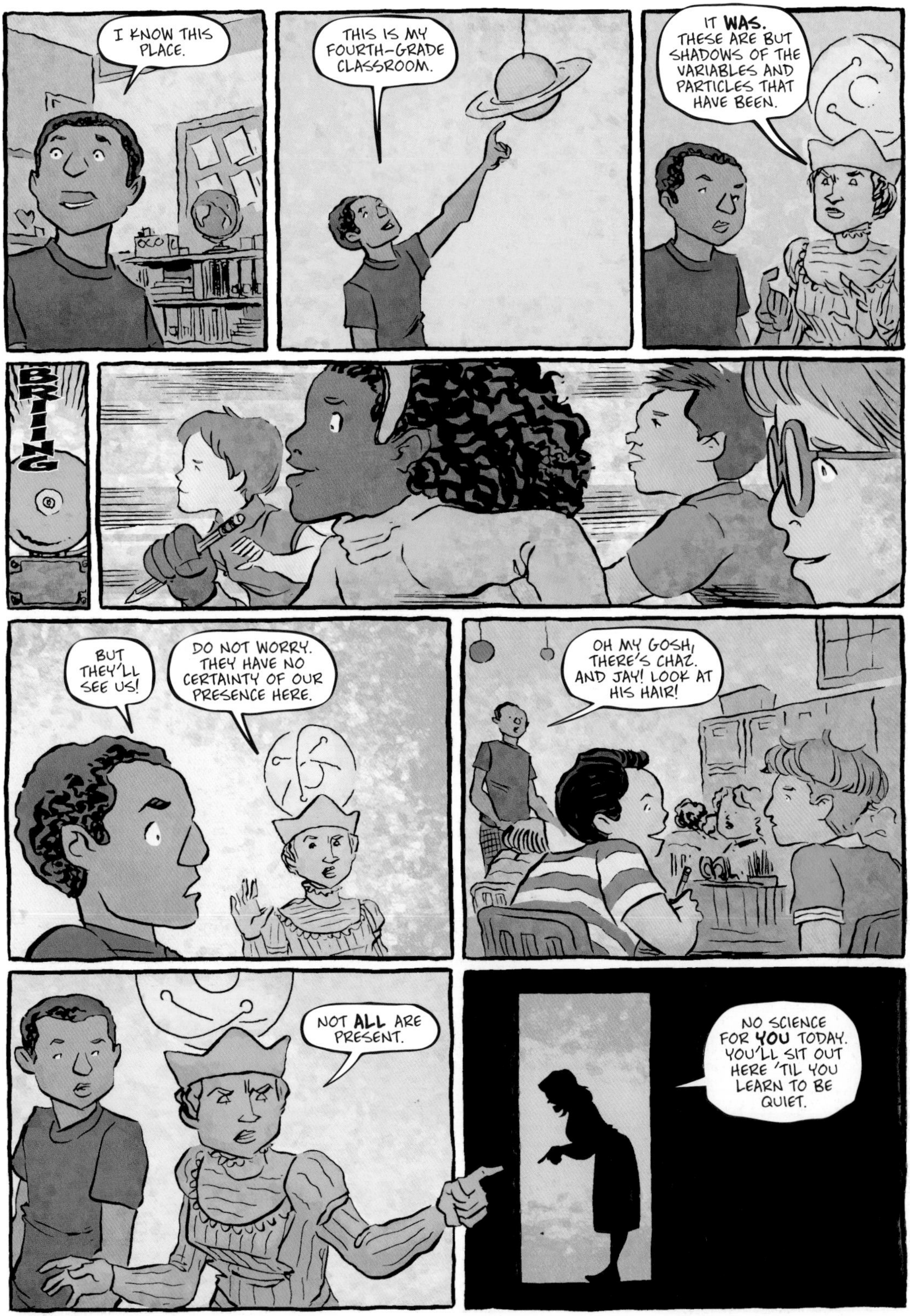
I KNOW THIS PLACE.
THIS IS MY FOURTH-GRADE CLASSROOM.
IT **WAS.** THESE ARE BUT SHADOWS OF THE VARIABLES AND PARTICLES THAT HAVE BEEN.
BRIING
BUT THEY'LL SEE US!
DO NOT WORRY. THEY HAVE NO CERTAINTY OF OUR PRESENCE HERE.
OH MY GOSH, THERE'S CHAZ. AND JAY! LOOK AT HIS HAIR!
NOT **ALL** ARE PRESENT.
NO SCIENCE FOR **YOU** TODAY. YOU'LL SIT OUT HERE 'TIL YOU LEARN TO BE QUIET.

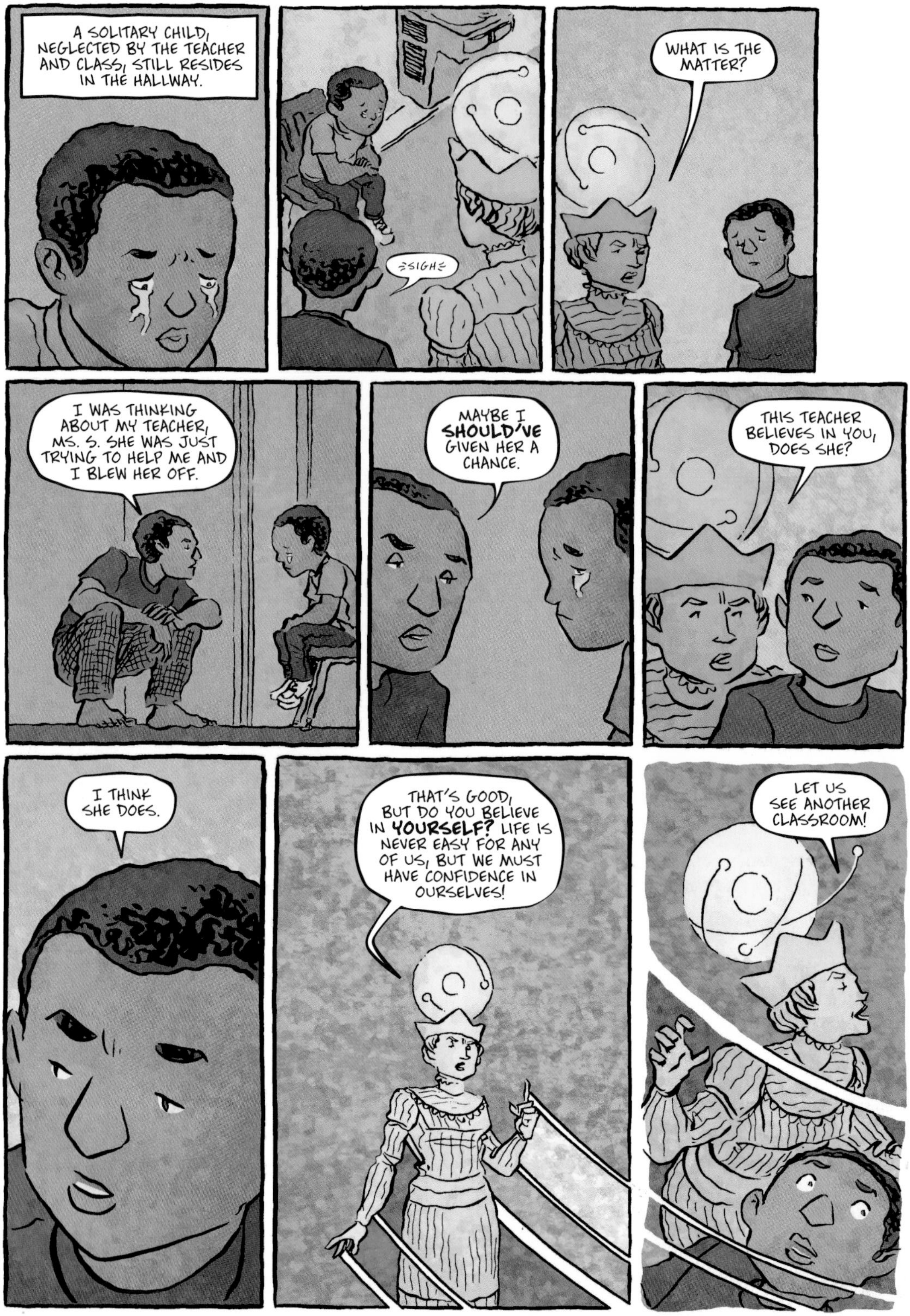
A SOLITARY CHILD, NEGLECTED BY THE TEACHER AND CLASS, STILL RESIDES IN THE HALLWAY.
SIGH
WHAT IS THE MATTER?
I WAS THINKING ABOUT MY TEACHER, MS. S. SHE WAS JUST TRYING TO HELP ME AND I BLEW HER OFF.
MAYBE I **SHOULD'VE** GIVEN HER A CHANCE.
THIS TEACHER BELIEVES IN YOU, DOES SHE?
I THINK SHE DOES.
THAT'S GOOD, BUT DO YOU BELIEVE IN **YOURSELF?** LIFE IS NEVER EASY FOR ANY OF US, BUT WE MUST HAVE CONFIDENCE IN OURSELVES!
LET US SEE ANOTHER CLASSROOM!

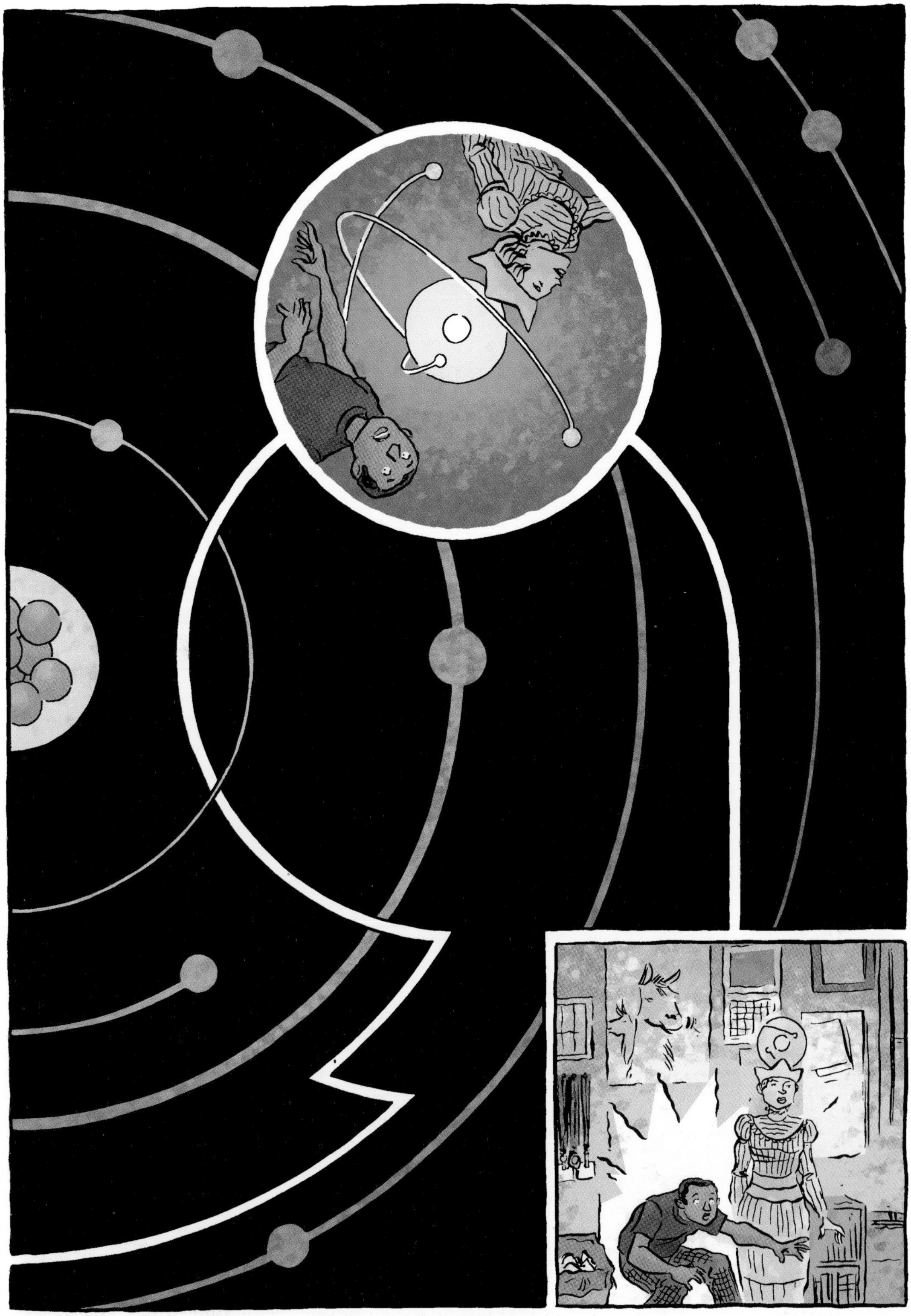

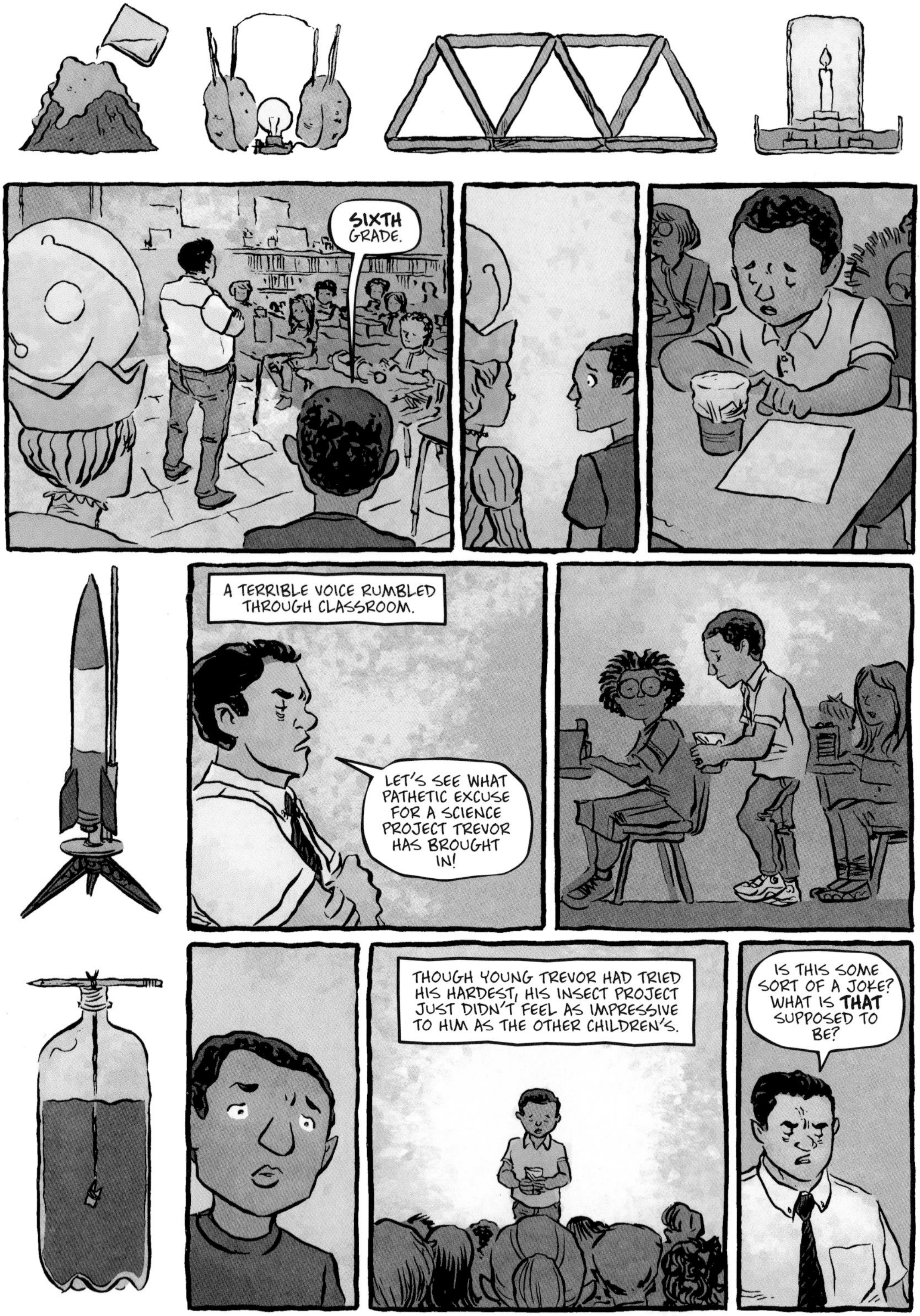
SIXTH GRADE.
A TERRIBLE VOICE RUMBLED THROUGH CLASSROOM.
LET'S SEE WHAT PATHETIC EXCUSE FOR A SCIENCE PROJECT TREVOR HAS BROUGHT IN!
THOUGH YOUNG TREVOR HAD TRIED HIS HARDEST, HIS INSECT PROJECT JUST DIDN'T FEEL AS IMPRESSIVE TO HIM AS THE OTHER CHILDREN'S.
IS THIS SOME SORT OF A JOKE? WHAT IS **THAT** SUPPOSED TO BE?

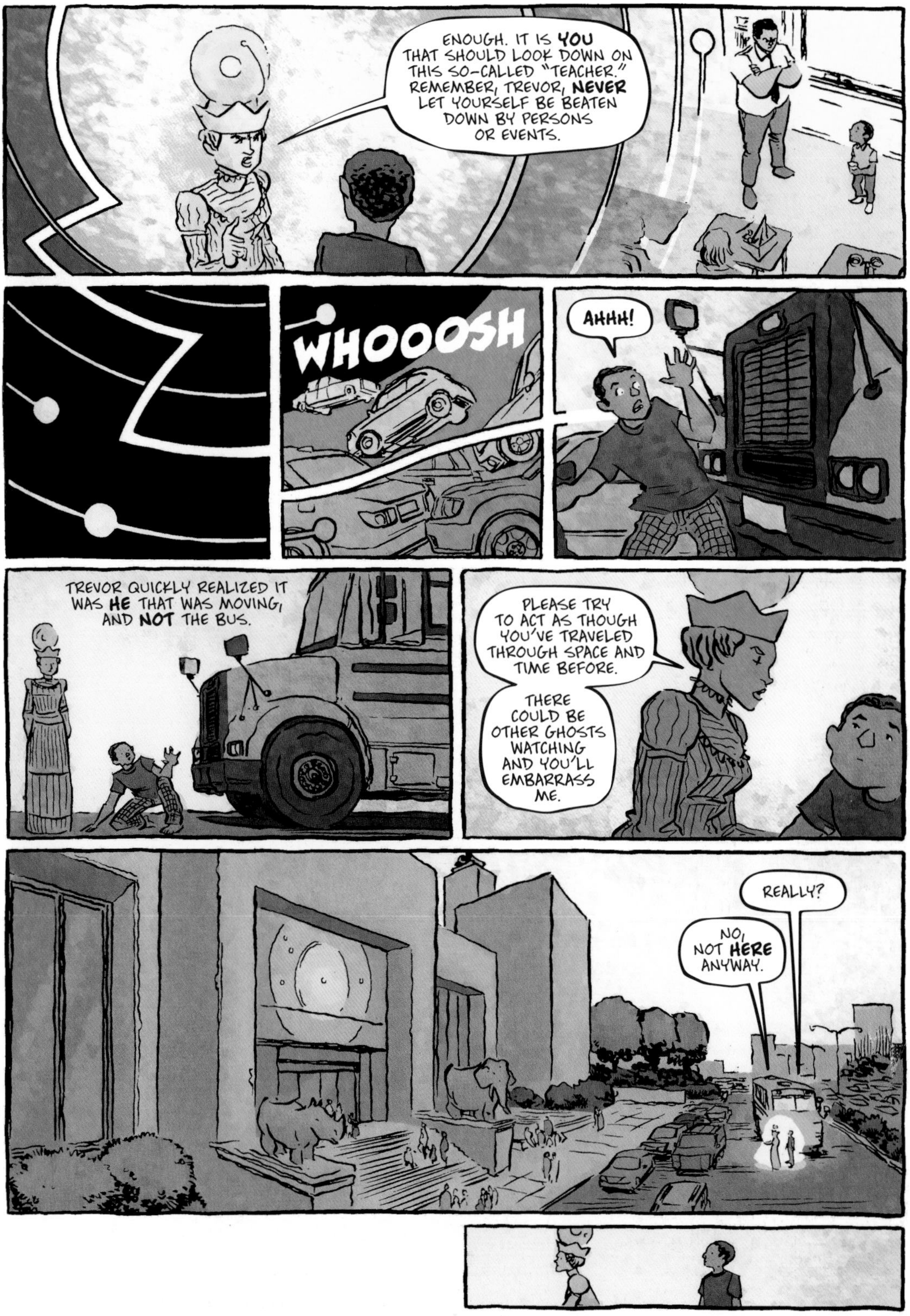
ENOUGH. IT IS YOU THAT SHOULD LOOK DOWN ON THIS SO-CALLED "TEACHER." REMEMBER, TREVOR, NEVER LET YOURSELF BE BEATEN DOWN BY PERSONS OR EVENTS.
WHOOOSH
AHHH!
TREVOR QUICKLY REALIZED IT WAS HE THAT WAS MOVING, AND NOT THE BUS.
PLEASE TRY TO ACT AS THOUGH YOU'VE TRAVELED THROUGH SPACE AND TIME BEFORE.
THERE COULD BE OTHER GHOSTS WATCHING AND YOU'LL EMBARRASS ME.
REALLY?
NO, NOT HERE ANYWAY.

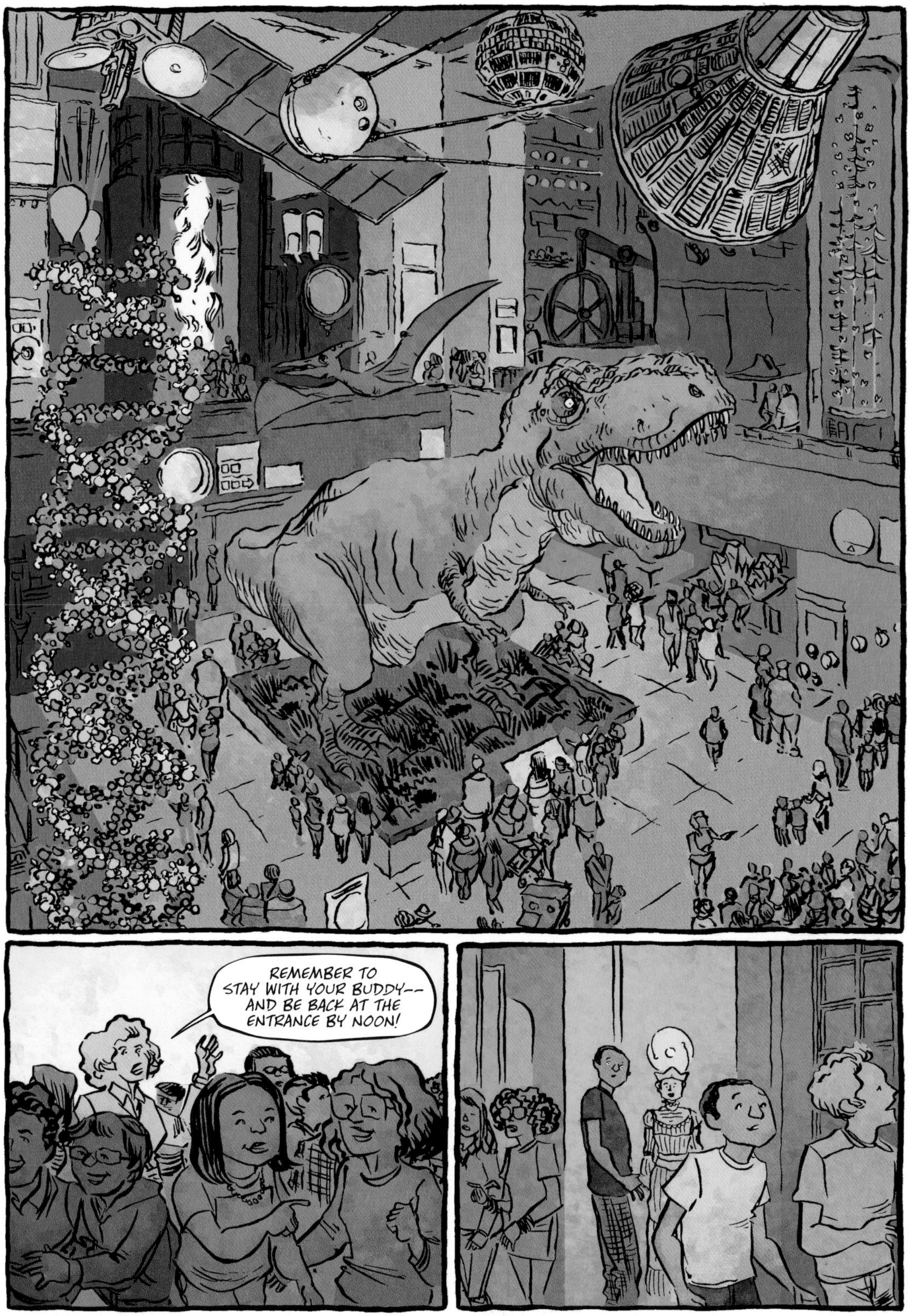
REMEMBER TO STAY WITH YOUR BUDDY-- AND BE BACK AT THE ENTRANCE BY NOON!

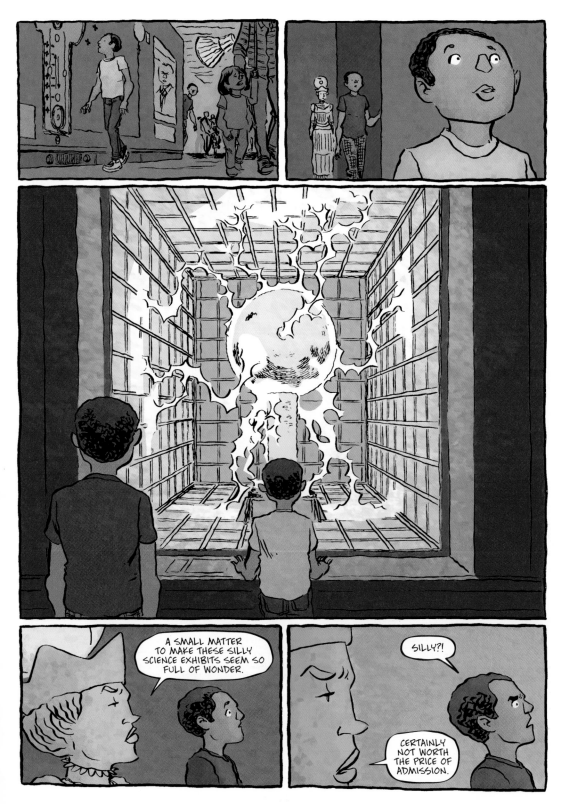

A SMALL MATTER TO MAKE THESE SILLY SCIENCE EXHIBITS SEEM SO FULL OF WONDER.

SILLY?!

CERTAINLY NOT WORTH THE PRICE OF ADMISSION.

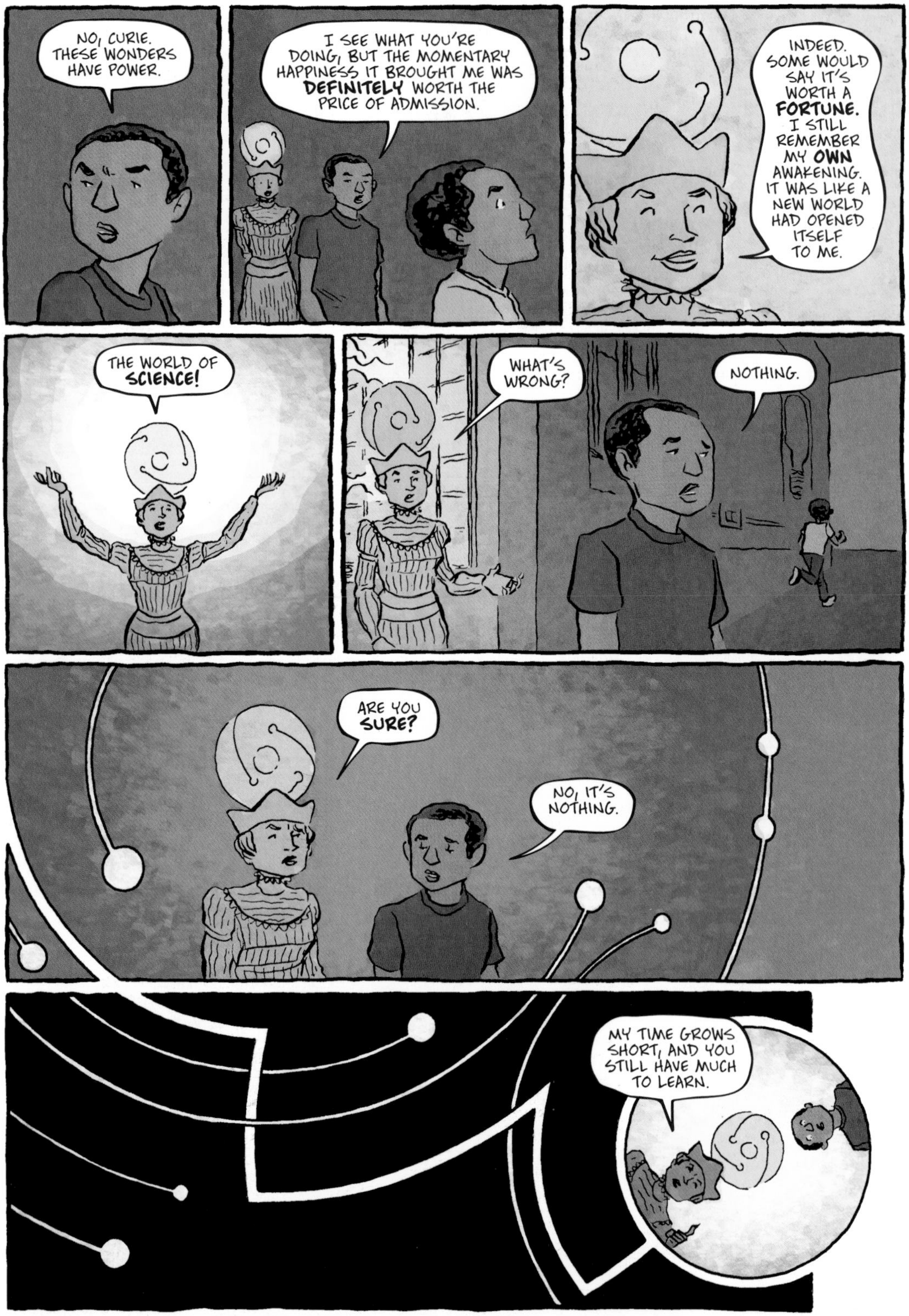
NO, CURIE. THESE WONDERS HAVE POWER.
I SEE WHAT YOU'RE DOING, BUT THE MOMENTARY HAPPINESS IT BROUGHT ME WAS **DEFINITELY** WORTH THE PRICE OF ADMISSION.
INDEED. SOME WOULD SAY IT'S WORTH A **FORTUNE.** I STILL REMEMBER MY **OWN** AWAKENING. IT WAS LIKE A NEW WORLD HAD OPENED ITSELF TO ME.
THE WORLD OF **SCIENCE!**
WHAT'S WRONG?
NOTHING.
ARE YOU **SURE?**
NO, IT'S NOTHING.
MY TIME GROWS SHORT, AND YOU STILL HAVE MUCH TO LEARN.

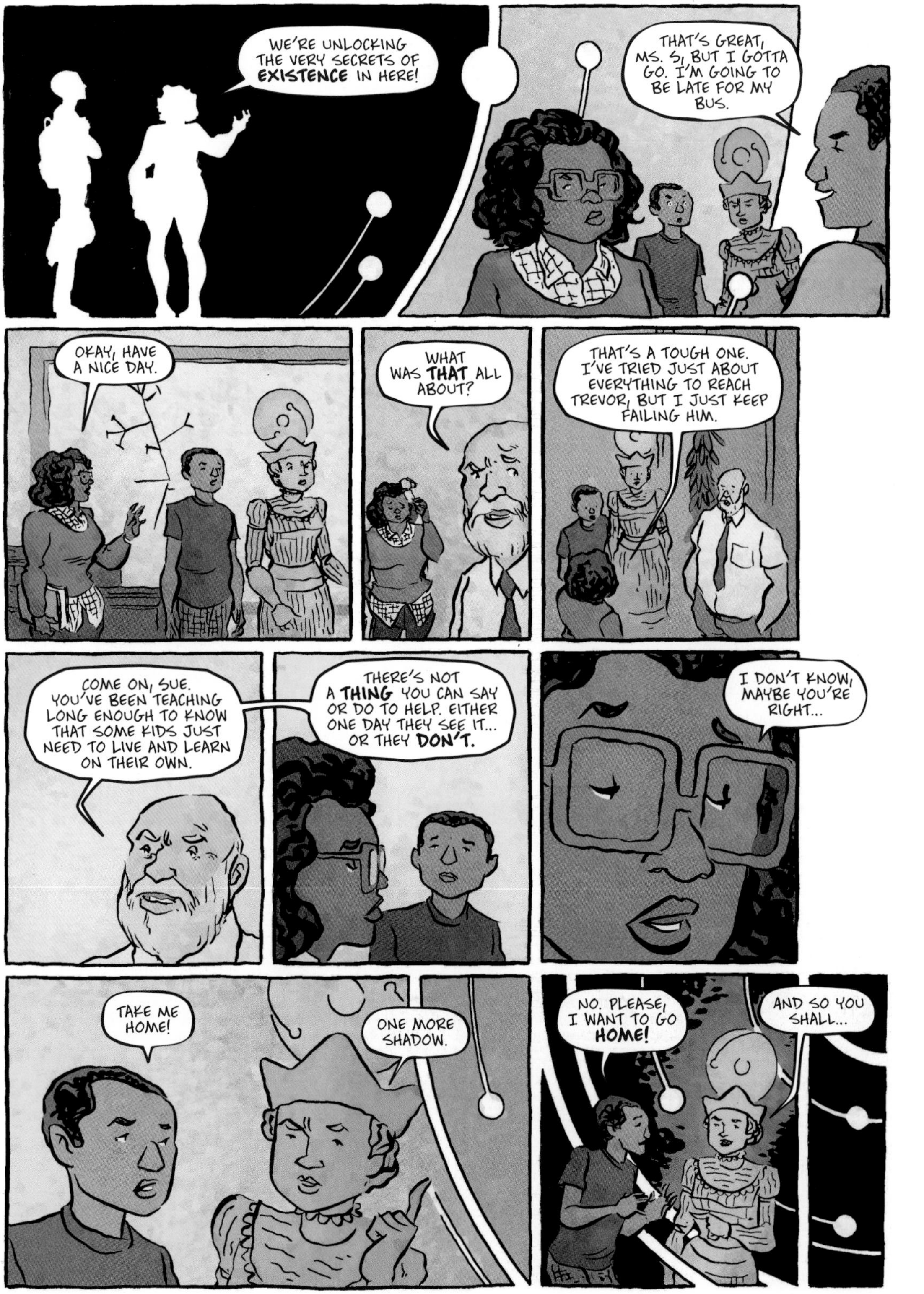
WE'RE UNLOCKING THE VERY SECRETS OF **EXISTENCE** IN HERE!
THAT'S GREAT, MS. S, BUT I GOTTA GO. I'M GOING TO BE LATE FOR MY BUS.
OKAY, HAVE A NICE DAY.
WHAT WAS **THAT** ALL ABOUT?
THAT'S A TOUGH ONE. I'VE TRIED JUST ABOUT EVERYTHING TO REACH TREVOR, BUT I JUST KEEP FAILING HIM.
COME ON, SUE. YOU'VE BEEN TEACHING LONG ENOUGH TO KNOW THAT SOME KIDS JUST NEED TO LIVE AND LEARN ON THEIR OWN.
THERE'S NOT A **THING** YOU CAN SAY OR DO TO HELP. EITHER ONE DAY THEY SEE IT... OR THEY **DON'T.**
I DON'T KNOW, MAYBE YOU'RE RIGHT...
TAKE ME HOME!
ONE MORE SHADOW.
NO. PLEASE, I WANT TO GO **HOME!**
AND SO YOU SHALL...

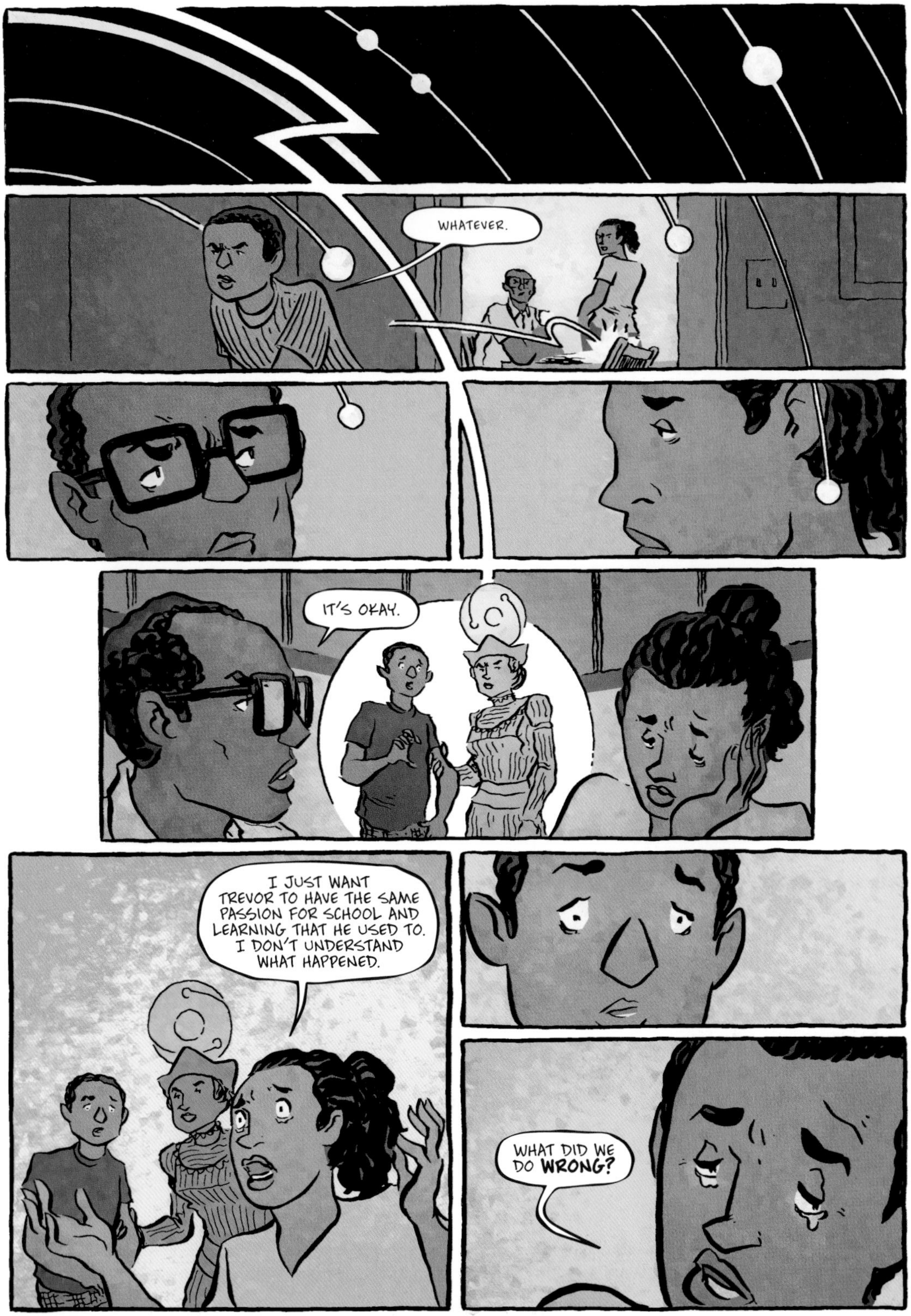
WHATEVER.
IT'S OKAY.
I JUST WANT TREVOR TO HAVE THE SAME PASSION FOR SCHOOL AND LEARNING THAT HE USED TO. I DON'T UNDERSTAND WHAT HAPPENED.
WHAT DID WE DO **WRONG?**

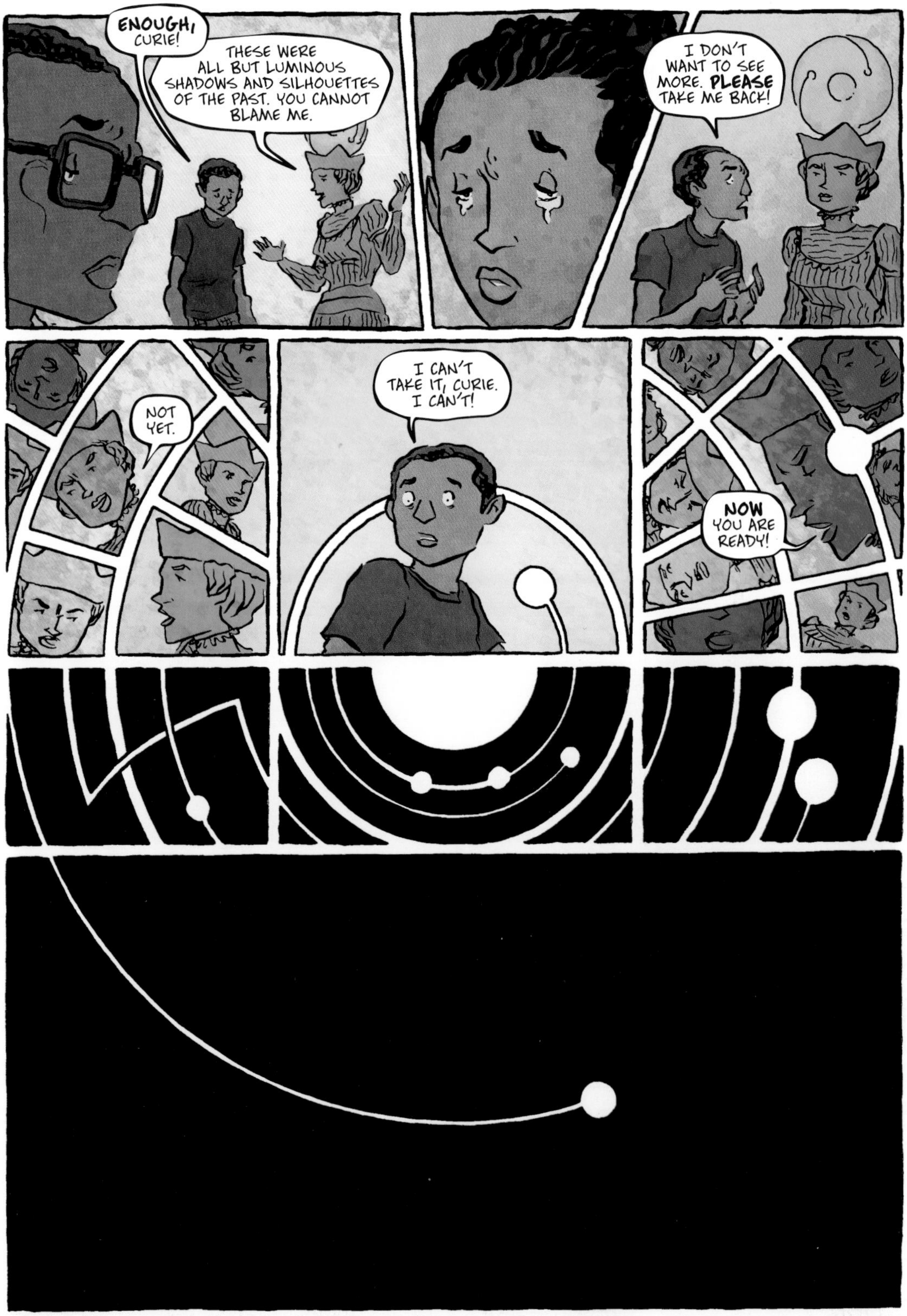
ENOUGH, CURIE!
THESE WERE ALL BUT LUMINOUS SHADOWS AND SILHOUETTES OF THE PAST. YOU CANNOT BLAME ME.
I DON'T WANT TO SEE MORE. PLEASE TAKE ME BACK!
NOT YET.
I CAN'T TAKE IT, CURIE. I CAN'T!
NOW YOU ARE READY!

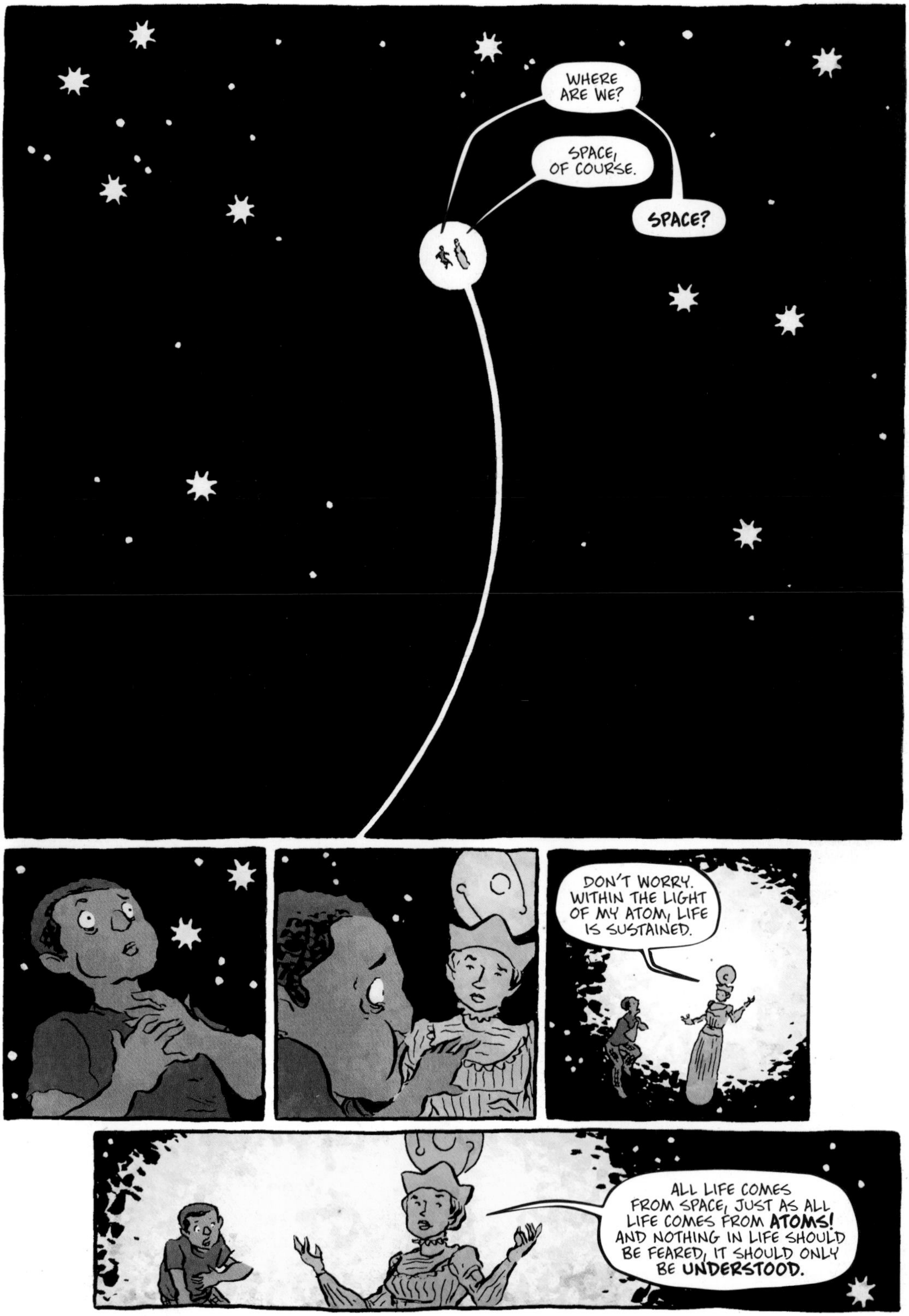
WHERE ARE WE?
SPACE, OF COURSE.
SPACE?
DON'T WORRY. WITHIN THE LIGHT OF MY ATOM, LIFE IS SUSTAINED.
ALL LIFE COMES FROM SPACE, JUST AS ALL LIFE COMES FROM **ATOMS!** AND NOTHING IN LIFE SHOULD BE FEARED, IT SHOULD ONLY BE **UNDERSTOOD.**

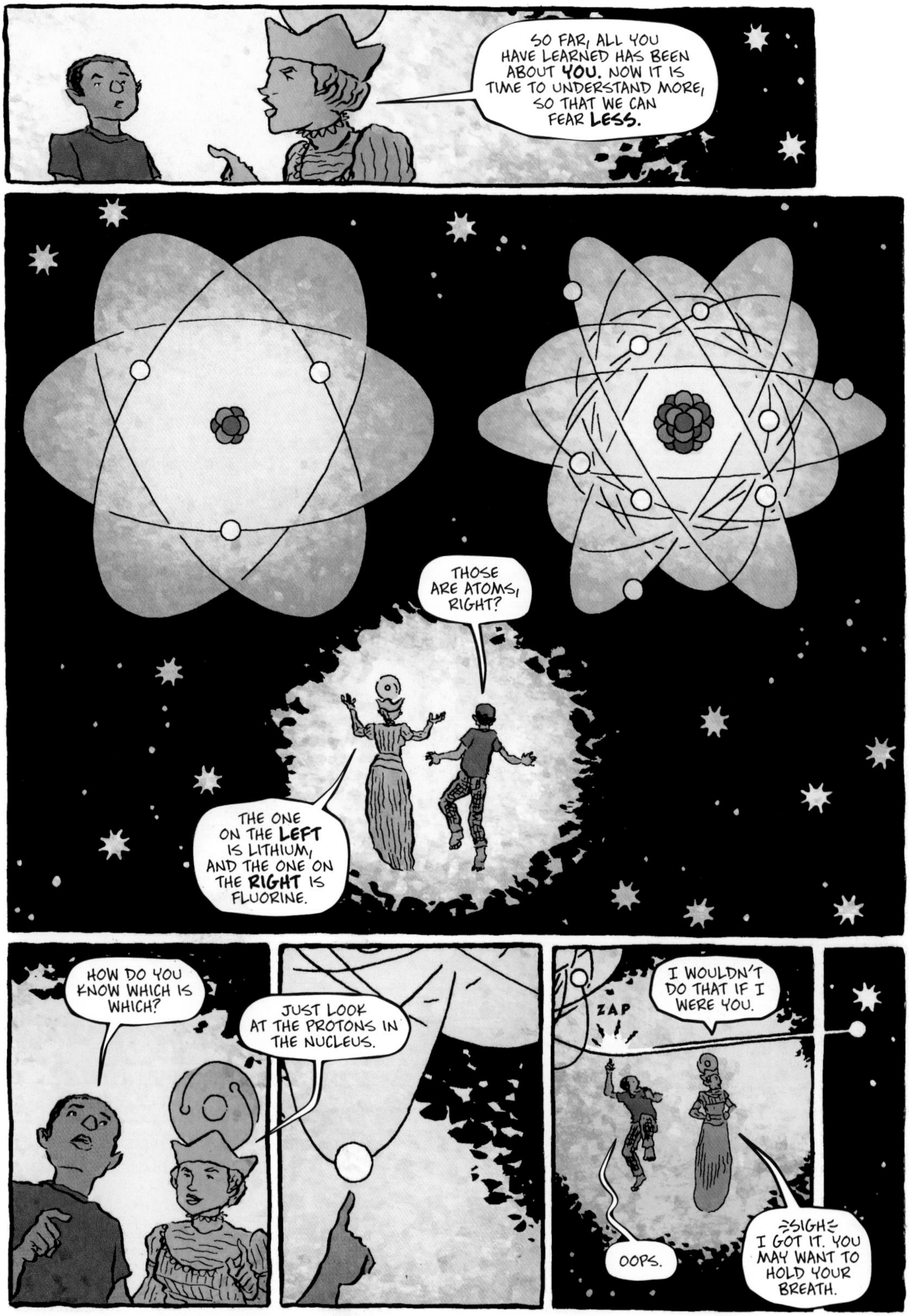
SO FAR, ALL YOU HAVE LEARNED HAS BEEN ABOUT **YOU.** NOW IT IS TIME TO UNDERSTAND MORE, SO THAT WE CAN FEAR **LESS.**
THOSE ARE ATOMS, RIGHT?
THE ONE ON THE **LEFT** IS LITHIUM, AND THE ONE ON THE **RIGHT** IS FLUORINE.
HOW DO YOU KNOW WHICH IS WHICH?
JUST LOOK AT THE PROTONS IN THE NUCLEUS.
I WOULDN'T DO THAT IF I WERE YOU.
ZAP
OOPS.
SIGH I GOT IT. YOU MAY WANT TO HOLD YOUR BREATH.

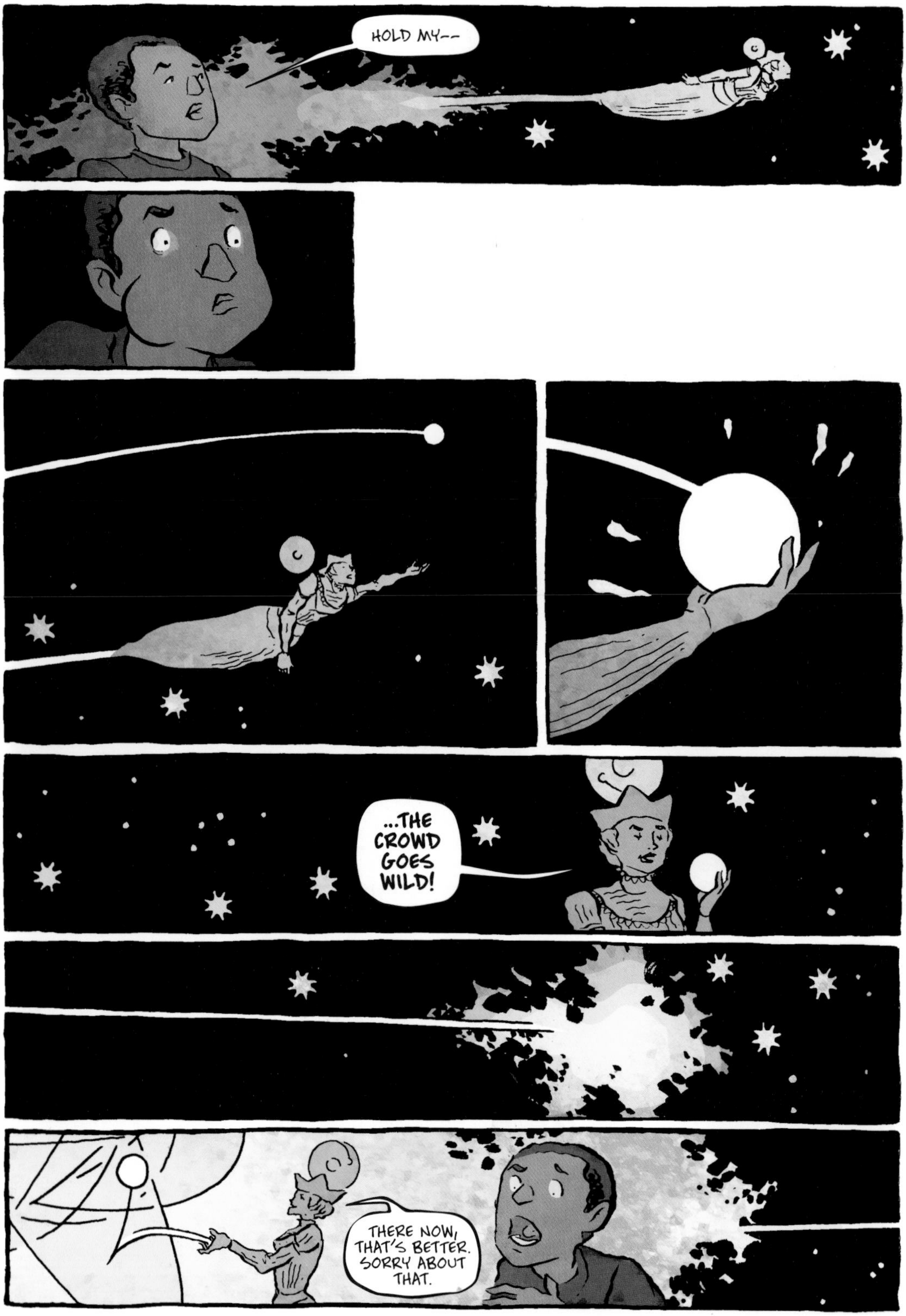
HOLD MY--
...THE CROWD GOES WILD!
THERE NOW, THAT'S BETTER. SORRY ABOUT THAT.

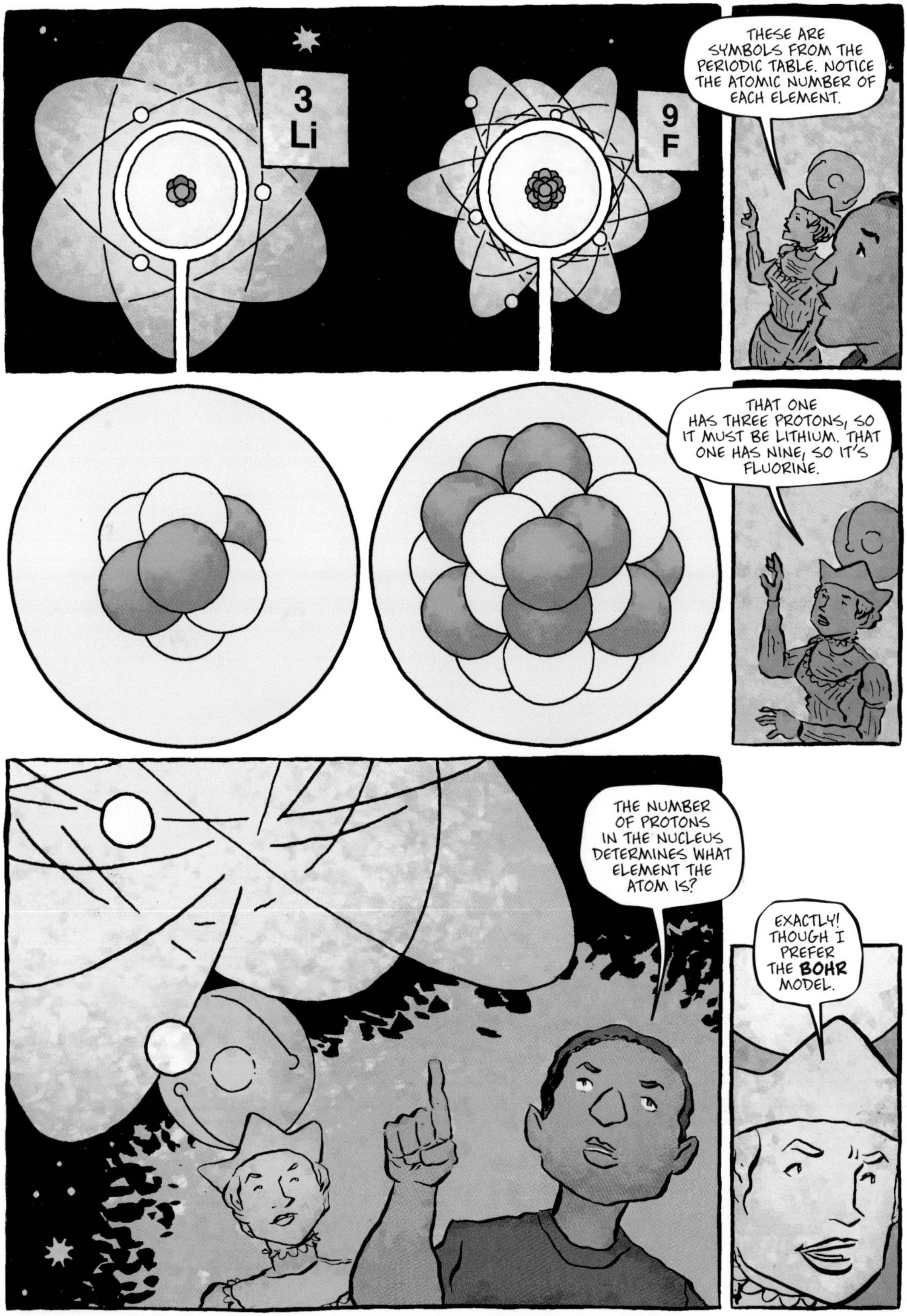
3 Li
9 F
THESE ARE SYMBOLS FROM THE PERIODIC TABLE. NOTICE THE ATOMIC NUMBER OF EACH ELEMENT.
THAT ONE HAS THREE PROTONS, SO IT MUST BE LITHIUM. THAT ONE HAS NINE, SO IT'S FLUORINE.
THE NUMBER OF PROTONS IN THE NUCLEUS DETERMINES WHAT ELEMENT THE ATOM IS?
EXACTLY! THOUGH I PREFER THE **BOHR** MODEL.

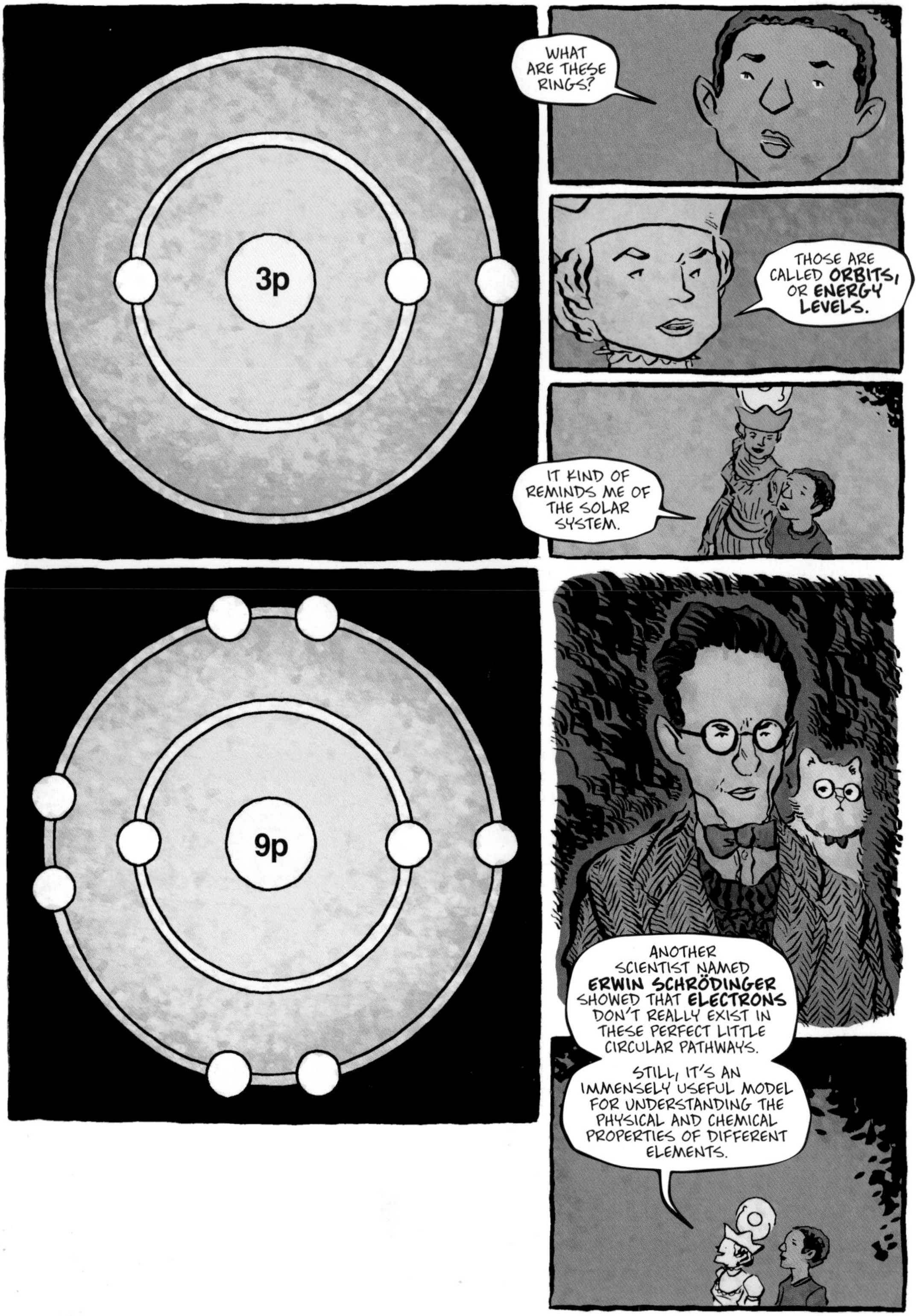
3p
WHAT ARE THESE RINGS?
THOSE ARE CALLED ORBITS, OR ENERGY LEVELS.
IT KIND OF REMINDS ME OF THE SOLAR SYSTEM.
9p
ANOTHER SCIENTIST NAMED ERWIN SCHRÖDINGER SHOWED THAT ELECTRONS DON'T REALLY EXIST IN THESE PERFECT LITTLE CIRCULAR PATHWAYS.
STILL, IT'S AN IMMENSELY USEFUL MODEL FOR UNDERSTANDING THE PHYSICAL AND CHEMICAL PROPERTIES OF DIFFERENT ELEMENTS.

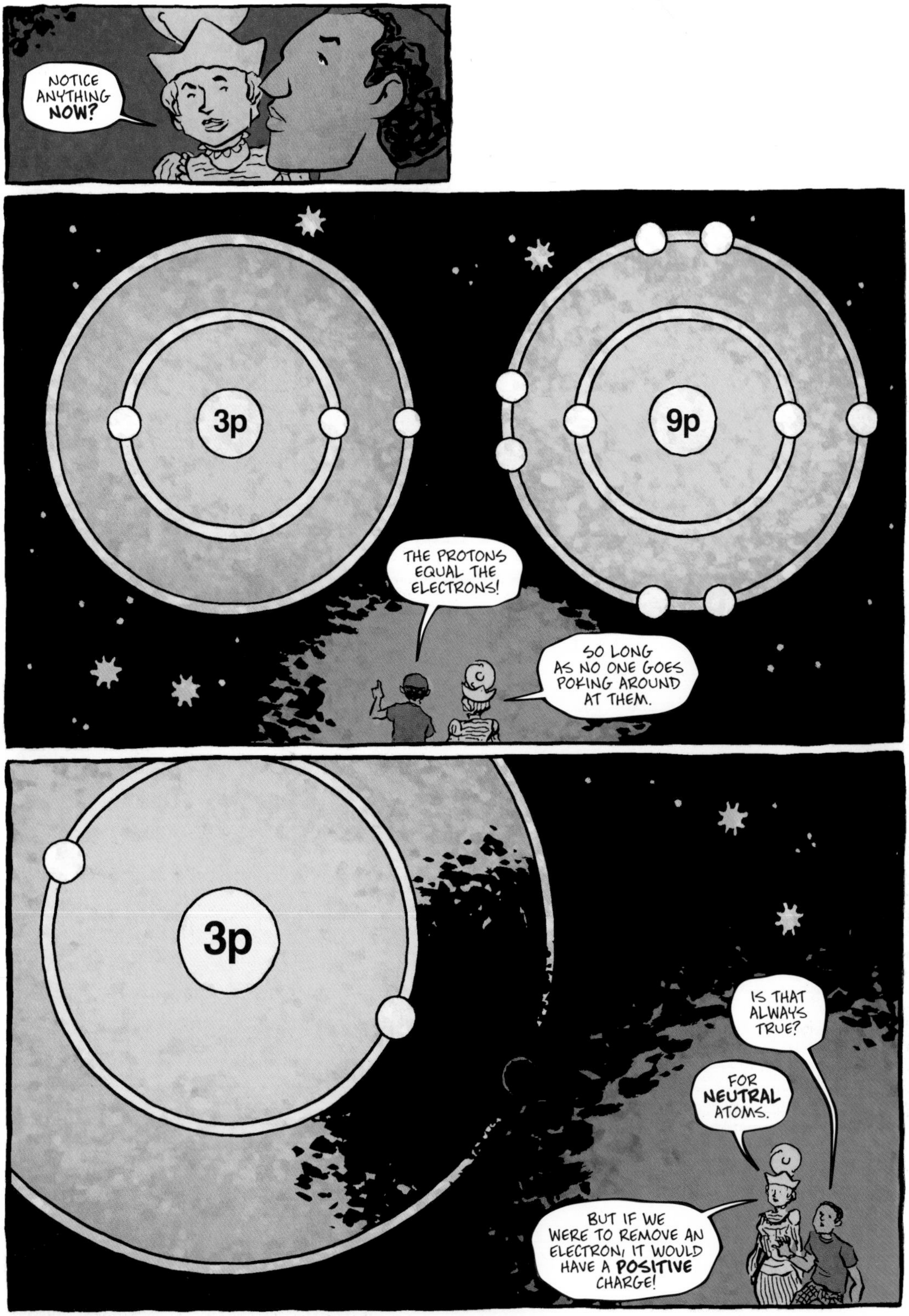
NOTICE ANYTHING **NOW?**
3p
9p
THE PROTONS EQUAL THE ELECTRONS!
SO LONG AS NO ONE GOES POKING AROUND AT THEM.
3p
IS THAT ALWAYS TRUE?
FOR **NEUTRAL** ATOMS.
BUT IF WE WERE TO REMOVE AN ELECTRON, IT WOULD HAVE A **POSITIVE** CHARGE!

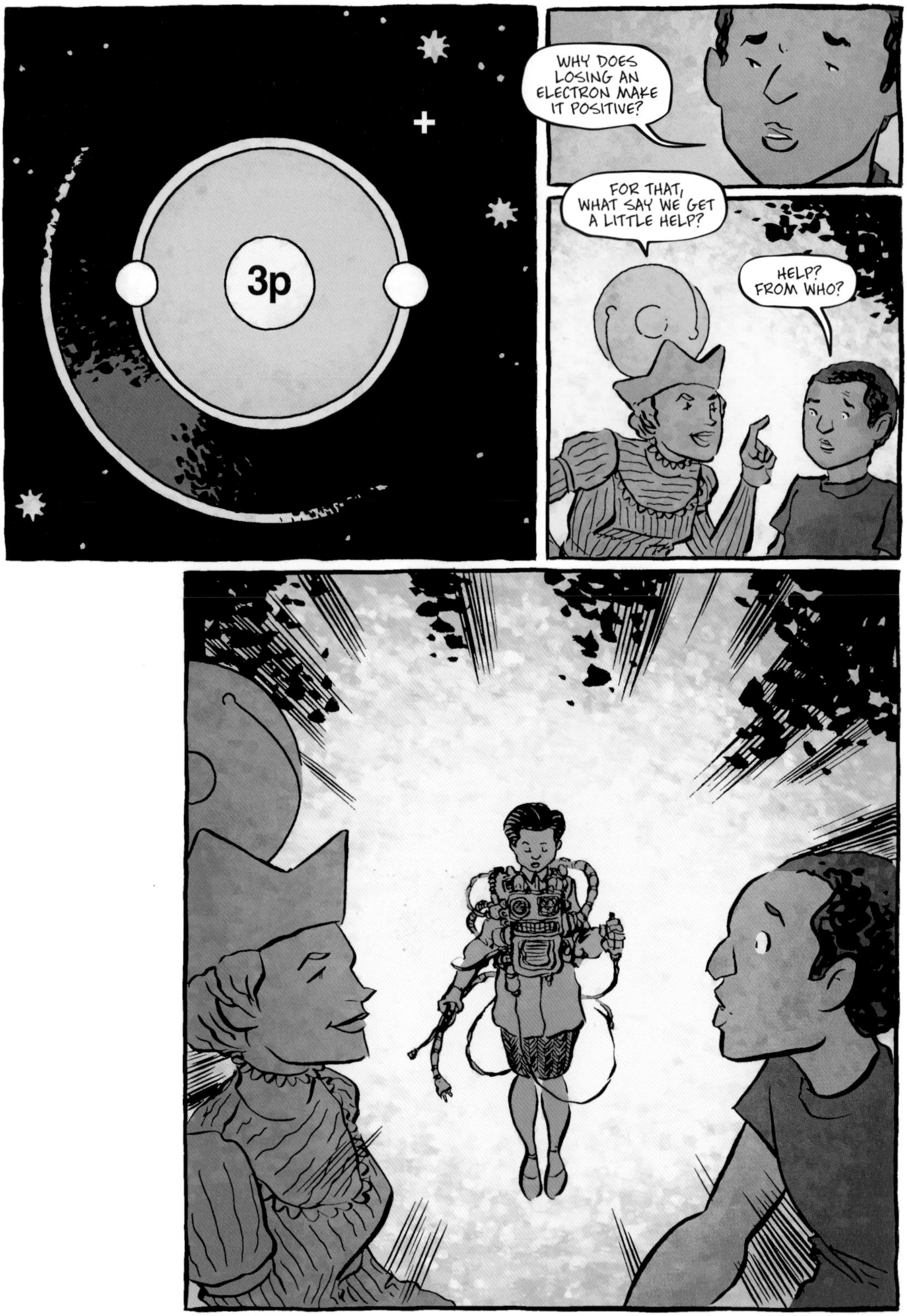
3p
+
WHY DOES LOSING AN ELECTRON MAKE IT POSITIVE?
FOR THAT, WHAT SAY WE GET A LITTLE HELP?
HELP? FROM WHO?

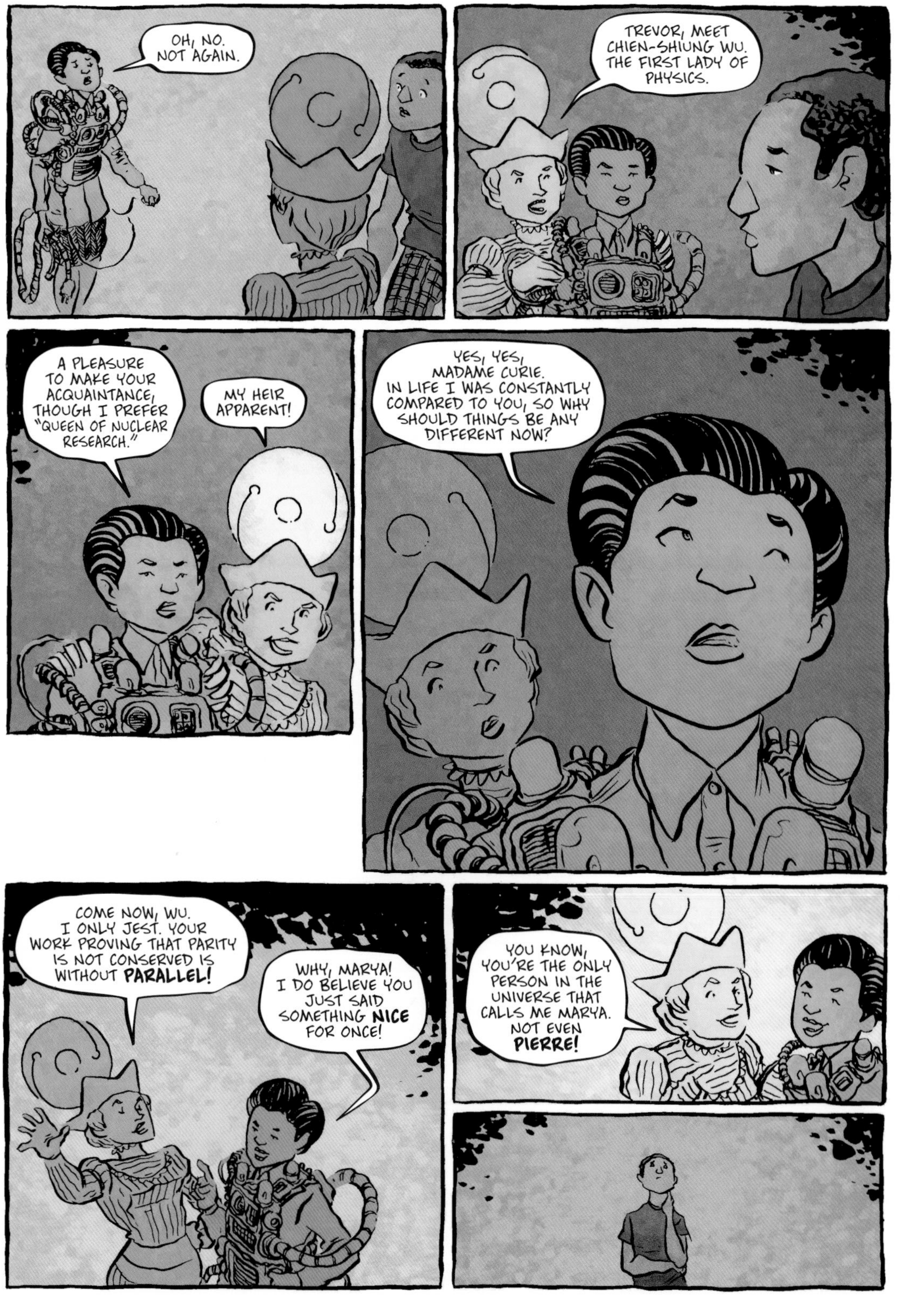
OH, NO. NOT AGAIN.
TREVOR, MEET CHIEN-SHIUNG WU. THE FIRST LADY OF PHYSICS.
A PLEASURE TO MAKE YOUR ACQUAINTANCE, THOUGH I PREFER "QUEEN OF NUCLEAR RESEARCH."
MY HEIR APPARENT!
YES, YES, MADAME CURIE. IN LIFE I WAS CONSTANTLY COMPARED TO YOU, SO WHY SHOULD THINGS BE ANY DIFFERENT NOW?
COME NOW, WU. I ONLY JEST. YOUR WORK PROVING THAT PARITY IS NOT CONSERVED IS WITHOUT **PARALLEL!**
WHY, MARYA! I DO BELIEVE YOU JUST SAID SOMETHING **NICE** FOR ONCE!
YOU KNOW, YOU'RE THE ONLY PERSON IN THE UNIVERSE THAT CALLS ME MARYA. NOT EVEN **PIERRE!**

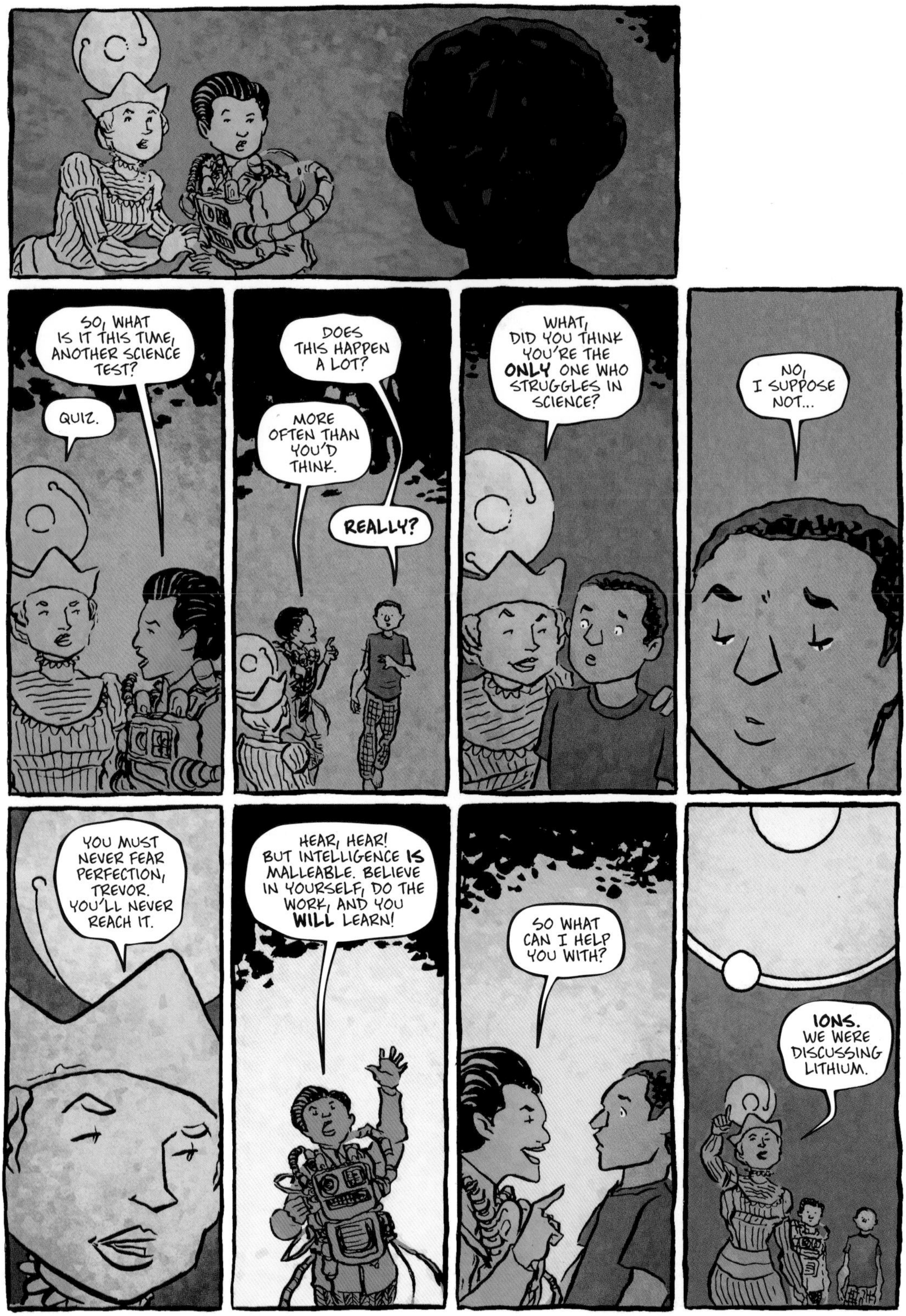
SO, WHAT IS IT THIS TIME, ANOTHER SCIENCE TEST?
QUIZ.
DOES THIS HAPPEN A LOT?
MORE OFTEN THAN YOU'D THINK.
REALLY?
WHAT, DID YOU THINK YOU'RE THE ONLY ONE WHO STRUGGLES IN SCIENCE?
NO, I SUPPOSE NOT...
YOU MUST NEVER FEAR PERFECTION, TREVOR. YOU'LL NEVER REACH IT.
HEAR, HEAR! BUT INTELLIGENCE IS MALLEABLE. BELIEVE IN YOURSELF, DO THE WORK, AND YOU WILL LEARN!
SO WHAT CAN I HELP YOU WITH?
IONS. WE WERE DISCUSSING LITHIUM.

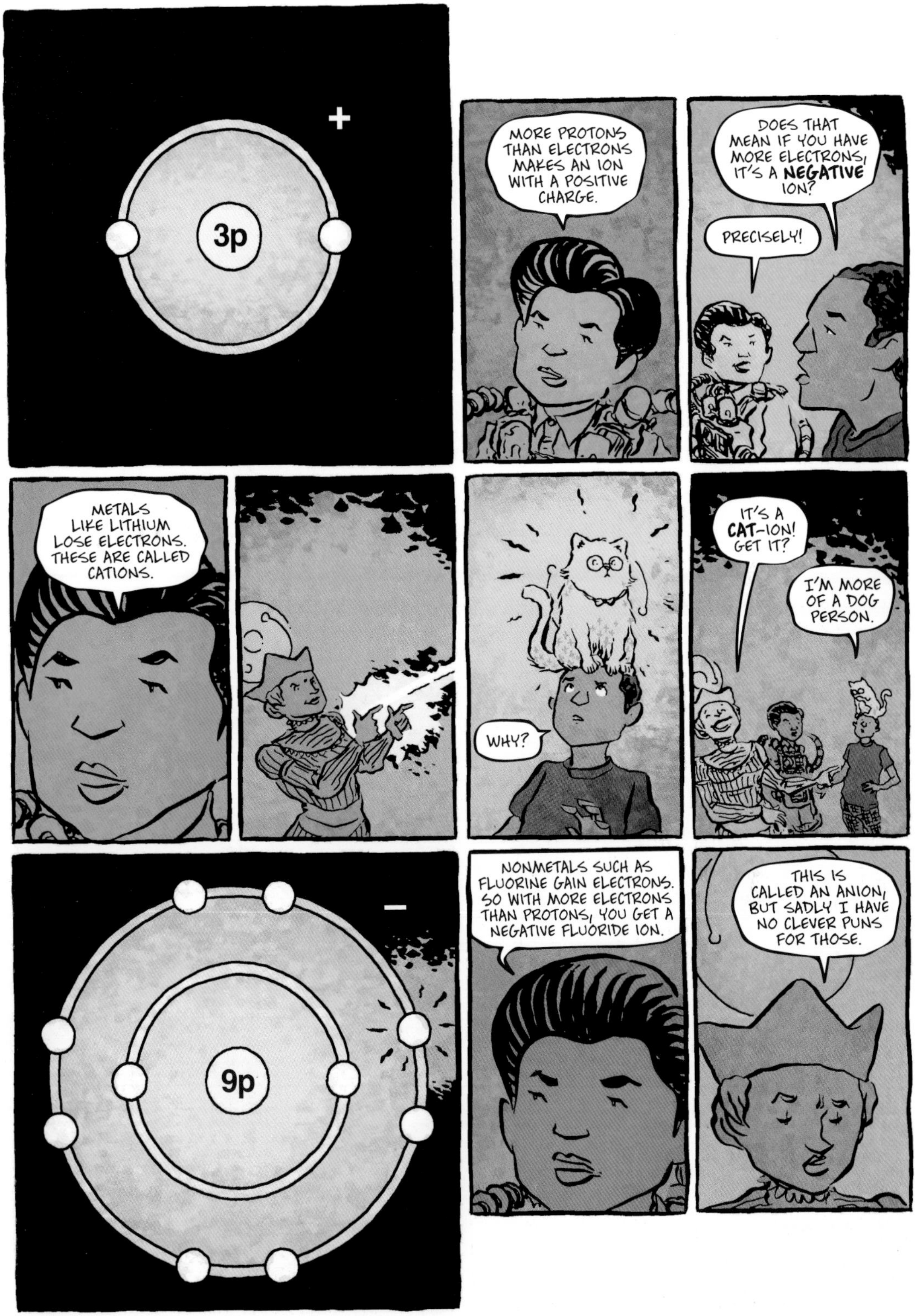
3p
+
MORE PROTONS THAN ELECTRONS MAKES AN ION WITH A POSITIVE CHARGE.
DOES THAT MEAN IF YOU HAVE MORE ELECTRONS, IT'S A **NEGATIVE** ION?
PRECISELY!
METALS LIKE LITHIUM LOSE ELECTRONS. THESE ARE CALLED CATIONS.
WHY?
IT'S A **CAT**-ION! GET IT?
I'M MORE OF A DOG PERSON.
9p
–
NONMETALS SUCH AS FLUORINE GAIN ELECTRONS. SO WITH MORE ELECTRONS THAN PROTONS, YOU GET A NEGATIVE FLUORIDE ION.
THIS IS CALLED AN ANION, BUT SADLY I HAVE NO CLEVER PUNS FOR THOSE.

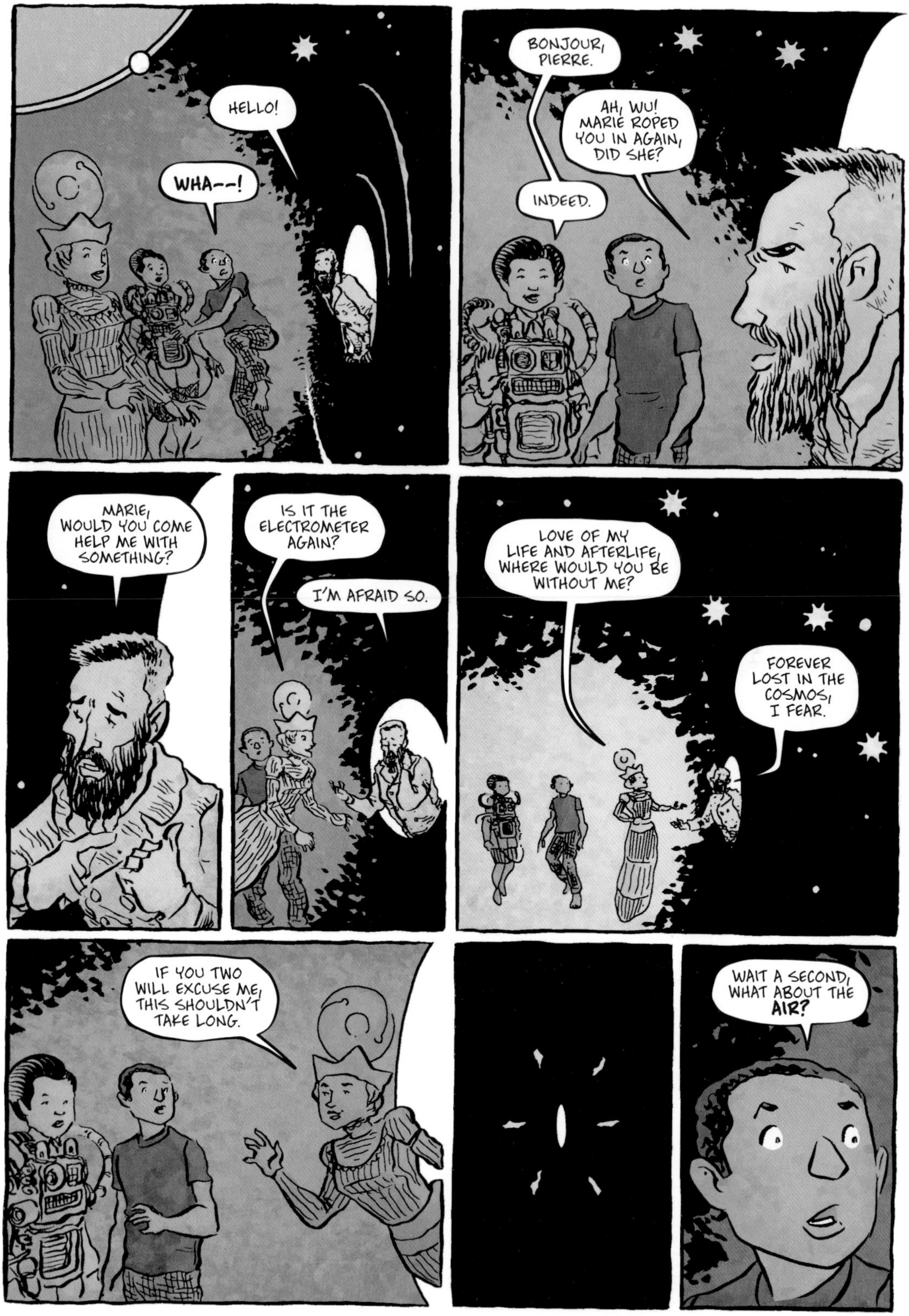
HELLO!
WHA--!
BONJOUR, PIERRE.
AH, WU! MARIE ROPED YOU IN AGAIN, DID SHE?
INDEED.
MARIE, WOULD YOU COME HELP ME WITH SOMETHING?
IS IT THE ELECTROMETER AGAIN?
I'M AFRAID SO.
LOVE OF MY LIFE AND AFTERLIFE, WHERE WOULD YOU BE WITHOUT ME?
FOREVER LOST IN THE COSMOS, I FEAR.
IF YOU TWO WILL EXCUSE ME, THIS SHOULDN'T TAKE LONG.
WAIT A SECOND, WHAT ABOUT THE **AIR?**

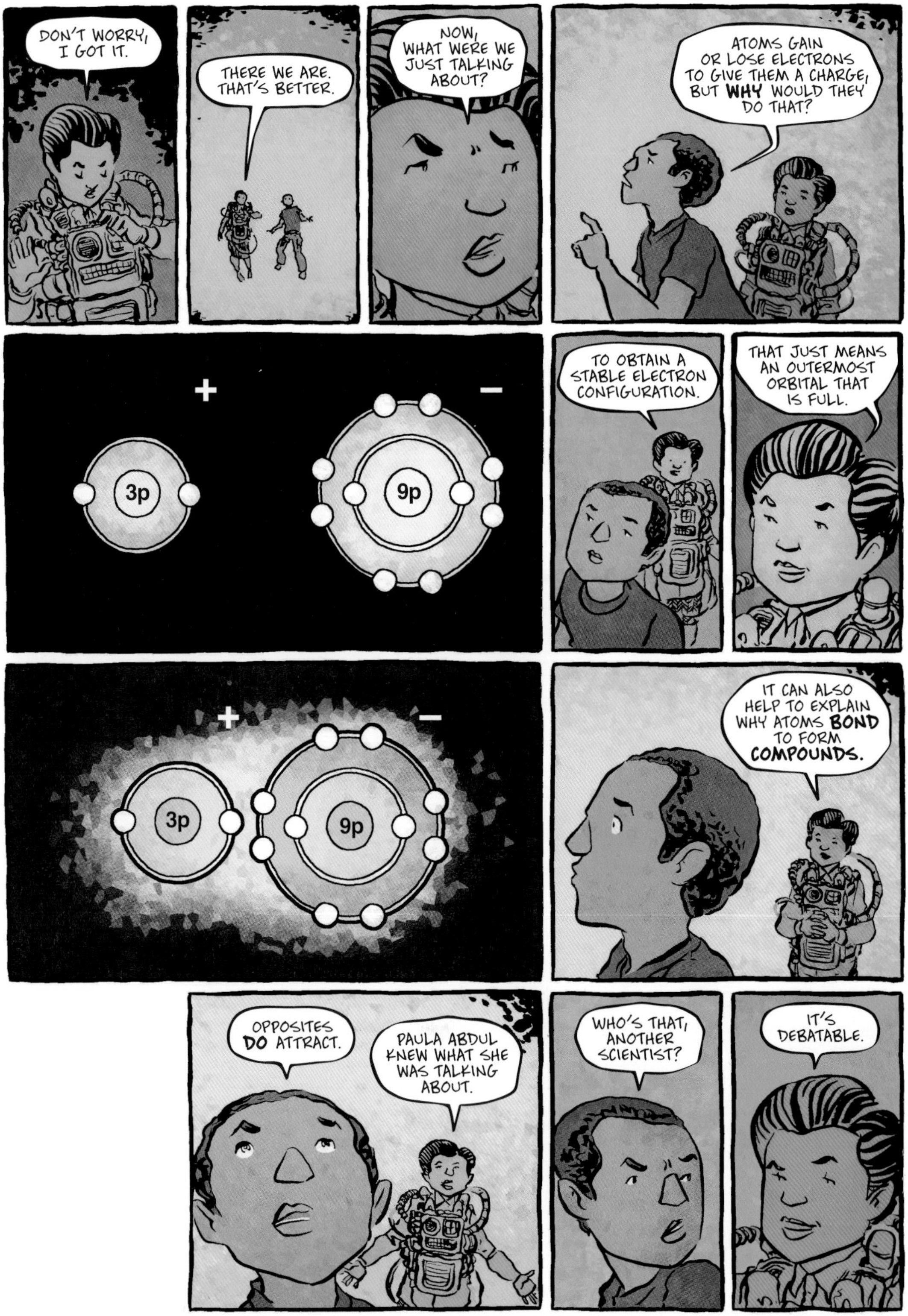
DON'T WORRY, I GOT IT.
THERE WE ARE. THAT'S BETTER.
NOW, WHAT WERE WE JUST TALKING ABOUT?
ATOMS GAIN OR LOSE ELECTRONS TO GIVE THEM A CHARGE, BUT **WHY** WOULD THEY DO THAT?
+
–
3p
9p
TO OBTAIN A STABLE ELECTRON CONFIGURATION.
THAT JUST MEANS AN OUTERMOST ORBITAL THAT IS FULL.
+
–
3p
9p
IT CAN ALSO HELP TO EXPLAIN WHY ATOMS **BOND** TO FORM **COMPOUNDS.**
OPPOSITES **DO** ATTRACT.
PAULA ABDUL KNEW WHAT SHE WAS TALKING ABOUT.
WHO'S THAT, ANOTHER SCIENTIST?
IT'S DEBATABLE.

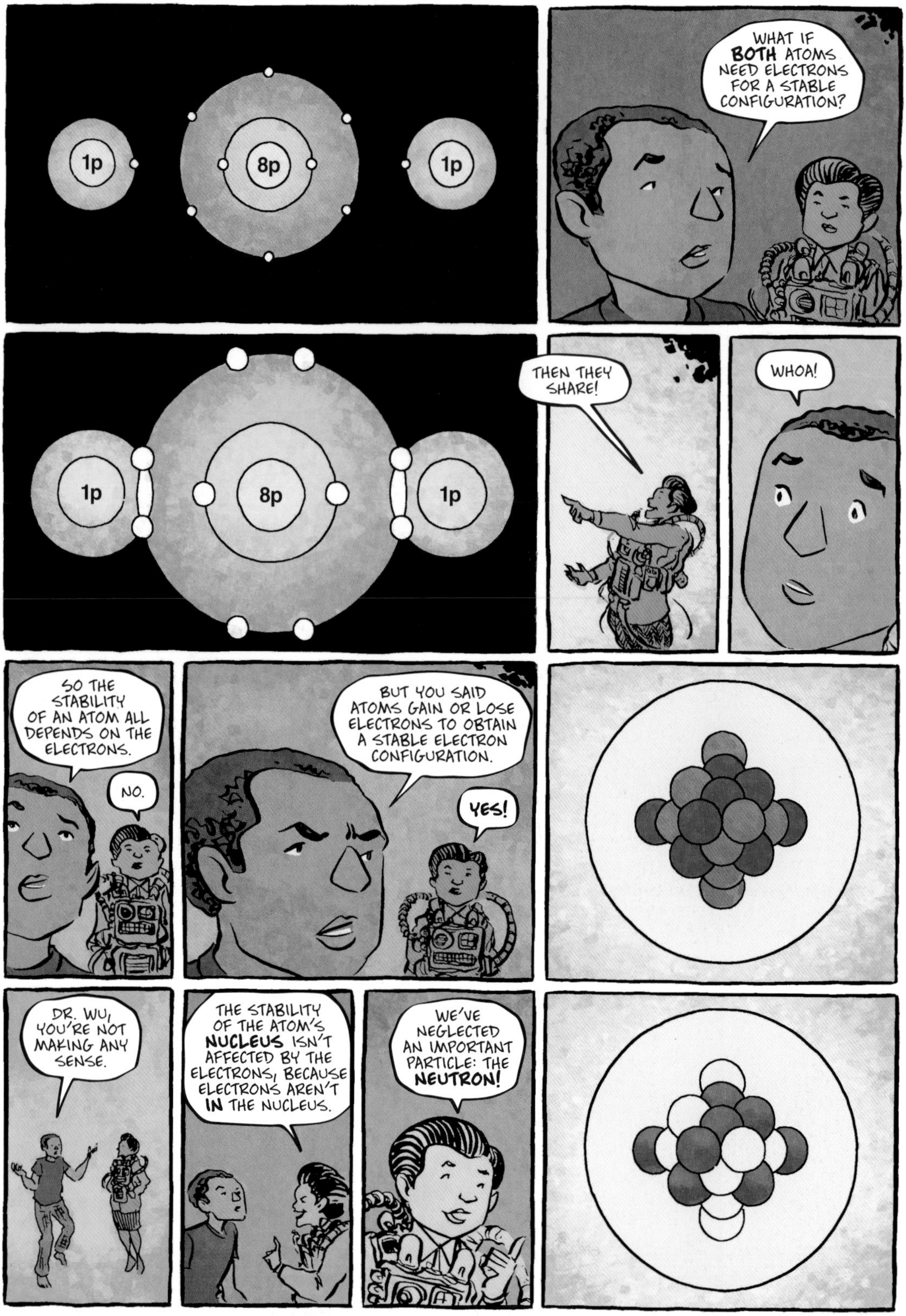
1p
8p
1p
WHAT IF **BOTH** ATOMS NEED ELECTRONS FOR A STABLE CONFIGURATION?
1p
8p
1p
THEN THEY SHARE!
WHOA!
SO THE STABILITY OF AN ATOM ALL DEPENDS ON THE ELECTRONS.
NO.
BUT YOU SAID ATOMS GAIN OR LOSE ELECTRONS TO OBTAIN A STABLE ELECTRON CONFIGURATION.
YES!
DR. WU, YOU'RE NOT MAKING ANY SENSE.
THE STABILITY OF THE ATOM'S **NUCLEUS** ISN'T AFFECTED BY THE ELECTRONS, BECAUSE ELECTRONS AREN'T **IN** THE NUCLEUS.
WE'VE NEGLECTED AN IMPORTANT PARTICLE: THE **NEUTRON!**

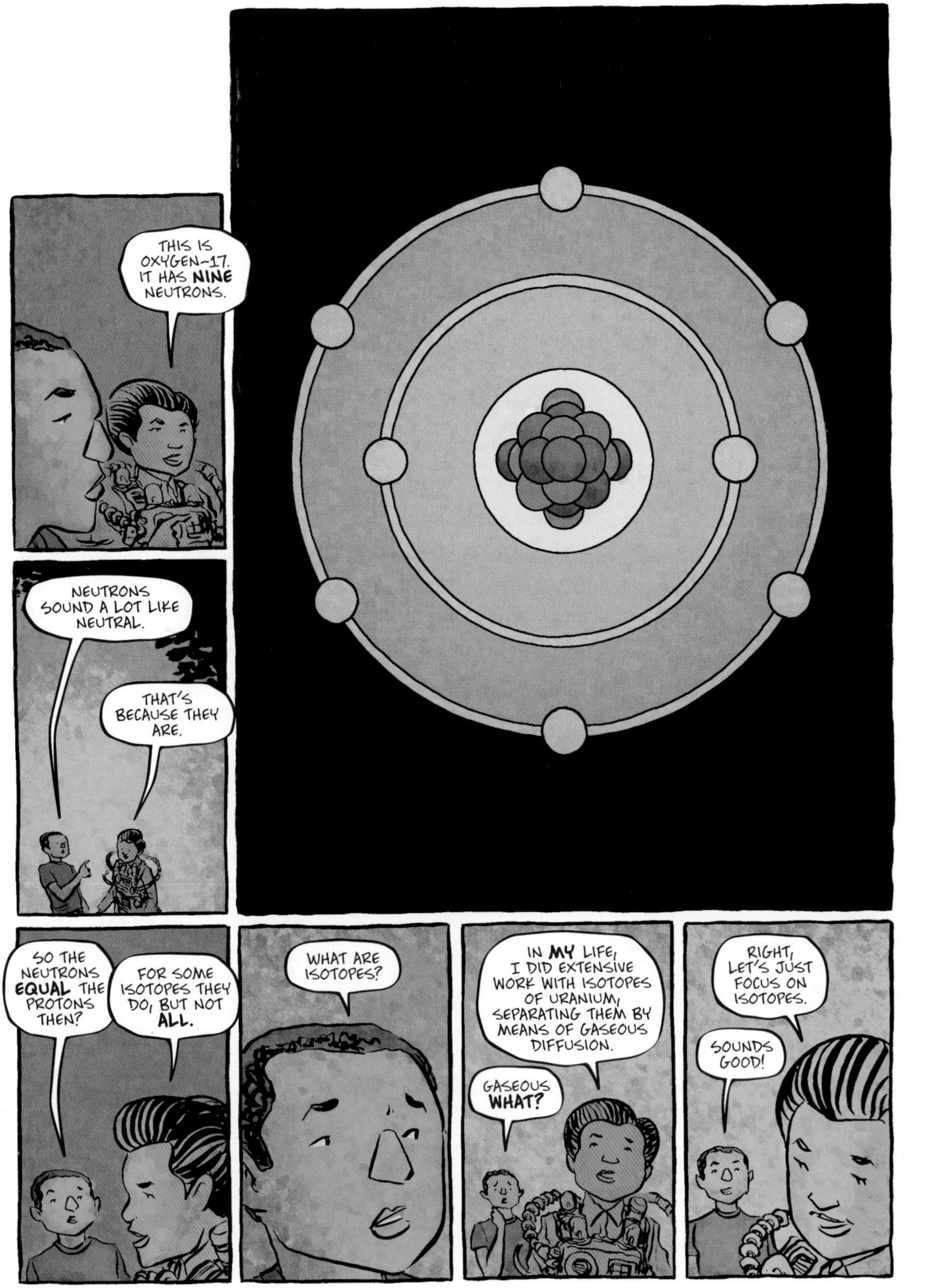

THIS IS OXYGEN-17. IT HAS **NINE** NEUTRONS.
NEUTRONS SOUND A LOT LIKE NEUTRAL.
THAT'S BECAUSE THEY ARE.
SO THE NEUTRONS **EQUAL** THE PROTONS THEN?
FOR SOME ISOTOPES THEY DO, BUT NOT **ALL**.
WHAT ARE ISOTOPES?
IN **MY** LIFE, I DID EXTENSIVE WORK WITH ISOTOPES OF URANIUM, SEPARATING THEM BY MEANS OF GASEOUS DIFFUSION.
GASEOUS **WHAT?**
RIGHT, LET'S JUST FOCUS ON ISOTOPES.
SOUNDS GOOD!

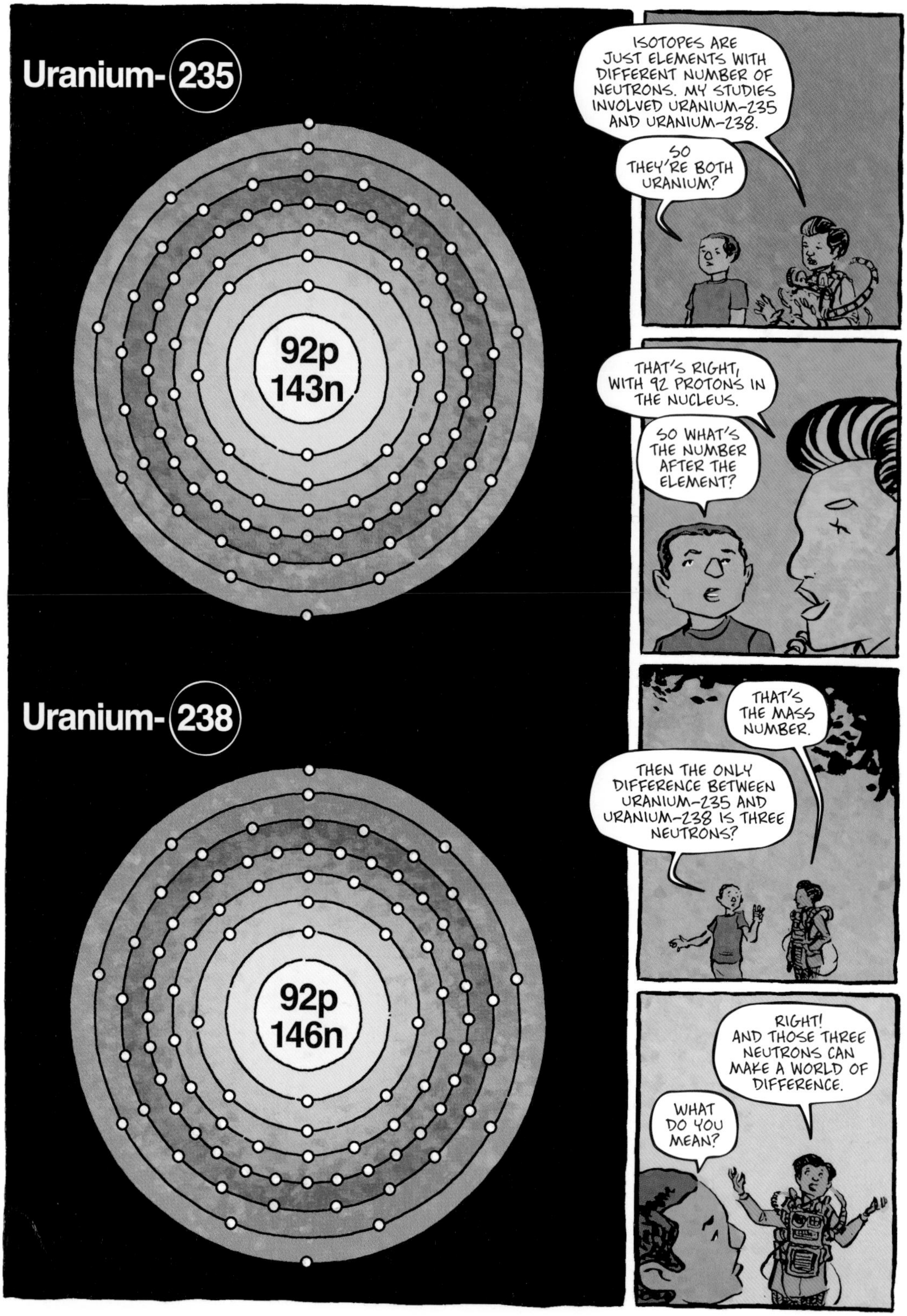
Uranium-235
92p
143n
Uranium-238
92p
146n
ISOTOPES ARE JUST ELEMENTS WITH DIFFERENT NUMBER OF NEUTRONS. MY STUDIES INVOLVED URANIUM-235 AND URANIUM-238.
SO THEY'RE BOTH URANIUM?
THAT'S RIGHT, WITH 92 PROTONS IN THE NUCLEUS.
SO WHAT'S THE NUMBER AFTER THE ELEMENT?
THAT'S THE MASS NUMBER.
THEN THE ONLY DIFFERENCE BETWEEN URANIUM-235 AND URANIUM-238 IS THREE NEUTRONS?
RIGHT! AND THOSE THREE NEUTRONS CAN MAKE A WORLD OF DIFFERENCE.
WHAT DO YOU MEAN?

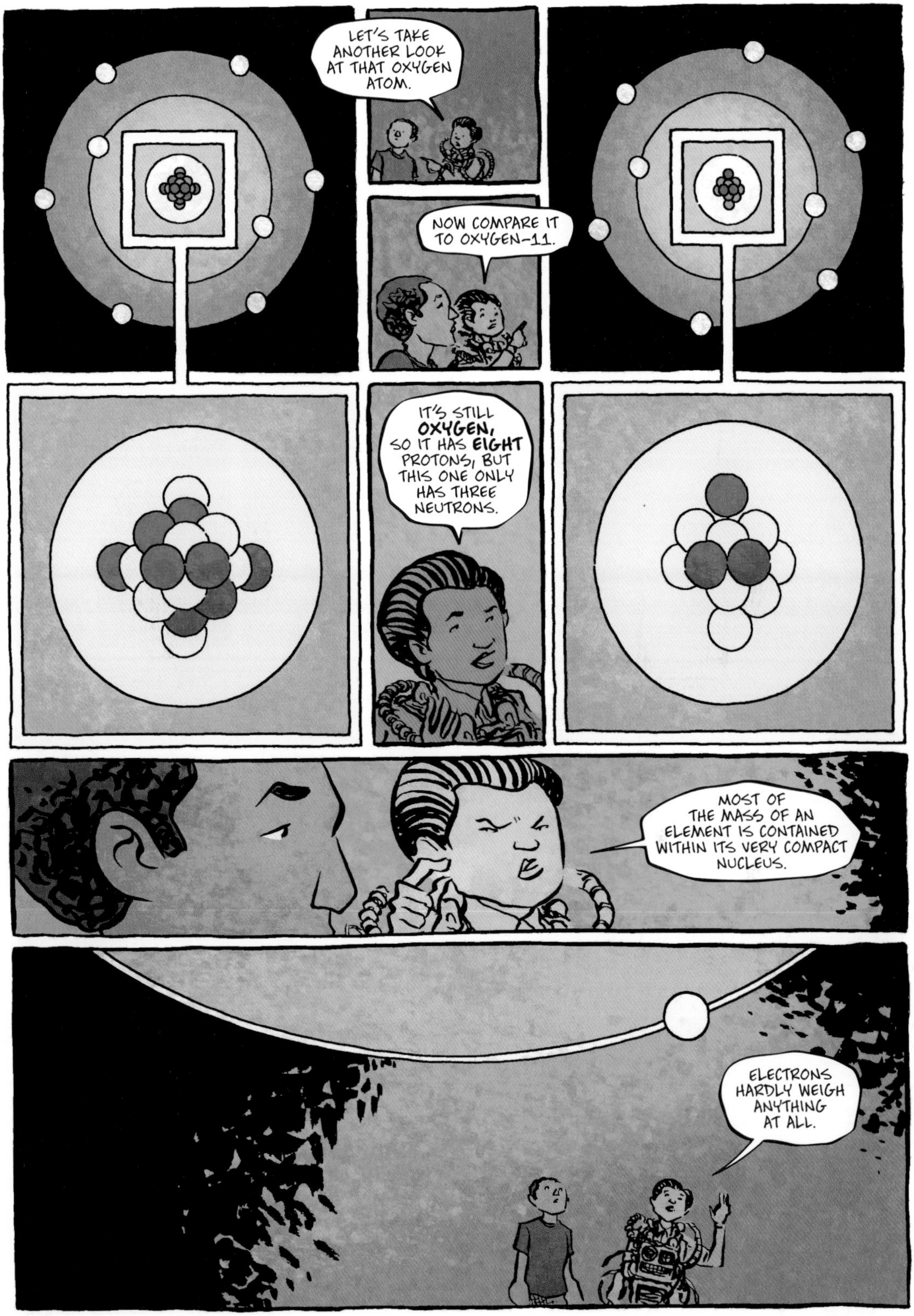
LET'S TAKE ANOTHER LOOK AT THAT OXYGEN ATOM.
NOW COMPARE IT TO OXYGEN-11.
IT'S STILL **OXYGEN,** SO IT HAS **EIGHT** PROTONS, BUT THIS ONE ONLY HAS THREE NEUTRONS.
MOST OF THE MASS OF AN ELEMENT IS CONTAINED WITHIN ITS VERY COMPACT NUCLEUS.
ELECTRONS HARDLY WEIGH ANYTHING AT ALL.

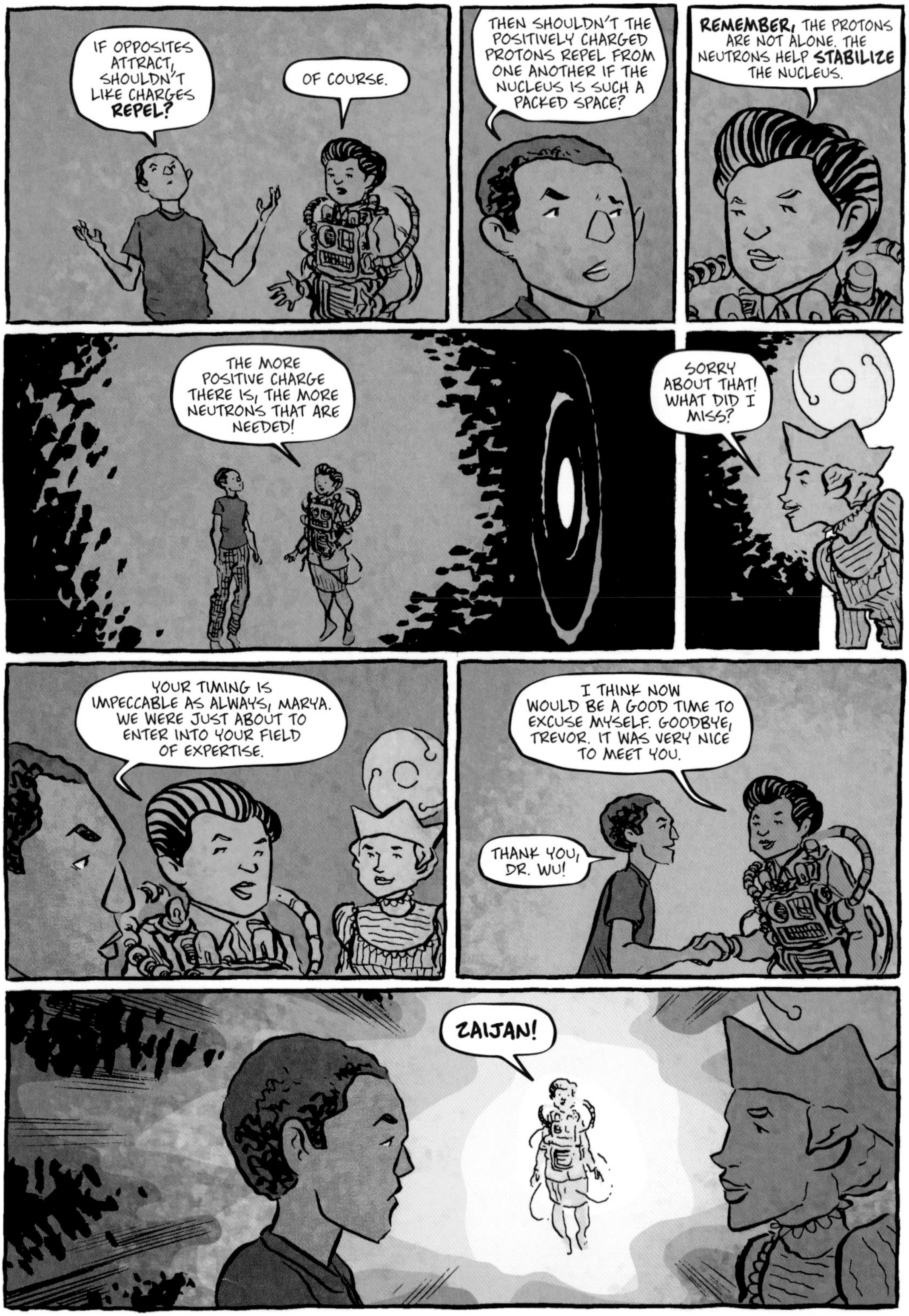
IF OPPOSITES ATTRACT, SHOULDN'T LIKE CHARGES **REPEL?**
OF COURSE.
THEN SHOULDN'T THE POSITIVELY CHARGED PROTONS REPEL FROM ONE ANOTHER IF THE NUCLEUS IS SUCH A PACKED SPACE?
REMEMBER, THE PROTONS ARE NOT ALONE. THE NEUTRONS HELP **STABILIZE** THE NUCLEUS.
THE MORE POSITIVE CHARGE THERE IS, THE MORE NEUTRONS THAT ARE NEEDED!
SORRY ABOUT THAT! WHAT DID I MISS?
YOUR TIMING IS IMPECCABLE AS ALWAYS, MARYA. WE WERE JUST ABOUT TO ENTER INTO YOUR FIELD OF EXPERTISE.
I THINK NOW WOULD BE A GOOD TIME TO EXCUSE MYSELF. GOODBYE, TREVOR. IT WAS VERY NICE TO MEET YOU.
THANK YOU, DR. WU!
ZAIJAN!

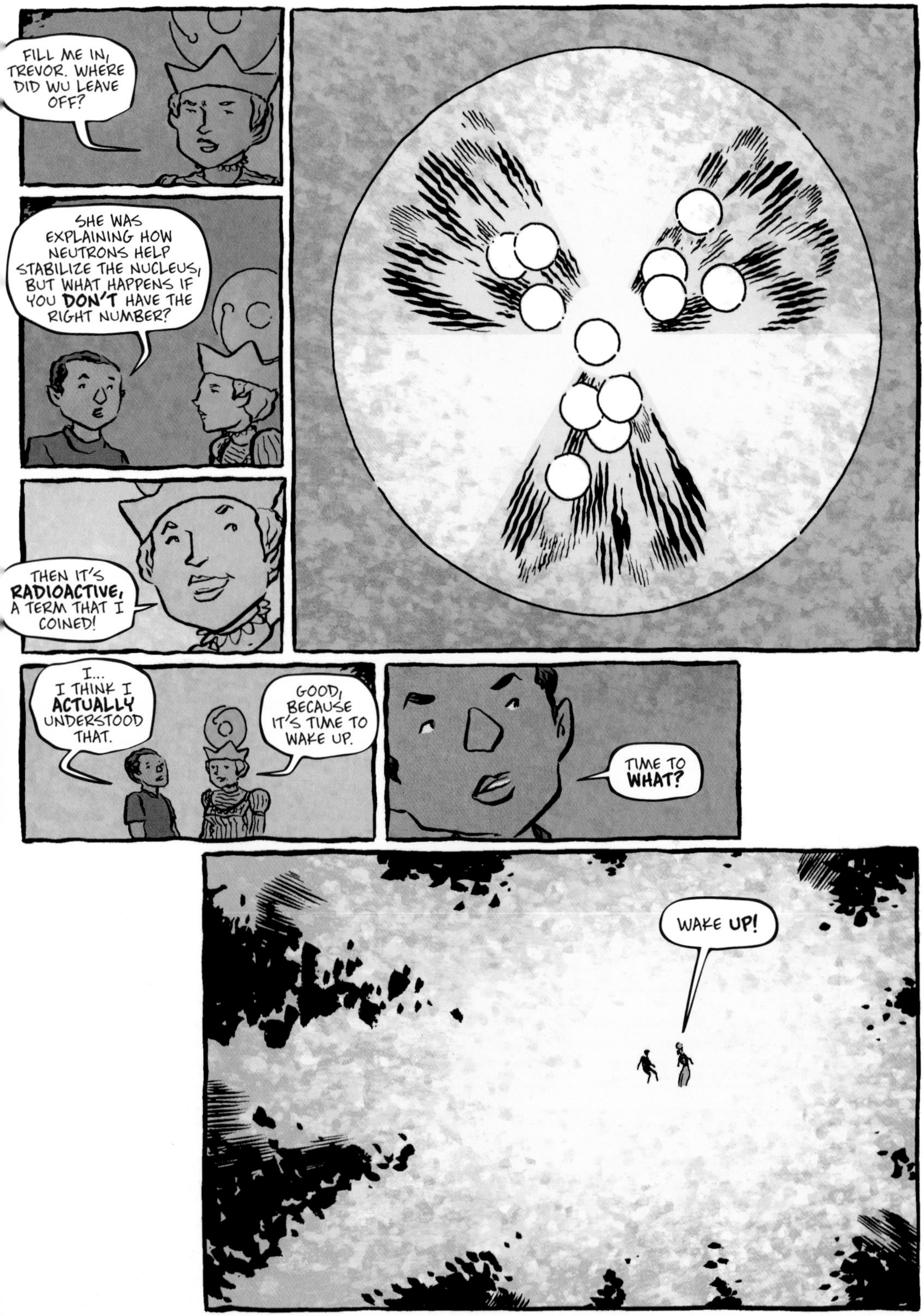
FILL ME IN, TREVOR. WHERE DID WU LEAVE OFF?
SHE WAS EXPLAINING HOW NEUTRONS HELP STABILIZE THE NUCLEUS, BUT WHAT HAPPENS IF YOU DON'T HAVE THE RIGHT NUMBER?
THEN IT'S RADIOACTIVE, A TERM THAT I COINED!
I... I THINK I ACTUALLY UNDERSTOOD THAT.
GOOD, BECAUSE IT'S TIME TO WAKE UP.
TIME TO WHAT?
WAKE UP!

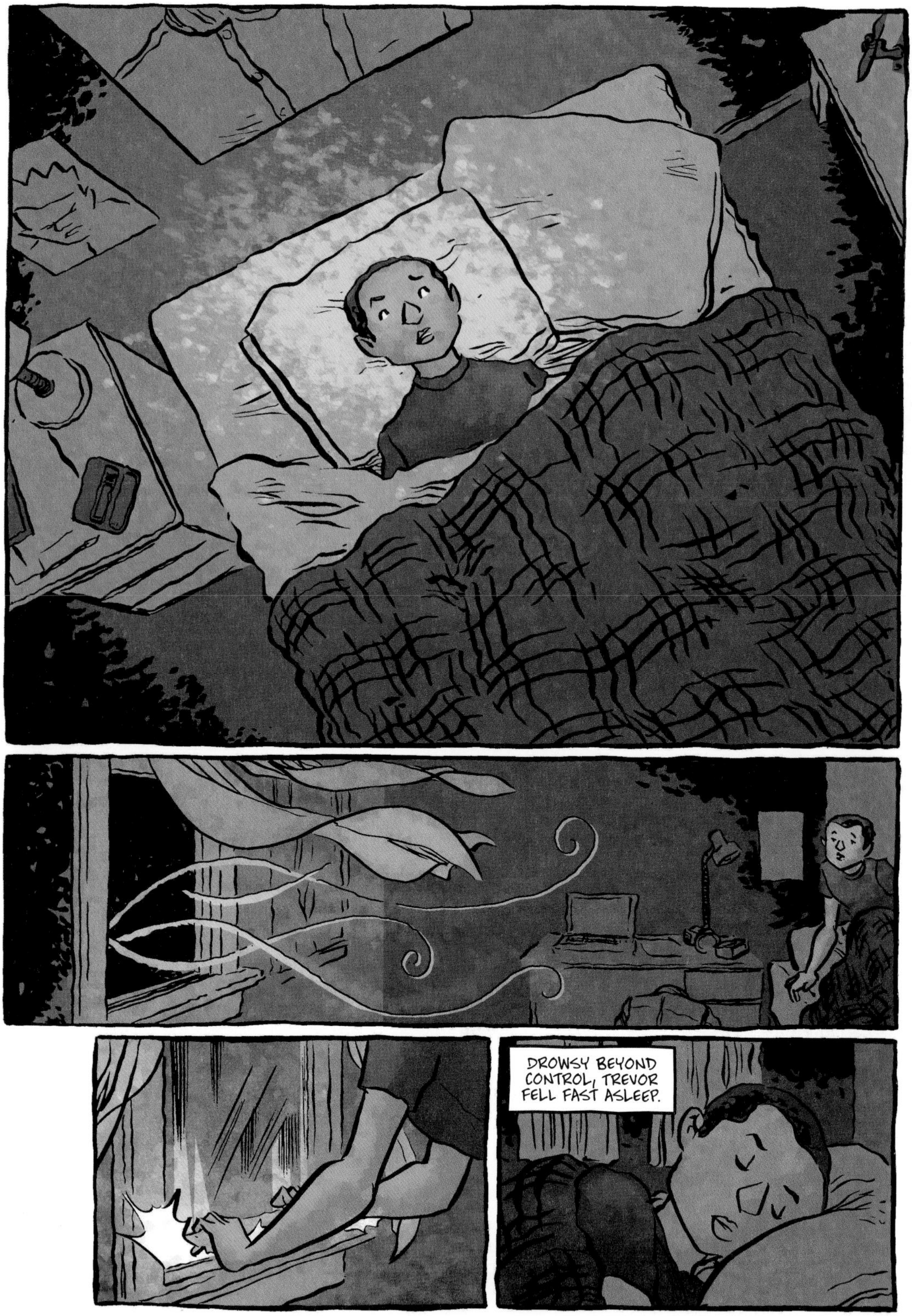
DROWSY BEYOND CONTROL, TREVOR FELL FAST ASLEEP.

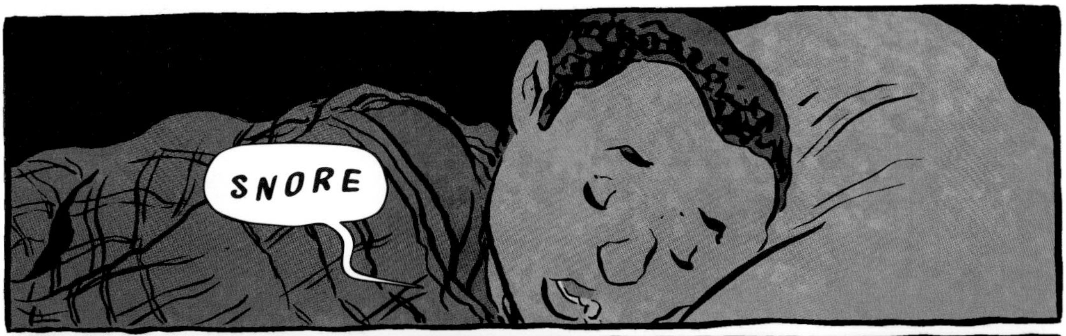
SNORE

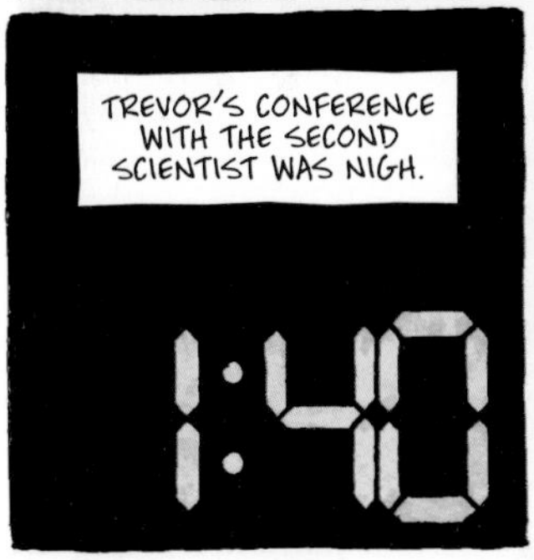
TREVOR'S CONFERENCE WITH THE SECOND SCIENTIST WAS NIGH.
1:40

Stave Three: The Second of the Three Scientists

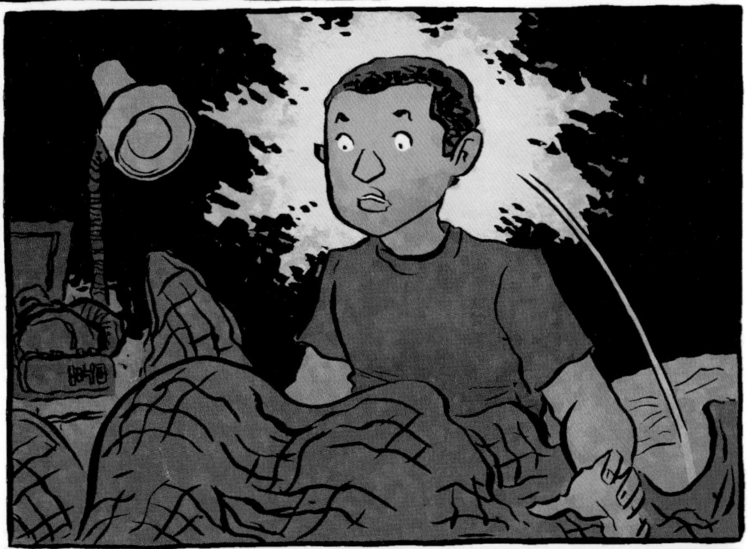

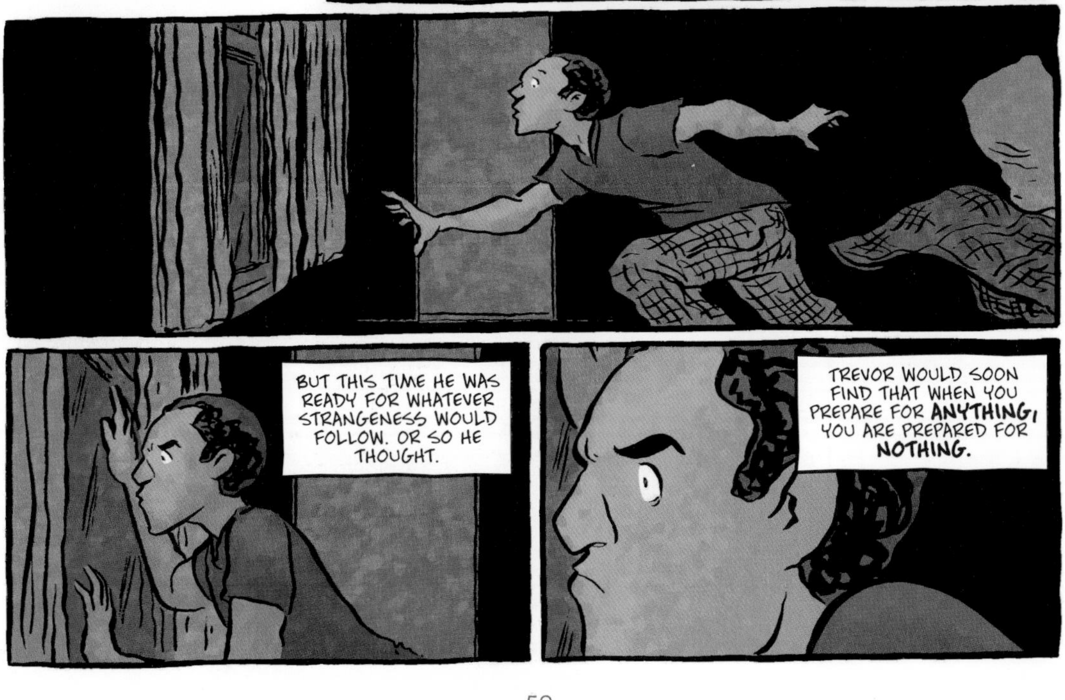
BUT THIS TIME HE WAS READY FOR WHATEVER STRANGENESS WOULD FOLLOW. OR SO HE THOUGHT.
TREVOR WOULD SOON FIND THAT WHEN YOU PREPARE FOR **ANYTHING**, YOU ARE PREPARED FOR **NOTHING**.

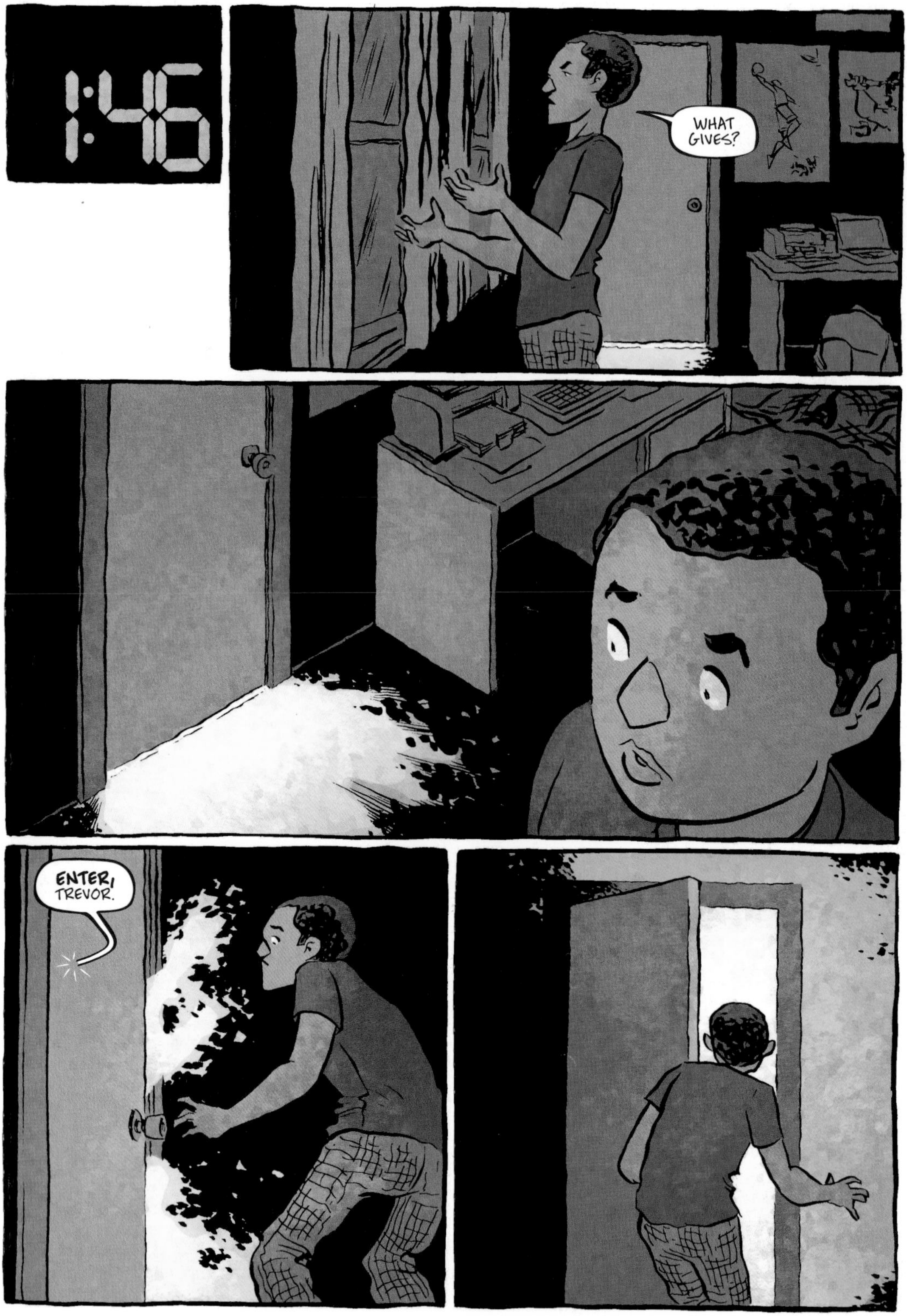
1:46
WHAT GIVES?
ENTER, TREVOR.

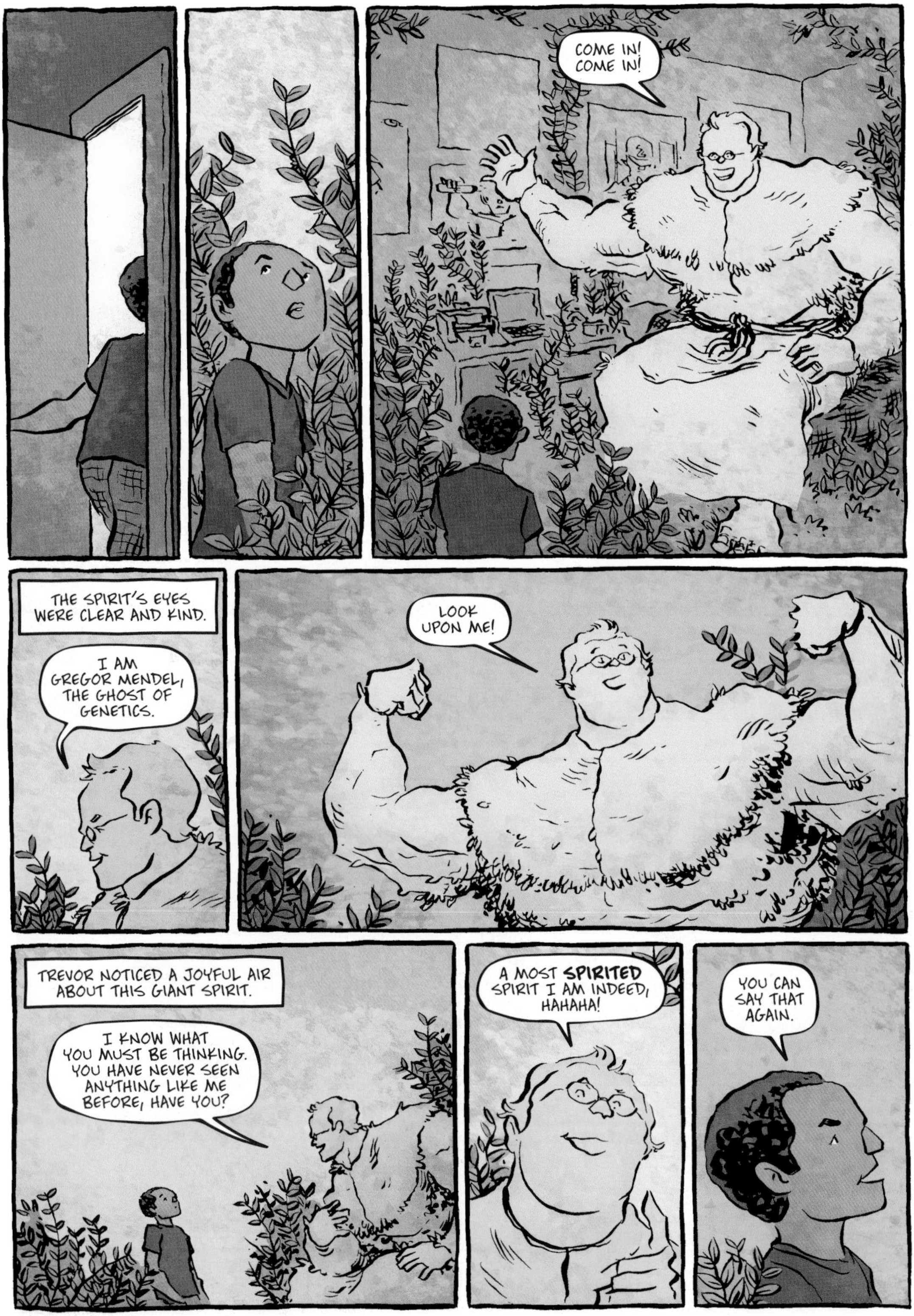
COME IN! COME IN!
THE SPIRIT'S EYES WERE CLEAR AND KIND.
I AM GREGOR MENDEL, THE GHOST OF GENETICS.
LOOK UPON ME!
TREVOR NOTICED A JOYFUL AIR ABOUT THIS GIANT SPIRIT.
I KNOW WHAT YOU MUST BE THINKING. YOU HAVE NEVER SEEN ANYTHING LIKE ME BEFORE, HAVE YOU?
A MOST **SPIRITED** SPIRIT I AM INDEED, HAHAHA!
YOU CAN SAY THAT AGAIN.

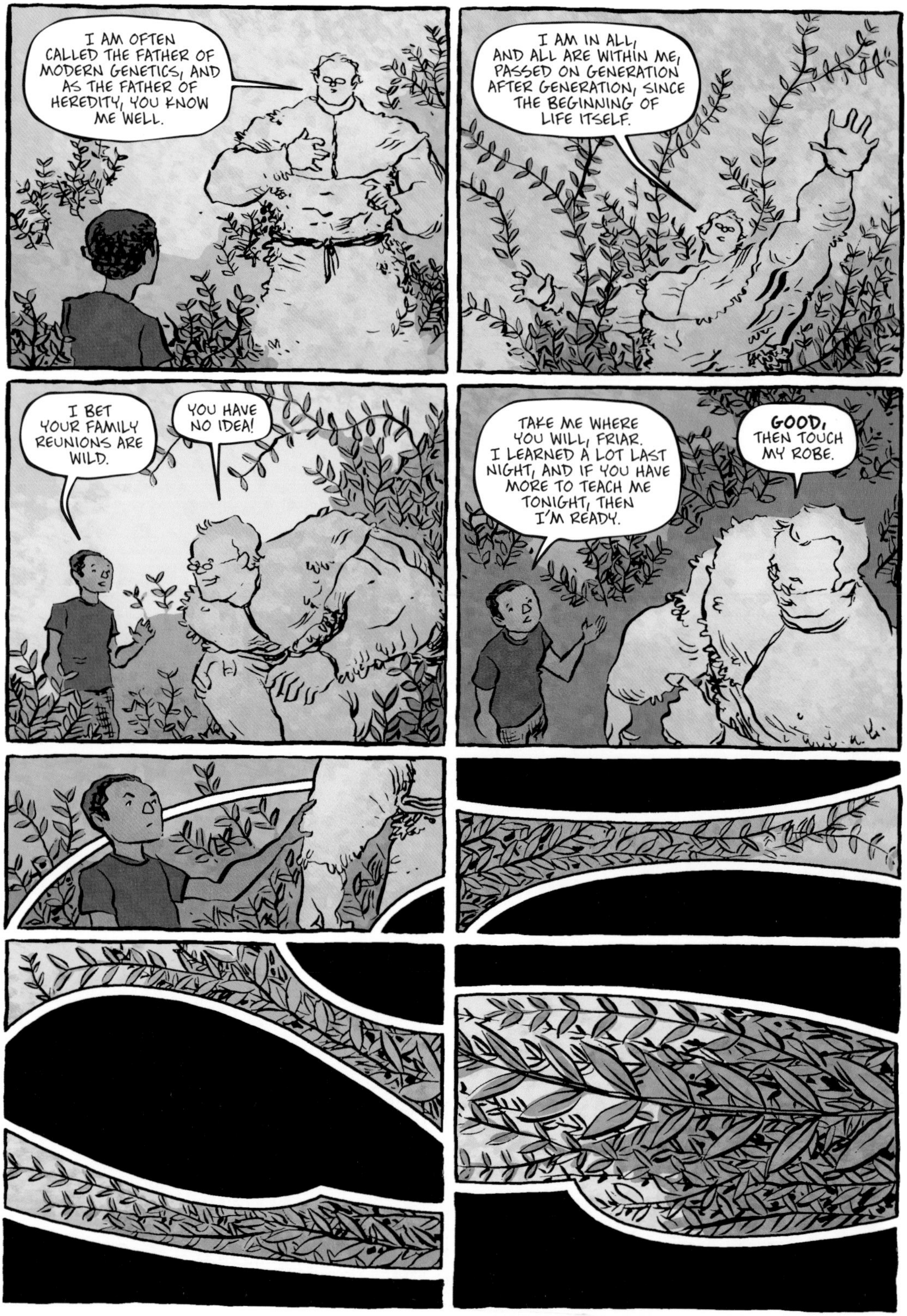
I AM OFTEN CALLED THE FATHER OF MODERN GENETICS, AND AS THE FATHER OF HEREDITY, YOU KNOW ME WELL.
I AM IN ALL, AND ALL ARE WITHIN ME, PASSED ON GENERATION AFTER GENERATION, SINCE THE BEGINNING OF LIFE ITSELF.
I BET YOUR FAMILY REUNIONS ARE WILD.
YOU HAVE NO IDEA!
TAKE ME WHERE YOU WILL, FRIAR. I LEARNED A LOT LAST NIGHT, AND IF YOU HAVE MORE TO TEACH ME TONIGHT, THEN I'M READY.
GOOD, THEN TOUCH MY ROBE.

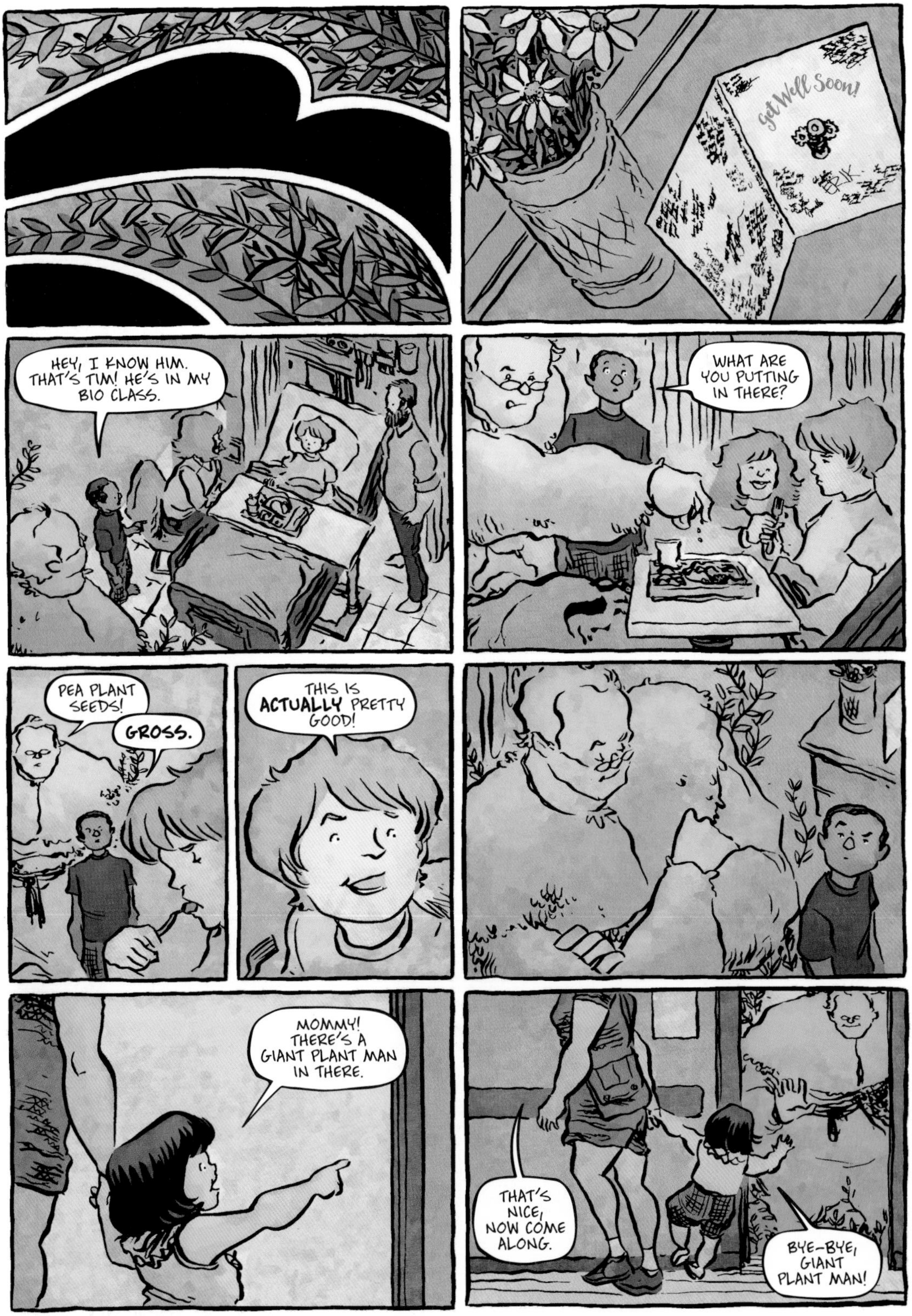
Get Well Soon!
HEY, I KNOW HIM. THAT'S TIM! HE'S IN MY BIO CLASS.
WHAT ARE YOU PUTTING IN THERE?
PEA PLANT SEEDS!
GROSS.
THIS IS **ACTUALLY** PRETTY GOOD!
MOMMY! THERE'S A GIANT PLANT MAN IN THERE.
THAT'S NICE, NOW COME ALONG.
BYE-BYE, GIANT PLANT MAN!

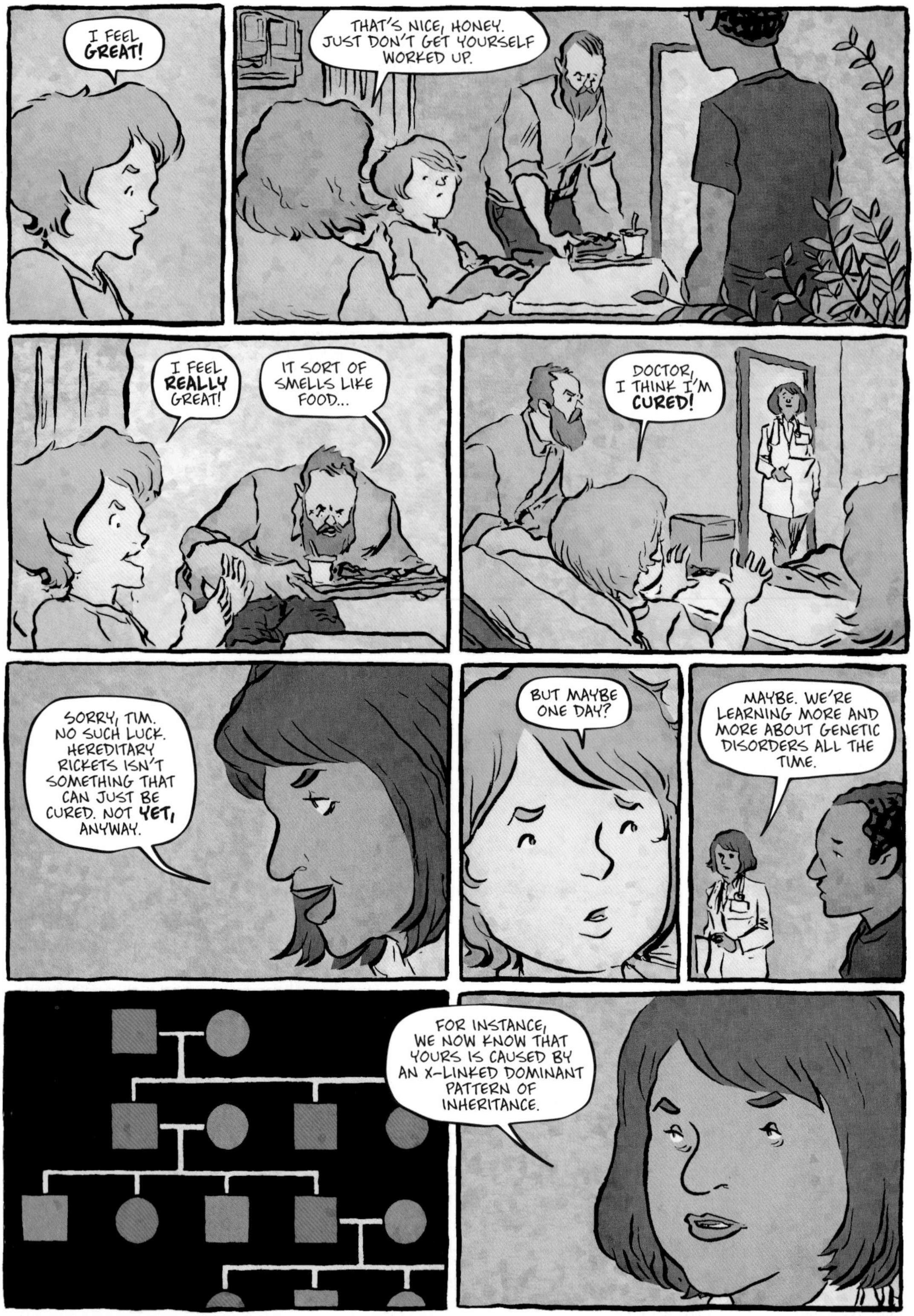
I FEEL **GREAT!**
THAT'S NICE, HONEY. JUST DON'T GET YOURSELF WORKED UP.
I FEEL **REALLY** GREAT!
IT SORT OF SMELLS LIKE FOOD...
DOCTOR, I THINK I'M **CURED!**
SORRY, TIM. NO SUCH LUCK. HEREDITARY RICKETS ISN'T SOMETHING THAT CAN JUST BE CURED. NOT **YET**, ANYWAY.
BUT MAYBE ONE DAY?
MAYBE. WE'RE LEARNING MORE AND MORE ABOUT GENETIC DISORDERS ALL THE TIME.
FOR INSTANCE, WE NOW KNOW THAT YOURS IS CAUSED BY AN X-LINKED DOMINANT PATTERN OF INHERITANCE.

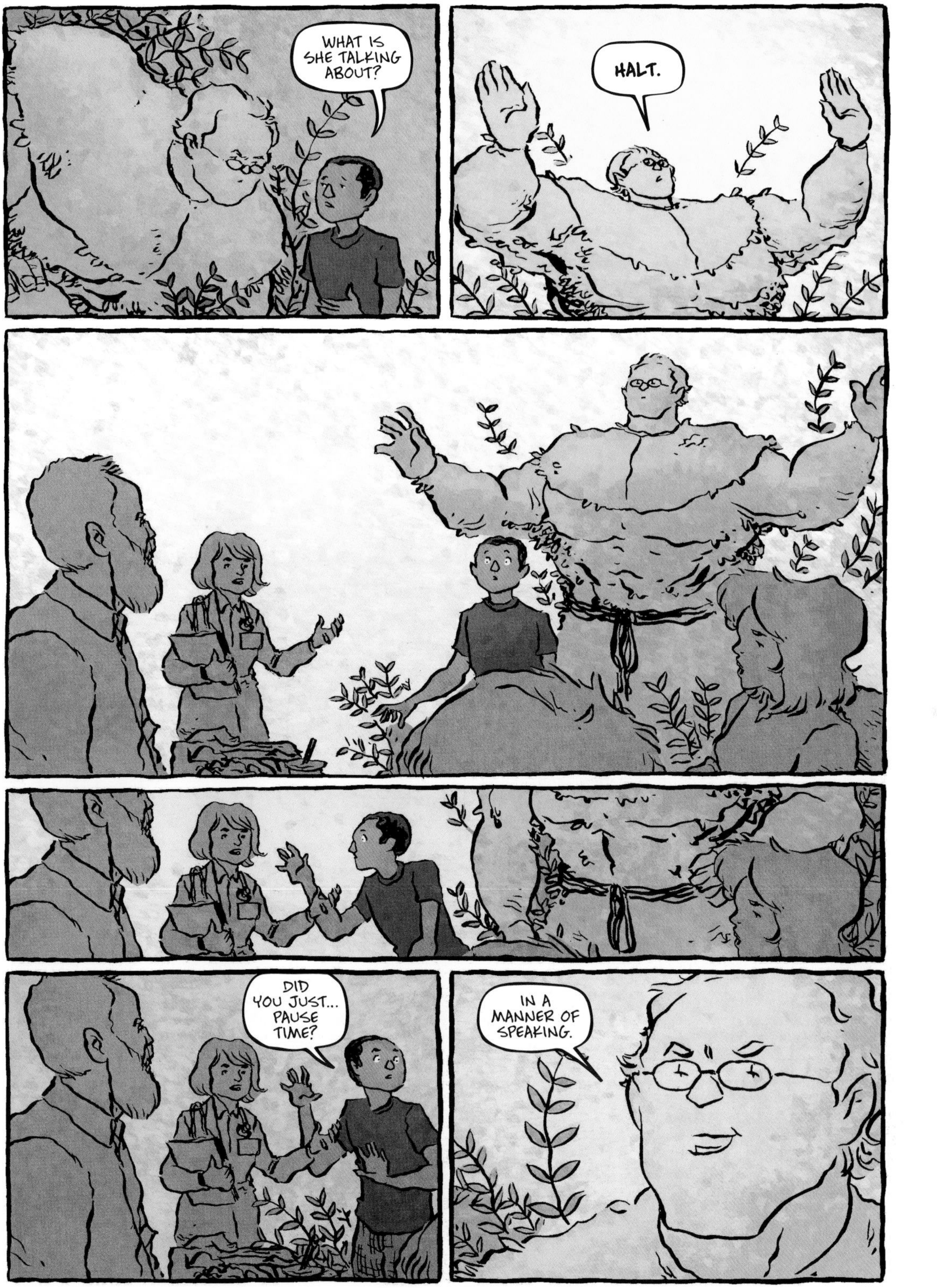
WHAT IS SHE TALKING ABOUT?
HALT.
DID YOU JUST... PAUSE TIME?
IN A MANNER OF SPEAKING.

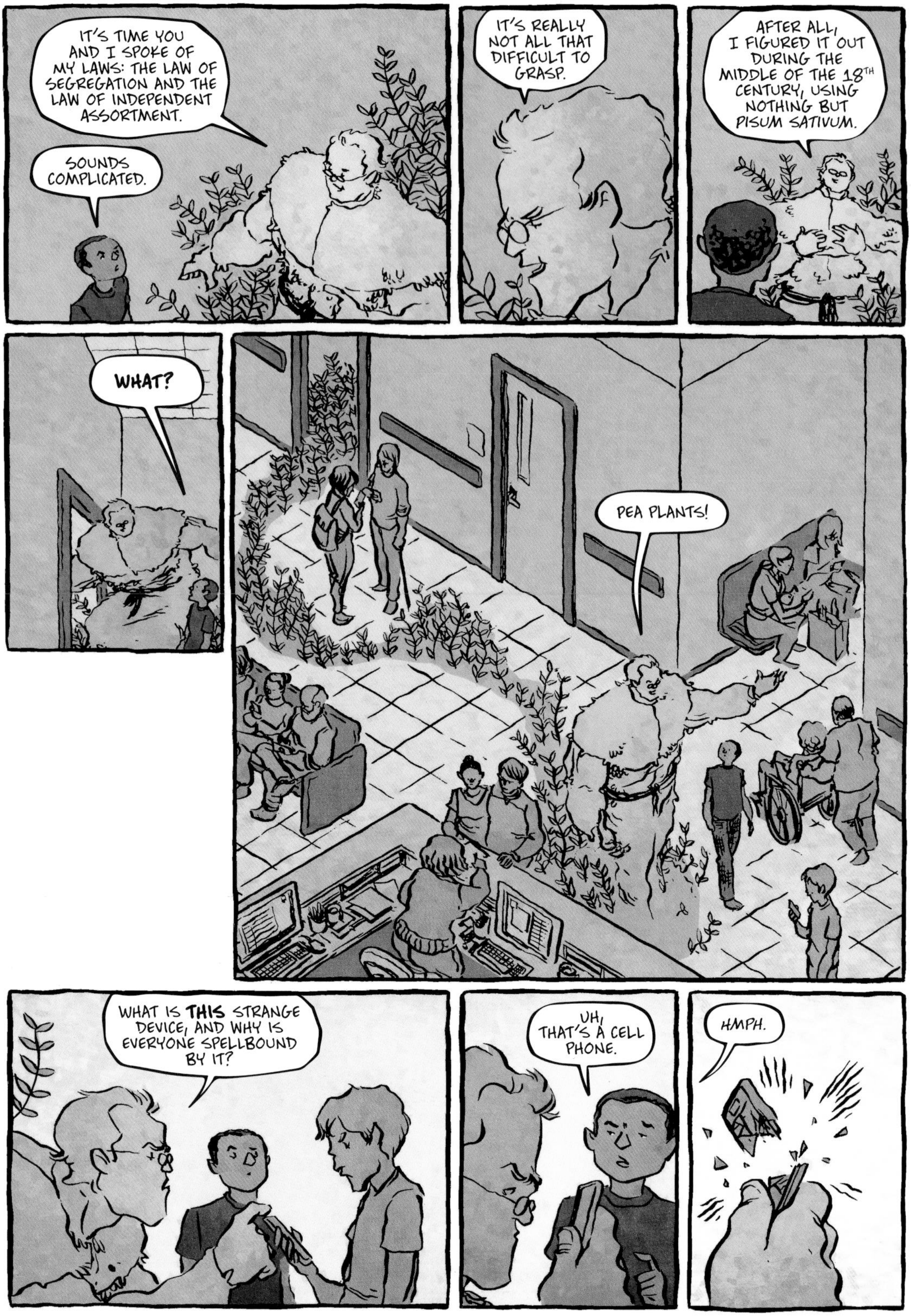
IT'S TIME YOU AND I SPOKE OF MY LAWS: THE LAW OF SEGREGATION AND THE LAW OF INDEPENDENT ASSORTMENT.
SOUNDS COMPLICATED.
IT'S REALLY NOT ALL THAT DIFFICULT TO GRASP.
AFTER ALL, I FIGURED IT OUT DURING THE MIDDLE OF THE 18TH CENTURY, USING NOTHING BUT PISUM SATIVUM.
WHAT?
PEA PLANTS!
WHAT IS THIS STRANGE DEVICE, AND WHY IS EVERYONE SPELLBOUND BY IT?
UH, THAT'S A CELL PHONE.
HMPH.

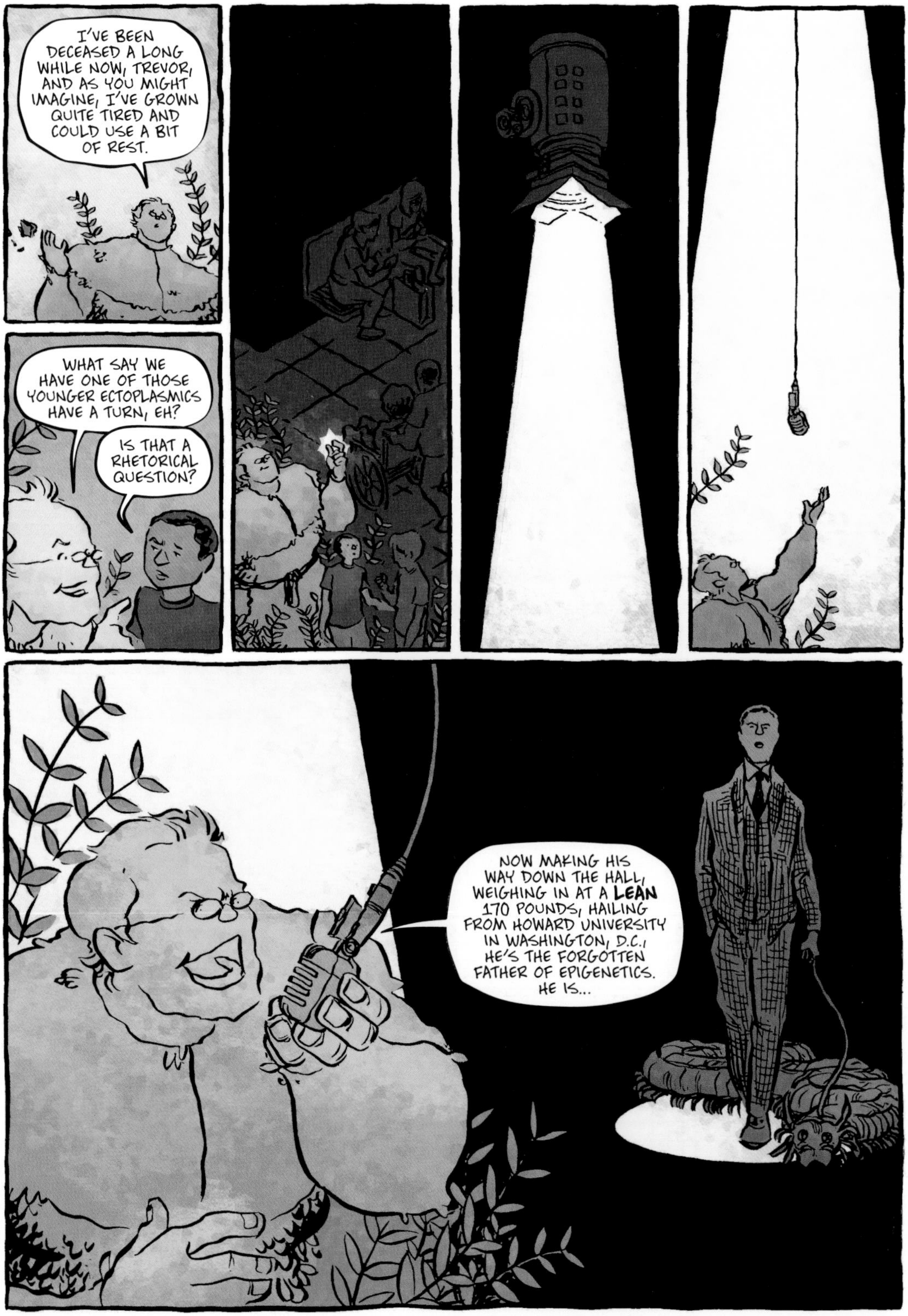
I'VE BEEN DECEASED A LONG WHILE NOW, TREVOR, AND AS YOU MIGHT IMAGINE, I'VE GROWN QUITE TIRED AND COULD USE A BIT OF REST.
WHAT SAY WE HAVE ONE OF THOSE YOUNGER ECTOPLASMICS HAVE A TURN, EH?
IS THAT A RHETORICAL QUESTION?
NOW MAKING HIS WAY DOWN THE HALL, WEIGHING IN AT A **LEAN** 170 POUNDS, HAILING FROM HOWARD UNIVERSITY IN WASHINGTON, D.C., HE'S THE FORGOTTEN FATHER OF EPIGENETICS. HE IS...

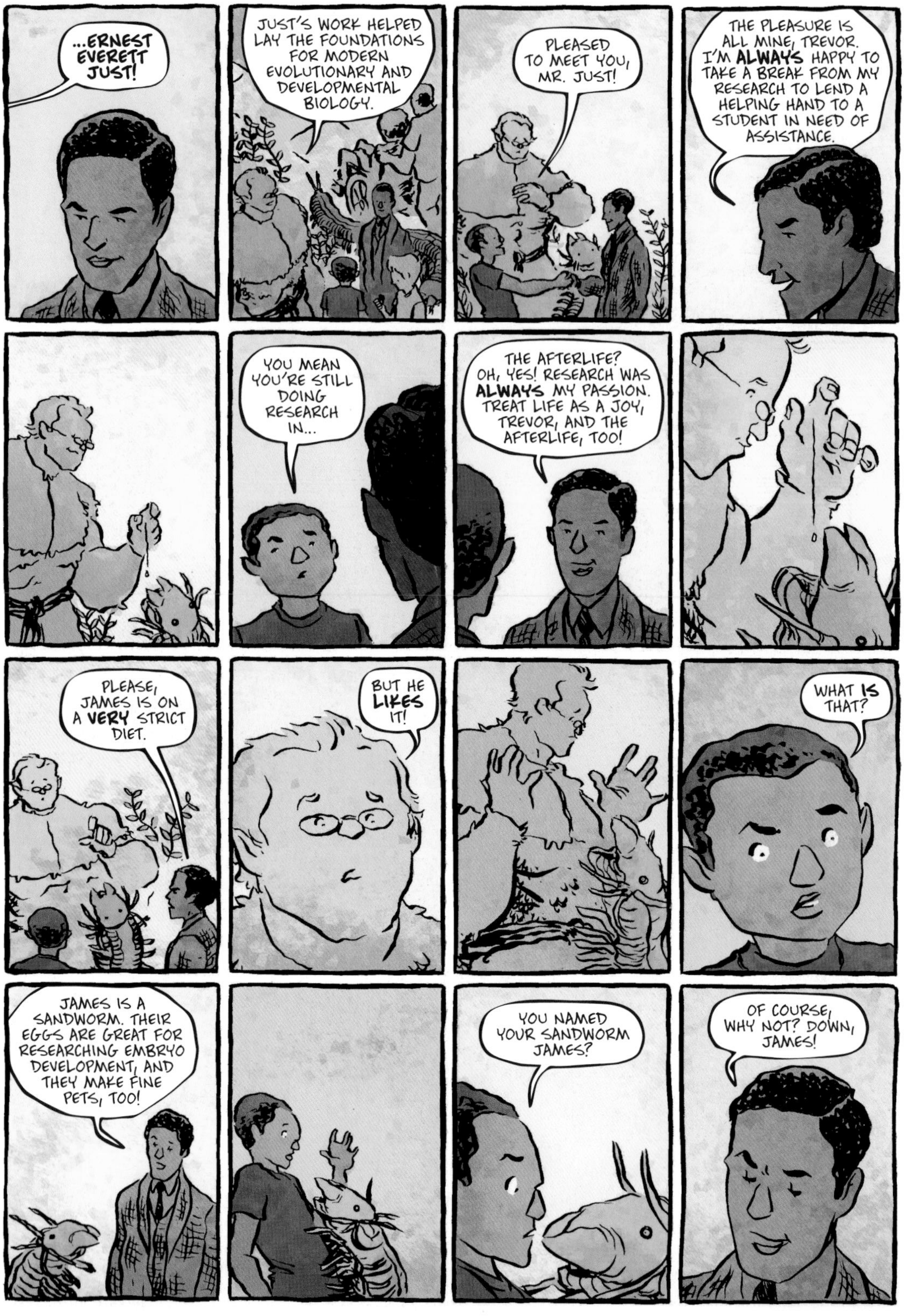

...ERNEST EVERETT JUST!
JUST'S WORK HELPED LAY THE FOUNDATIONS FOR MODERN EVOLUTIONARY AND DEVELOPMENTAL BIOLOGY.
PLEASED TO MEET YOU, MR. JUST!
THE PLEASURE IS ALL MINE, TREVOR. I'M ALWAYS HAPPY TO TAKE A BREAK FROM MY RESEARCH TO LEND A HELPING HAND TO A STUDENT IN NEED OF ASSISTANCE.
YOU MEAN YOU'RE STILL DOING RESEARCH IN...
THE AFTERLIFE? OH, YES! RESEARCH WAS ALWAYS MY PASSION. TREAT LIFE AS A JOY, TREVOR, AND THE AFTERLIFE, TOO!
PLEASE, JAMES IS ON A VERY STRICT DIET.
BUT HE LIKES IT!
WHAT IS THAT?
JAMES IS A SANDWORM. THEIR EGGS ARE GREAT FOR RESEARCHING EMBRYO DEVELOPMENT, AND THEY MAKE FINE PETS, TOO!
YOU NAMED YOUR SANDWORM JAMES?
OF COURSE, WHY NOT? DOWN, JAMES!

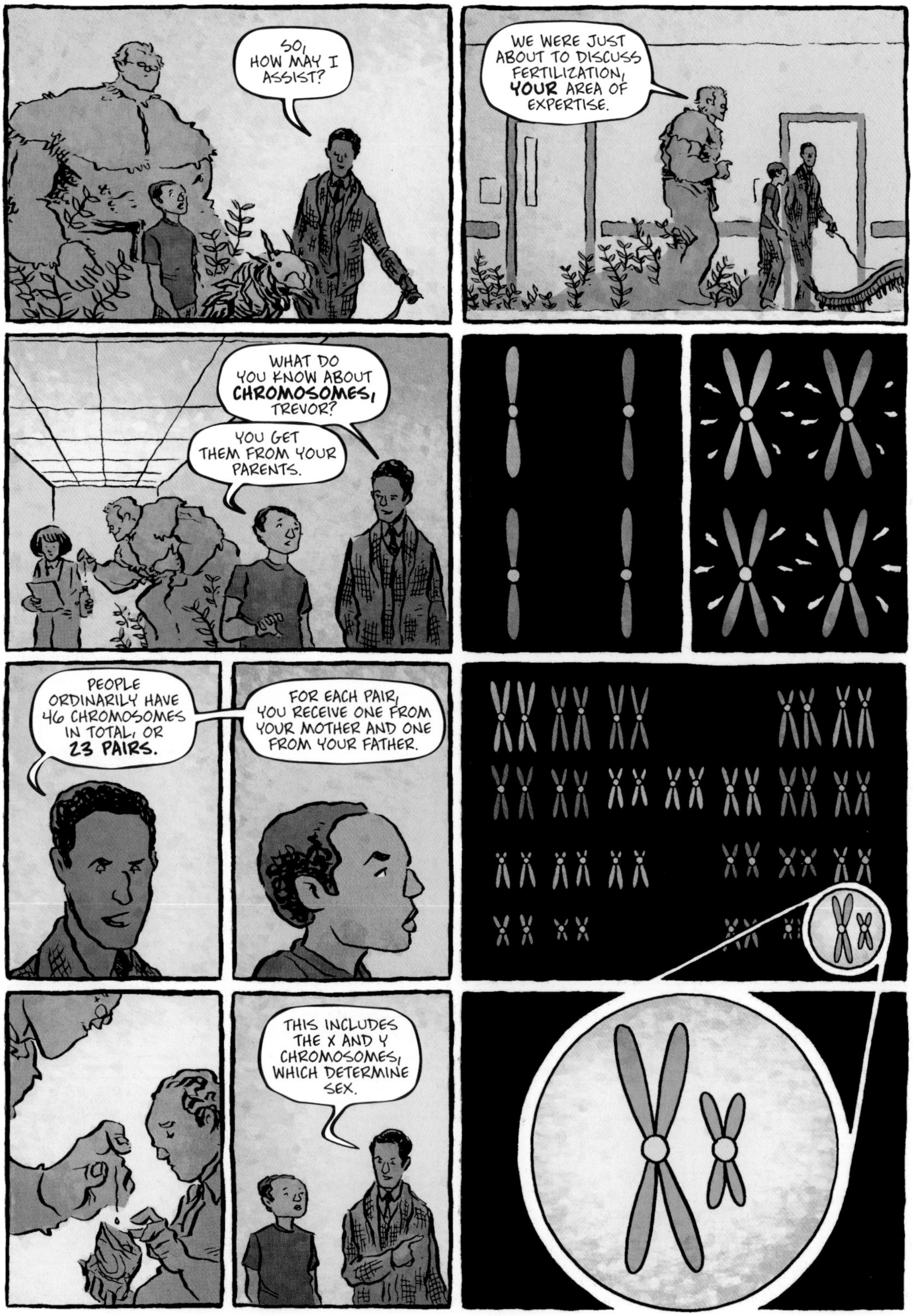
SO, HOW MAY I ASSIST?
WE WERE JUST ABOUT TO DISCUSS FERTILIZATION, **YOUR** AREA OF EXPERTISE.
WHAT DO YOU KNOW ABOUT **CHROMOSOMES**, TREVOR?
YOU GET THEM FROM YOUR PARENTS.
PEOPLE ORDINARILY HAVE 46 CHROMOSOMES IN TOTAL, OR **23 PAIRS.**
FOR EACH PAIR, YOU RECEIVE ONE FROM YOUR MOTHER AND ONE FROM YOUR FATHER.
THIS INCLUDES THE X AND Y CHROMOSOMES, WHICH DETERMINE SEX.

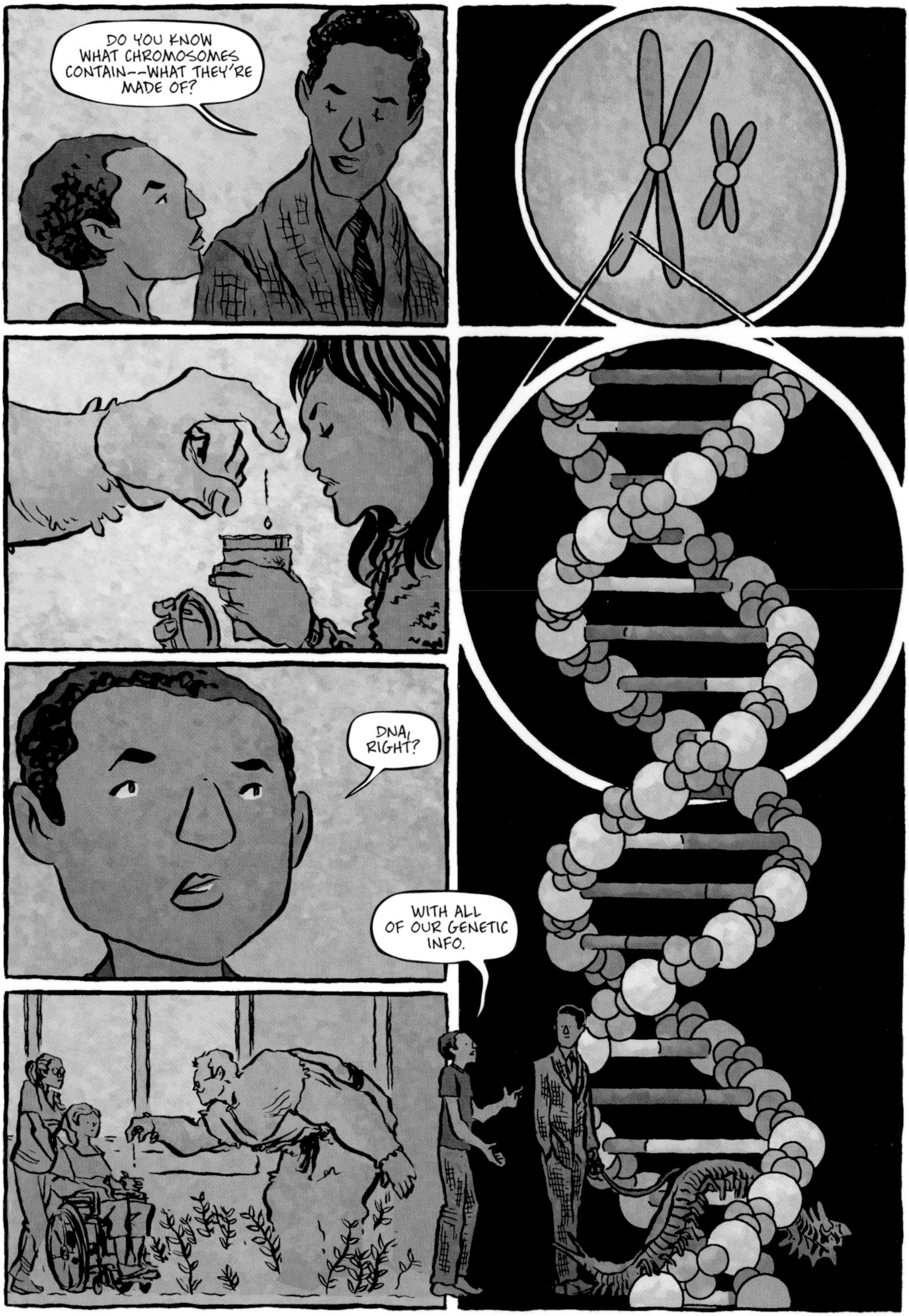
DO YOU KNOW WHAT CHROMOSOMES CONTAIN--WHAT THEY'RE MADE OF?
DNA, RIGHT?
WITH ALL OF OUR GENETIC INFO.

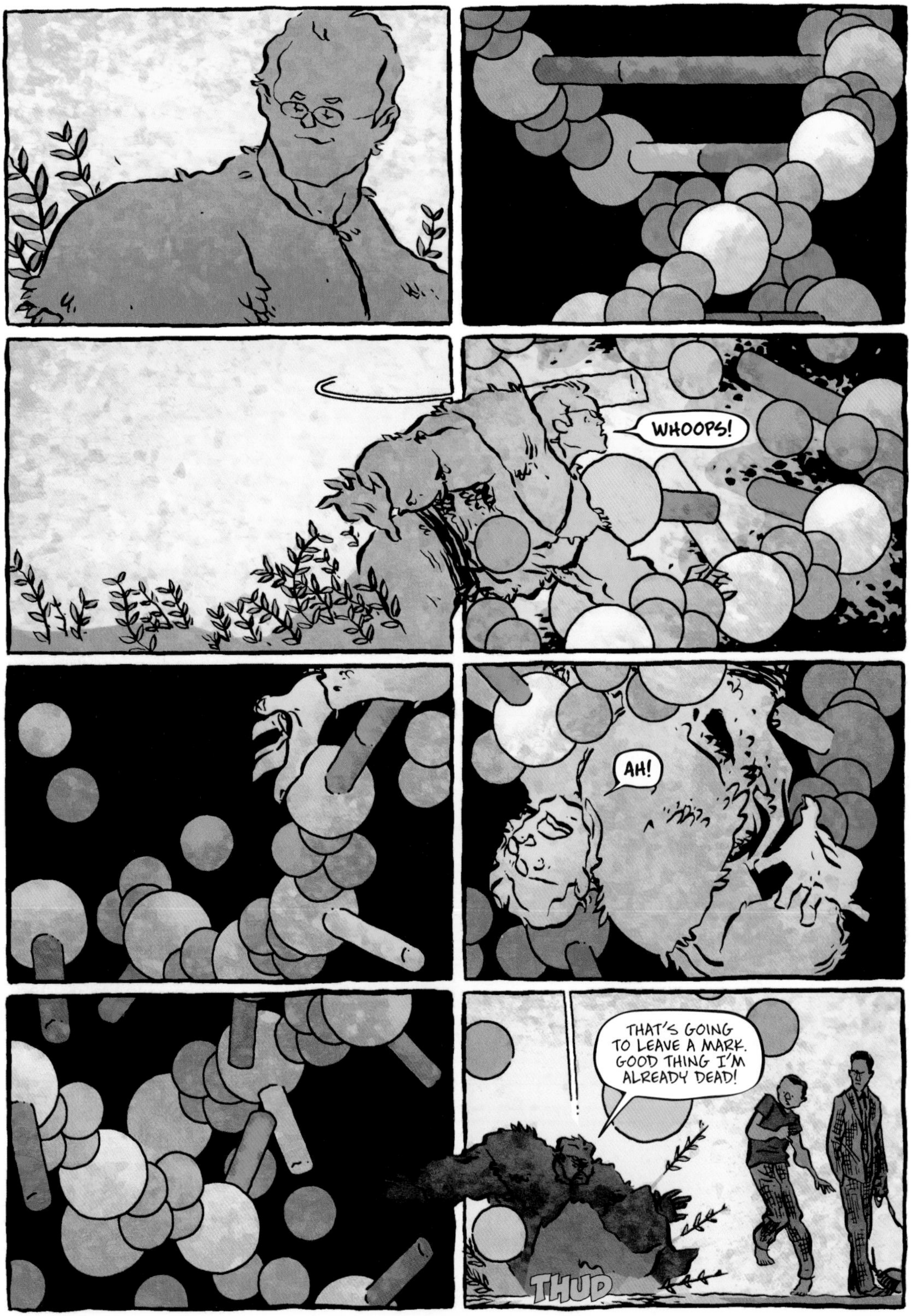
WHOOPS!
AH!
THAT'S GOING TO LEAVE A MARK. GOOD THING I'M ALREADY DEAD!
THUD

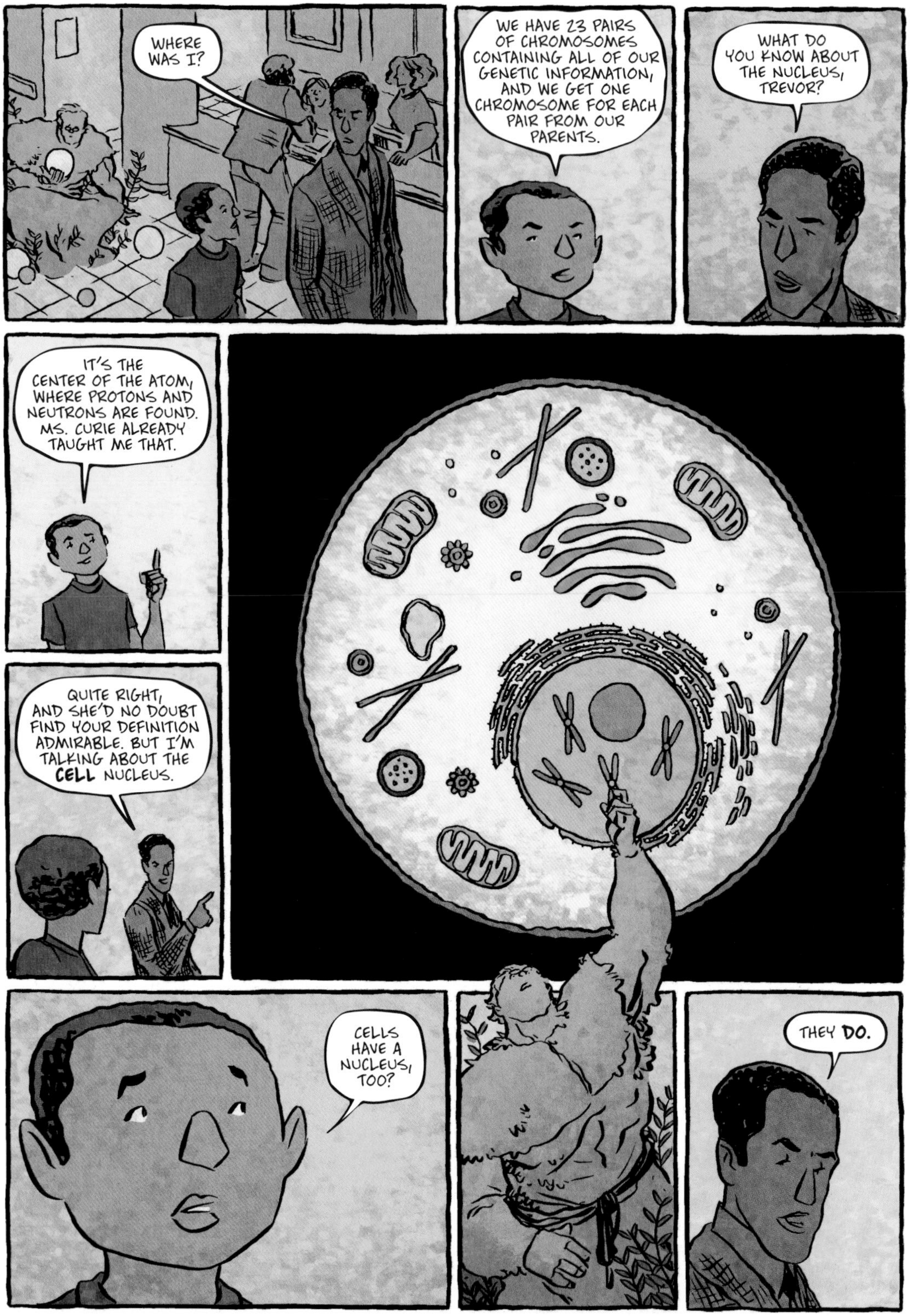
WHERE WAS I?
WE HAVE 23 PAIRS OF CHROMOSOMES CONTAINING ALL OF OUR GENETIC INFORMATION, AND WE GET ONE CHROMOSOME FOR EACH PAIR FROM OUR PARENTS.
WHAT DO YOU KNOW ABOUT THE NUCLEUS, TREVOR?
IT'S THE CENTER OF THE ATOM, WHERE PROTONS AND NEUTRONS ARE FOUND. MS. CURIE ALREADY TAUGHT ME THAT.
QUITE RIGHT, AND SHE'D NO DOUBT FIND YOUR DEFINITION ADMIRABLE. BUT I'M TALKING ABOUT THE **CELL** NUCLEUS.
CELLS HAVE A NUCLEUS, TOO?
THEY **DO.**

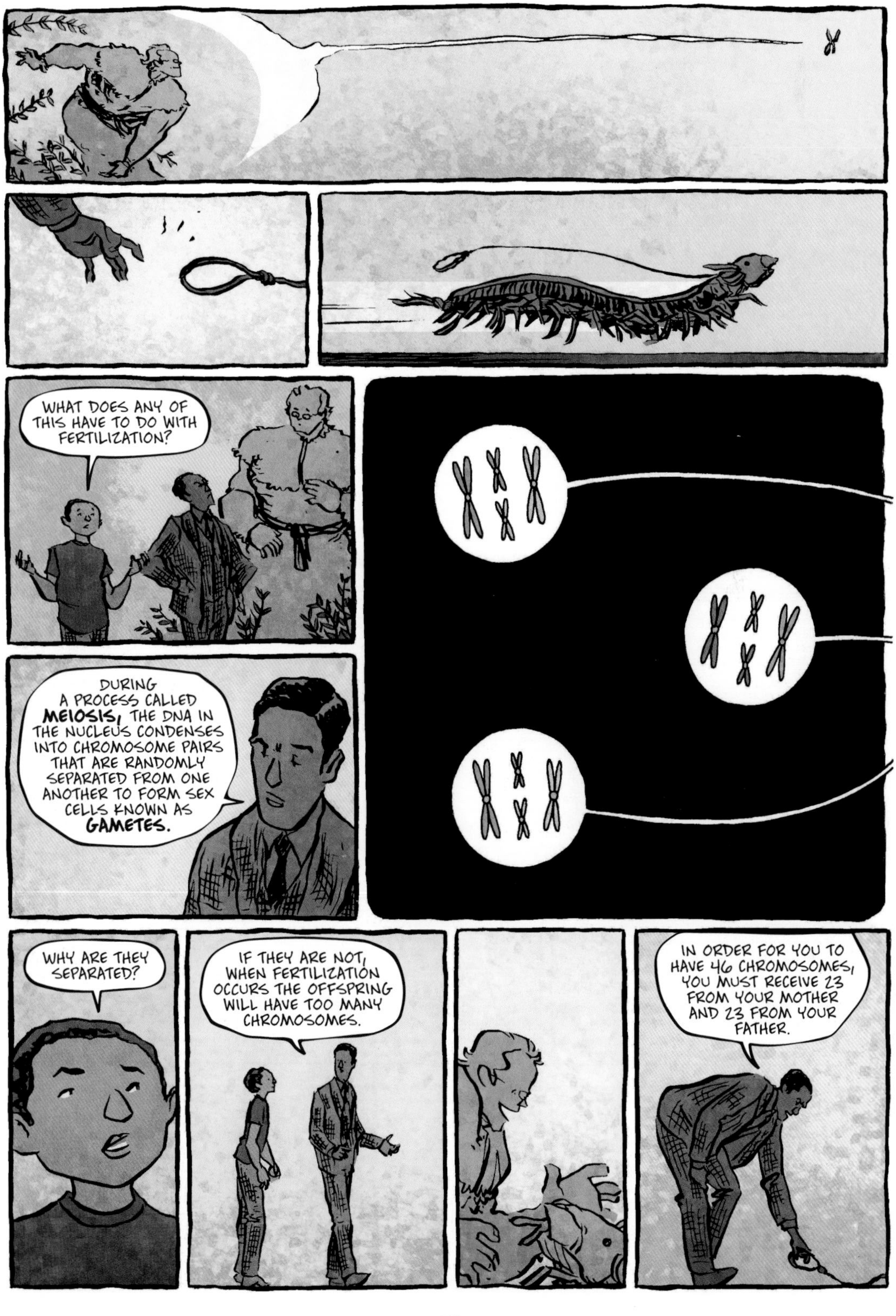
WHAT DOES ANY OF THIS HAVE TO DO WITH FERTILIZATION?
DURING A PROCESS CALLED **MEIOSIS**, THE DNA IN THE NUCLEUS CONDENSES INTO CHROMOSOME PAIRS THAT ARE RANDOMLY SEPARATED FROM ONE ANOTHER TO FORM SEX CELLS KNOWN AS **GAMETES**.
WHY ARE THEY SEPARATED?
IF THEY ARE NOT, WHEN FERTILIZATION OCCURS THE OFFSPRING WILL HAVE TOO MANY CHROMOSOMES.
IN ORDER FOR YOU TO HAVE 46 CHROMOSOMES, YOU MUST RECEIVE 23 FROM YOUR MOTHER AND 23 FROM YOUR FATHER.

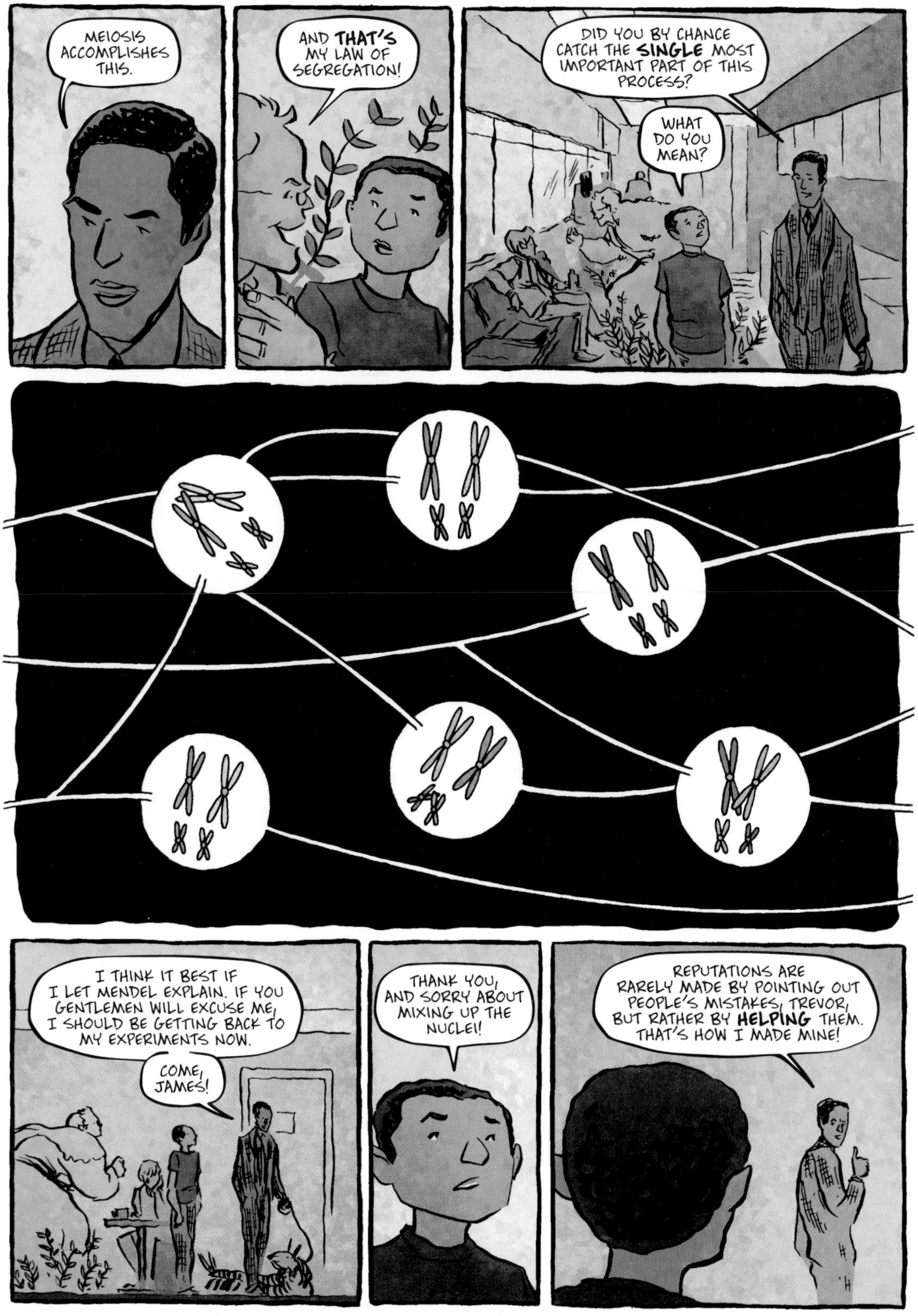
MEIOSIS ACCOMPLISHES THIS.
AND THAT'S MY LAW OF SEGREGATION!
DID YOU BY CHANCE CATCH THE SINGLE MOST IMPORTANT PART OF THIS PROCESS?
WHAT DO YOU MEAN?
I THINK IT BEST IF I LET MENDEL EXPLAIN. IF YOU GENTLEMEN WILL EXCUSE ME, I SHOULD BE GETTING BACK TO MY EXPERIMENTS NOW.
COME, JAMES!
THANK YOU, AND SORRY ABOUT MIXING UP THE NUCLEI!
REPUTATIONS ARE RARELY MADE BY POINTING OUT PEOPLE'S MISTAKES, TREVOR, BUT RATHER BY HELPING THEM. THAT'S HOW I MADE MINE!

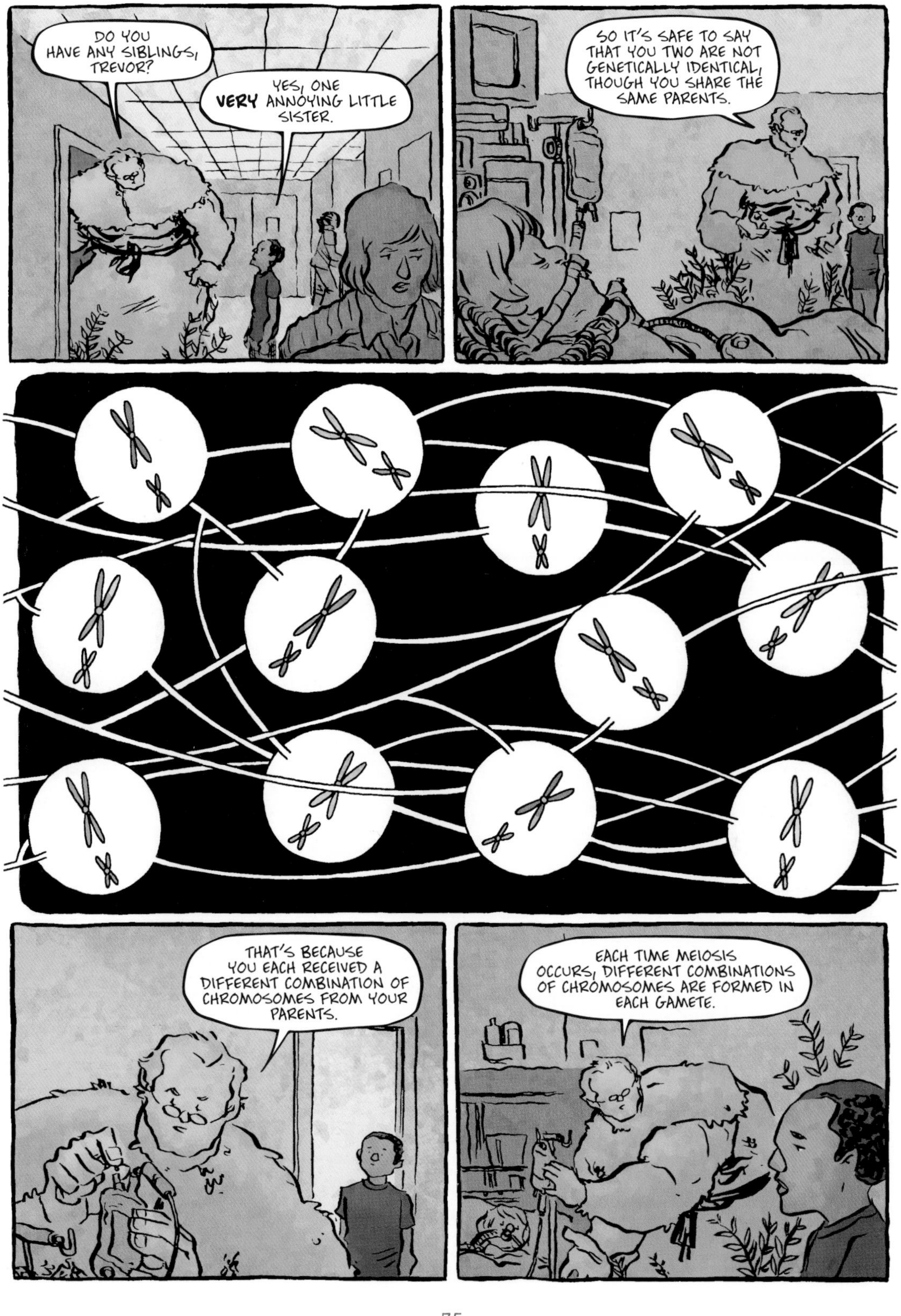
DO YOU HAVE ANY SIBLINGS, TREVOR?
YES, ONE VERY ANNOYING LITTLE SISTER.
SO IT'S SAFE TO SAY THAT YOU TWO ARE NOT GENETICALLY IDENTICAL, THOUGH YOU SHARE THE SAME PARENTS.
THAT'S BECAUSE YOU EACH RECEIVED A DIFFERENT COMBINATION OF CHROMOSOMES FROM YOUR PARENTS.
EACH TIME MEIOSIS OCCURS, DIFFERENT COMBINATIONS OF CHROMOSOMES ARE FORMED IN EACH GAMETE.

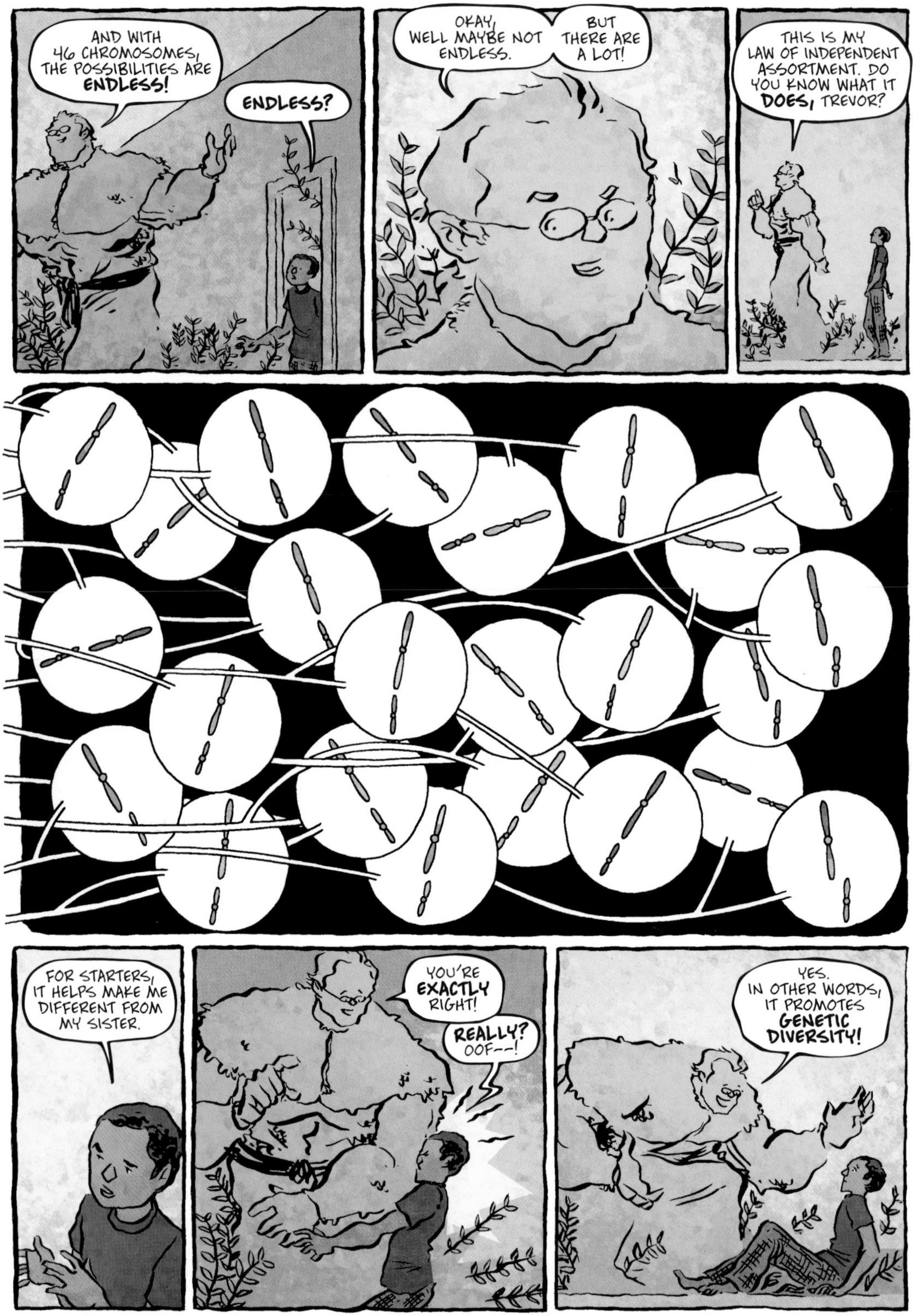
AND WITH 46 CHROMOSOMES, THE POSSIBILITIES ARE ENDLESS!
ENDLESS?
OKAY, WELL MAYBE NOT ENDLESS.
BUT THERE ARE A LOT!
THIS IS MY LAW OF INDEPENDENT ASSORTMENT. DO YOU KNOW WHAT IT DOES, TREVOR?
FOR STARTERS, IT HELPS MAKE ME DIFFERENT FROM MY SISTER.
YOU'RE EXACTLY RIGHT!
REALLY? OOF--!
YES. IN OTHER WORDS, IT PROMOTES GENETIC DIVERSITY!

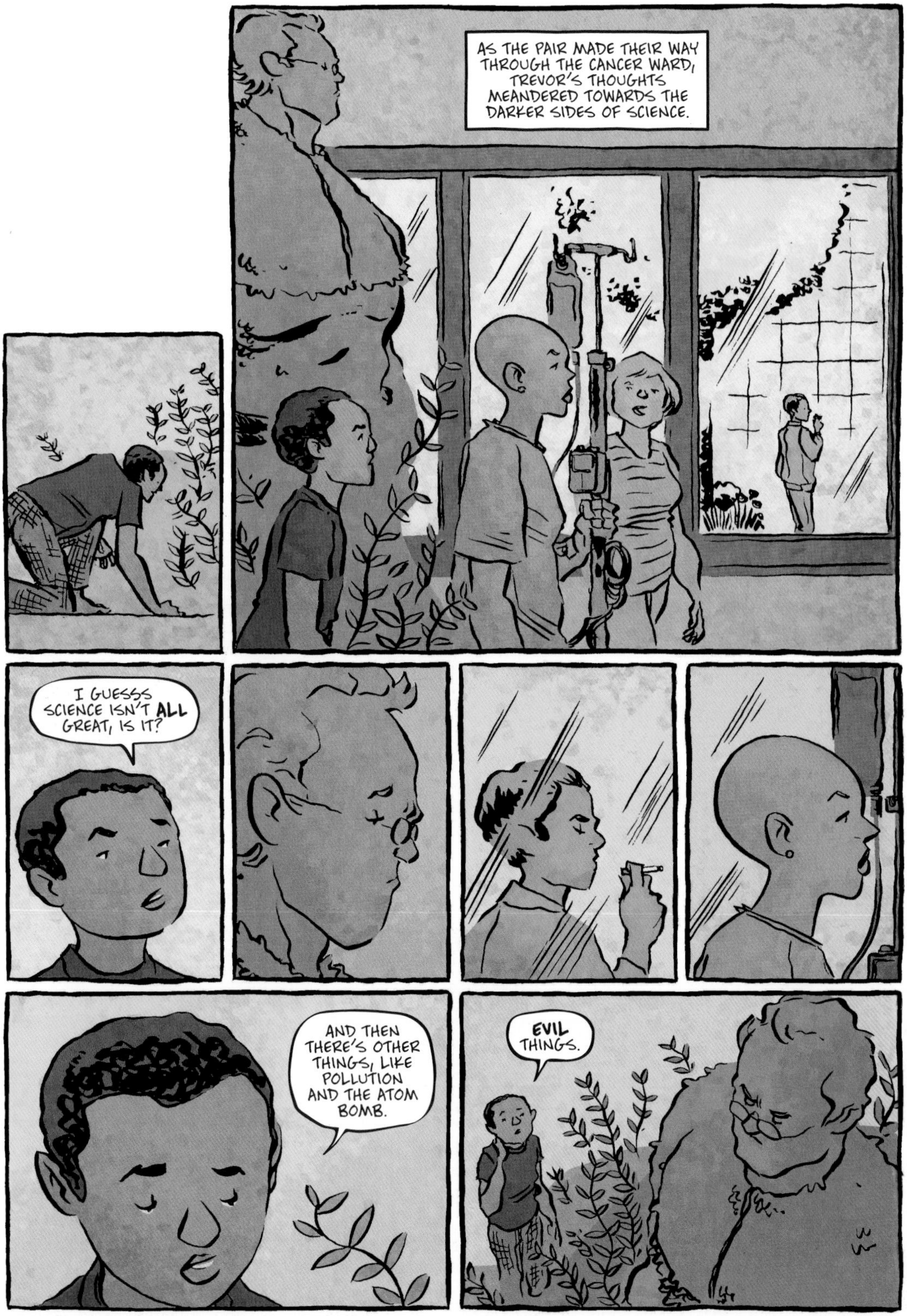
AS THE PAIR MADE THEIR WAY THROUGH THE CANCER WARD, TREVOR'S THOUGHTS MEANDERED TOWARDS THE DARKER SIDES OF SCIENCE.
I GUESSS SCIENCE ISN'T **ALL** GREAT, IS IT?
AND THEN THERE'S OTHER THINGS, LIKE POLLUTION AND THE ATOM BOMB.
EVIL THINGS.

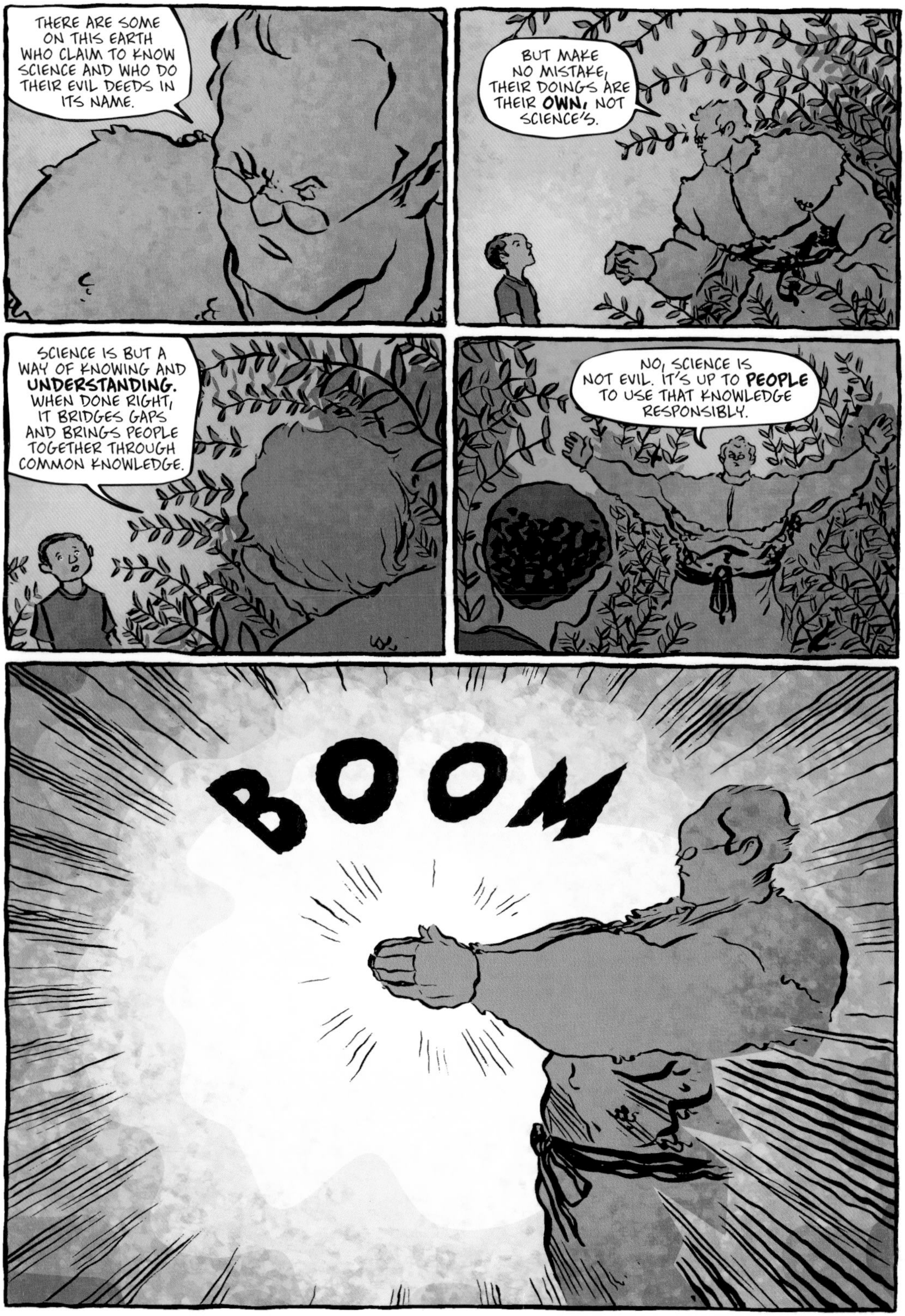
THERE ARE SOME ON THIS EARTH WHO CLAIM TO KNOW SCIENCE AND WHO DO THEIR EVIL DEEDS IN ITS NAME.
BUT MAKE NO MISTAKE, THEIR DOINGS ARE THEIR **OWN**, NOT SCIENCE'S.
SCIENCE IS BUT A WAY OF KNOWING AND **UNDERSTANDING.** WHEN DONE RIGHT, IT BRIDGES GAPS AND BRINGS PEOPLE TOGETHER THROUGH COMMON KNOWLEDGE.
NO, SCIENCE IS NOT EVIL. IT'S UP TO **PEOPLE** TO USE THAT KNOWLEDGE RESPONSIBLY.
BOOM

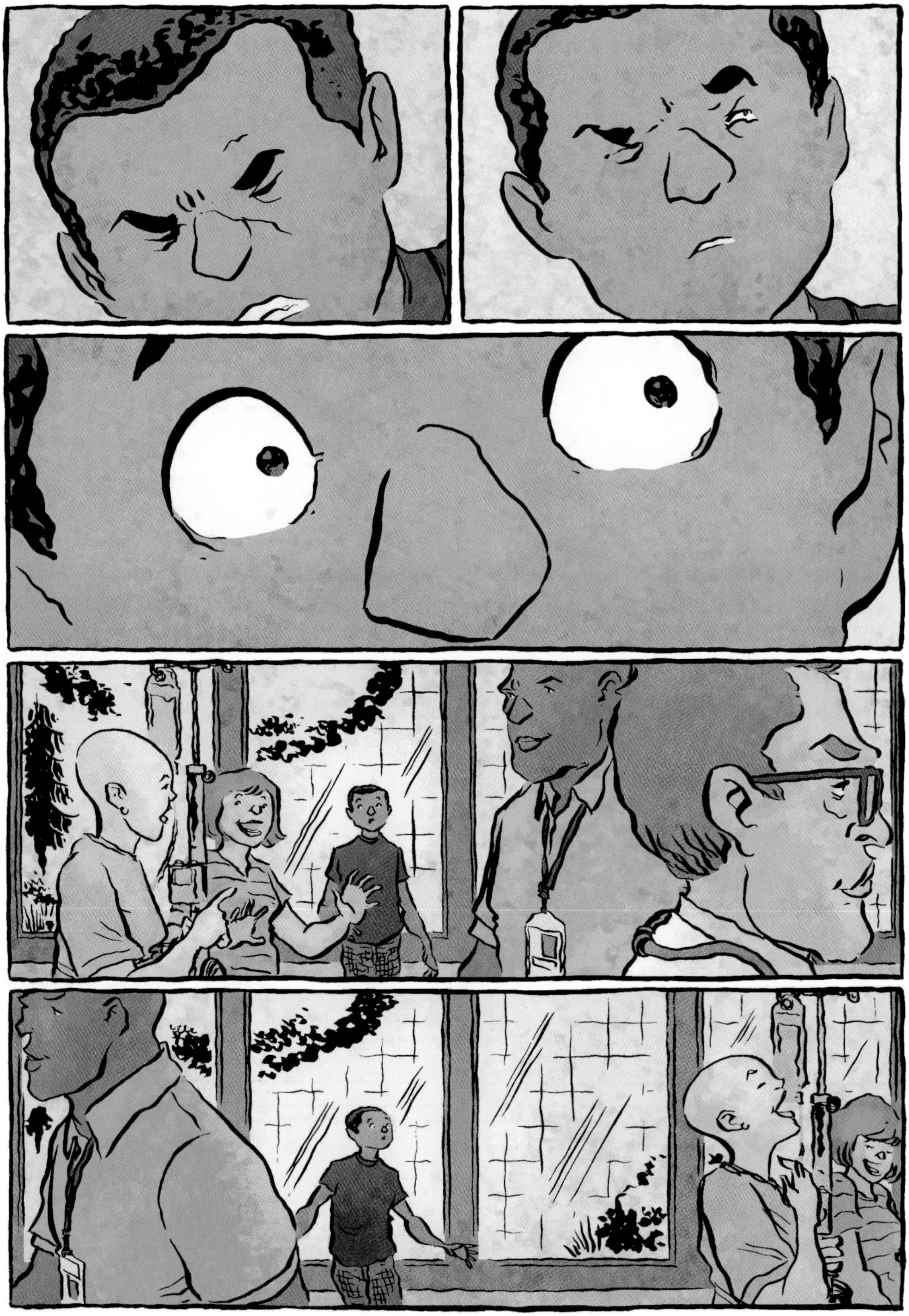

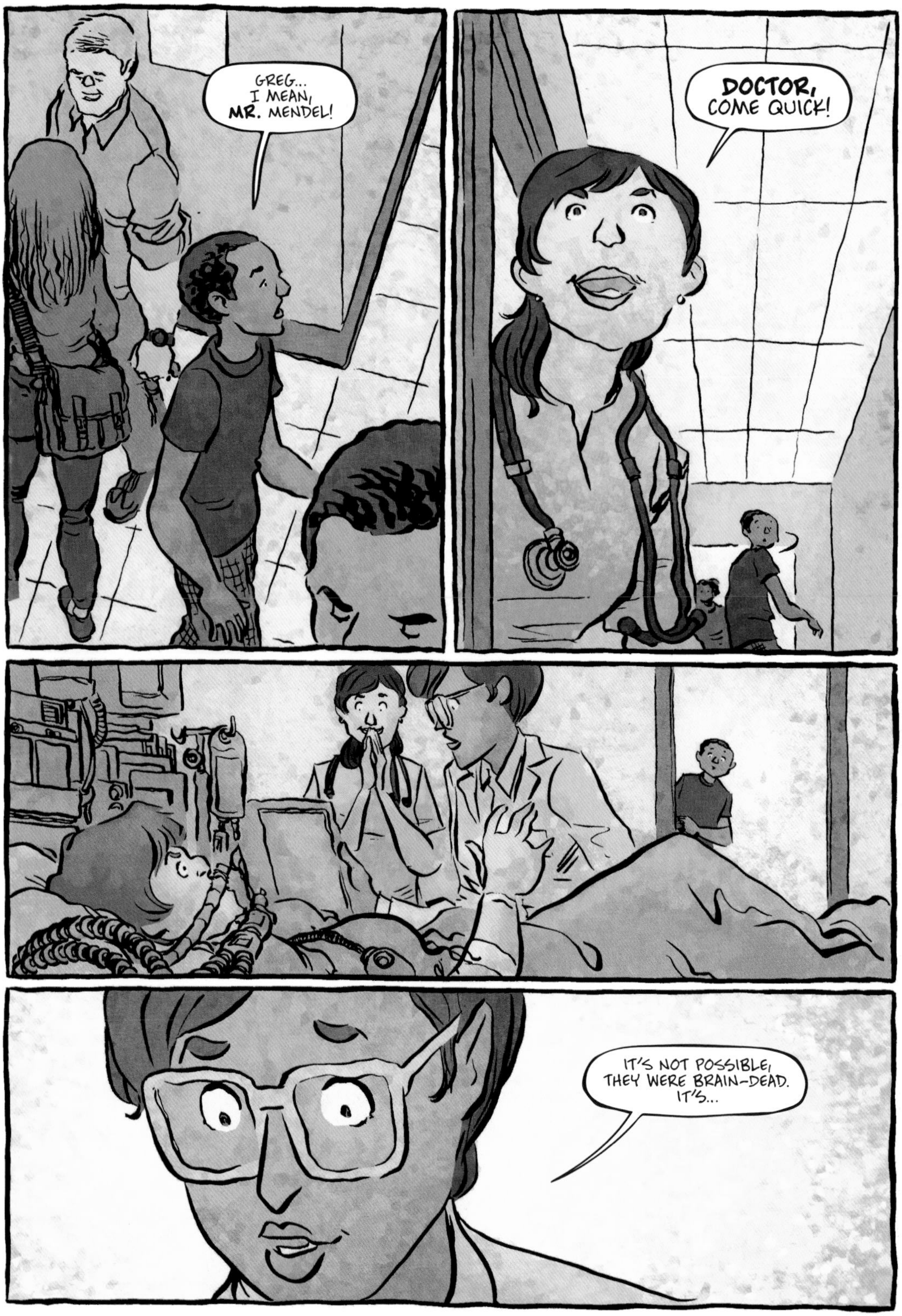
GREG... I MEAN, MR. MENDEL!
DOCTOR, COME QUICK!
IT'S NOT POSSIBLE, THEY WERE BRAIN-DEAD. IT'S...

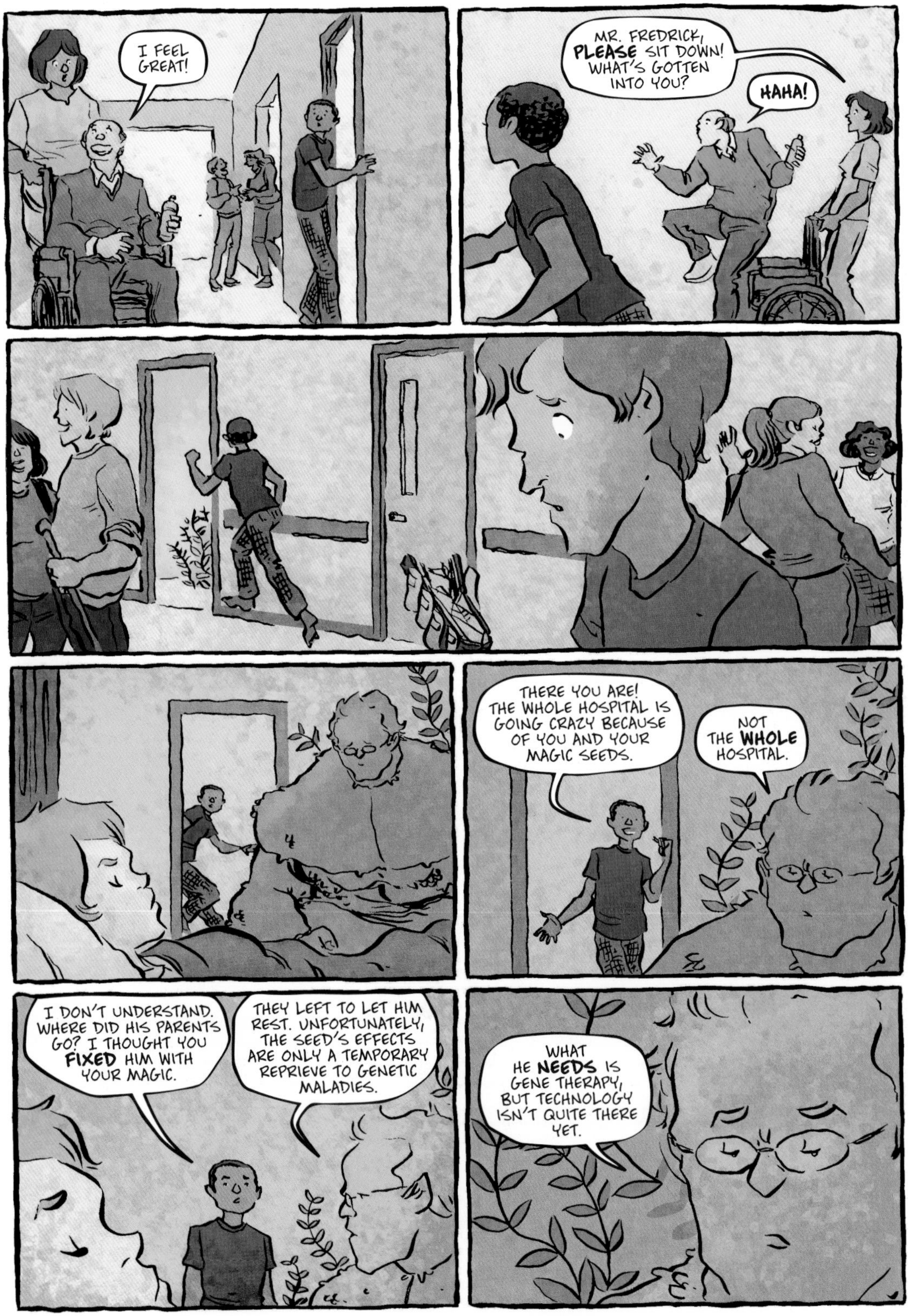
I FEEL GREAT!
MR. FREDRICK, **PLEASE** SIT DOWN! WHAT'S GOTTEN INTO YOU?
HAHA!
THERE YOU ARE! THE WHOLE HOSPITAL IS GOING CRAZY BECAUSE OF YOU AND YOUR MAGIC SEEDS.
NOT THE **WHOLE** HOSPITAL.
I DON'T UNDERSTAND. WHERE DID HIS PARENTS GO? I THOUGHT YOU **FIXED** HIM WITH YOUR MAGIC.
THEY LEFT TO LET HIM REST. UNFORTUNATELY, THE SEED'S EFFECTS ARE ONLY A TEMPORARY REPRIEVE TO GENETIC MALADIES.
WHAT HE **NEEDS** IS GENE THERAPY, BUT TECHNOLOGY ISN'T QUITE THERE YET.

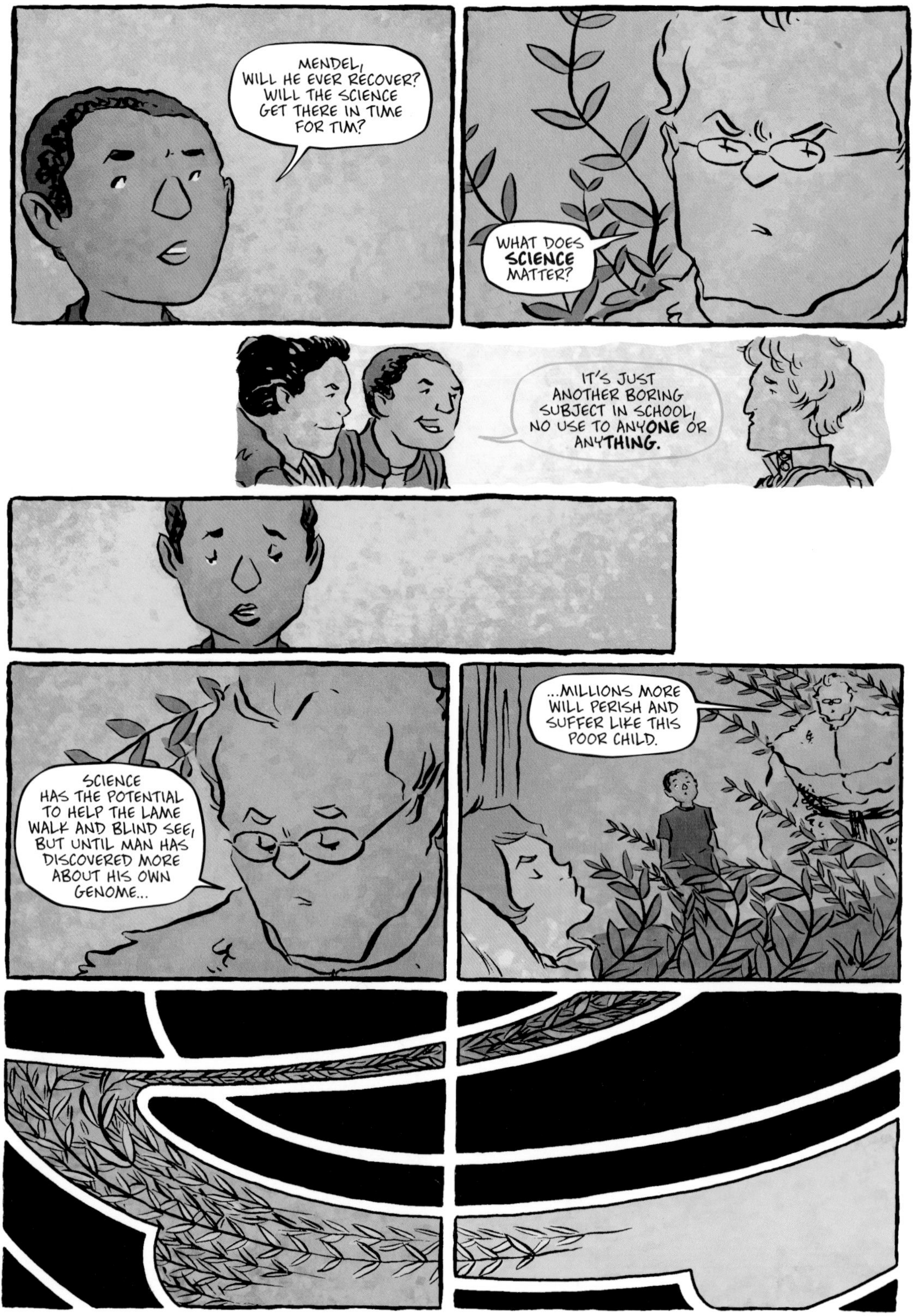
MENDEL, WILL HE EVER RECOVER? WILL THE SCIENCE GET THERE IN TIME FOR TIM?
WHAT DOES **SCIENCE** MATTER?
IT'S JUST ANOTHER BORING SUBJECT IN SCHOOL, NO USE TO ANY**ONE** OR ANY**THING.**
SCIENCE HAS THE POTENTIAL TO HELP THE LAME WALK AND BLIND SEE, BUT UNTIL MAN HAS DISCOVERED MORE ABOUT HIS OWN GENOME...
...MILLIONS MORE WILL PERISH AND SUFFER LIKE THIS POOR CHILD.

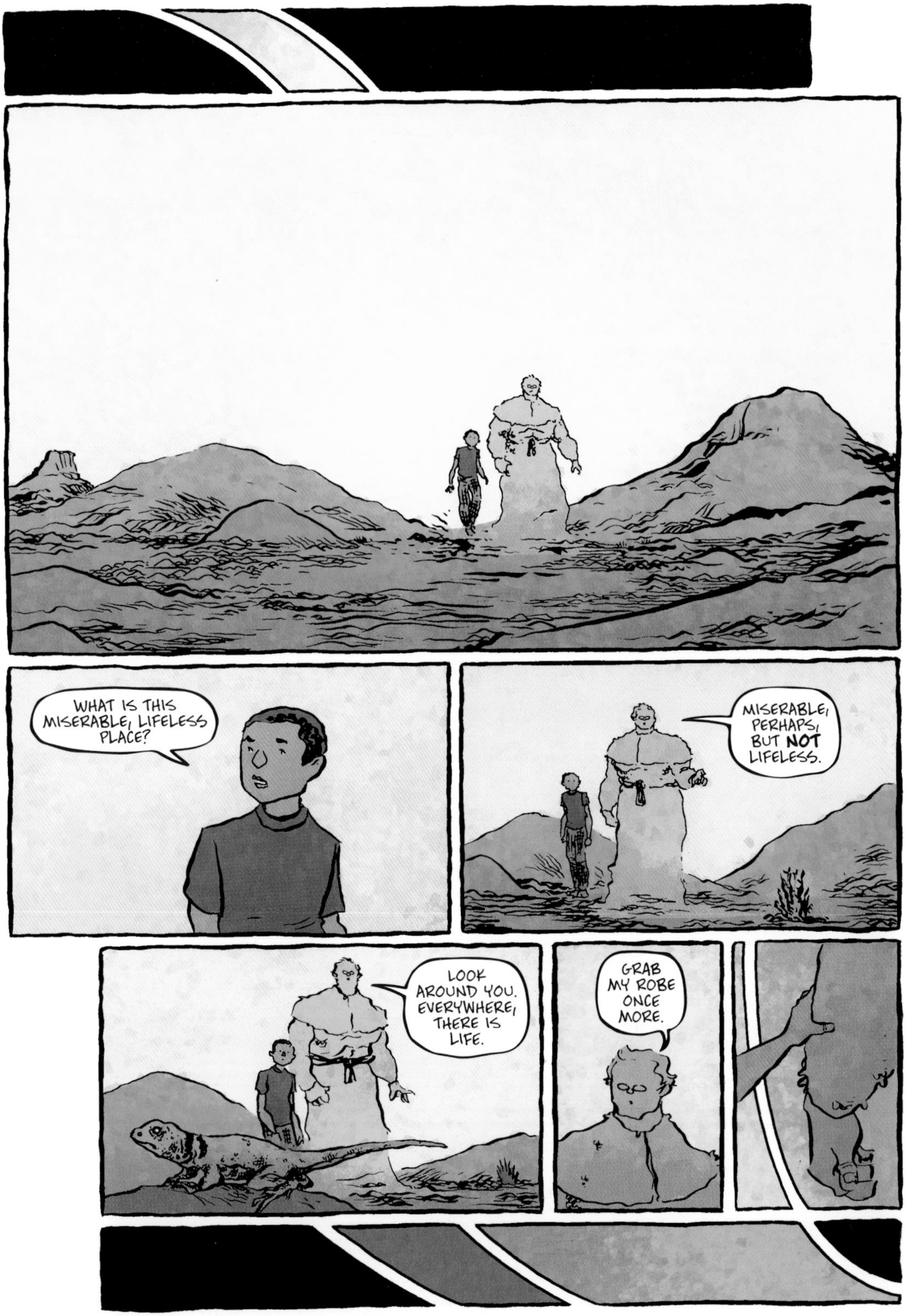
WHAT IS THIS MISERABLE, LIFELESS PLACE?
MISERABLE, PERHAPS, BUT **NOT** LIFELESS.
LOOK AROUND YOU. EVERYWHERE, THERE IS LIFE.
GRAB MY ROBE ONCE MORE.

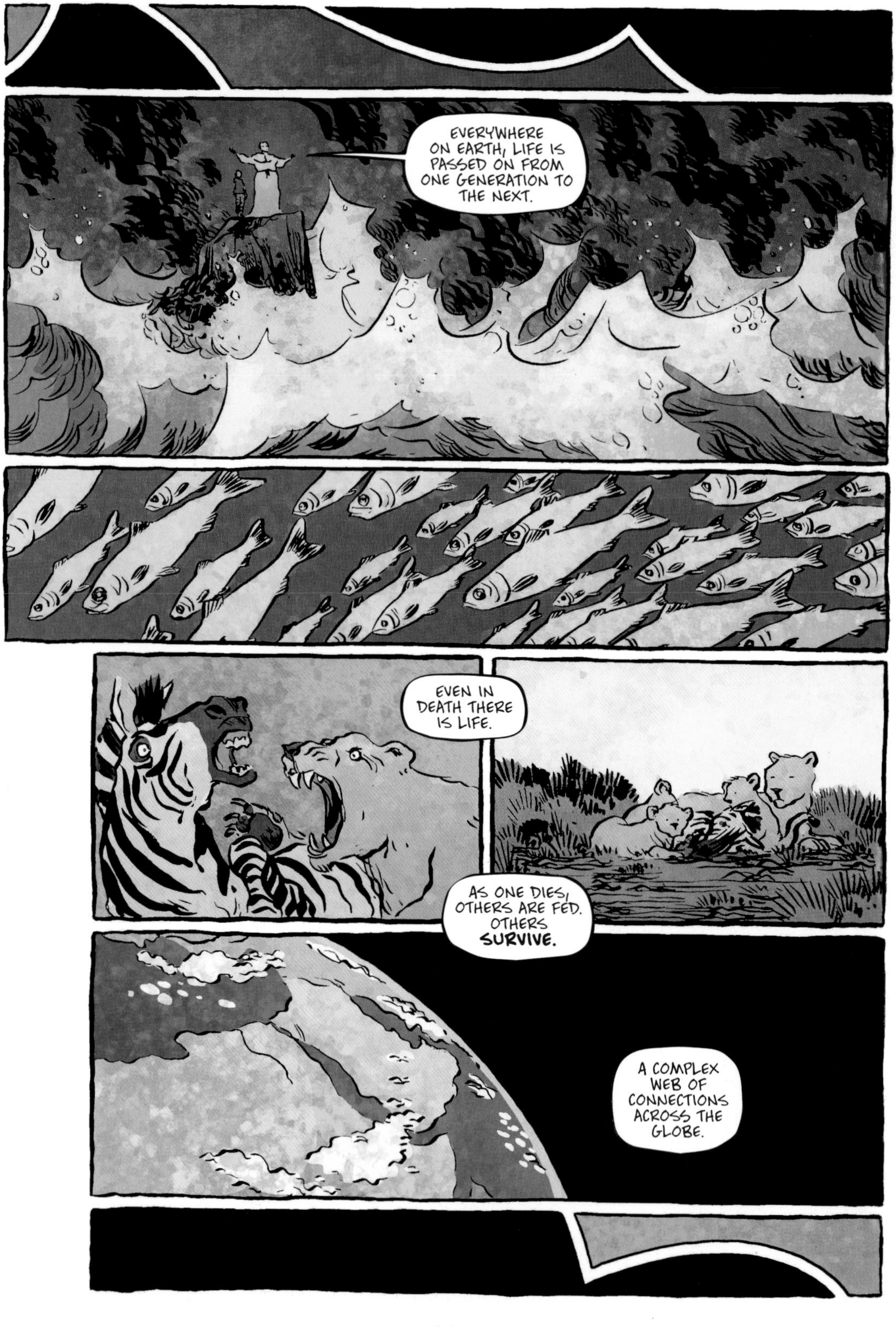
EVERYWHERE ON EARTH, LIFE IS PASSED ON FROM ONE GENERATION TO THE NEXT.
EVEN IN DEATH THERE IS LIFE.
AS ONE DIES, OTHERS ARE FED. OTHERS **SURVIVE.**
A COMPLEX WEB OF CONNECTIONS ACROSS THE GLOBE.

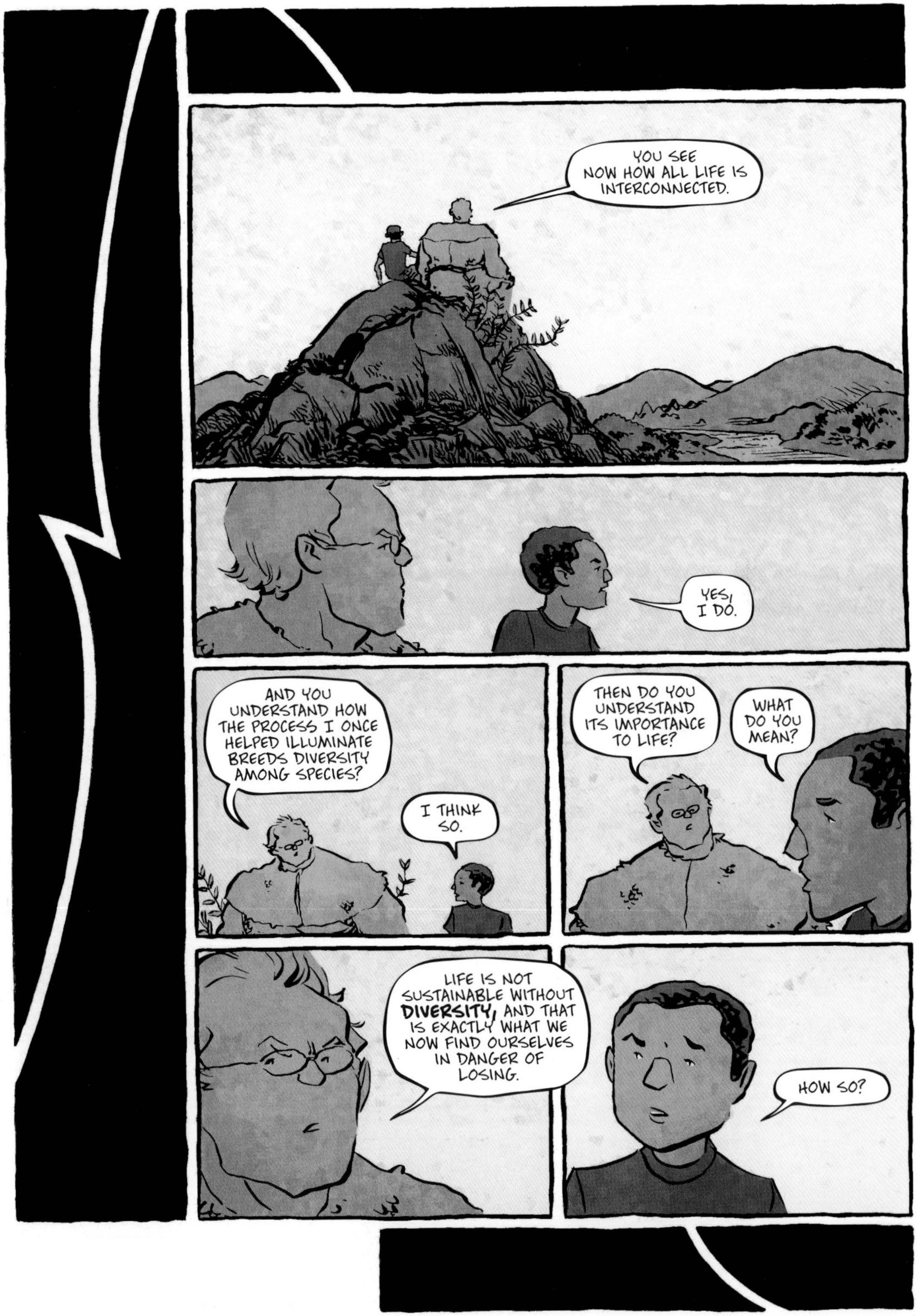
YOU SEE NOW HOW ALL LIFE IS INTERCONNECTED.
YES, I DO.
AND YOU UNDERSTAND HOW THE PROCESS I ONCE HELPED ILLUMINATE BREEDS DIVERSITY AMONG SPECIES?
I THINK SO.
THEN DO YOU UNDERSTAND ITS IMPORTANCE TO LIFE?
WHAT DO YOU MEAN?
LIFE IS NOT SUSTAINABLE WITHOUT **DIVERSITY,** AND THAT IS EXACTLY WHAT WE NOW FIND OURSELVES IN DANGER OF LOSING.
HOW SO?

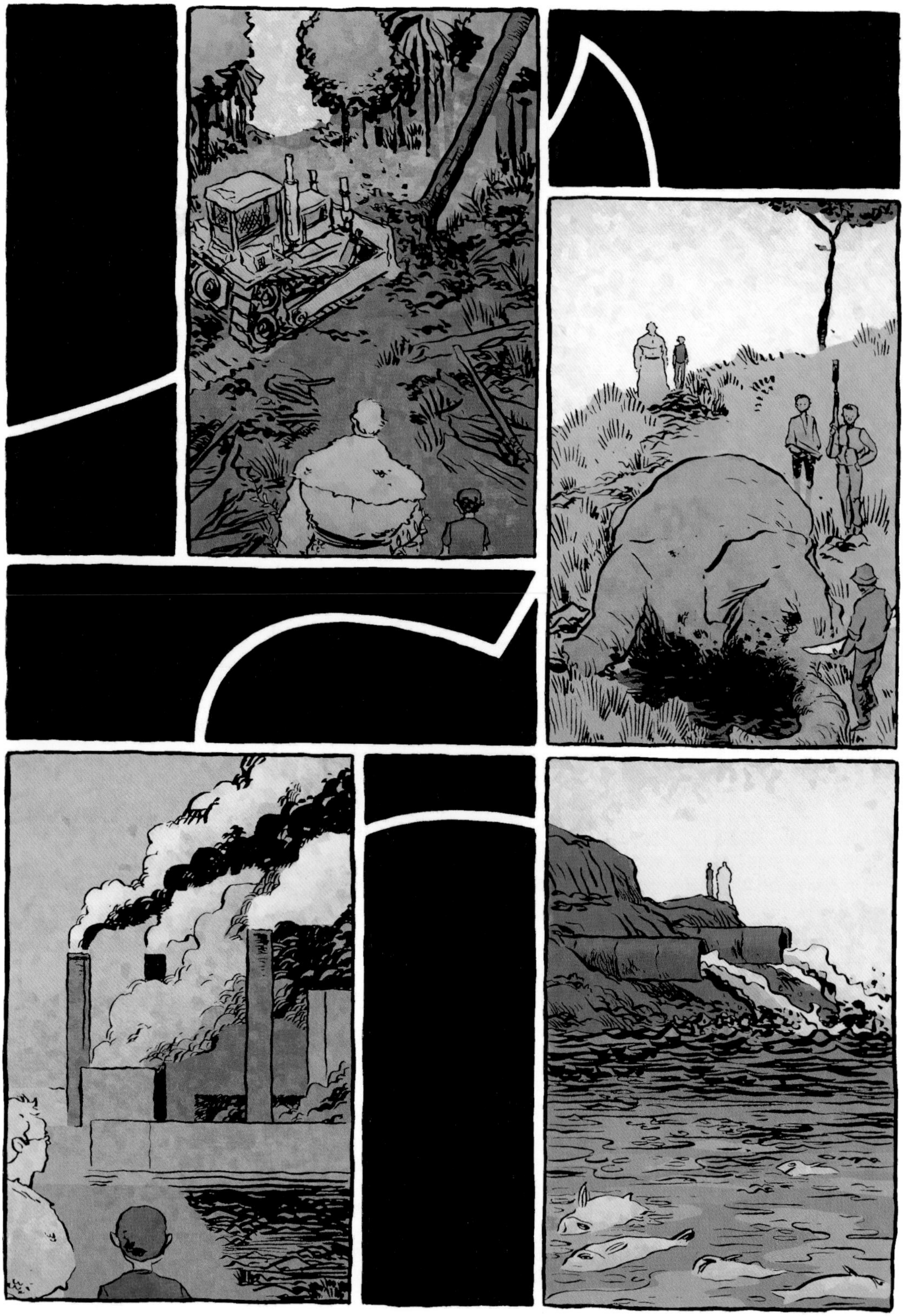

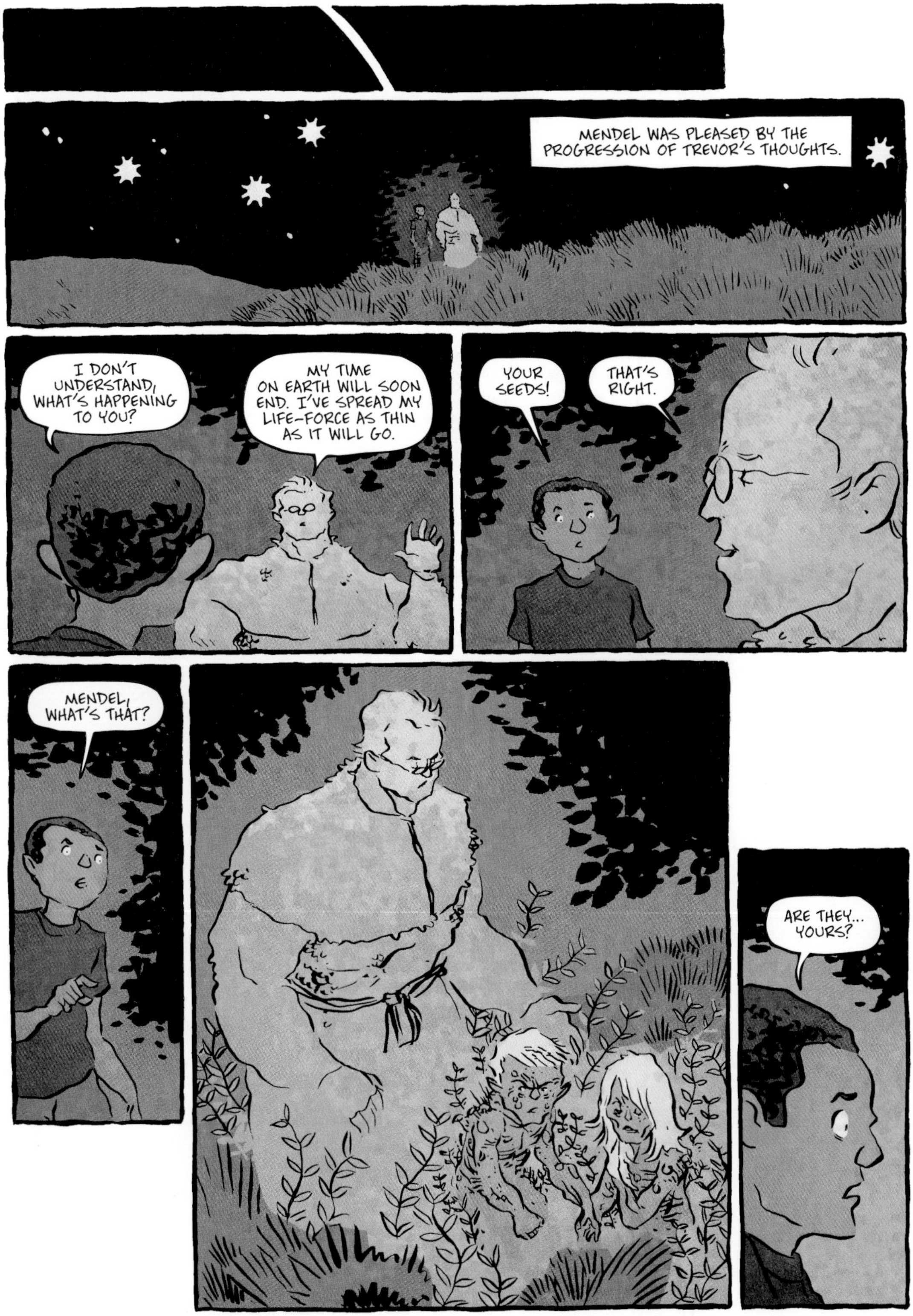
MENDEL WAS PLEASED BY THE PROGRESSION OF TREVOR'S THOUGHTS.
I DON'T UNDERSTAND, WHAT'S HAPPENING TO YOU?
MY TIME ON EARTH WILL SOON END. I'VE SPREAD MY LIFE-FORCE AS THIN AS IT WILL GO.
YOUR SEEDS!
THAT'S RIGHT.
MENDEL, WHAT'S THAT?
ARE THEY... YOURS?

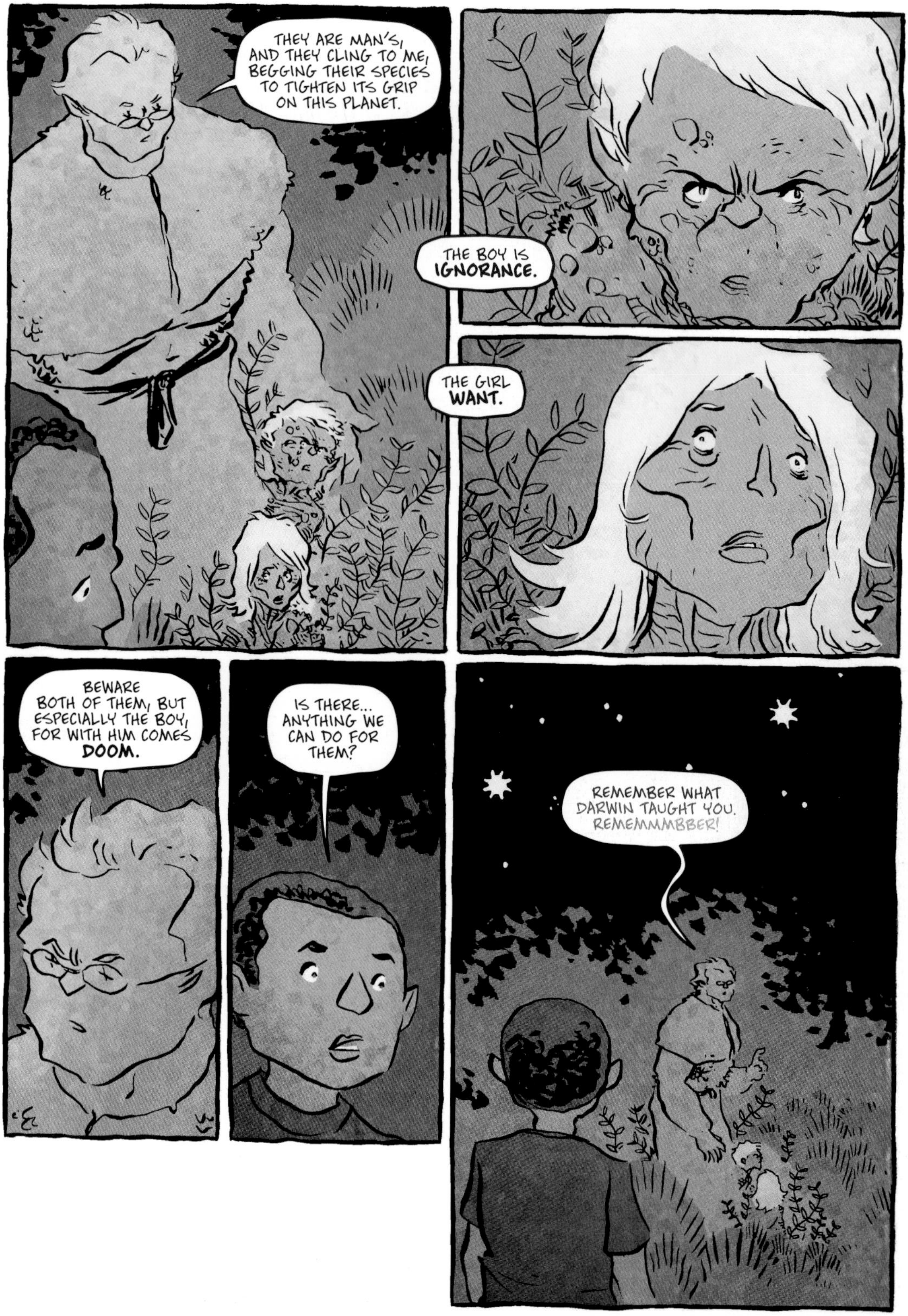
THEY ARE MAN'S, AND THEY CLING TO ME, BEGGING THEIR SPECIES TO TIGHTEN ITS GRIP ON THIS PLANET.
THE BOY IS **IGNORANCE.**
THE GIRL **WANT.**
BEWARE BOTH OF THEM, BUT ESPECIALLY THE BOY, FOR WITH HIM COMES **DOOM.**
IS THERE... ANYTHING WE CAN DO FOR THEM?
REMEMBER WHAT DARWIN TAUGHT YOU. REMEMMMBBER!

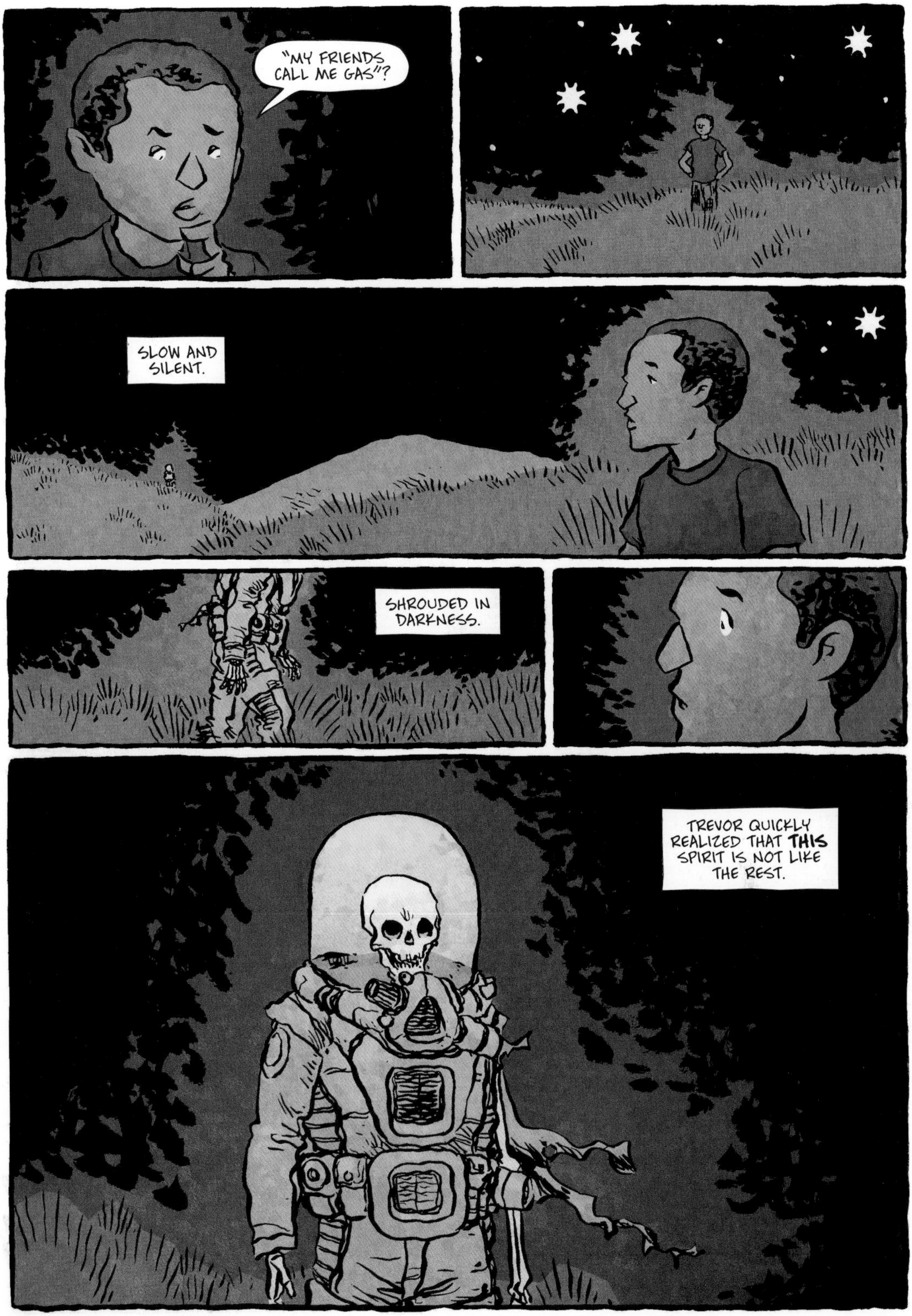
"MY FRIENDS CALL ME GAS"?
SLOW AND SILENT.
SHROUDED IN DARKNESS.
TREVOR QUICKLY REALIZED THAT **THIS** SPIRIT IS NOT LIKE THE REST.

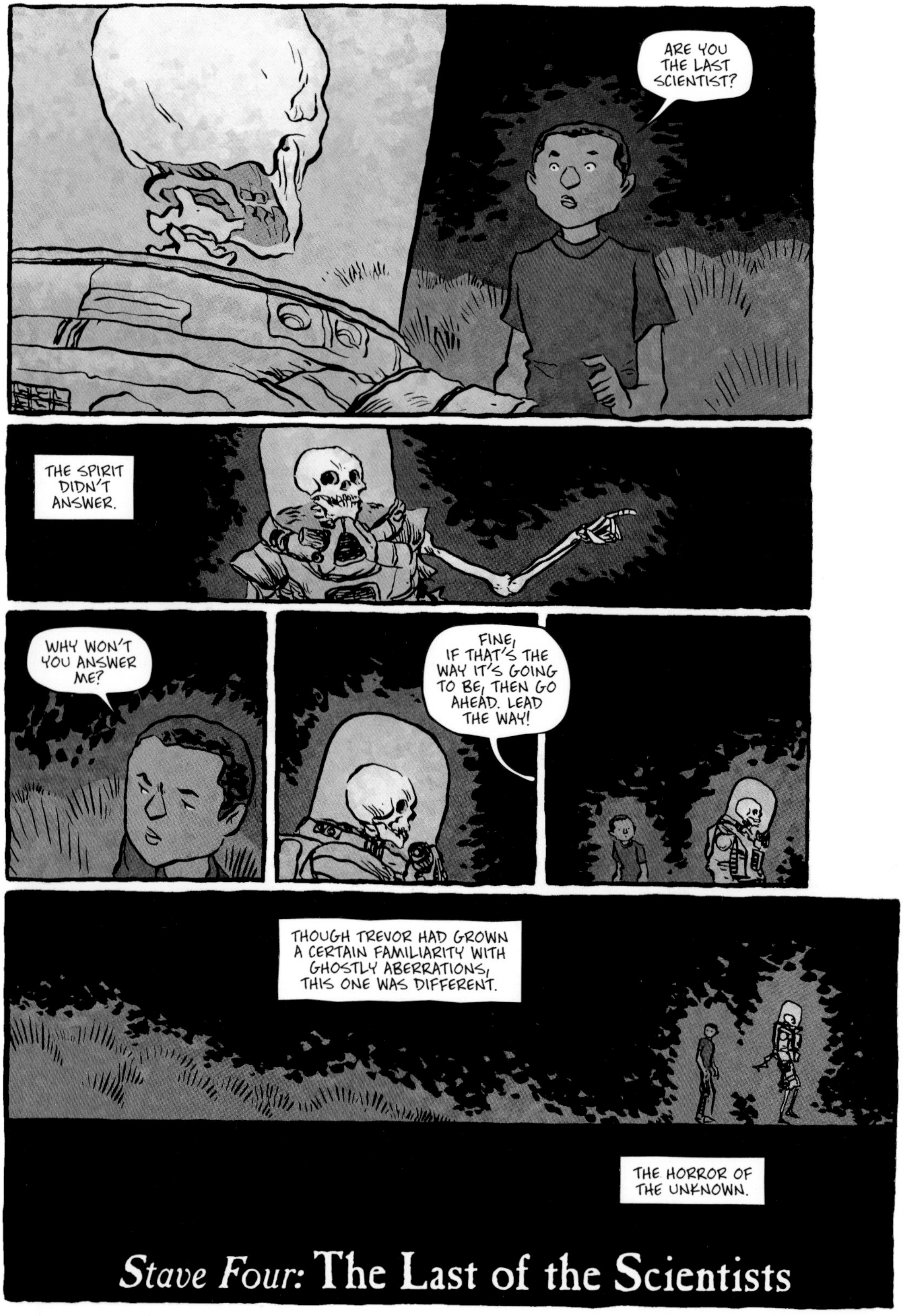
ARE YOU THE LAST SCIENTIST?
THE SPIRIT DIDN'T ANSWER.
WHY WON'T YOU ANSWER ME?
FINE, IF THAT'S THE WAY IT'S GOING TO BE, THEN GO AHEAD. LEAD THE WAY!
THOUGH TREVOR HAD GROWN A CERTAIN FAMILIARITY WITH GHOSTLY ABERRATIONS, THIS ONE WAS DIFFERENT.
THE HORROR OF THE UNKNOWN.
Stave Four: The Last of the Scientists

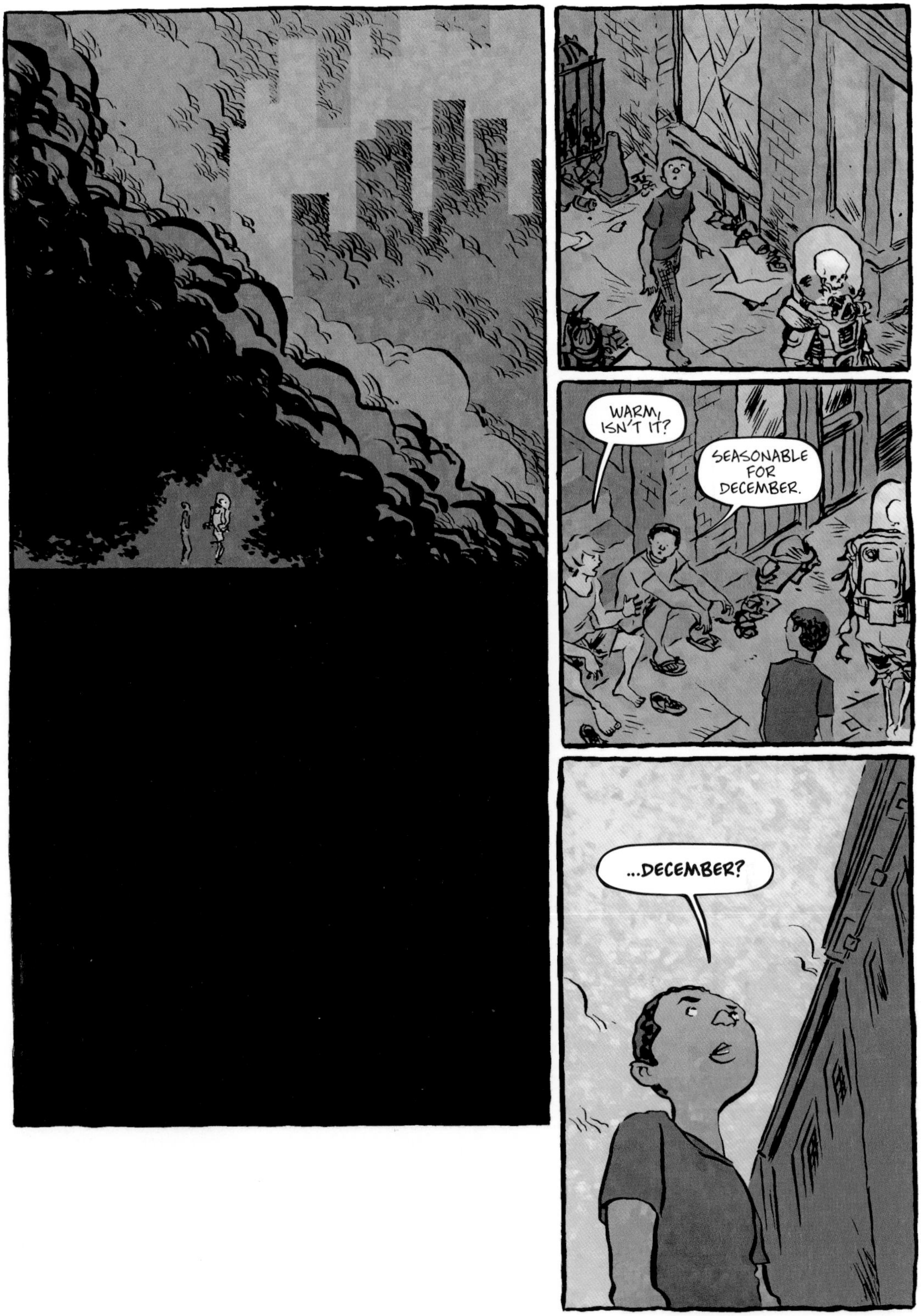
WARM, ISN'T IT?
SEASONABLE FOR DECEMBER.
...DECEMBER?

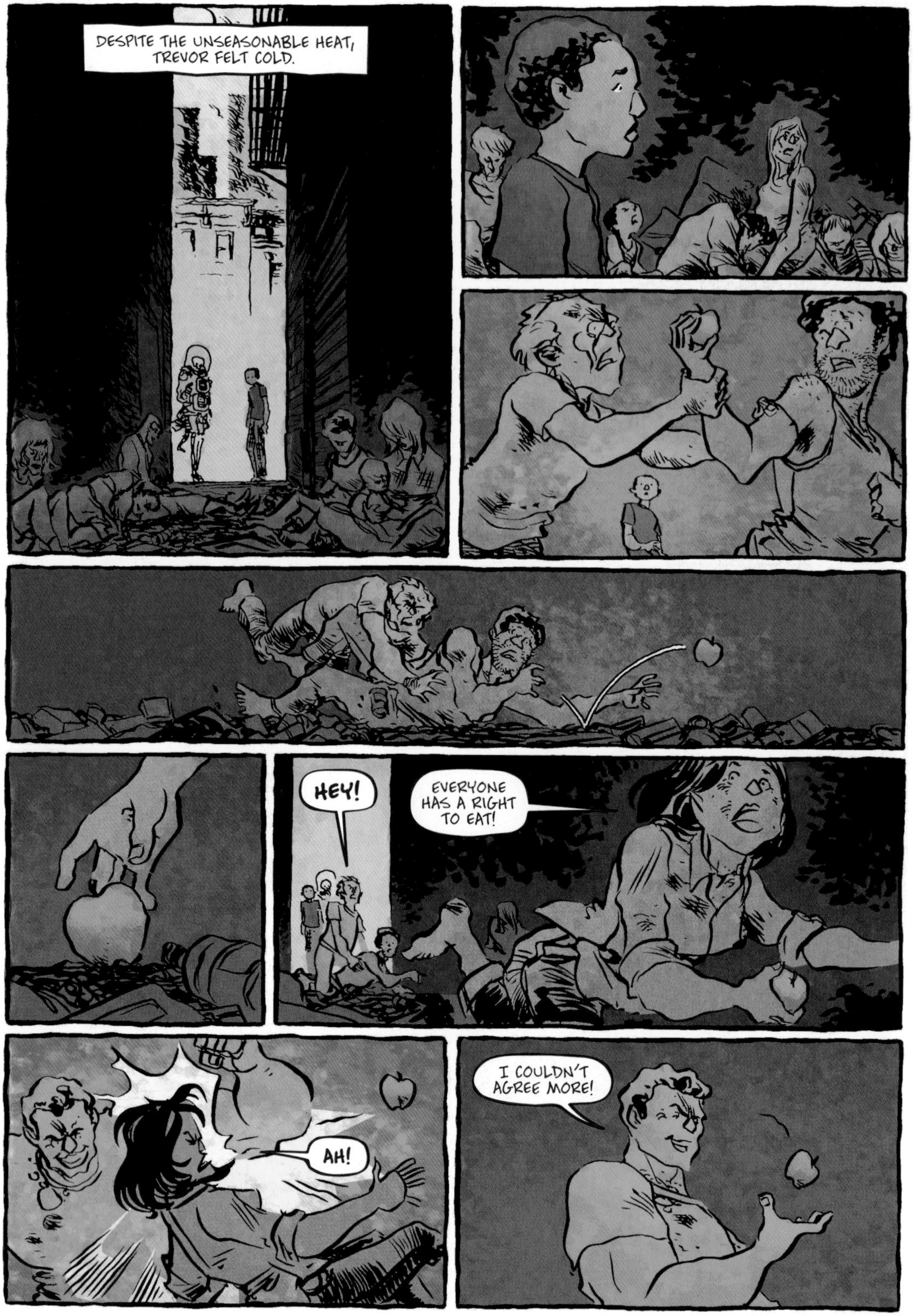
DESPITE THE UNSEASONABLE HEAT, TREVOR FELT COLD.
HEY!
EVERYONE HAS A RIGHT TO EAT!
AH!
I COULDN'T AGREE MORE!

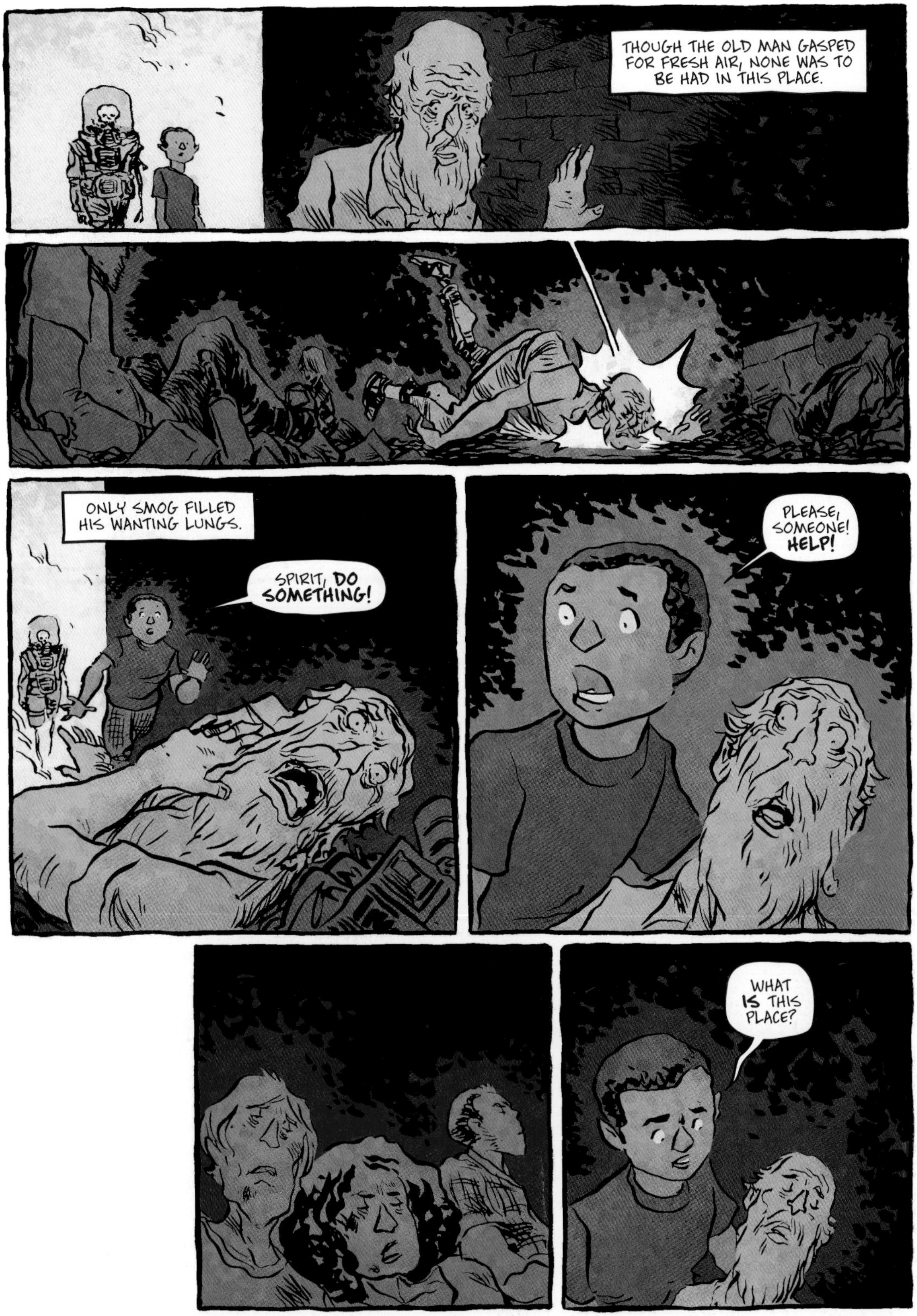
THOUGH THE OLD MAN GASPED FOR FRESH AIR, NONE WAS TO BE HAD IN THIS PLACE.
ONLY SMOG FILLED HIS WANTING LUNGS.
SPIRIT, DO SOMETHING!
PLEASE, SOMEONE! HELP!
WHAT IS THIS PLACE?

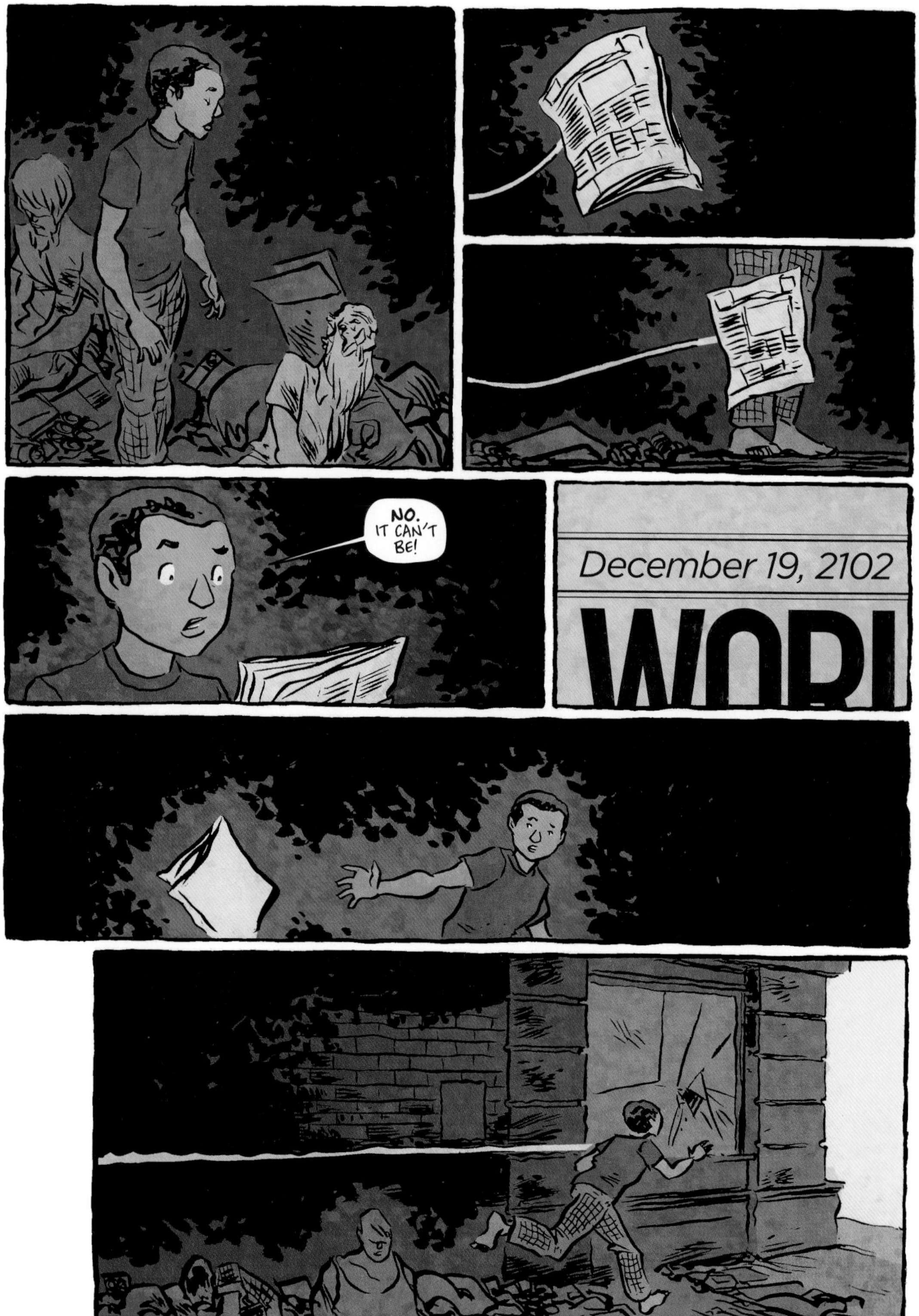
NO. IT CAN'T BE!
December 19, 2102
WORL

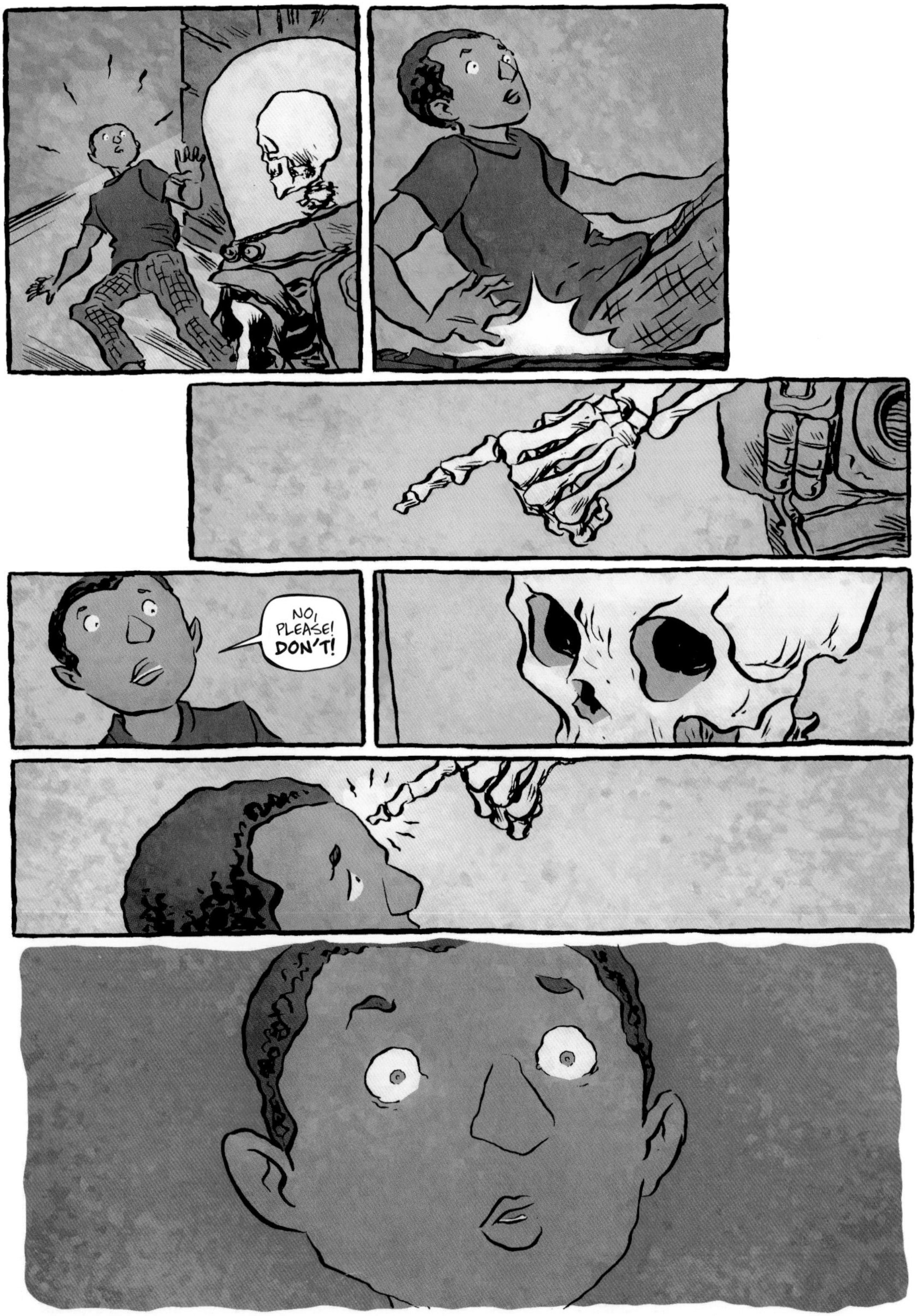
NO, PLEASE! DON'T!

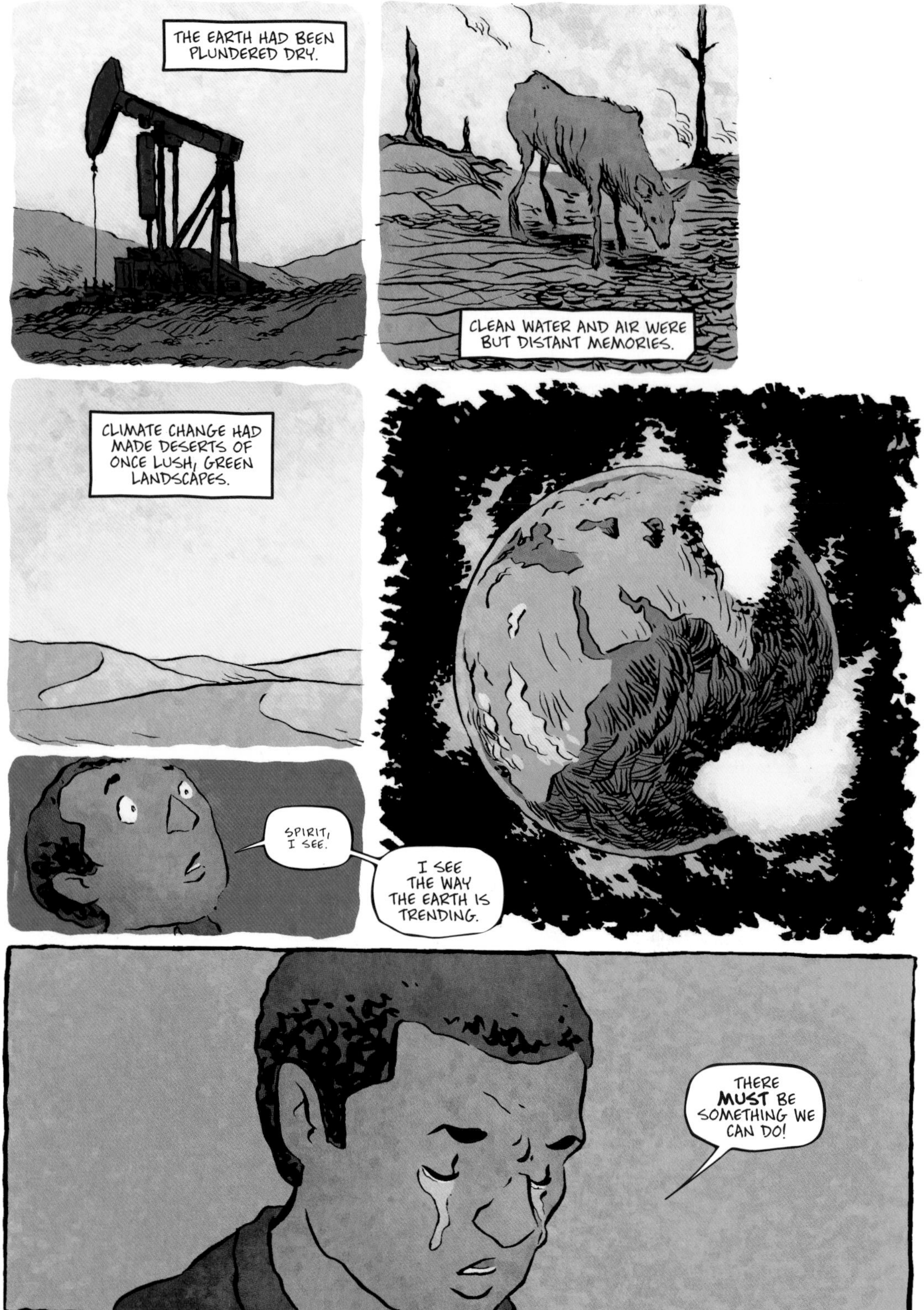
THE EARTH HAD BEEN PLUNDERED DRY.
CLEAN WATER AND AIR WERE BUT DISTANT MEMORIES.
CLIMATE CHANGE HAD MADE DESERTS OF ONCE LUSH, GREEN LANDSCAPES.
SPIRIT, I SEE.
I SEE THE WAY THE EARTH IS TRENDING.
THERE **MUST** BE SOMETHING WE CAN DO!

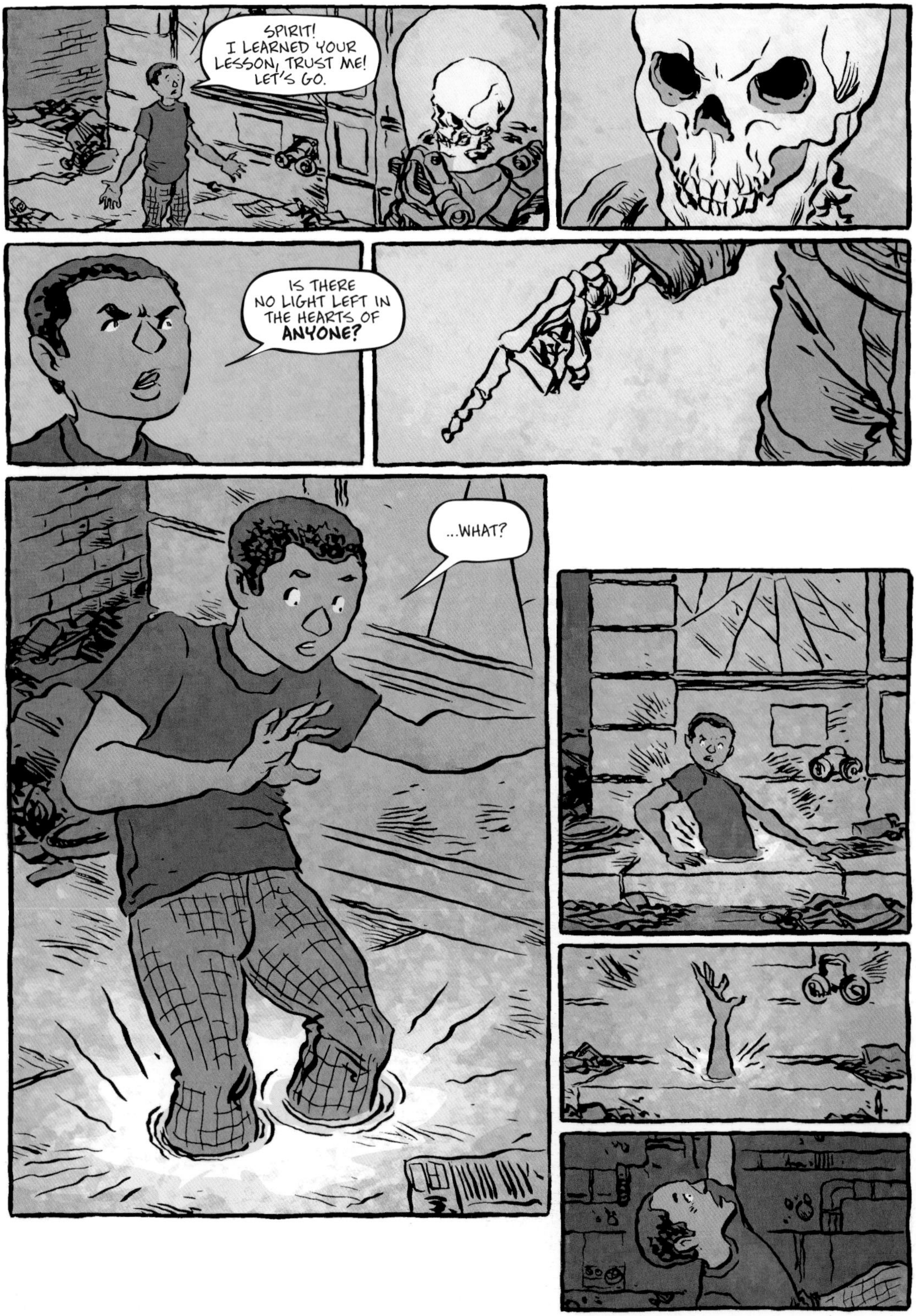
SPIRIT! I LEARNED YOUR LESSON, TRUST ME! LET'S GO.
IS THERE NO LIGHT LEFT IN THE HEARTS OF **ANYONE?**
...WHAT?

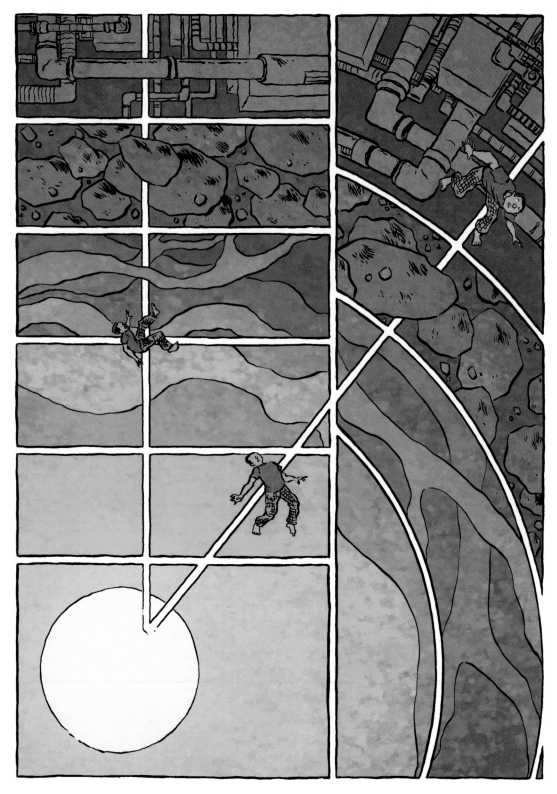

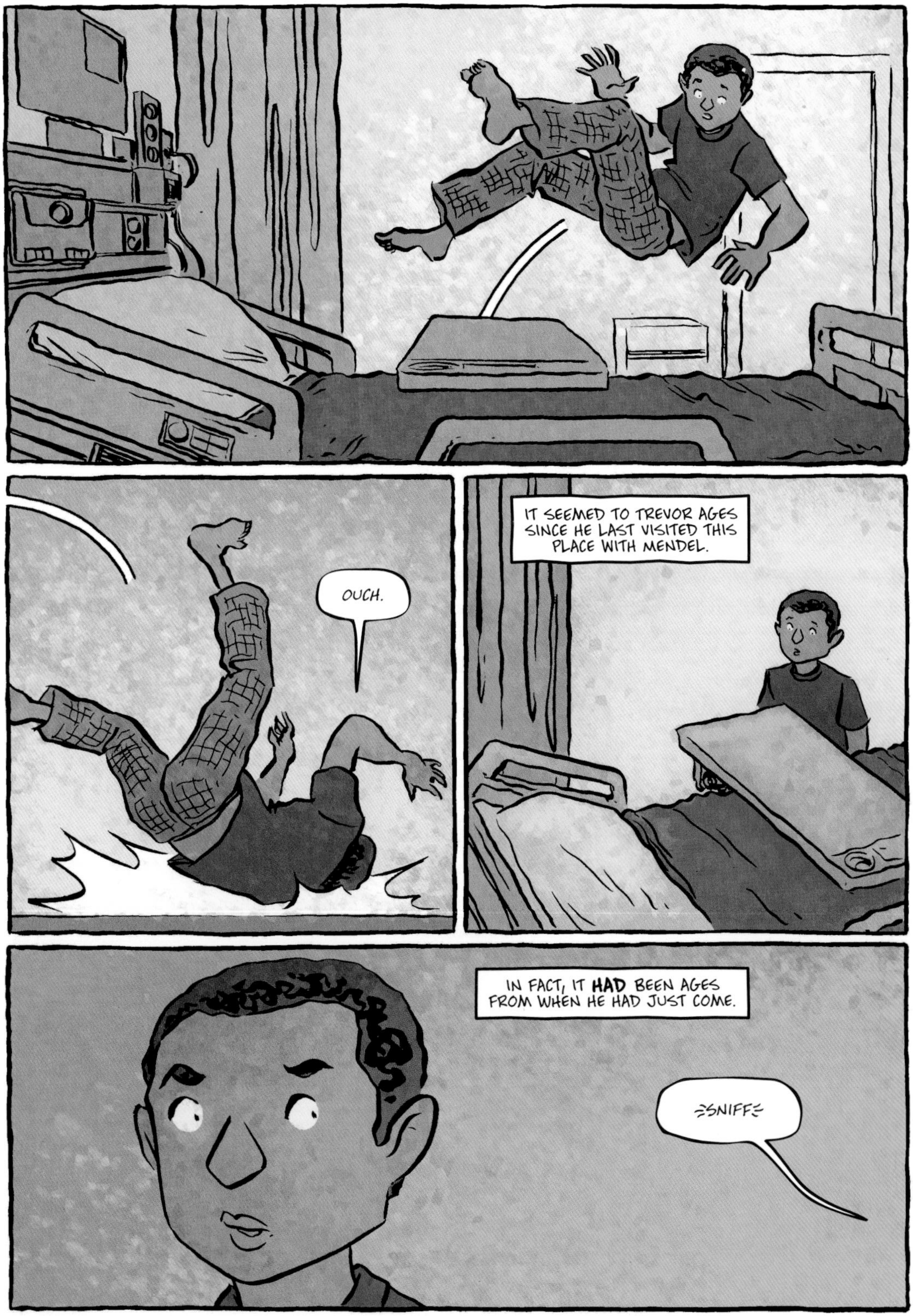
OUCH.
IT SEEMED TO TREVOR AGES SINCE HE LAST VISITED THIS PLACE WITH MENDEL.
IN FACT, IT **HAD** BEEN AGES FROM WHEN HE HAD JUST COME.
≈SNIFF≈

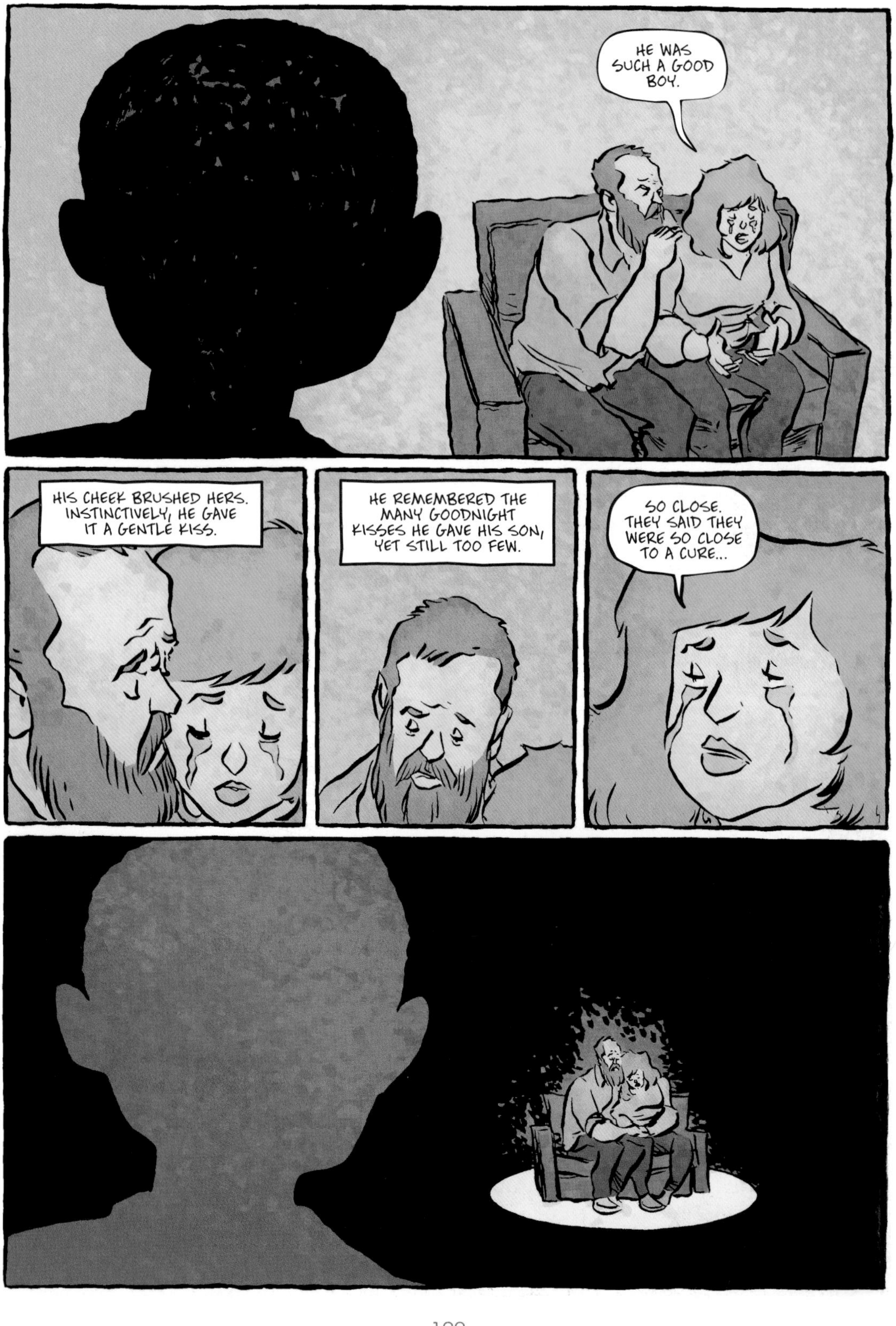
HE WAS SUCH A GOOD BOY.
HIS CHEEK BRUSHED HERS. INSTINCTIVELY, HE GAVE IT A GENTLE KISS.
HE REMEMBERED THE MANY GOODNIGHT KISSES HE GAVE HIS SON, YET STILL TOO FEW.
SO CLOSE. THEY SAID THEY WERE SO CLOSE TO A CURE...

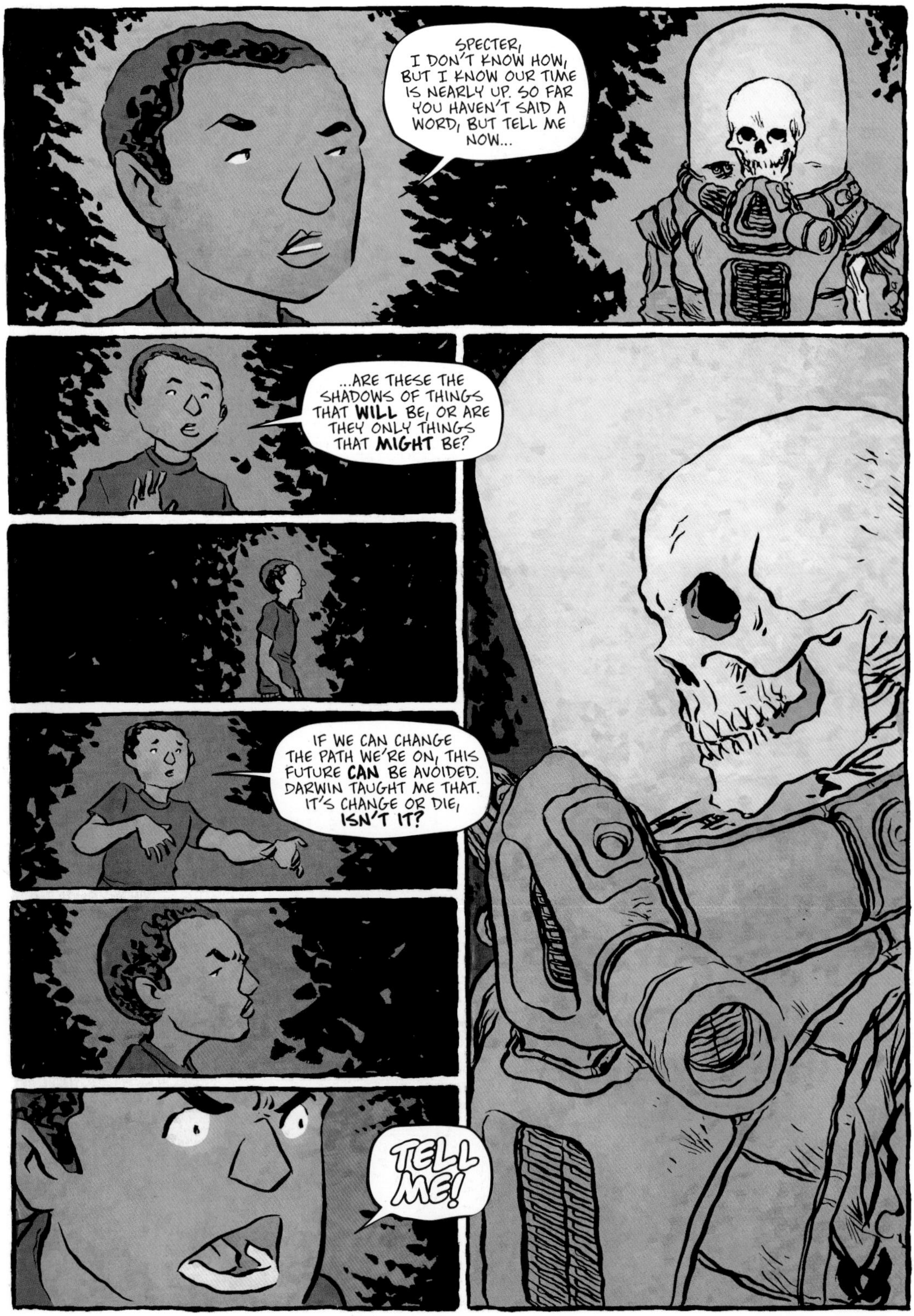
SPECTER, I DON'T KNOW HOW, BUT I KNOW OUR TIME IS NEARLY UP. SO FAR YOU HAVEN'T SAID A WORD, BUT TELL ME NOW...
...ARE THESE THE SHADOWS OF THINGS THAT **WILL** BE, OR ARE THEY ONLY THINGS THAT **MIGHT** BE?
IF WE CAN CHANGE THE PATH WE'RE ON, THIS FUTURE **CAN** BE AVOIDED. DARWIN TAUGHT ME THAT. IT'S CHANGE OR DIE, **ISN'T IT?**
TELL ME!

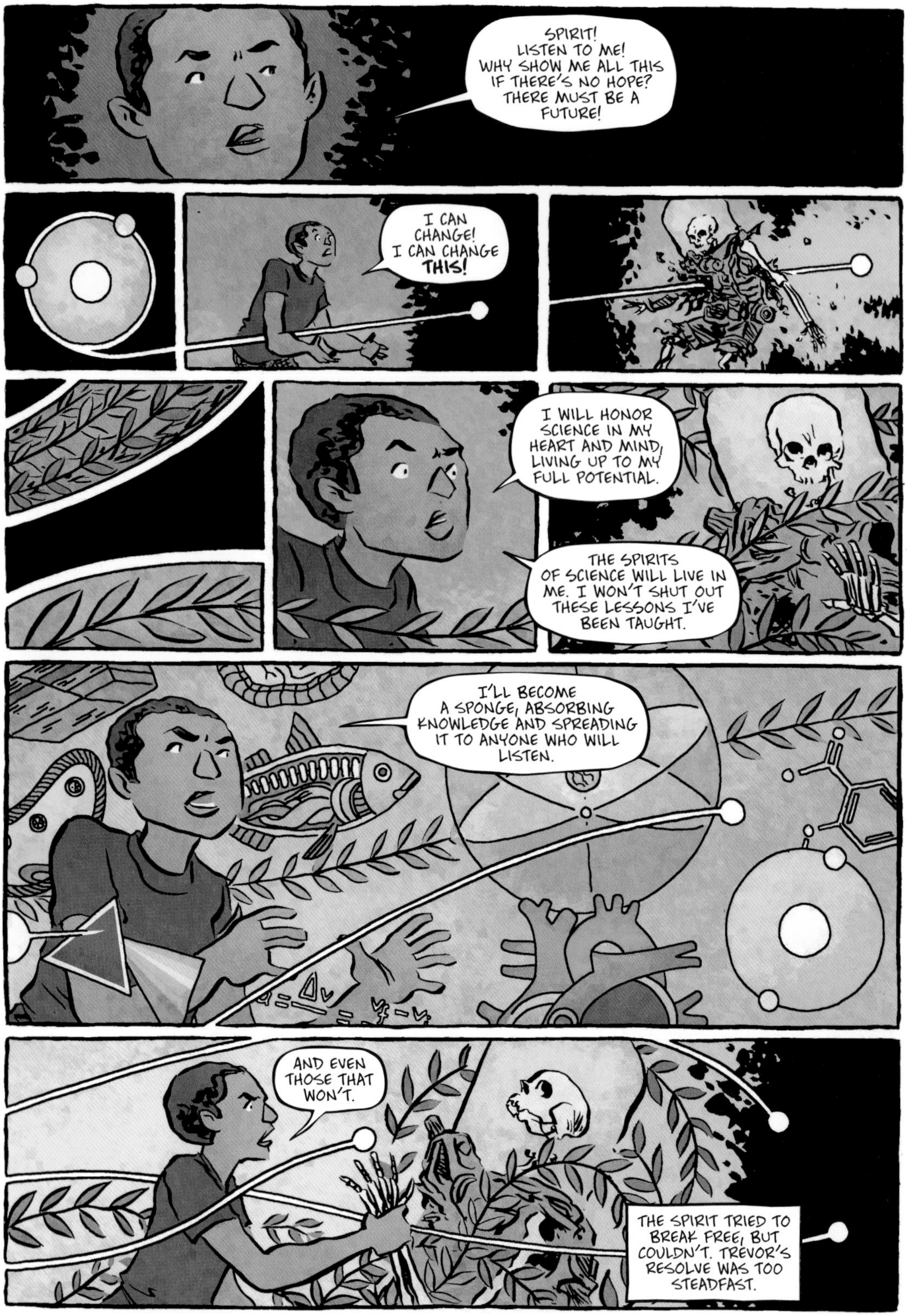
SPIRIT! LISTEN TO ME! WHY SHOW ME ALL THIS IF THERE'S NO HOPE? THERE MUST BE A FUTURE!
I CAN CHANGE! I CAN CHANGE **THIS!**
I WILL HONOR SCIENCE IN MY HEART AND MIND, LIVING UP TO MY FULL POTENTIAL.
THE SPIRITS OF SCIENCE WILL LIVE IN ME. I WON'T SHUT OUT THESE LESSONS I'VE BEEN TAUGHT.
I'LL BECOME A SPONGE, ABSORBING KNOWLEDGE AND SPREADING IT TO ANYONE WHO WILL LISTEN.
AND EVEN THOSE THAT WON'T.
THE SPIRIT TRIED TO BREAK FREE, BUT COULDN'T. TREVOR'S RESOLVE WAS TOO STEADFAST.

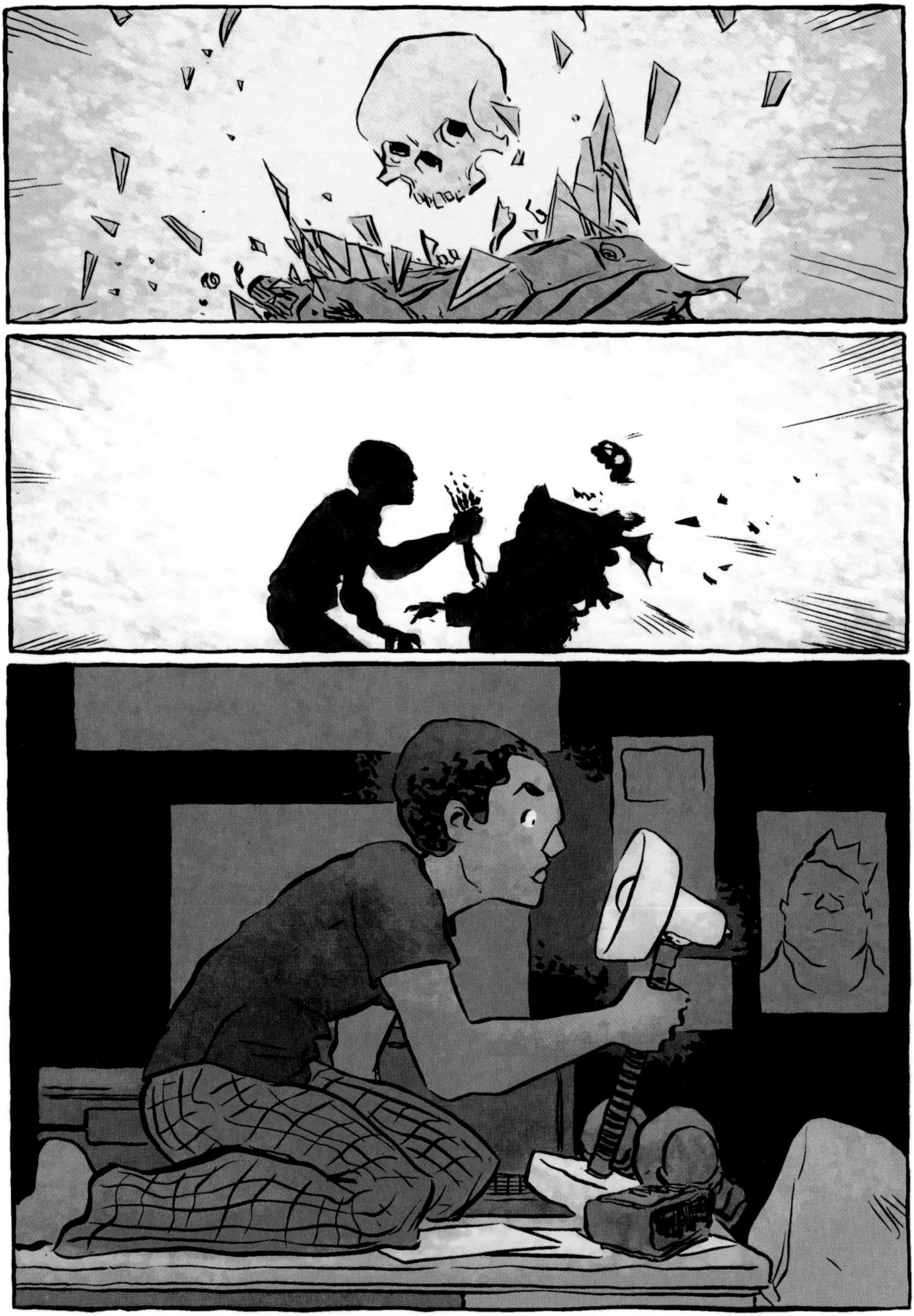

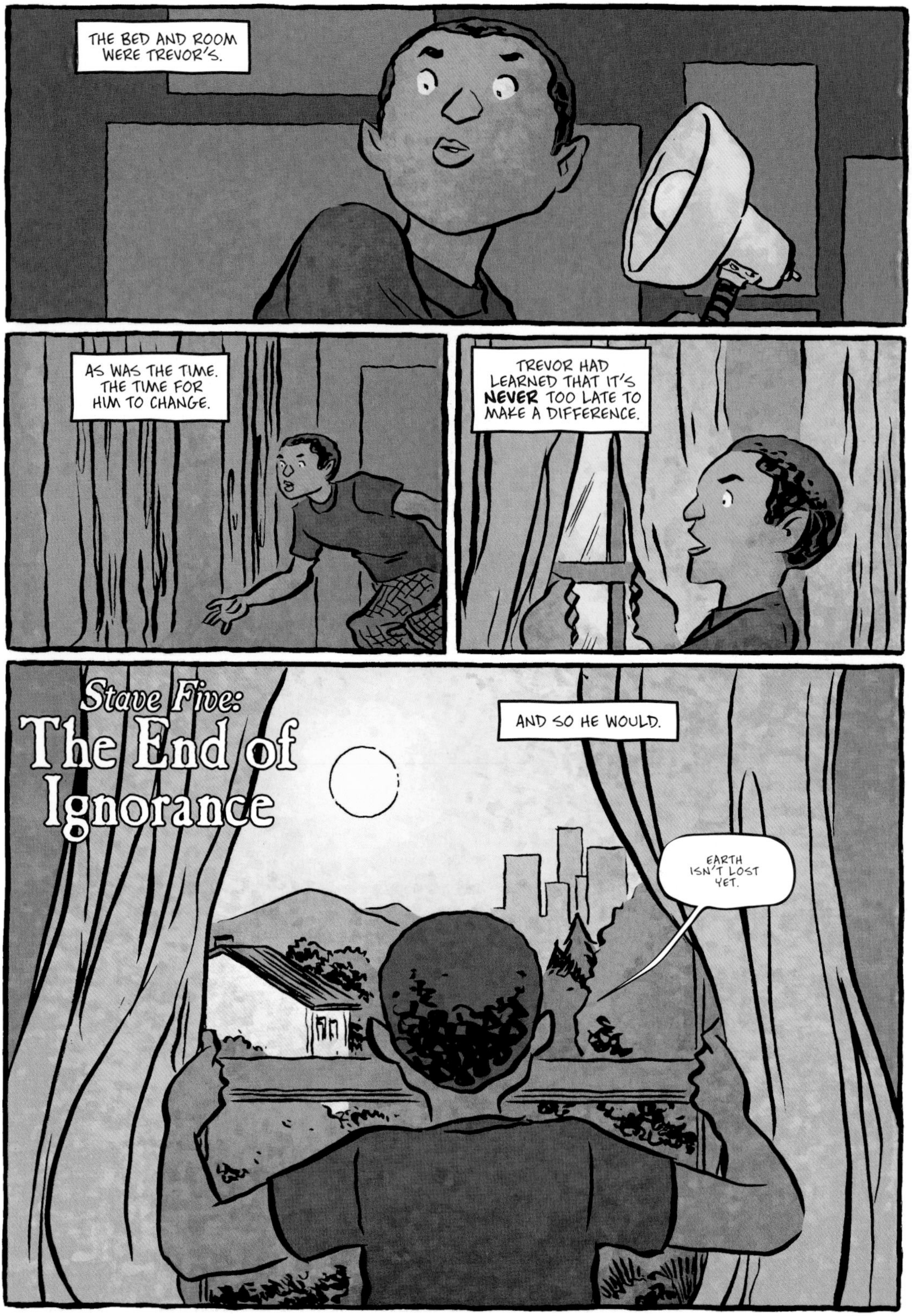
THE BED AND ROOM WERE TREVOR'S.
AS WAS THE TIME. THE TIME FOR HIM TO CHANGE.
TREVOR HAD LEARNED THAT IT'S **NEVER** TOO LATE TO MAKE A DIFFERENCE.
Stave Five:
The End of Ignorance
AND SO HE WOULD.
EARTH ISN'T LOST YET.

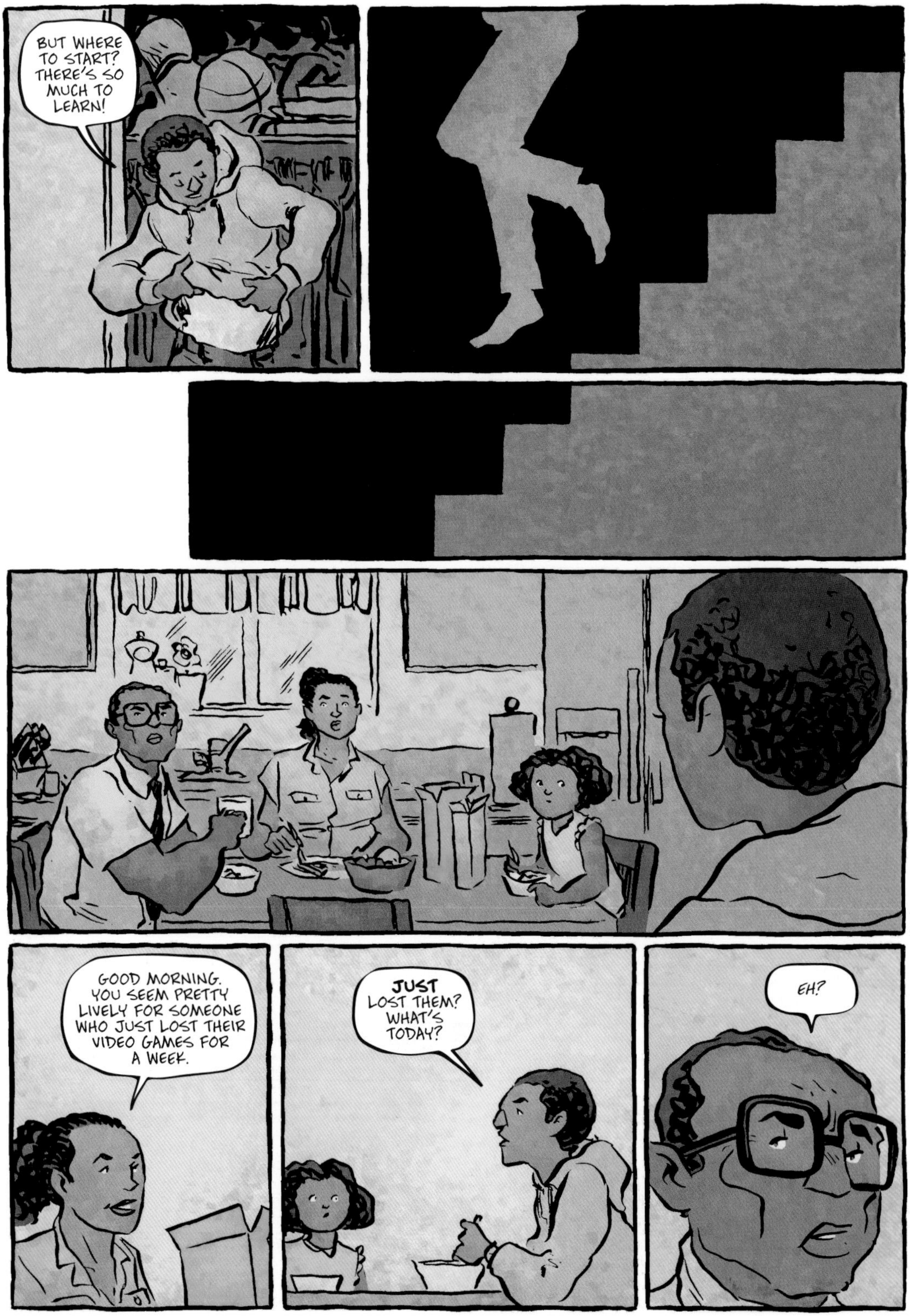
BUT WHERE TO START? THERE'S SO MUCH TO LEARN!
GOOD MORNING. YOU SEEM PRETTY LIVELY FOR SOMEONE WHO JUST LOST THEIR VIDEO GAMES FOR A WEEK.
JUST LOST THEM? WHAT'S TODAY?
EH?

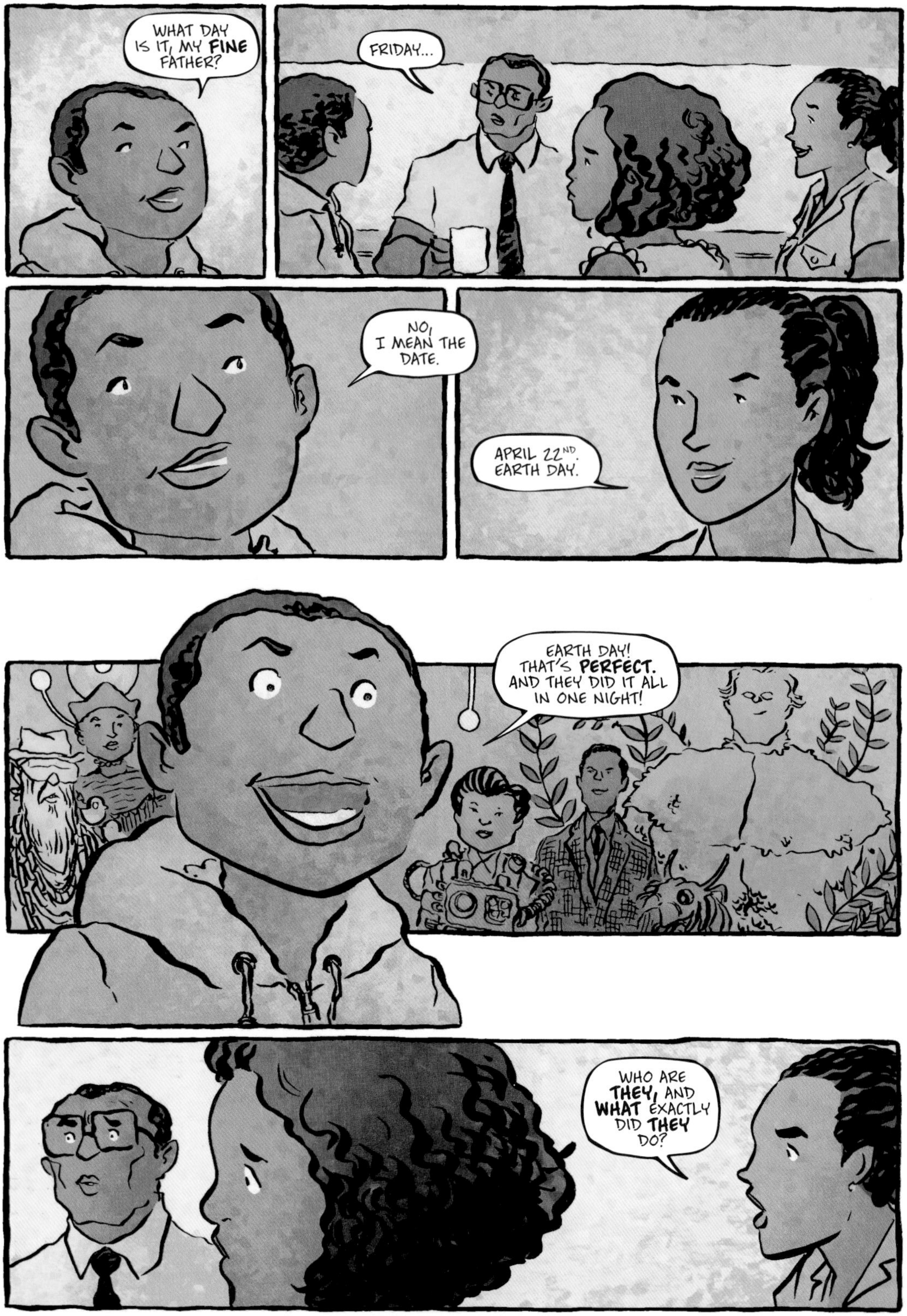

WHAT DAY IS IT, MY **FINE** FATHER?
FRIDAY...
NO, I MEAN THE DATE.
APRIL 22ND. EARTH DAY.
EARTH DAY! THAT'S **PERFECT.** AND THEY DID IT ALL IN ONE NIGHT!
WHO ARE **THEY,** AND **WHAT** EXACTLY DID **THEY** DO?

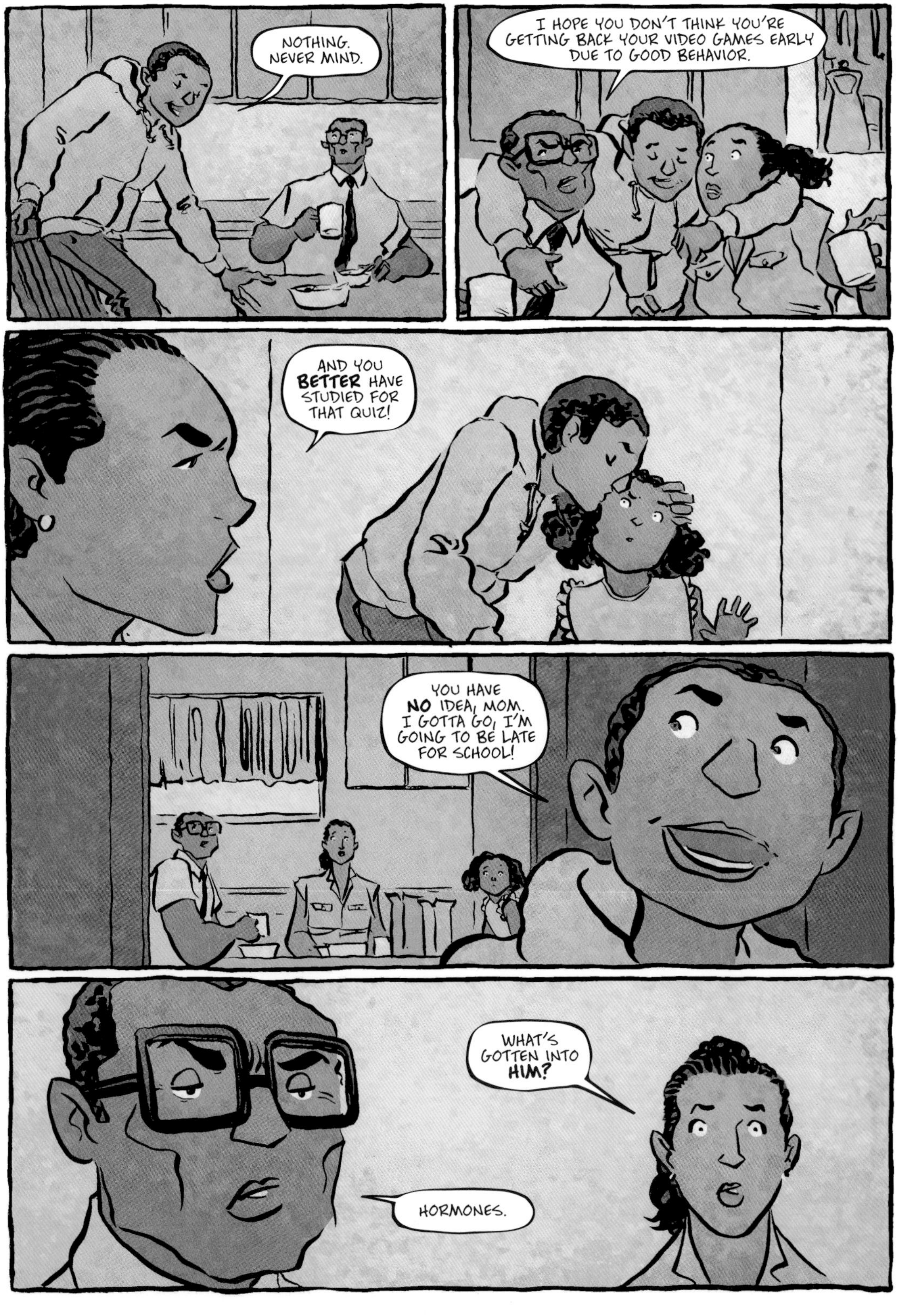
NOTHING. NEVER MIND.
I HOPE YOU DON'T THINK YOU'RE GETTING BACK YOUR VIDEO GAMES EARLY DUE TO GOOD BEHAVIOR.
AND YOU **BETTER** HAVE STUDIED FOR THAT QUIZ!
YOU HAVE **NO** IDEA, MOM. I GOTTA GO, I'M GOING TO BE LATE FOR SCHOOL!
WHAT'S GOTTEN INTO **HIM?**
HORMONES.

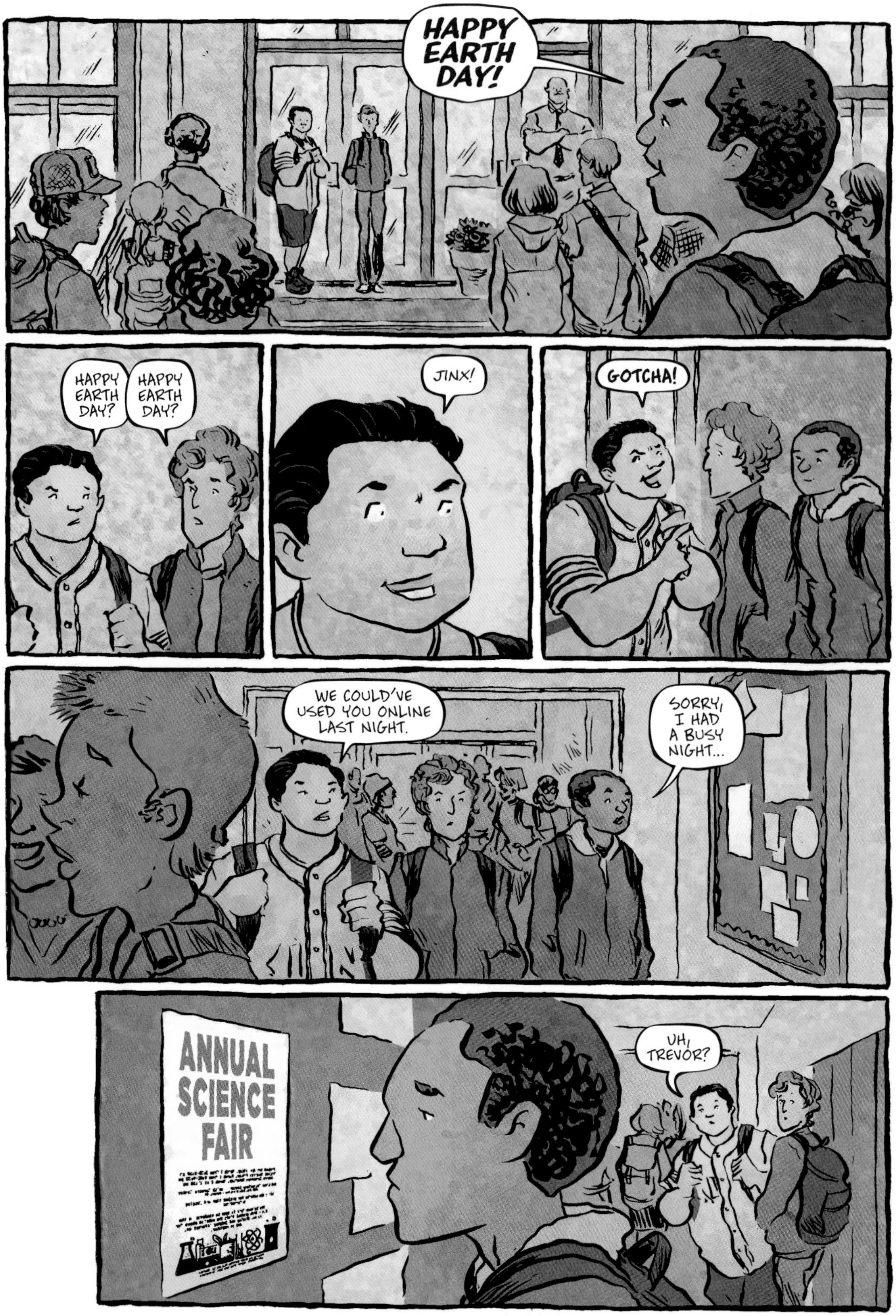
HAPPY EARTH DAY!
HAPPY EARTH DAY?
HAPPY EARTH DAY?
JINX!
GOTCHA!
WE COULD'VE USED YOU ONLINE LAST NIGHT.
SORRY, I HAD A BUSY NIGHT...
ANNUAL SCIENCE FAIR
UH, TREVOR?

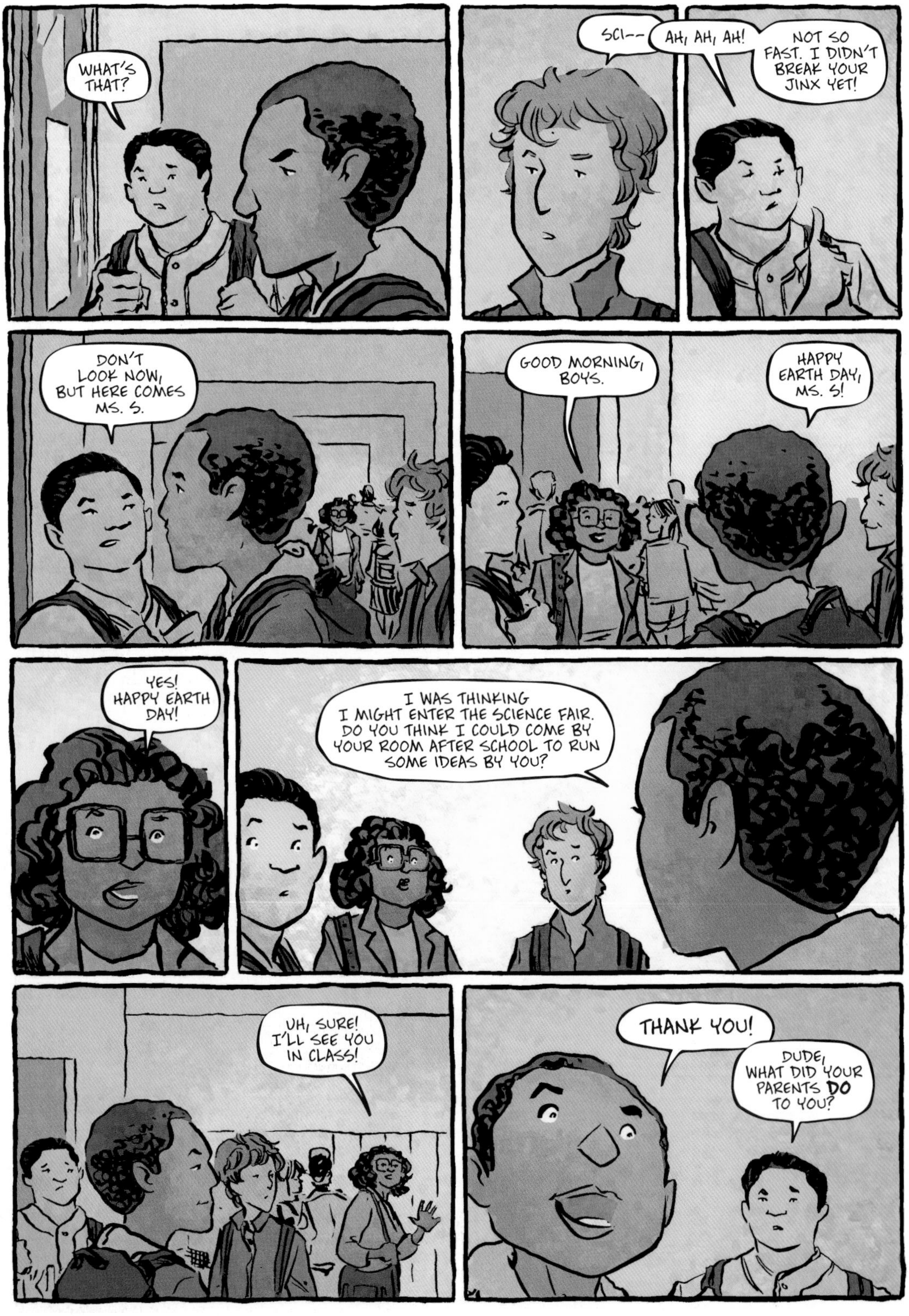
WHAT'S THAT?
SCI--
AH, AH, AH!
NOT SO FAST. I DIDN'T BREAK YOUR JINX YET!
DON'T LOOK NOW, BUT HERE COMES MS. S.
GOOD MORNING, BOYS.
HAPPY EARTH DAY, MS. S!
YES! HAPPY EARTH DAY!
I WAS THINKING I MIGHT ENTER THE SCIENCE FAIR. DO YOU THINK I COULD COME BY YOUR ROOM AFTER SCHOOL TO RUN SOME IDEAS BY YOU?
UH, SURE! I'LL SEE YOU IN CLASS!
THANK YOU!
DUDE, WHAT DID YOUR PARENTS **DO** TO YOU?

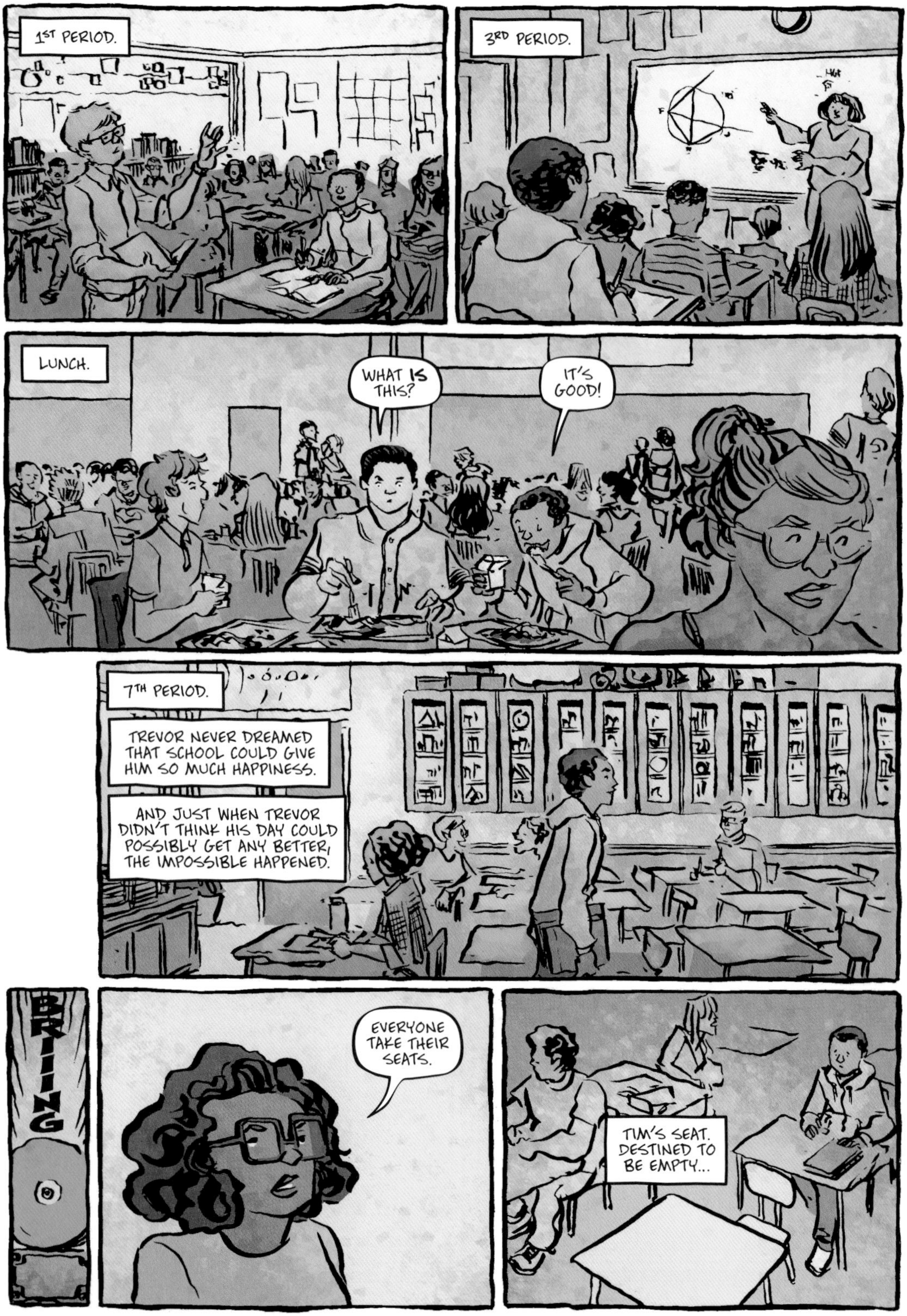

1ST PERIOD.
3RD PERIOD.
LUNCH.
WHAT IS THIS?
IT'S GOOD!
7TH PERIOD.
TREVOR NEVER DREAMED THAT SCHOOL COULD GIVE HIM SO MUCH HAPPINESS.
AND JUST WHEN TREVOR DIDN'T THINK HIS DAY COULD POSSIBLY GET ANY BETTER, THE IMPOSSIBLE HAPPENED.
BRIIING
EVERYONE TAKE THEIR SEATS.
TIM'S SEAT. DESTINED TO BE EMPTY...

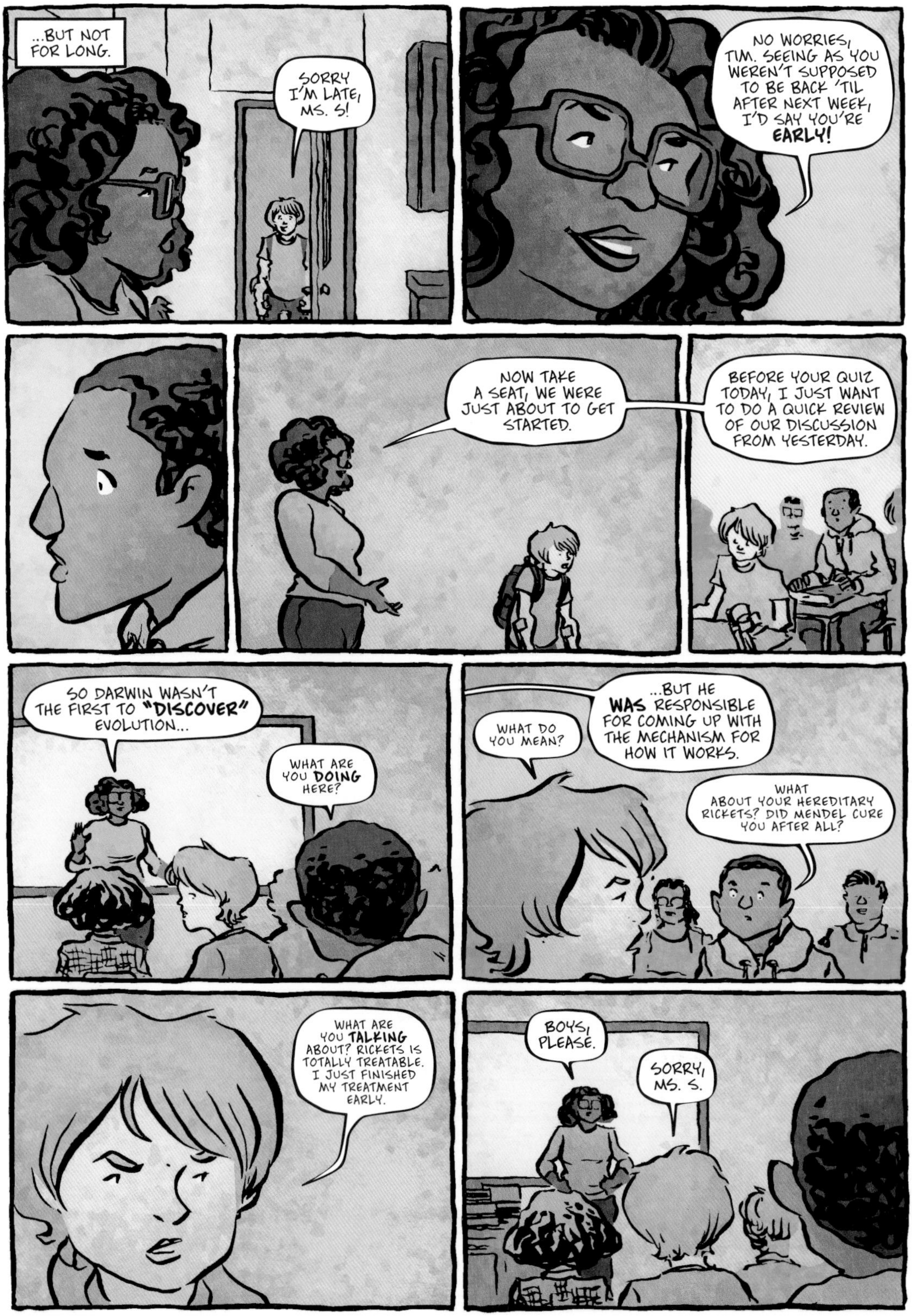
...BUT NOT FOR LONG.
SORRY I'M LATE, MS. S!
NO WORRIES, TIM. SEEING AS YOU WEREN'T SUPPOSED TO BE BACK 'TIL AFTER NEXT WEEK, I'D SAY YOU'RE **EARLY!**
NOW TAKE A SEAT, WE WERE JUST ABOUT TO GET STARTED.
BEFORE YOUR QUIZ TODAY, I JUST WANT TO DO A QUICK REVIEW OF OUR DISCUSSION FROM YESTERDAY.
SO DARWIN WASN'T THE FIRST TO **"DISCOVER"** EVOLUTION...
WHAT ARE YOU **DOING** HERE?
...BUT HE **WAS** RESPONSIBLE FOR COMING UP WITH THE MECHANISM FOR HOW IT WORKS.
WHAT DO YOU MEAN?
WHAT ABOUT YOUR HEREDITARY RICKETS? DID MENDEL CURE YOU AFTER ALL?
WHAT ARE YOU **TALKING** ABOUT? RICKETS IS TOTALLY TREATABLE. I JUST FINISHED MY TREATMENT EARLY.
BOYS, PLEASE.
SORRY, MS. S.

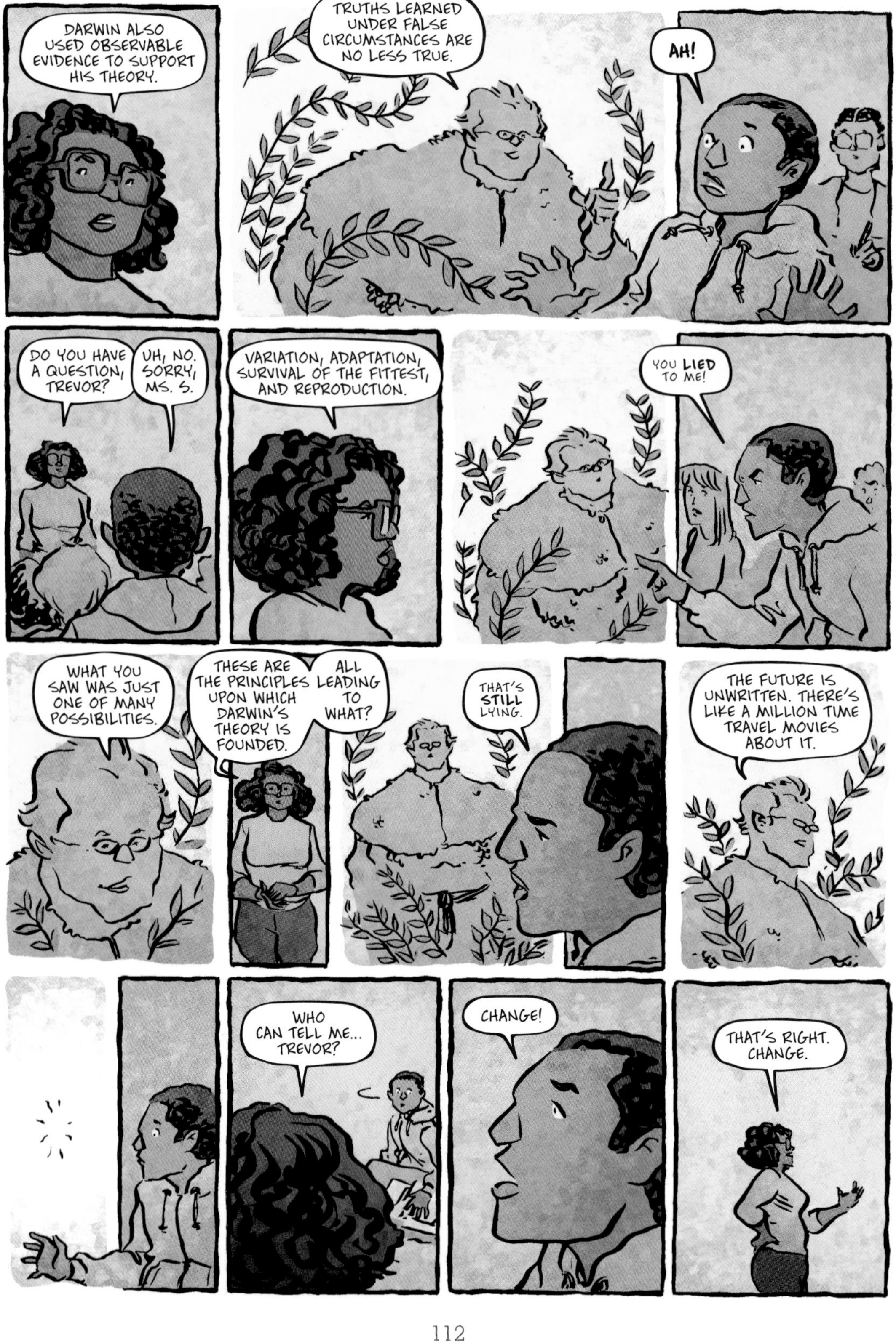

DARWIN ALSO USED OBSERVABLE EVIDENCE TO SUPPORT HIS THEORY.
TRUTHS LEARNED UNDER FALSE CIRCUMSTANCES ARE NO LESS TRUE.
AH!
DO YOU HAVE A QUESTION, TREVOR?
UH, NO. SORRY, MS. S.
VARIATION, ADAPTATION, SURVIVAL OF THE FITTEST, AND REPRODUCTION.
YOU LIED TO ME!
WHAT YOU SAW WAS JUST ONE OF MANY POSSIBILITIES.
THESE ARE THE PRINCIPLES UPON WHICH DARWIN'S THEORY IS FOUNDED.
ALL LEADING TO WHAT?
THAT'S STILL LYING.
THE FUTURE IS UNWRITTEN. THERE'S LIKE A MILLION TIME TRAVEL MOVIES ABOUT IT.
WHO CAN TELL ME... TREVOR?
CHANGE!
THAT'S RIGHT. CHANGE.

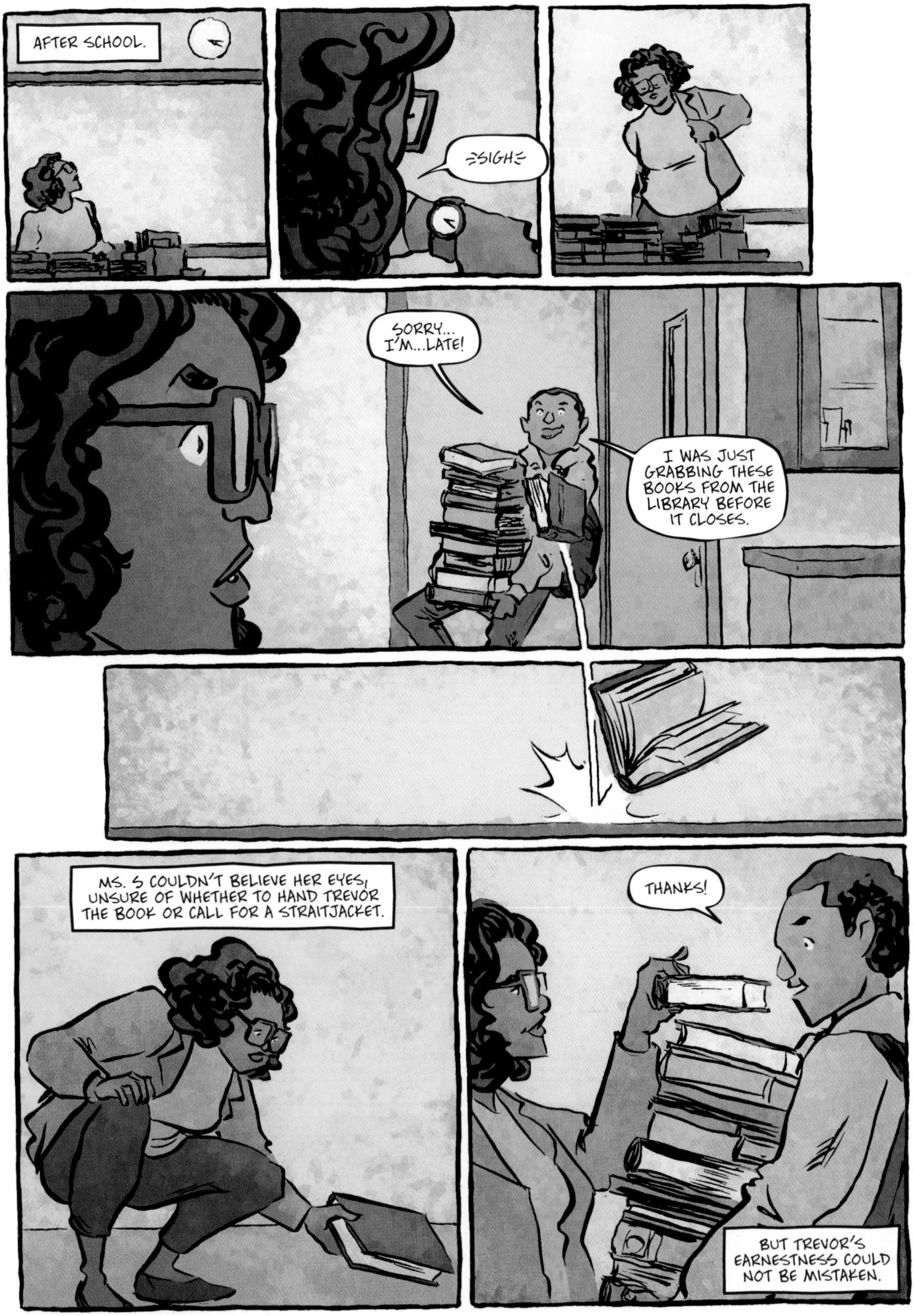

AFTER SCHOOL.
=SIGH=
SORRY... I'M...LATE!
I WAS JUST GRABBING THESE BOOKS FROM THE LIBRARY BEFORE IT CLOSES.
MS. S COULDN'T BELIEVE HER EYES, UNSURE OF WHETHER TO HAND TREVOR THE BOOK OR CALL FOR A STRAITJACKET.
THANKS!
BUT TREVOR'S EARNESTNESS COULD NOT BE MISTAKEN.

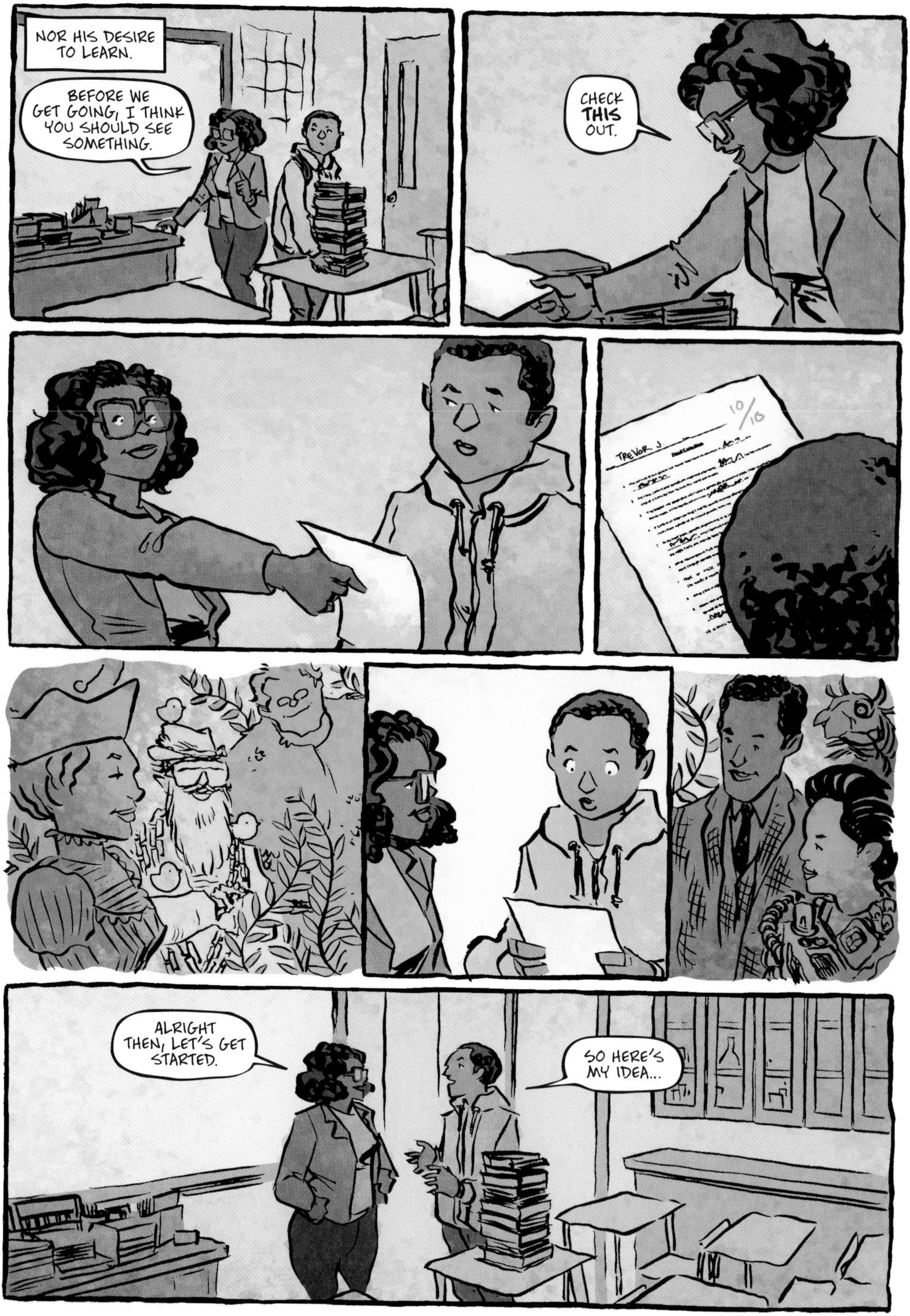
NOR HIS DESIRE TO LEARN.
BEFORE WE GET GOING, I THINK YOU SHOULD SEE SOMETHING.
CHECK THIS OUT.
ALRIGHT THEN, LET'S GET STARTED.
SO HERE'S MY IDEA...

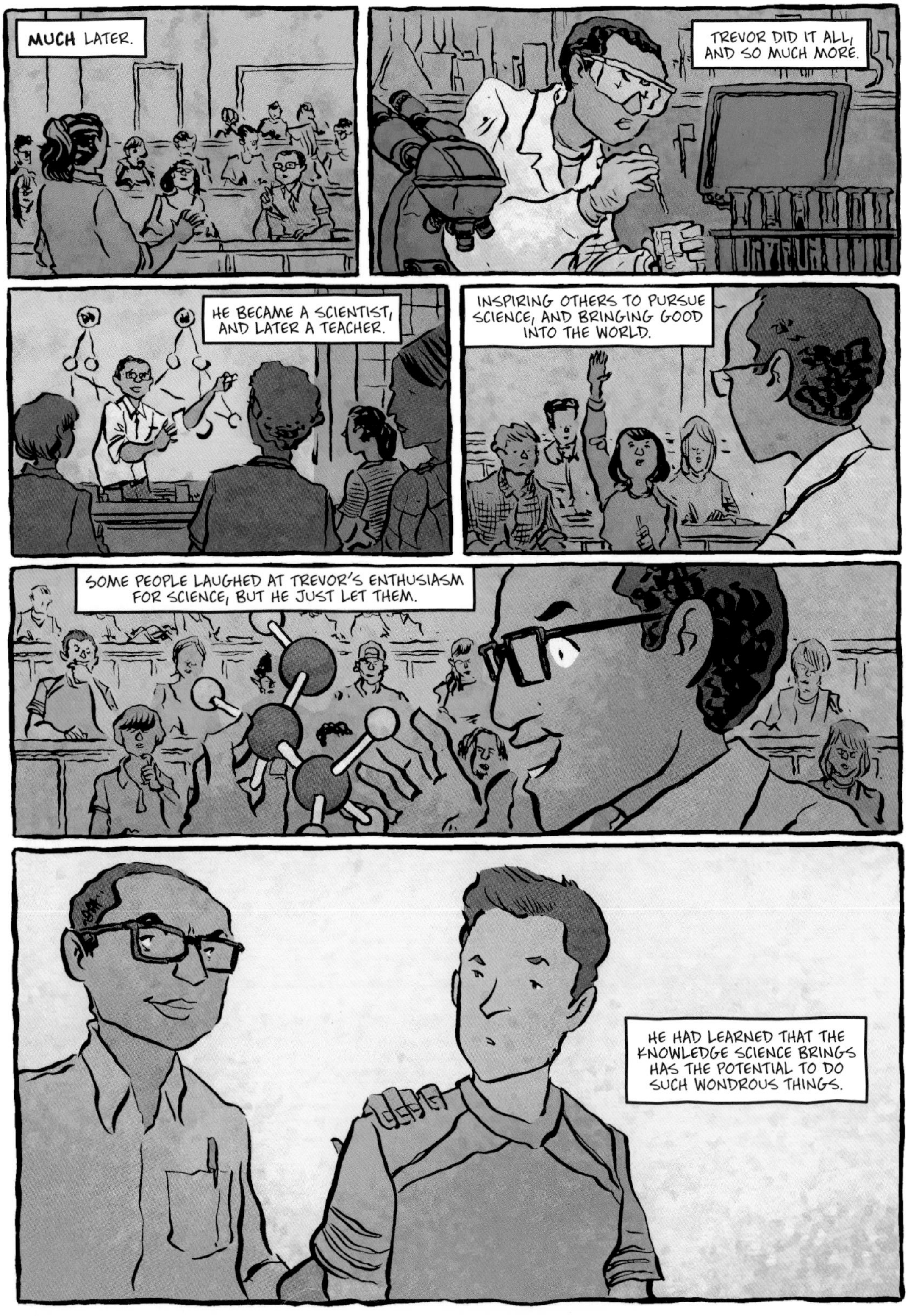
MUCH LATER.
TREVOR DID IT ALL, AND SO MUCH MORE.
HE BECAME A SCIENTIST, AND LATER A TEACHER.
INSPIRING OTHERS TO PURSUE SCIENCE, AND BRINGING GOOD INTO THE WORLD.
SOME PEOPLE LAUGHED AT TREVOR'S ENTHUSIASM FOR SCIENCE, BUT HE JUST LET THEM.
HE HAD LEARNED THAT THE KNOWLEDGE SCIENCE BRINGS HAS THE POTENTIAL TO DO SUCH WONDROUS THINGS.

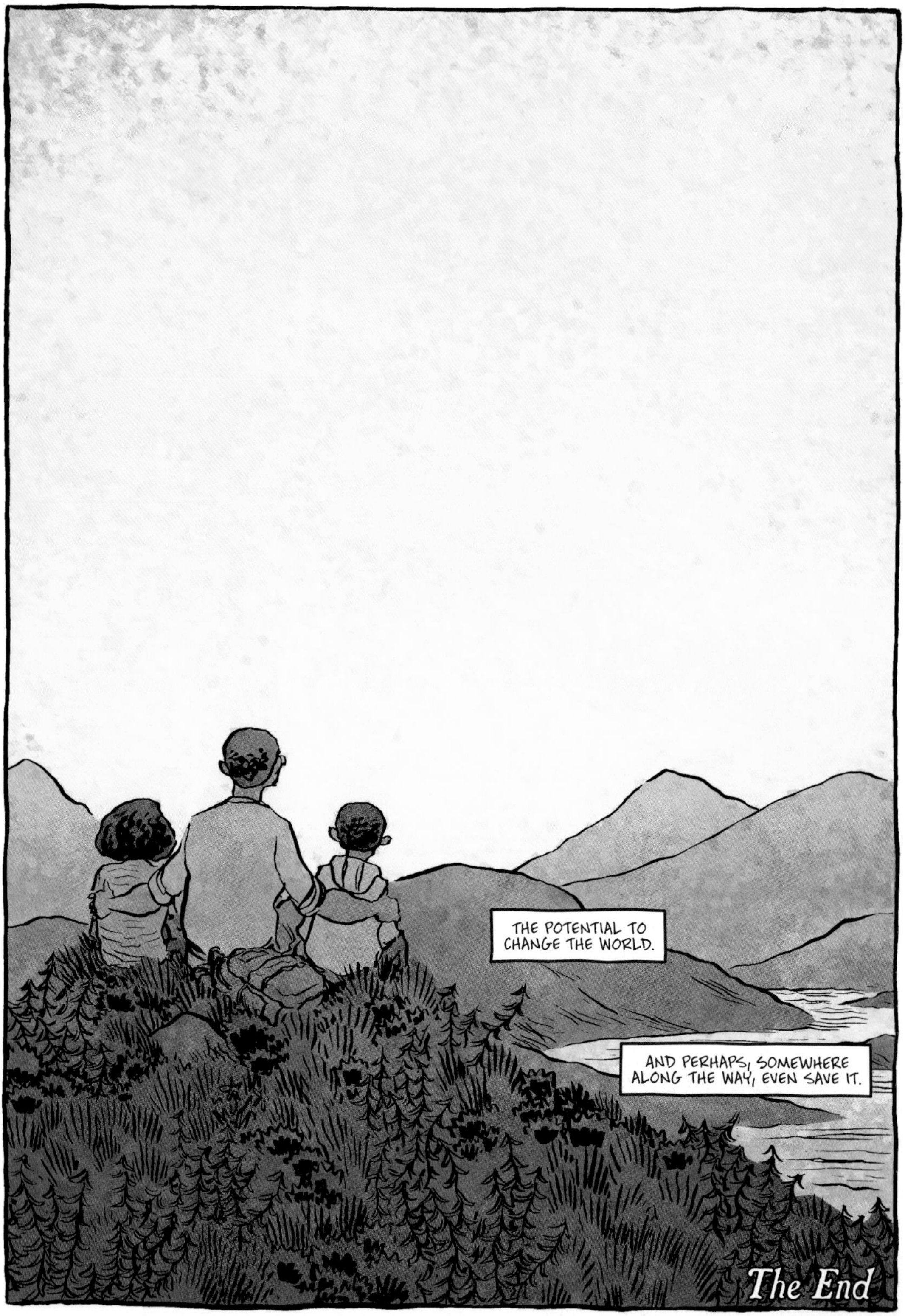
THE POTENTIAL TO CHANGE THE WORLD.
AND PERHAPS, SOMEWHERE ALONG THE WAY, EVEN SAVE IT.
The End

EXTRA CREDIT: MEET THE GHOSTS!

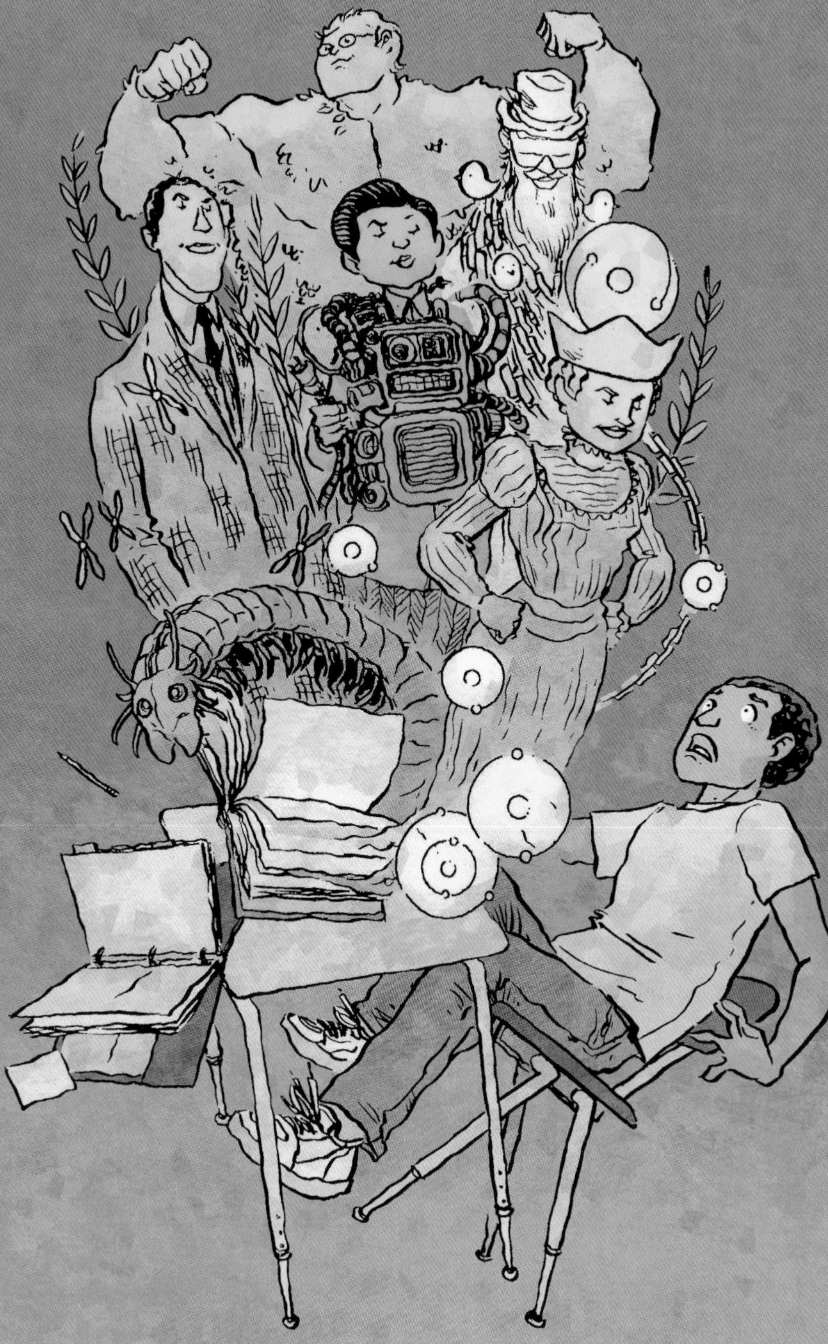

CHARLES "GAS" DARWIN

Hello, Reader. It's me, your old pal, Gas! I'm here to ask you a couple of questions to see what you learned from my time with Trevor. I'll also tell you a bit more about myself, if you can dig it. And yes, you can expect much of the same from the other Ghosts of Science. Let's get to business!

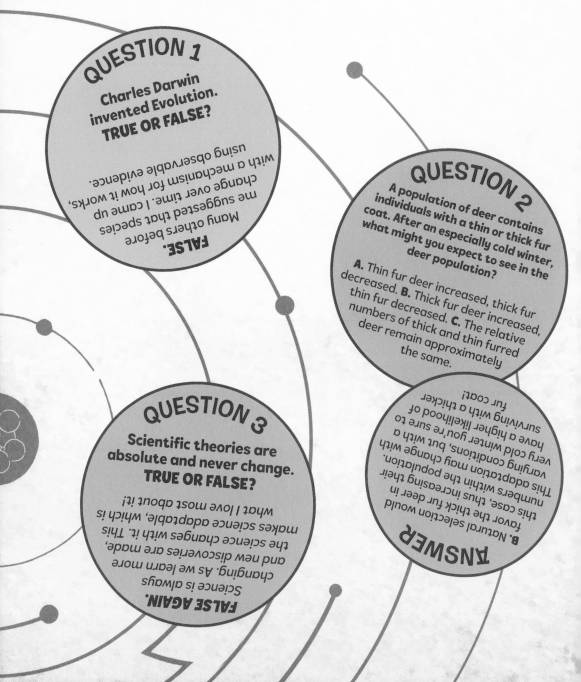

QUESTION 1

Charles Darwin invented Evolution. **TRUE OR FALSE?**

FALSE. Many others before me suggested that species change over time. I came up with a mechanism for how it works, using observable evidence.

QUESTION 2

A population of deer contains individuals with a thin or thick fur coat. After an especially cold winter, what might you expect to see in the deer population?

A. Thin fur deer increased, thick fur decreased. **B.** Thick fur deer increased, thin fur decreased. **C.** The relative numbers of thick and thin furred deer remain approximately the same.

ANSWER

B. Natural selection would favor the thick fur deer in this case, thus increasing their numbers within the population. This adaptation may change with varying conditions, but with a very cold winter you're sure to have a higher likelihood of surviving with a thicker fur coat!

QUESTION 3

Scientific theories are absolute and never change. **TRUE OR FALSE?**

FALSE AGAIN. Science is always changing. As we learn more and new discoveries are made, the science changes with it. This makes science adaptable, which is what I love most about it!

Not bad, Reader! Now let me tell you about the hippest of ghosts. I was born in 1809. As a young man I took an epic trip on the HMS Beagle that would shape the rest of my life. I went to the Galapagos Islands, where I encountered all sorts of interesting wildlife. None captured my imagination more than the finch! From those birds I would develop my theory of evolution and descent with modification, published in *On the Origin of Species* in 1859.

I owe much to the other scientists of my time, such as Thomas Malthus and my friend Charles Lyell. Their respective work on principles shaping populations and geology were integral to my own. I must also make mention of all I learned by observing common dog breeders selecting specific traits to be passed to the offspring. Why shouldn't nature contain a similar mechanism for change? It was almost too simple!

I would pass from life at the age of 72, with my beloved wife, Emma, by my side. I did not fear death as it approached, as mine was a complete life filled with the love of my children, friendship, adventure, and an everlasting passion for nature. My work is still considered controversial by some today, and to that I can only smile.

MARIE CURIE

Dzień dobry. I understand you require additional information about my life. Well, knowledge has its price, so you will first have to answer a few questions to demonstrate that you have learned from my lessons. Shall we begin?

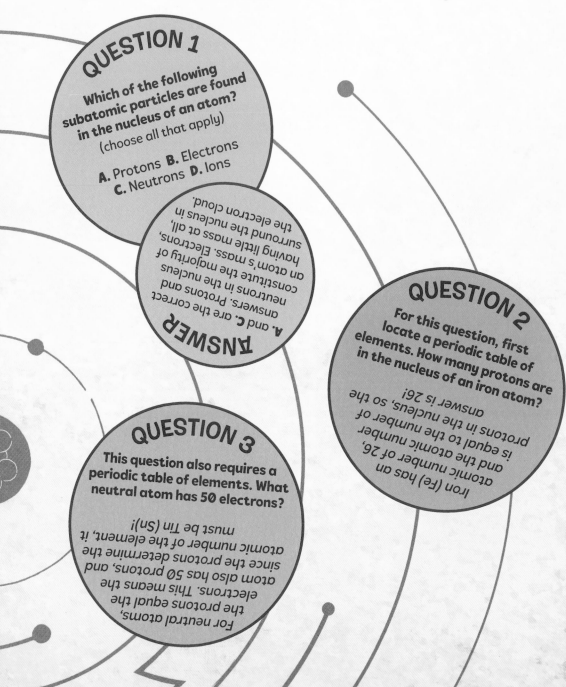

QUESTION 1

Which of the following subatomic particles are found in the nucleus of an atom? (choose all that apply)

A. Protons **B.** Electrons **C.** Neutrons **D.** Ions

ANSWER

A. and **C.** are the correct answers. Protons and neutrons in the nucleus constitute the majority of an atom's mass. Electrons, having little mass at all, surround the nucleus in the electron cloud.

QUESTION 2

For this question, first locate a periodic table of elements. How many protons are in the nucleus of an iron atom?

Iron (Fe) has an atomic number of 26, and the atomic number is equal to the number of protons in the nucleus, so the answer is 26!

QUESTION 3

This question also requires a periodic table of elements. What neutral atom has 50 electrons?

For neutral atoms, the protons equal the electrons. This means the atom also has 50 protons, and since the protons determine the atomic number of the element, it must be Tin (Sn)!

Well done! Without further ado... I began my life in Poland, where I could not be admitted to a standard Polish University because of my gender. Instead, I attended an illegal Polish Floating University where women hid their studies.

At 24, I left Poland to continue my studies at the University of Paris, where I earned a degree in physics. Not long after that I met my future husband, Pierre. We would discover the elements polonium and radium, both of which are radioactive. We realized radium is useful in treating tumors, using Pierre as a test subject!

Together we decided to share our findings with the people instead of patenting them for profit. At the first international conference on physics in France we presented our glowing block of radium, but I had to remain offstage because of my gender. Similarly, I was not allowed to present with Pierre at the British Royal Institution in London. Some opposed my inclusion in the Nobel Prize for our work with Henri Becquerel, and I was not allowed to participate in a lecture for the committee.

Despite all that, I was the first woman in France to receive a doctoral degree and the first female professor of the University of Paris. I was also the first person to be honored with a Nobel Prize in two scientific fields. Unfortunately, I had no concept of the dangers of radiation, sleeping with a sample of radium on my nightstand and carrying extracts in my pockets. My workspace was so contaminated that a hazmat suit is required to enter even today. I would die of aplastic anemia at 67, proud of everything I accomplished and confident in my legacy.

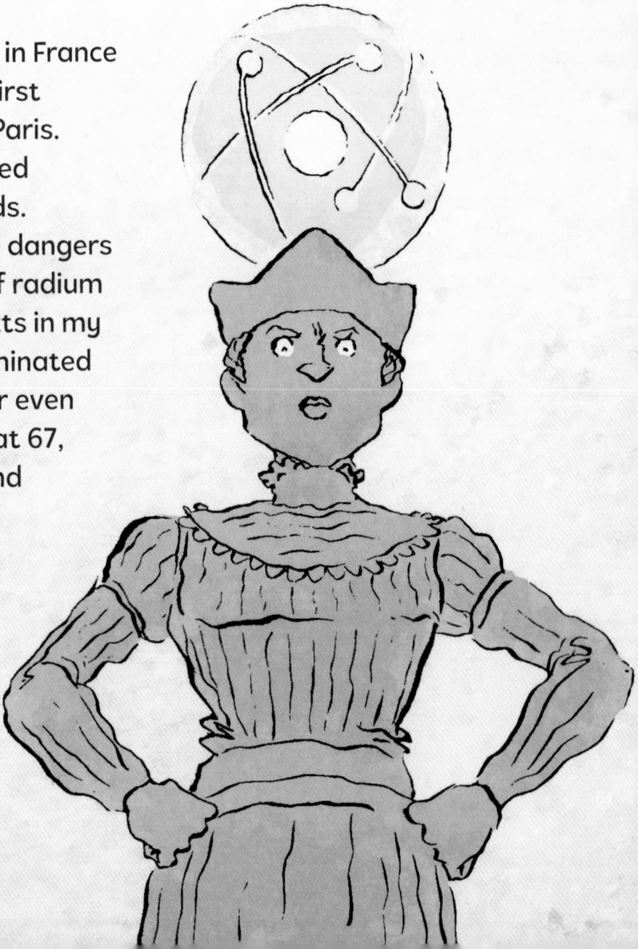

CHIEN-SHIUNG WU

Welcome! I am Chien-Shiung Wu, but you can just call me Dr. Wu. I'd be happy to share a bit about my life, but first, let's see what you've learned so far.

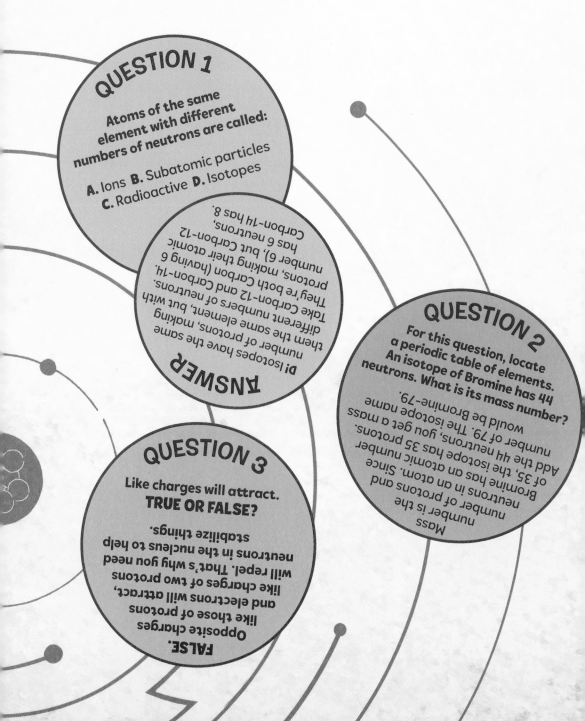

QUESTION 1

Atoms of the same element with different numbers of neutrons are called:

A. Ions **B.** Subatomic particles **C.** Radioactive **D.** Isotopes

ANSWER

D) Isotopes have the same number of protons, making them the same element, but with different numbers of neutrons. Take Carbon-12 and Carbon-14. They're both Carbon, making their atomic number 6), but Carbon-12 has 6 neutrons, Carbon-14 has 8.

QUESTION 2

For this question, locate a periodic table of elements. An isotope of Bromine has 44 neutrons. What is its mass number?

Mass number is the number of protons and neutrons in an atom. Since Bromine has an atomic number of 35, the isotope has 35 protons. Add the 44 neutrons, you get a mass number of 79. The isotope name would be Bromine-79.

QUESTION 3

Like charges will attract. **TRUE OR FALSE?**

FALSE. Opposite charges like those of protons and electrons will attract, like charges of two protons will repel. That's why you need neutrons in the nucleus to help stabilize things.

Great job, Reader! My life was one of science and compassion. I was born in a province of China in 1912. I had two very encouraging parents who fought for gender equality, helping to shape my own views on politics and feminism. Between my studies of mathematics and physics I would lead sit-ins and protests. In 1936 I went to America to attend the University of California, Berkeley to earn my PhD.

I made many strides in the research of beta decay, despite facing sexism and prejudice against Asian students. My thesis impressed Robert Oppenheimer, leading to my involvement, much to my regret, in the development of the atomic bomb. After World War II, I accepted a position at Columbia, where I would become the first woman with a tenured physics professorship. I experimentally confirmed Einstein's famous quantum entanglement thought experiment. I would use experimental evidence to show that the "law of conservation of parity" is not conserved under weaker nuclear interactions, a major contribution to particle physics. Proposed by Tsung-Dao Lee and Chen Ning Yang, my experiment would help earn them the Nobel Prize for Physics in 1957. Despite their acknowledgement of my contributions, I was denied consideration by the Nobel committee.

I would remain one of the world's top experimental physicists while speaking out against gender discrimination. I also advocated for human rights, promoting STEM teaching for all students. When I passed in 1997, I was widely regarded as one of the top *female* physicists of all time. It is my hope that one day, such a distinction will no longer be deemed necessary and scientists will be considered solely by the merits of their work.

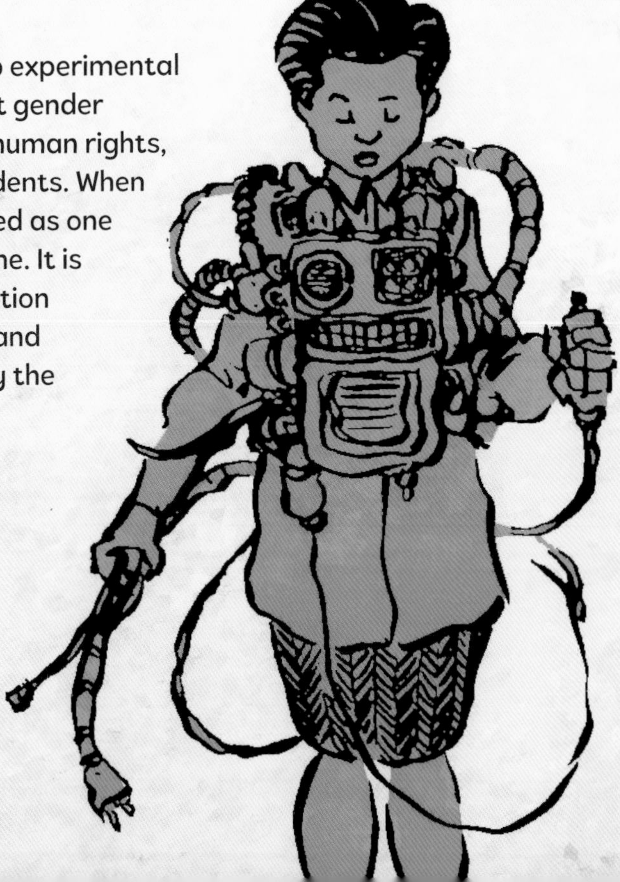

GREGOR MENDEL

Guten Tag! You've made it to me, Gregor Mendel. I will gladly share my story, but you are supposed to answer a few questions first. One of Darwin's silly rules. But don't worry, no matter how you fare, the knowledge you seek will be yours.

According to this law, only one of the two genes is placed in each gamete sex cell.

A. Law of gravity
B. Law of independent assortment
C. Law of segregation
D. Law of thermodynamics

ANSWER

The answer is c! Homologous chromosomes are separated during meiosis, halving the number of chromosomes. This results in gametes randomly receiving one gene copy.

QUESTION 2

Here's an easy one. What did I study in order to come up with my laws of inheritance?

Peas! Why? Because they're fun, they're tasty, and I just love them. Give peas a chance!

QUESTION 3

Alleles are different forms of a gene. **TRUE OR FALSE?**

TRUE. Alleles of genes are found in the same location on homologous pairs of chromosomes. Your parents each give you a gene for all the traits that make you YOU! Because they may not give you the same version of that gene, sexual reproduction increases variation in offspring. And that's a good thing, because diversity is what makes us unique!

Spectacular! You are a lively one! Having been dead for well over 100 years, I should know! Born to a Czech family of farmers in 1822, what we lacked in money we made up in our devotion to one another, but I thirsted for knowledge beyond farm life. I realized my family could not afford the education I desired, so I turned to the cloth to help ease the financial burden. I entered the Augustinian St Thomas's Abbey in Brno to begin my priesthood, eventually progressing to abbot in 1868. But before that, I had my garden...

At the monastery, I grew and experimented with thousands of pea plants. I studied several traits, demonstrating what would later be named Mendel's laws of inheritance. I cleverly crossed true-breeding varieties of pea plants for different pairs of traits, recording the resulting offspring. In the second generation of plants, I continuously found that a quarter of them were purebred dominant, half of them were hybrids, and a quarter purebred recessive for each pair of traits that I crossed. While in my mind this clearly illuminated principles governing inheritance, it was unfortunately not seen as such by the rest of the scientific community. My work was widely discounted during my lifetime, only to be rediscovered long after I passed.

My work, along with Darwin's theory of natural selection, would go on to inspire modern evolutionary biology. If only Darwin had known about my findings in his own time, there's no telling what progress he could have made in genetics! Be sure not to mention it in his presence, though, for he is certain to glare at you from those luminous eye sockets of his! My time with the living ended in 1884, but what is now known as Mendelian inheritance continues to play an important role in modern genetics today. And to think, it all came from peas!

ERNEST EVERETT JUST

Oh, hi! I was just tending to the lab, but I'd be happy to spare a moment to tell you about myself. First, let's get to the questions.

QUESTION 1

Crossing over occurs during meiosis, not mitosis.
TRUE OR FALSE?

TRUE. When homologous chromosomes pair in meiosis, parts of the chromosomes exchange DNA and recombine, creating new combinations of genetic information that lead to unique cells and offspring. During mitosis this would simply result in daughter cells that would simply be copies.

QUESTION 2

Of the 46 chromosomes usually found in a human cell, how many are sex chromosomes?

A. 2 **B.** 23 **C.** 44 **D.** 46

ANSWER

The answer is **A.** Humans typically have 44 autosomes, determining nearly everything about us except our sex. The remaining two chromosomes are sex chromosomes, which help determine the sex of the individual. There are other traits attached to these chromosomes as well, but they are unique in that function.

QUESTION 3

Chromosomes are made of condensed DNA.
TRUE OR FALSE?

TRUE. The DNA is coiled around proteins called histones. The two halves of the chromosome are called sister chromatids, and are genetically identical. They are held together by a centromere, and formed during the S phase of interphase when the DNA is copied.

Excellent work! As for me, I was born in 1883. I lost my father at a young age. My mother taught me to put my education first and never to settle. Sadly, I lost her, too, while I was away at school. I was only 16. I'd go on to graduate from Dartmouth with honors in zoology, but it was fertilization and egg development that really captured my wonder.

In 1907, I accepted a teaching position at Howard University in Washington, D.C. It wasn't long before I became head of the Zoology Department. Around that time, I was introduced to Frank Lillie, a pioneer in the newly emerging field of embryology, and the two of us became fast friends. I'd join him each summer at the Marine Biological Laboratory in Woods Hole, researching the fertilization of invertebrate marine eggs. As my notoriety expanded I enrolled at the University of Chicago, where I would earn my Ph.D. I was one of only a few African Americans to do so at the time. Despite my growing reputation I was unable to teach at any major American universities because of my race. That is why I so enjoyed my time working in Europe, where I was free from the racism and discrimination that I experienced back home.

Throughout my life, I authored over 70 scientific papers and two books, including my seminal work, *The Biology of the Cell Surface*. I am perhaps best known for my discoveries regarding egg cell surface changes during fertilization and the adhesiveness of early embryonic cells. With superior technical skills as a scientist, it was oft said that I was a genius in the design of experiments. Though I would die of pancreatic cancer in 1941, my legacy would live on, contributing to the understanding of epigenetics and how genes work.

FUTURE GHOST

Salutations! Surprised to hear me speechify? Tragically, before my encounter with young Trevor I lost a jinx to that infernal Charles Darwin, so I was sorrowfully silent in my lesson to Trevor. Unlike my fellow Ghosts, the answer to my query you alone can discover!

CHALLENGE!

Draw two monsters with 5 distinct differences for 2 contrasting traits (i.e. one has four legs and the other eight, one has spots and the other stripes, one has wings and the other doesn't, etc.). Randomly label one variation "dominant," the other "recessive." Assume the genotype for the dominant trait is heterozygous, meaning that the monster has both a dominant and recessive allele (Pp). In order to have a recessive version of a trait, they must be homozygous for the recessive alleles (pp). We will flip a coin using "heads" for the dominant allele and "tails" for the recessive. So if you flip heads, the offspring with be heterozygous with the dominant trait. If you flip tails, the offspring will be homozygous recessive with the recessive trait. Flip a coin for each of the 5 differences, then draw the new monster made from the assembled 5 coin flips. See how different they are from their parents? Which law that Gregor Mendel mentions applies here? What environmental factors might favor one trait over another?

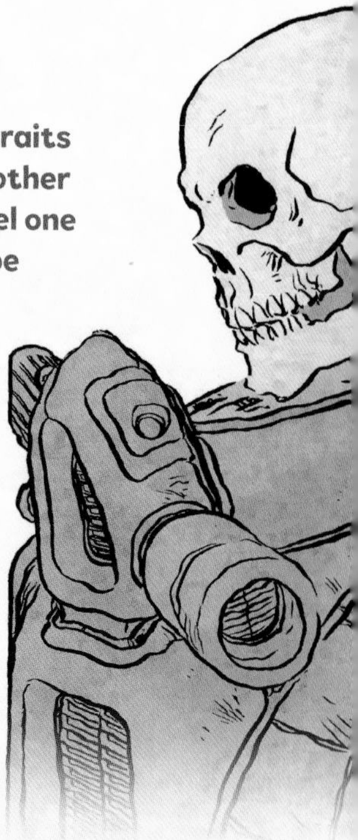

I did not "live" like the other scientists, I have always existed as a concept of change. Some change is good, like the eukaryotic cells forming from their prokaryotic ancestors. Some change is tragic, like the extinction of species and destruction of habitats. Every sentient being is an agent of change, good or ill. Trevor decided to make a change in favor of knowledge and creation. What choices will you make?

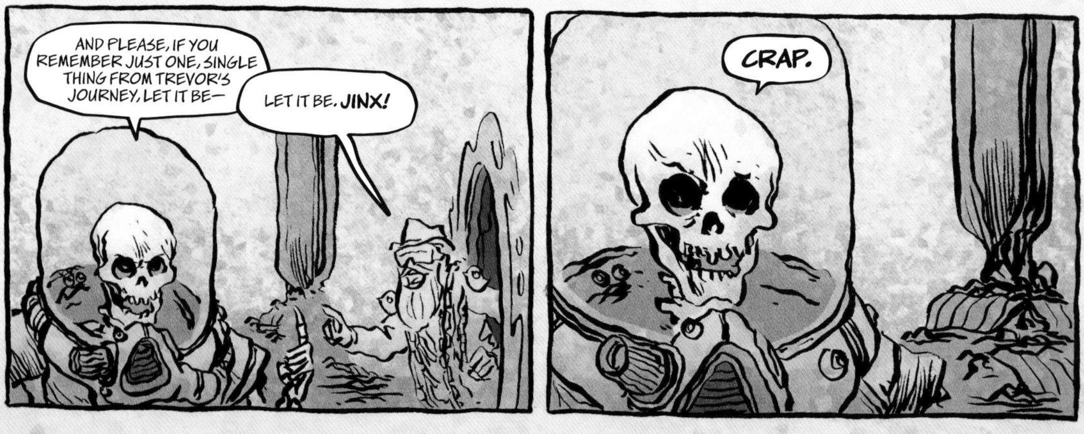
AND PLEASE, IF YOU REMEMBER JUST ONE, SINGLE THING FROM TREVOR'S JOURNEY, LET IT BE—
LET IT BE. JINX!
CRAP.